Uncle Remus
THE COMPLETE TALES

Uncle Remus

THE COMPLETE TALES

WITH A NEW INTRODUCTION

as told by JULIUS LESTER

illustrated by Jerry Pinkney

·

PHYLLIS FOGELMAN BOOKS

·

New York

Phyllis Fogelman Books
An imprint of Penguin Putnam Books for Young Readers
345 Hudson Street
New York, New York 10014

Introduction copyright © 1999 by Julius Lester
Frontispiece © 1990 by Jerry Pinkney
Case cover illustration © 1999 by Jerry Pinkney
Printed in Hong Kong
First Edition
10 9 8 7 6 5 4 3 2 1

Library of Congress Cataloging in Publication Data
Lester, Julius.
Uncle Remus: the complete tales/as told by Julius Lester;
illustrated by Jerry Pinkney.—1st ed.
p.   cm.
Reprint in one volume of works originally published separately,
1987–1994.
Contents: Bk. 1. The tales of Uncle Remus—Bk. 2. More tales of Uncle
Remus—Bk. 3. Further tales of Uncle Remus—Bk. 4. The last tales of
Uncle Remus.
ISBN 0-8037-2451-9
1. Afro-Americans—Folklore. 2. Tales—United States.
[1. Afro-Americans—Folklore. 2. Animals—Folklore.
3. Folklore—United States.] I. Pinkney, Jerry, ill. II. Title.
PZ8.1.L434Un 1999 [398.2'089'96073]—dc21   99-17121   CIP

Each black-and-white drawing is made of pencil and graphite; and
each full-color picture consists of a pencil, graphite, and watercolor
painting that is color-separated and reproduced in full color.

Contents

When I undertook the challenge of retelling Joel Chandler
Harris's Uncle Remus tales, I was not sure what the response
would be. On the one hand, there were those who remembered
the tales from childhood and retained an almost sacred affection
for them in their original form. Others associated the tales with
slavery and saw no reason why anyone would want to resurrect
them.

However, I was also aware that there were several generations that had never heard of Joel Chandler Harris and Uncle Remus, generations that had never encountered the adventures of Brer Rabbit, Brer Fox, Brer Wolf, and all the others. So it was primarily for them that I set out to retell these stories, but in a way that hopefully would have the same affectionate sense of play and fun as the original, but without evoking associations with slavery. I am gratified that the critical and popular response to these retellings has been universally warm and enthusiastic.

The power of folk tales is that they transcend their social origins, and that is certainly true of these tales. They are as funny, delightful, and wise in the twenty-first century as they were in the nineteenth. They can be told as well in the vernacular of that era as in the vernacular of our own. And probably in a century or so, someone else will sit down and retell these tales in the vernacular of that time. And that is as it should be.

Folk tales live only as long as we roll the words around on our tongues and let them spiral into the ears of a listener, even if that listener is only ourselves. So I invite you to do just that—to make these tales live in your hearts, for it is the heart which is the home of a story, not the words on the page.

Julius Lester
Belchertown, Massachusetts
January 1, 1999

The Tales of Uncle Remus
THE ADVENTURES OF BRER RABBIT

The Tales of Uncle Remus

The Adventures of Brer Rabbit

as told by JULIUS LESTER

illustrated by Jerry Pinkney

DIAL BOOKS

New York

Published by Dial Books
375 Hudson Street
New York, New York 10014

Text copyright © 1987 by Julius Lester
Illustrations copyright © 1987 by Jerry Pinkney
All rights reserved
Design by Jane Byers Bierhorst
First Edition

Library of Congress Cataloging in Publication Data

Lester, Julius.
The tales of Uncle Remus.

Contents : The adventures of Brer Rabbit.
1. Afro-Americans—Folklore. 2. Tales—United States.
[1. Folklore, Afro-American. 2. Animals—Fiction.]
I. Jerry Pinkney, ill. II. Title.
PZ8.1.L434Tal 1987 [398.2] 85.20449
ISBN 0-8037-0271-X
ISBN 0-8037-0272-8 (lib. bdg.)

The publisher wishes to express its sincere thanks to the estate
of Joel Chandler Harris for its gracious support during the
publication of this new version of *The Tales of Uncle Remus.*

*Each black-and-white drawing is made of pencil and graphite; and
each full-color picture consists of a pencil, graphite, and watercolor
painting that is color-separated and reproduced in full color.*

To the memory of my father
J. L.

For my children,
Troy, Brian, Scott, and Myles
J. P.

My lasting memories of my grandmother are of her telling me stories. I know that she told folktales and fairy tales from many parts of the world. I cried when she told Andersen's "Little Match Girl"—it was so beautiful and so sad. But my favorites, and I'm sure they were hers as well, were the Brer Rabbit stories. I howled with laughter when Brer Rabbit asked the Tar Baby "and how does your symptoms segashuate?" My grandmother did not attempt to use the dialect of Joel Chandler Harris because, even though she had been born on a Maryland plantation in 1862, she did not speak the way Harris interpreted slave speech. Her mother had told her the stories and she told them to me with love and affection as she sat in her favorite rocking chair in the middle of a large, old-fashioned kitchen. It was a way for her to entertain me as she watched her cooking.

In 1917 when I was old enough to go to school I still wanted to hear about Brer Rabbit and Miz Meadows and the gals, so I would rush home to be there by "pot-watching" time. "Grandma," I'd ask, "tell about how Brer Rabbit tricked Brer Fox." We would get comfortable and start down Brer Rabbit's road. Small, helpless Brer Rabbit always defeated his adversaries—the large animals—with his wit, humor, and wisdom. In my smallness I related to the clever little hare who could always get out of the most difficult situations through his sharp wit.

I soon wanted to read these stories myself, which led me to

the only collections available, by Joel Chandler Harris. They were in a dialect that was like a foreign language and I could not handle it. I was frustrated and, although I loved the stories, I was too impatient to struggle with the words. Grandmother died and the Brer Rabbit stories were put into the storage of my mind.

It wasn't until several years later, in college, that I learned about the importance of these stories as true American folklore. Dr. Harold Thompson, a leading American folklorist, gave a lecture on people from the West Coast of Africa who had been captured and sold as slaves. Some were settled in the southern states where they took stories from home about a hare—Wakaima—and adapted them to their new surroundings. Wakaima became Brer Rabbit and the clay man became the Tar Baby. Learning about this made me turn to the books again, and once again I tried unsuccessfully to read them.

In 1937 I found myself in the 135th Street branch of the New York Public Library located in the heart of Harlem as a children's librarian. One of the prerequisites of this position was to tell stories. I soon learned that these black boys and girls needed to be introduced to the humor and hidden philosophies of Brer Rabbit and his cohorts. Here was a contribution to their racial pride—to know that their black forefathers had first told these stories and, in so doing, had added to the body of American folklore. Many of them were sensitive to the slave setting that showed Uncle Remus telling the stories to the little white boy, so I eliminated that frame. It became obvious that the tales stood on their own as their African counterparts about Wakaima did.

One day a young, dynamic woman came to the children's room and told me that she was a student in Lucy Sprague Mitchell's Bank Street writing course. She had decided that her project would be to retell the Uncle Remus stories. Her name was Margaret Wise Brown, who later became an outstanding author of books for the very young. She too realized that the stories could be removed from their slave setting without losing any of their unique qualities. So she eliminated the figure of Uncle Remus and titled her project simply "Brer Rabbit" and subsequently had it published under the same title. But she retained the phrasing and speech patterns of Joel Chandler Harris because she did not have the rhythm and natural speech patterns of the southern blacks. A true translation and interpretation would come from within the black experience.

Despite the drawbacks in Harris's text, I still loved the stories and appreciated Brer Rabbit as a cultural hero and a significant part of my heritage. However, I was telling the stories less and less often because of the dialect. Then in the late forties and early fifties the Harlem schools along with others with liberal philosophies in New York City were asking that their classes be given lectures on black history. How could I represent our African background and the relationship between Africa and black America to primary grades? How could I show the fusion of the different African cultures and the cultures existing in America and the West Indies?

The answer came one day as I was planning a story hour. I would tell "Wakaima and the Clay Man," discuss in simple terms the middle passage (the slaves' experiences on slave ships), relate Wakaima to Brer Rabbit, and finally tell "Brer Rabbit and the Tar Baby." Once again I would be telling the animal stories without a truly satisfactory book for the children. As a librarian and one who feels that storytelling is an ideal way to bring together children and books, my frustration grew.

In 1972 a book was placed on my desk and I knew immediately that I had found the answer to years of seeking. Julius Lester had written *The Knee-High Man and Other Tales*, published by Dial. Here were black folktales told perfectly. Lester had used the voice and the language of black people. And he does so again in his tellings of the Uncle Remus stories. In the foreword to this book he calls it "a modified contemporary southern black English, a combination of standard English and black English where sound is as important as meaning." He has preserved the story lines, the wit, the humor—all of the attributes which have made the stories so much a part of my life— while making them accessible to readers. It is interesting to read the foreword to this collection, preferably before reading the stories. Much research and personal feeling have been distilled into a concise, historical, and chronological explanation of the Uncle Remus stories. This foreword is invaluable to the appreciation of the tales.

I can not emphasize enough the importance of telling the stories. As you listen to yourself the rhythm and melodic language of Lester's telling will come forth. The contemporary approach to some of the stories brings them into today's lifestyle. They fit into the traditional and bring a modern humor to the stories. They must be told and I look forward to sharing them with children.

Augusta Baker

Columbia, South Carolina
August 1985

Augusta Baker is former Coordinator of Children's Services of
The New York Public Library and Storyteller-in-Residence
at the University of South Carolina.

Contents

"The tale is not beautiful if nothing is added.
Folktales remain merely dumb until you realize you are required to
complete them yourself, to fill in your own particulars."

ITALO CALVINO

The Uncle Remus stories of Joel Chandler Harris represent the largest single collection of Afro-American folktales ever collected and published. Their place and importance in Afro-American culture is singular and undisputed.

Harris (1848–1908) was a newspaperman, who, after stints on papers in Macon, Forsyth, and Savannah, Georgia, and New Orleans, wrote for the *Atlanta Constitution* for twenty-four years beginning in 1876. It was in its pages that stories told by a character called Uncle Remus first appeared to immediate acclaim.

Between 1896 and 1918, eight volumes of black folktales as told by Uncle Remus were published. There are 263 tales in these eight volumes, with the inestimable Brer Rabbit as the central character in 113, more or less. (The number is necessarily imprecise because of the stories in which Brer Rabbit plays an important role without being the central character.) Although Harris never studied folklore, and was embarrassed when others acclaimed him a folklorist, his integrity regarding the tales was exemplary and remarkable.

All of the tales were collected from blacks. Often Harris collected two or three versions of the same tale, and then chose the best version to publish. If he doubted a story's Afro-American roots, he did not use it.

Harris's other concern was language. Possessing a remarkable ear, he recognized that the tales could not be divorced from the language of the people who told them. Thus, he made a conscious and diligent effort to put this language on paper. In the absence of actual recordings, the Uncle Remus tales as put down by Harris are the most conscientious attempt to reproduce how the slaves talked, at least in one area of the South.

It is questionable whether the tales would have been so popular if Harris had not created a character named Uncle Remus as storyteller. By Harris's own admission, Uncle Remus was a composite of three former slaves he knew who had told him some of the tales.

As a character, Uncle Remus represents the "faithful darky" who, in Harris's words, "has nothing but pleasant memories of the discipline of slavery." He identifies wholly with his white master and mistress, espouses their value system, and is derisive of other blacks. There are no inaccuracies in Harris's characterization of Uncle Remus. Even the most cursory reading of the slave narratives collected by the Federal Writer's Project of the 1930s reveals that there were many slaves who fit the Uncle Remus mold.

Uncle Remus became a stereotype, and therefore negative, not because of inaccuracies in Harris's characterization, but because he was used as a symbol of slavery and a retrospective justification for it. This reflects the times in which the Uncle Remus tales appeared.

In 1876, the year the first Uncle Remus tale was published in the *Atlanta Constitution,* Rutherford B. Hayes "stole" the Presidency by promising the South that he would end Reconstruction and withdraw Federal troops in return for the South's votes in the electoral college. Beginning the following year, the nation's attitude was to let the South deal with its problems—meaning the freed slaves—as it saw fit, in an attempt to heal the wounds inflicted by the Civil War.

In such a political and moral climate Uncle Remus became a symbol of that reconciliation. He was the freed slave who not only had no bitterness toward his former enslavement, but looked back nostalgically to a time he considered better. The white majority could take comfort in Uncle Remus because he affirmed white superiority and confirmed an image of black inferiority many whites needed. Harris's Uncle Remus permitted whites to look to the future free of guilt about the past.

Uncle Remus is the most remembered character from a literature that justified slavery by portraying blacks who found slavery a haven, and freedom a threat and imposition.

It would be unfair and inaccurate to ascribe unseemly motives to Joel Chandler Harris in his creation of Uncle Remus. A writer should be judged on his total oeuvre. In this context, Harris's work is varied in its depiction of blacks and their attitudes toward slavery.

If there is one aspect of the Uncle Remus stories with which one could seriously disagree, it is the social setting in which the tales are told. Uncle Remus, and sometimes other blacks, tell the stories to an audience of one—a little white boy, the son of the plantation owner. While such a setting added to the appeal and accessibility of the tales for whites, it leaves the reader with no sense of the important role the tales played in black life.

The telling of black folktales, and indeed tales of all cultures, was a social event bringing together adults and children. That folktales are now considered primarily stories for children is an indication of our society's spiritual impoverishment. Traditionally, tales were told by adults to adults. If the children were quiet, they might be allowed to listen. Clearly, black folktales were not created and told for the entertainment of little white children, as the Uncle Remus tales would lead one to believe.

Reading the original Uncle Remus tales today is not an easy

task. The contemporary reader is offended by the dialect, if that reader is able to decipher it. (It is almost like reading a foreign language.) The reader is also uncomfortable with the figure of Uncle Remus, his attitudes, his use of the word "nigger," and his sycophancy. Because Uncle Remus is a character with whom blacks and whites are uneasy today, the tales themselves have become tainted in many minds. This is unfortunate. Whatever one may think about how Harris chose to present the tales, the fact remains that they are a cornerstone of Afro-American culture and continue to be vital.

The purpose in my retelling of the Uncle Remus tales is simple: to make the tales accessible again, to be told in the living rooms of condominiums as well as on front porches in the South.

2

Books have curious beginnings. This one began with the suggestion of Augusta Baker, the venerable children's librarian of the New York Public Library, to my editor, Phyllis Fogelman, that I retell the Uncle Remus stories. Having published two books of black folktales, *Black Folktales* and *The Knee-High Man and Other Tales,* such a project seemed logical. My background was southern and I had grown up hearing tales from my father and other black ministers. I had collected tales in Mississippi, and before the resurgence of interest in black culture, I had published essays on black traditional music and tales.

There were important questions that had to be answered about how to tell the tales before I could begin writing. Should Uncle Remus tell the tales in a black social setting or should several people in the same setting tell them? What language should be used—"straight" English, so that the tales would exist only as tales, without reference to their cultural roots? Or, should I use "black English," and if so, which black English? That spoken in northern urban areas, or that which I grew up hearing and speaking in the South? Should I retell all the tales, or should I choose from among them? On what basis would such choices be made?

The answers came once I decided that what is most important are the tales themselves. They are extraordinary and should be a part of people's lives again. They are funny, touching, horrifying, and some partake of that quality of magic found in myth.

Once I knew that the book should be the tales, the question of changing the characterization of Uncle Remus became irrelevant. Reportraying him would have been a distraction for those readers fond of Harris's Uncle Remus, or those who simply might not like my Uncle Remus. (I did have fun thinking about a new Uncle Remus, and couldn't decide whether to make him a Harlem barbershop owner, a hip dude "hanging out" on the corner, or even an old woman sitting on her Mississippi front porch, dipping snuff. For a while I seriously considered putting Uncle Remus in a slave setting and attempting a portrayal of slavery from the slave's point of view. Any of these approaches would have been interesting and fun, but ultimately irrelevant to my purpose, which was to tell the tales.)

The Uncle Remus presented here is a voice. I hesitate to call it my voice, because it is also the voice of a people, the black people of Kansas City, Kansas; Pine Bluff, Arkansas; Nashville, Tennessee; and the state of Mississippi. The first three places are where I grew up, and the latter is where I feel most at home and closest to my roots as a black person.

Yet, I have not attempted to duplicate black speech precisely, as Harris did. I have not even written the stories as I would tell them before an audience. (A frustration was realizing that the many inflections that can be brought to the word *well* as a transition between parts of a story, simply do not communicate on the printed page.) Instead, I have attempted to find a mean point so that the stories will read easily, whether they are read silently or aloud.

Thus, the stories are written in a modified contemporary southern black English, which is a combination of standard English and black English. Sometimes *kind of* is used, and other times *kinna*. How a word is pronounced depends on where it is in a sentence and whether the sentence requires the harder sound of *kind of* or the softer flow of *kinna*. In black English sound is as important as meaning. Thus, *their hands* and *they hands* mean the same thing, but the music is different. What is incorrect grammatically in standard English, e.g., *They was married,* is correct black English because of sound.

The other inconsistency the reader will notice is a shifting from past to present tense in some stories. Black English does not make hard distinctions between past and present. Is something that happened in the past but is present in the emotions, past or present? It is both, according to black people. Thus, some stories begin in the past tense and end in the present tense, reflecting the storyteller's excitement (mine) as the story reaches its climax.

The decision not to retell all of the Uncle Remus tales was a difficult one, but I made it on a very simple basis. I cannot tell a story I do not consider good, and some of the stories aren't. Harris himself became bored with the stories after a time, especially as it became difficult to find good ones.

There are 110 stories I have classified as having Brer Rabbit as the central character, including four found in Harris's papers and published in 1948 in *Seven Tales of Uncle Remus*. These four are excluded because Harris questioned their authenticity as black folktales. Of the remaining 106, I have combined eleven stories into five and omitted fifteen. Forty-eight tales appear in this volume, and thirty-seven tales will appear in the second volume. (For the interested reader, omitted stories and combined stories will be listed in the Appendix of the second volume.) I have created new titles for most of the stories.

Because the stories were published in eight volumes over twenty-two years, they were not presented in any particular order. Continuity between stories in each volume is provided by events on the plantation, happenings in the lives of the little boy and the blacks that allow Uncle Remus to say, "That reminds me of the time Brer Rabbit did," etc. In reading the tales, however, they suggest their own order, since many of the stories revolve around similar themes—courting, stealing from Mr. Man's garden, famine. I have attempted to give the tales an order in two ways: (1) By bringing together these related stories scattered through the eight volumes, and (2) By introductory paragraphs connecting a story to the one preceding, where it was warranted. Each stands as a separate story, however, whole unto itself.

Because these are authentic folktales, I have not changed the story lines. Thus there may be some tales that contemporary readers will find cruel. But as any reader of folktales knows, cruelty, too, has its place in the world of the imagination. I have also retained the language of the original stories where it was especially vivid or funny. Retelling the tales has involved sharpening story lines, i.e., eliminating irrelevant details and many archaic references and images that would be familiar only to someone with an intimate knowledge of slave life. Primarily, however, retelling the tales was a matter of finding the language that would allow the stories to live as the wonderful creations they have always been.

Some readers might be disturbed by my Uncle Remus making reference to things that are decidedly contemporary, such as shopping malls. This is a characteristic of black storytelling, and it was also used in the Uncle Remus tales as told by Harris. Black folktales exist in time, unlike myth, which reflects supratime. Thus, I am telling these tales now, and being true to the black tradition, there are contemporary references in them. Folktales are not cultural artifacts. In actuality, we are the tale and folktales are a mirror in which we can see (if we know how to see) our particular story. When I tell tales before audiences, the number of such references tends to increase because I tailor tales to the audience before me. I am well aware that such contemporary references will date the tales as they appear on the printed page. That is as it should be, because tales do not exist wholly on the printed page. The page preserves a particular telling of a tale, but not the tale itself. The tale is merely the theme on which the storyteller improvises, revitalizing the tale and making it ever new. The tale can never be what is on the printed page because what cannot be printed are the movement of the arms, the body motions, the gestures of the hands, which are as important and integral to the tales as the words. Stories are told in equal parts by the voice and the body.

The contemporary references also reflect that the tales were originally adult stories. Thus, there are lines and references in my telling of these tales that are for the enjoyment of adults, references that children may not understand. You as teller of these tales should feel free, are encouraged to feel free, to omit the contemporary references or any descriptions with which you may be uncomfortable. You are the storyteller; I am merely your guide to these stories.

One final word: I have been asked many times whether it is all right for a white person to tell black folktales. "I can't tell them the way you do," is the inevitable plaint. Of course not, but why should that be a consideration? Undoubtedly, a black person with roots in the southern black tradition will bring an added dimension to the telling of these tales to which most whites will not have access. That does not bar whites from telling them.

The most important element in telling these tales, or any folktale, is, do you love the tale? After all, what is a tale except a means of expressing love for this experience we call being human. If you love the tale, and tell it with love, the tale will communicate. If the language you speak is different from the language I speak, tell the tale in your language. Tell the tale as you would, not I, and believe in the tale. It will communicate its riches and its wonders, regardless of who you are. Trust the tale. Trust your love for the tale. That is all any good storyteller can do.

These tales are printed in a book merely to get them into the minds and hearts of as many people as possible. Don't mistake the tales in this book for the tales themselves. The tales will live only if they flow through your voice. The suffering of those slaves who created the tales will be redeemed (to a degree at least) if you receive their offering and make it a part of your life.

Julius Lester
Amherst, Massachusetts
August 1985

How the Animals Came to Earth

Most folks don't know it, but the animals didn't always live on earth. Way back before "In the beginning" and "Once upon a time," they lived next door to the Moon. They'd probably still be there if Brer Rabbit and Sister Moon hadn't started squabbling with one another like they were married. The way it come about was like this:

The animals liked to sit out in their yards every evening and look at Sister Moon. They thought she was just about the prettiest thing they'd ever seen, and Sister Moon never argued with them. Well, the animals started noticing that she was losing weight. To tell the truth, she was looking downright puny, like she had gone on a cottage cheese diet.

Brer Rabbit decided to climb over the fence to find out what was going on. "What's the matter, Sister Moon? I don't mean to hurt your feelings or nothing like that, but you look po' as Job's turkey."

Sister Moon said, "I ain't been feeling like myself of late."

"Is there anything I can do to help you?"

"Thank you, Brer Rabbit, but I don't believe you the man to do what I need doing."

Brer Rabbit was insulted. "I'm more man than Brer Sun who you chase all over the sky every month and can't catch up to."

Sister Moon smiled tightly. "All right, Brer Rabbit. I'll try you out. I need to get word to Mr. Man that I ain't feeling like myself. I believe I done caught cold from being out in the night air so much. If I don't put my light out and take a little vacation, I'm going to be in a bad way. I don't want Mr. Man to look up and see my light out one night and get scared."

"I'll take the word to him. I been wanting to see what a something called Mr. Man look like anyway."

"Tell Mr. Man I said, 'I'm getting weak for to be more strong. I'm going in the shade for to get more light.' "

Brer Rabbit said it over a couple of times and off he went.

He took a running start and jumped a long jump. He fell through space, past the stars and down through the firmament, tumbling tail over head and head over behind. This was no place for a rabbit! He was so scared, his eyes got big and wide and almost popped out of his head and they been that way ever since. This was the last time his mouth was going to get him into something his feet couldn't do.

He landed on Earth and waited a few minutes to make sure he had all his parts and they were in working order. Then he looked around. The first thing he saw was Mr. Man's garden. It was filled with green peas, lettuce, cabbage, collard greens, and sparrow grass. Over in the field were sheep, cows, goats, and pigs. Brer Rabbit's mouth started trembling and dribbling at the same time.

He went up to Mr. Man's house, knocked on the door, and said, "I got a message for you from Sister Moon."

"What is it?"

Brer Rabbit thought for a minute. "She say, 'I'm getting weak; I got no strength. I'm going to where the shadows stay.' "

Mr. Man got indignant. "Tell Sister Moon I said, 'Seldom seen and soon forgot; when Sister Moon dies her feet get cold.' "

Brer Rabbit nodded and took a long jump back up to Sister Moon. He told her what Mr. Man said. Sister Moon was angry. She hauled off and hit Brer Rabbit with a shovel and split his lip. Brer Rabbit don't take no stuff off nobody and he clawed and scratched Sister Moon. And to this day you can seek the marks—rabbits have split lips and the face of the moon is all scratched up and got holes in it.

Brer Rabbit went and told the animals about all the vegetables and sheep and goats and fat pigs he'd seen on Mr. Man's place. They decided right then that Sister Moon was on her own from now on.

They took the long jump and this is where they've been ever since.

How Brer Fox and Brer Dog Became Enemies

When the animals started living here on Earth, something seemed to happen to them. Where before they had gotten along with each other, now they started having little arguments and disagreements. It was only a matter of time before they weren't much different from people.

Brer Fox and Brer Rabbit were sitting alongside the road one day talking about much of nothing when they heard a strange sound—*blim, blim, blim.*

"What's that?" Brer Fox wanted to know. He didn't know whether to get scared or not.

"That?" answered Brer Rabbit. "Sound like Sister Goose."

"What she be doing?"

"Battling clothes," said Brer Rabbit.

I know y'all don't know what I'm talking about. You take your clothes to the Laundromat, or have a washing machine and dryer sitting right in the house. Way back yonder folks took their clothes down to the creek or stream or what'nsoever, got them real wet, laid 'em across a big rock or something, took a stick and *beat* the dirt out of them. You don't know nothing about no clean clothes until you put on some what been cleaned with a battlin' stick.

Well, when Brer Fox heard that Sister Goose was down at the stream, his eyes got big and Brer Rabbit knew his mind had just gotten fixed on supper. Brer Fox said he reckoned he better be getting home. Brer Rabbit said he supposed he should do the same, and they went their separate ways.

Brer Rabbit doubled back, however, and went down to the stream where Sister Goose was.

"How you today, Sister Goose?"

"Just fine, Brer Rabbit. Excuse me for not shaking hands with you, but I got all these suds on my hands."

Brer Rabbit said he understood.

I suppose I got to stop the story, 'cause I can hear you thinking that a goose don't have hands. And next thing I know you be trying to get me to believe that snakes don't have feet and cats don't have wings, and I know better! So, if you don't mind, you can keep your thoughts to yourself and I'll get back to the story.

After Brer Rabbit and Sister Goose had finished exchanging the pleasantries of the day, Brer Rabbit said, "I got to talk with you about Brer Fox. He's coming for you, Sister Goose, and it'll probably be before daybreak."

Sister Goose got all nervous and scared. "What am I gon' do, Brer Rabbit? My husband is dead and ain't no man around the house. What am I gon' do?"

Brer Rabbit thought for a minute. "Take all your clothes and roll 'em up in a nice clean white sheet and put that on your bed tonight. Then you go spend the night up in the rafters."

So, that's what Sister Goose did. But she also sent for her friend, Brer Dog, and asked him if he'd keep watch that night. He said he'd be glad to.

Just before daybreak Brer Fox creeped up to the house, looked around, eased the front door open and slipped inside. He saw something big and white on the bed. He grabbed it and ran out the door. Soon as he jumped off the porch, Brer Dog came out from under the house growling and scratching up dirt. Brer Fox dropped that bundle of clothes like it was a burning log and took off! It's a good thing, too, 'cause it had taken Brer Dog four months to find somebody who could wash and iron his pajamas as good as Sister Goose, and he wasn't about to let nothing happen to her.

Next day when the news got around that Brer Fox had tried to steal Sister Goose's laundry, he couldn't go no-where for a week. Brer Fox blamed Brer Dog for spreading the news through the community, and ever since that day, the Dog and the Fox haven't gotten along with each other.

"Hold'im Down, Brer Fox"

Brer Fox couldn't prove it, but he knew Brer Rabbit had warned Sister Goose he was coming, and he made up his mind to get even. Brer Rabbit got word about what Brer Fox was thinking on, so he stayed away from his regular habitats for a while.

On this particular day he was somewhere up around Lost Forty and saw a great big Horse laying dead out in a pasture. Or he thought it was dead until he saw the Horse's tail switch.

Brer Rabbit went on his way, but who should he see coming toward him but Brer Fox!

"Brer Fox! Brer Fox! Come here! Quick! I got some good news! Come here!"

Brer Fox didn't care what kind of good news Brer Rabbit had. The good news was that he had found that rabbit! Just as Brer Fox got in grabbing distance, Brer Rabbit said:

"Come on, Brer Fox! I done found how we can have enough fresh meat to last us until the middle of next Sep-terrary."

Brer Fox, being a prudent man, thought he should check this out. "What you talking about, Brer Rabbit?"

"I just found a Horse laying on the ground where we can catch him and tie him up."

Sounded good to Brer Fox. "Let's go!"

Brer Rabbit led him over to the pasture, and sho' nuf', there was the Horse laying on the ground like he was waiting for them. Brer Rabbit and Brer Fox got to talking about how to tie him up. They argued back and forth for a while until finally Brer Rabbit said:

"Listen. I tell you the way we do it. I'll tie you to his tail and when he tries to get up, you can hold him down. If I was a big strong man like you, I'd do it, and you know, if I was to hold him, he would be held. But I ain't got your strength. Of course, if you scared to do it, then I reckon we got to come up with another plan."

There was something about the plan that Brer Fox didn't like, but he couldn't think of what it was. Not wanting Brer Rabbit to think he wasn't strong and brave, he said O.K.

Brer Rabbit tied him to the Horse's tail. "Brer Fox! That Horse don't know it, but he caught!" Brer Fox grinned weakly.

Brer Rabbit got him a great, long switch and hit the Horse on the rump—POW! The Horse jumped up and landed on his feet and there was Brer Fox, dangling upside down in the air, too far off the ground for peace of mind.

"Hold'im down, Brer Fox! Hold'im down!"

The Horse felt something on his tail. He started jumping and raring and bucking and Brer Fox knew now what was wrong with Brer Rabbit's idea.

"Hold'im down, Brer Fox! Hold'im down!"

The Horse jumped and twirled and snorted and bucked, but Brer Fox hung on.

"Hold'im down, Brer Fox! Hold'im down!"

One time Brer Fox managed to shout back, "If I got *him* down, who got hold of *me?*"

But Brer Rabbit just yelled, "Hold'im down, Brer Fox! You got him now! Hold'im down!"

The Horse started kicking with his hind legs and Brer Fox slid down the tail. The Horse kicked him in the stomach once, twice, three times, and Brer Fox went sailing through the air. It was a week and four days before Brer Fox finally come to earth, which gave him a whole lot of time to realize that Brer Rabbit had bested him again.

Brer Rabbit Comes to Dinner

It took Brer Fox a while to recuperate, but that gave him a lot of time to scheme and plan on how he was going to get Brer Rabbit.

The very first day Brer Fox was up and about, he sauntered down the road. Coming toward him looking as plump and fat as a Christmas turkey was Brer Rabbit.

"Just a minute there!" Brer Fox said as Brer Rabbit started to walk past without speaking.

"I'm busy," said Brer Rabbit. "I'm full of fleas today and got to go to town and get some ointment."

"This won't take more than a minute," Brer Fox answered, falling into step beside him.

"All right. What's on your mind?"

Brer Fox gave a sheepish grin. "Well, Brer Rabbit. I saw Brer Bear yesterday and he said I ought to make friends with you. I felt so bad when he finished with me that I promised I'd make up with you the first chance I got."

Brer Rabbit scratched his head real slow like. "Awright, Brer Fox. I believe Brer Bear got a point. To show you I mean business, why don't you drop over to the house to-morrow and take supper with me and the family?"

Next day Brer Rabbit helped his wife fix up a big meal of cabbages, roasting ears, and sparrow grass. Long about supper time the children came in the house all excited, hollering, "Here come Brer Fox!"

Brer Rabbit told them to sit down to the table, mind their manners, and be quiet. He wanted everything to be just right. So everybody sat down and waited for Brer Fox to knock on the door. They waited a long time, but no knock came.

"Are you sure that was Brer Fox you saw coming up the road?" he asked his children.

"We sure. He was drooling at the mouth."

No mistake. That was Brer Fox.

Brer Rabbit got out of his chair very quietly and cracked the door open. He peeped one of his eyeballs out. He rolled his eyeballs from one side of the yard to the other until they stopped on a bush that looked like it was growing a fox's tail. Fox's tail! Brer Rabbit slammed the door real quick.

Next day Brer Fox sent word by Brer Mink that he had been low-down sick the day before and was sorry he couldn't come. To make up for it, he'd sho' be pleased if Brer Rabbit would take supper with him that very same evening.

When the shadows were at their shortest, Brer Rabbit went over to Brer Fox's. He'd scarcely set one foot on the porch when he heard groaning from inside. He opened the door and saw Brer Fox sitting in his rocking chair, a blanket over his shoulder, looking like Death eating soda crackers in the graveyard. Brer Rabbit looked around and didn't see any supper on the stove. He did notice the butcher knife and roasting pan on the counter, however.

"Looks like you planning on us having chicken for supper, Brer Fox," says Brer Rabbit like nothing was wrong.

"Sho' nuf'," says Brer Fox.

"You know what goes good with chicken, Brer Fox?"

"What's that?"

"Calamus root! Seems like I can't eat chicken no other way nowadays." And before Brer Fox could blink, Brer Rabbit was out the door and into the bushes where he hid to see if Brer Fox was sho' nuf' sick.

A minute later Brer Fox come out on the porch looking as healthy as a rat in a tuxedo. Brer Rabbit stuck his head out of the bushes and said, "I leave you some calamus root right here, Brer Fox. You ought to try it with your chicken tonight!"

Brer Fox leaped off the porch and took off after Brer Rabbit, but that rabbit was halfway to Philly-Me-York before Brer Fox's claws touched the ground. All Brer Fox had for supper that night was an air sandwich.

Brer Rabbit and the Tar Baby

Early one morning, even before Sister Moon had put on her negligee, Brer Fox was up and moving around. He had a glint in his eye, so you know he was up to no good.

He mixed up a big batch of tar and made it into the shape of a baby. By the time he finished, Brer Sun was yawning himself awake and peeping one eye over the topside of the earth.

Brer Fox took his Tar Baby down to the road, the very road Brer Rabbit walked along every morning. He sat the Tar Baby in the road, put a hat on it, and then hid in a ditch.

He had scarcely gotten comfortable (as comfortable as one can get in a ditch), before Brer Rabbit came strutting along like he owned the world and was collecting rent from everybody in it.

Seeing the Tar Baby, Brer Rabbit tipped his hat. "Good morning! Nice day, ain't it? Of course, any day I wake up and find I'm still alive is a nice day far as I'm concerned." He laughed at his joke, which he thought was pretty good. (Ain't too bad if I say so myself.)

Tar Baby don't say a word. Brer Fox stuck his head up out of the ditch, grinning.

"You deaf?" Brer Rabbit asked the Tar Baby. "If you are, I can talk louder." He yelled, *"How you this morning? Nice day, ain't it?"*

Tar Baby still don't say nothing.

Brer Rabbit was getting kinna annoyed. "I don't know what's wrong with this young generation. Didn't your parents teach you no manners?"

Tar Baby don't say nothing.

"Well, I reckon I'll teach you some!" He hauls off and hits the Tar Baby. BIP! And his fist was stuck to the side of the Tar Baby's face.

"You let me go!" Brer Rabbit yelled. "Let me go or I'll really pop you one." He twisted and turned, but he couldn't get loose. "All right! I warned you!" And he smacked the

Tar Baby on the other side of its head. BIP! His other fist was stuck.

Brer Rabbit was sho' nuf' mad now. "You turn me loose or I'll make you wish you'd never been born." THUNK! He kicked the Tar Baby and his foot was caught. He was cussing and carrying on something terrible and kicked the Tar Baby with the other foot and THUNK! That foot was caught. "You let me go or I'll butt you with my head." He butted the Tar Baby under the chin and THUNK! His head was stuck.

Brer Fox sauntered out of the ditch just as cool as the sweat on the side of a glass of ice tea. He looked at Brer Rabbit stuck to the Tar Baby and laughed until he was almost sick.

"Well, I got you now," Brer Fox said when he was able to catch his breath. "You floppy-eared, pom-pom-tailed good-for-nothing! I guess you know who's having rabbit for dinner this night!"

Brer Rabbit would've turned around and looked at him if he could've unstuck his head. Didn't matter. He heard the drool in Brer Fox's voice and knew he was in a world of trouble.

"You ain't gon' be going around through the community raising commotion anymore, Brer Rabbit. And it's your own fault too. Didn't nobody tell you to be so friendly with the Tar Baby. You stuck yourself on that Tar Baby without so much as an invitation. There you are and there you'll be until I get my fire started and my barbecue sauce ready."

Brer Rabbit always got enough lip for anybody and everybody. He even told God once what He'd done wrong on the third day of Creation. This time, though, Brer Rabbit talked mighty humble. "Well, Brer Fox. No doubt about it. You got me and no point my saying that I would improve my ways if you spared me."

"No point at all," Brer Fox agreed as he started gathering kindling for the fire.

"I guess I'm going to be barbecue this day." Brer Rabbit sighed. "But getting barbecued is a whole lot better than getting thrown in the briar patch." He sighed again. "No doubt about it. Getting barbecued is almost a blessing compared to being thrown in that briar patch on the other side of the road. If you got to go, go in a barbecue sauce. That's what I always say. How much lemon juice and brown sugar you put in yours?"

When Brer Fox heard this, he had to do some more thinking, because he wanted the worst death possible for that rabbit. "Now that I thinks on it, it's too hot to be standing over a hot fire. I think I'll hang you."

Brer Rabbit shuddered. "Hanging is a terrible way to die! Just terrible! But I thank you for being so considerate. Hanging is better than being thrown in the briar patch."

Brer Fox thought that over a minute. "Come to think of it, I can't hang you, 'cause I didn't bring my rope. I'll drown you in the creek over yonder."

Brer Rabbit sniffed like he was about to cry. "No, no, Brer Fox. You know I can't stand water, but I guess drowning, awful as it is, is better than the briar patch."

"I got it!" Brer Fox exclaimed. "I don't feel like dragging you all the way down to the creek. I got my knife right here. I'm going to skin you!" He pulled out his knife.

Brer Rabbit's ears shivered. "That's all right, Brer Fox. It'll hurt something awful, but go ahead and skin me. Scratch out my eyeballs! Tear out my ears by the roots! Cut off my legs! Do what'nsoever you want to with me,

Brer Fox, but please, please, please! Don't throw me in that briar patch!"

Brer Fox was convinced now that the worst thing he could do to Brer Rabbit was the very thing Brer Rabbit didn't want him to do. He snatched him off the Tar Baby and wound up his arm like he was trying to throw a fast-ball past Hank Aaron and chunked that rabbit across the road and smack dab in the middle of the briar patch.

Brer Fox waited. Didn't hear a thing. He waited a little longer. Still no sound. And just about the time he decided he was rid of Brer Rabbit, just about the time a big grin started to spread across his face, he heard a little giggle.

"Tee-hee! Tee-hee!" And the giggles broke into the loudest laughing you've ever heard.

Brer Fox looked up to see Brer Rabbit sitting on top of the hill on the other side of the briar patch.

Brer Rabbit waved. "I was born and raised in the briar patch, Brer Fox! Born and raised in the briar patch!" And he hopped on over the hill and out of sight.

Brer Rabbit Gets Even

About a week later Brer Rabbit decided to visit with Miz Meadows and the girls. Don't come asking me who Miz Meadows and her girls were. I don't know, but then again, ain't no reason I got to know. Miz Meadows and the girls were in the tale when it was handed to me, and they gon' be in it when I hand it to you. And that's the way the rain falls on that one.

Brer Rabbit was sitting on the porch with Miz Meadows and the girls, and Miz Meadows said that Brer Fox was going through the community telling how he'd tricked Brer Rabbit with the Tar Baby. Miz Meadows and the girls thought that was about the funniest thing they'd ever heard and they just laughed and laughed.

Brer Rabbit was as cool as Joshua when he blew on the trumpet 'round the walls of Jericho. Just rocked in the rocking chair as if the girls were admiring his good looks.

When they got done with their giggling, he looked at them and winked his eye real slow. "Ladies, Brer Fox was my daddy's riding horse for thirty years. Might've been thirty-five or forty, but thirty, for sure." He got up, tipped his hat, said, "Good day, ladies," and walked on off up the road like he was the Easter Parade.

Next day Brer Fox came by to see Miz Meadows and the girls. No sooner had he tipped his hat than they told him what Brer Rabbit had said. Brer Fox got so hot it was all he could do to keep from biting through his tongue.

"Ladies, I'm going to make Brer Rabbit eat his words and spit'em out where you can see'em!"

Brer Fox took off down the road, through the woods, down the valley, up the hill, down the hill, round the bend, through the creek, and past the shopping mall, until he came to Brer Rabbit's house. (Wasn't no shopping mall there. I just put that in to see if you was listening.)

Brer Rabbit saw him coming. He ran in the house and shut the door tight as midnight. Brer Fox knocked on the door. BAM! BAM! BAM! No answer. BAM! BAM! BAM! Still no answer. BLAMMITY BLAM BLAM BLAM!

From inside came this weak voice. "Is that you, Brer Fox? If it is, please run and get the doctor. I ate some parsley this morning, and it ain't setting too well on my stomach. Please, Brer Fox. Run and get the doctor."

"I'm sho' sorry to hear that, Brer Rabbit. Miz Meadows asked me to come tell you that she and the girls are having a party today. They said it wouldn't be a party worth a dead leaf if you weren't there. They sent me to come get you."

Brer Rabbit allowed as to how he was too sick, and Brer Fox said he couldn't be too sick to go partying. (God knows, that's the truth! I ain't never been too sick to party. Even when I'm dead, I'll get up out of the grave to party. And when I get sick, the blues are the best doctor God put on earth. The blues can cure athlete's foot, hangnail, and the heartbreak of psoriasis.)

Well, Brer Rabbit and Brer Fox got to arguing back and forth and forth and back about whether he was too sick to come to the party. Finally, Brer Rabbit said, "Well, all right, Brer Fox. I don't want to hurt nobody's feelings by not coming to the party, but I can't walk."

Brer Fox said, "That's all right. I'll carry you in my arms."

"I'm afraid you'll drop me."

"I wouldn't do a thing like that, Brer Rabbit. I'm stronger than bad breath."

"I wouldn't argue with you there, but I'm still afraid. I'll go if you carry me on your back."

"Well, all right," Brer Fox said reluctantly.

"But I can't ride without a saddle."

"I'll get the saddle."

"But I can't get in the saddle without a bridle."

Brer Fox was getting a little tired of this, but he agreed to get a bridle.

"And I can't keep my balance unless you got some

blinders on. How I know you won't try to throw me off?"

That's just what Brer Fox was planning on doing, but he said he'd put the blinders on.

Brer Fox went off to get all the riding gear, and Brer Rabbit combed his hair, greased his mustache, put on his best suit (the purple one with the yellow vest), shined his toenails, and fluffed out his cottontail. He was definitely ready to party!

He went outside and Brer Fox had the saddle, bridle, and blinders on and was down on all fours. Brer Rabbit got on and away they went. They hadn't gone far when Brer Fox felt Brer Rabbit raise his foot.

"What you doing, Brer Rabbit?"

"Shortening up the left stirrup."

Brer Rabbit raised the other foot.

"What you doing now?" Brer Fox wanted to know.

"Shortening up the right stirrup."

What Brer Rabbit was really doing was putting on spurs. When they got close to Miz Meadows's house, Brer Rabbit stuck them spurs into Brer Fox's flanks and Brer Fox took off *buckity-buckity-buckity!*

Miz Meadows and the girls were sitting on the porch when Brer Rabbit come riding by like he was carrying mail on the Pony Express. He galloped up the road until he was almost out of sight, turned Brer Fox around and came back by the house a-whooping and a-hollering like he'd just discovered gold.

He turned Brer Fox around again, slowed him to a trot and rode on up to Miz Meadows's house, where he got off and tied Brer Fox to the hitching post. He sauntered up the steps, tipped his hat to the ladies, lit a cigar, and sat down in the rocking chair.

"Ladies, didn't I tell you that Brer Fox was the riding horse for our family! Of course, he don't keep his gait like he used to, but in a month or so he'll have it back."

Miz Meadows and the gals laughed so hard and so long, they liked to broke out of their underclothes.

Brer Rabbit must've stayed with Miz Meadows and the girls half the day. They had tea and cookies, and Brer Rabbit entertained them with some old-time barrelhouse piano. Finally it was time to go. He kissed the ladies' hands, got on Brer Fox, and with a little nudge of the spurs, rode away.

Soon as they were out of sight, Brer Fox started rarin' and buckin' to get Brer Rabbit off. Every time he rared, Brer Rabbit jabbed him with the spurs, and every time he bucked, Brer Rabbit yanked hard on the bridle. Finally, Brer

Fox rolled over on the ground and that got Brer Rabbit off in a hurry.

Brer Rabbit didn't waste no time getting through the underbrush, and Brer Fox was after him like the wet on water. Brer Rabbit saw a tree with a hole and ran in it just as the shadow of Brer Fox's teeth was going up his back.

The hole was too little for Brer Fox to get into, so he lay down on the ground beside it to do some serious thinking.

He was lying there with his eyes closed (a fox always closes his eyes when he's doing *serious* thinking), when Brer Buzzard came flopping along. He saw Brer Fox lying there like he was dead, and said, "Looks like supper has come to me."

"No, it ain't, fool!" said Brer Fox, opening his eyes. "I ain't dead. I got Brer Rabbit trapped in this tree here, and I ain't letting him get away this time if it takes me six Christmases."

Brer Buzzard and Brer Fox talked over the situation for a while. Finally, Brer Buzzard said he'd watch the tree if Brer Fox wanted to go get his axe to chop the tree down.

Soon as Brer Fox was gone and everything was quiet, Brer Rabbit moved close to the hole and yelled, "Brer Fox! Brer Fox!"

Brer Rabbit acted like he was annoyed when Brer Fox didn't answer. "I know you out there, Brer Fox. Can't fool me. I just wanted to tell you how much I wish Brer Turkey Buzzard was here."

Brer Buzzard's ears got kind of sharp. He put on his best Brer Fox voice and said, "What you want with Brer Buzzard?"

"Oh, nothing, except there's the fattest gray squirrel in

here that I've ever seen. If Brer Buzzard was here, I'd drive the squirrel out the other side of the tree to him."

"Well," said Brer Buzzard, still trying to sound like Brer Fox and not doing too good a job, "you drive him out and I'll catch him for Brer Buzzard."

Brer Rabbit started making all kinds of noises like he was trying to drive the squirrel out and Brer Buzzard ran around to the other side of the tree. Quite naturally, Brer Rabbit ran out of the tree and headed straight for home.

Brer Buzzard was mighty embarrassed when he realized he'd been tricked. Before he could think of what to tell Brer Fox, Brer Fox came marching up with his axe on his shoulder.

"How's Brer Rabbit?" Brer Fox wanted to know.

"Oh, he doing fine, I reckon. He's mighty quiet, but he's in there."

Brer Fox took his axe and—POW!—started in on the tree. He was swinging that axe so hard and so fast, the chips were piling up like snowflakes.

"He's in there!" Brer Buzzard yelled. "He's in there!" The sweat was pouring off Brer Fox like grease coming out of a Christmas goose what's been in the oven all day. Finally, Brer Buzzard couldn't hold it in any longer and he bust out laughing.

"What's so doggone funny?" Brer Fox wanted to know, putting his axe down.

"He's in there, Brer Fox! He's in there!" Brer Buzzard exclaimed, still laughing.

Brer Fox was suspicious now. He stuck his head in the hole and didn't see a thing. "It's dark in there, Brer Buzzard. Your neck is longer than mine. You stick your head in. Maybe you can see where he's at."

Brer Buzzard didn't want to do it, but he didn't have no choice. He walked over real careful like, stuck his head in the hole, and soon as he did, Brer Fox grabbed his neck and pulled him out.

"Let me go, Brer Fox! I ain't done nothing to you. I got to get home to my wife. She be worrying about me."

"She don't have to do that, 'cause you gon' be dead if you don't tell me where that rabbit is."

Brer Buzzard told him what had happened and how sorry he was.

"Well, it don't make no never mind," said Brer Fox. "You'll do just as good. I'm gon' throw you on a fire and burn you up."

"If you do, I'll fly away."

"Well, if that's the case, I better take care of you right here and now."

Brer Fox grabbed Brer Buzzard by the tail to throw him on the ground and break his neck. Soon as he raised his arm, however, Brer Buzzard's tail feathers came out and he flew away.

Po' Brer Fox. If it wasn't for bad luck, he wouldn't have no luck at all.

Brer Rabbit and Sister Cow

While Brer Fox was sitting on the ground with Brer Buzzard's tail feathers in his hand, wondering if God had something against him, Brer Rabbit was eleventeen miles away. He was tired, sweaty, and out of breath, and when he saw Sister Cow grazing in a field, he thought how nice it would be if she gave him some milk to drink. But he knew she wouldn't. One time his wife had been sick and Brer Rabbit had asked her for some milk and she'd refused him. But that didn't make no never mind. He was going to get him some of her milk.

"How you, Sister Cow?" asked Brer Rabbit, walking up to her.

"Reckon I be getting on all right, Brer Rabbit. How you be?"

"Fair to middling. Fair to middling."

"How's your family?"

" 'Bout the same, I reckon. How's Brer Bull and all your young'uns?"

"They doing fine, just fine."

"Glad to hear it."

Brer Rabbit looked around for a minute and noticed a persimmon tree. "There's some mighty nice persimmons on that tree. I'd love to have some."

"How you gon' get'em?" Sister Cow wanted to know.

"Well, I was wondering if you would butt the tree for me a time or two and shake some down."

Sister Cow allowed as to how she thought she could do that. She took a running start and banged her head into the tree, but no persimmons fell. And there was a good reason too. The persimmons were green and weren't ready to fall, which Brer Rabbit knew. Sister Cow backed up farther and galloped toward the tree like a racehorse and—BAM!—hit that tree so hard that one of her horns got stuck. Brer Rabbit jumped up and did the shimmy, 'cause that was just what he'd been waiting for.

"I'm stuck," called out Sister Cow. "Come give me a hand, Brer Rabbit."

"Don't believe there's much I can do, but I'll run and get Brer Bull." Brer Rabbit ran all right, ran straight home to get his wife and all the children. They come back with buckets and milked Sister Cow dry.

"You have a good night, Sister Cow!" Brer Rabbit called out as him and his family were leaving. "I be back in the morning."

Sister Cow worked hard all through the night trying to get her horn unstuck, and nigh on to daybreak she finally got loose. She grazed around in the field for a while, because she was mighty hungry. Long before the time she thought Brer Rabbit would be coming back, she stuck her horn back in the hole. However, Sister Cow didn't know that Brer Rabbit had been watching all the while.

"Good morning, Sister Cow!" says Brer Rabbit, coming up to her. "How you this morning?"

"Ain't doing too good, Brer Rabbit. Couldn't sleep last night for trying to get out of this hole. Brer Rabbit? You suppose you could grab on to my tail and yank it real hard? I believe if you did that, I might be able to get free."

"Tell you what, Sister Cow. You do the pulling and I'll do the grunting."

Sister Cow had had enough. She turned around and took off after Brer Rabbit. She was a lot faster than Brer Rabbit had given her credit for and it was all he could do to stay a hop in front of her horns. He dived into the first briar patch he saw, and Sister Cow come to a screeching halt.

After a while she saw two big eyes staring out at her. "How you this morning, Brer Big-Eyes?" she says. "You seen Brer Rabbit pass here?"

"I did. He was looking mighty scared too."

Sister Cow went galloping down the road. Brer Rabbit lay there in the briar patch just laughing and laughing. Brer Fox was mad at him; Brer Buzzard was mad at him; and now, Sister Cow was mad at him. And he just laughed and laughed.

Brer Turtle, Brer Rabbit, and Brer Fox

First thing next morning Brer Rabbit went to see Miz Meadows and the girls. He wasn't far from their house when he came upon Brer Turtle. He knocked on Brer Turtle's roof.

You know, Brer Turtle is a cautious kind of creature and he always carries his house with him. Don't know whether he's afraid of robbers or just what. (The way folks be breaking into houses these days, seems to me Brer Turtle got the right idea.)

Anyway, Brer Rabbit knocked on the roof and asked if anybody was in. Brer Turtle allowed as to how he was. Brer Rabbit wanted to know where he was going.

Brer Turtle thought that was an interesting question, 'cause he hadn't thought about it. Going was so much of a problem that *where* he went wasn't important. Chances were he wasn't gon' get there anyway. As far as he was concerned, he was going to wherever he got to. That being the case, Brer Rabbit said he'd carry him along and they could call on Miz Meadows and the girls. That was all right with Brer Turtle.

Miz Meadows and the girls were glad to have some company and invited them in to set a spell. Brer Turtle was too low to sit on the floor and take part in the conversation, and when they sat him in a chair, he still wasn't high enough. Finally, Miz Meadows put him on the mantelpiece above the fireplace, where he could take part in everything that was going on.

Very quickly the conversation got around to Brer Rabbit riding Brer Fox like a horse the day before.

"I would've ridden him over this morning," said Brer Rabbit, "but I rode him so hard yesterday that he's kinna lame in one leg this morning. I may be forced to sell him."

Brer Turtle spoke up. "Well, Brer Rabbit, please sell him out of the neighborhood. Why, day before yesterday Brer Fox passed me on the road, and do you know what he said?"

Quite naturally nobody did, since they weren't there.

"He looked at me and said, 'Hello, Stinkin' Jim!' "

"He didn't!" exclaimed Miz Meadows. She and the girls were dismayed that Brer Fox would talk like that to a fine gentleman like Brer Turtle.

Now, while all this was going on, Brer Fox was standing in the back door, hearing every word. He sho' heard more than he bargained for, which is always how it is with folks who put their ears in other folks' conversations. The talk about him got so bad that the only way to stop it was to walk in like he'd just got there.

"Good day, everybody!" he said, grinning, and having taken care of all the pleasantries, he made a grab for Brer Rabbit.

Miz Meadows and the girls commenced to hollering and screaming and carrying on. Brer Turtle was scampering around on the mantelpiece and he got so excited that he tripped, fell off, and landed right on Brer Fox's head.

That brought all the commotion to a halt. Brer Fox rubbed the knot on his head, looked around, and Brer Rabbit was nowhere to be seen. Brer Fox looked and looked until finally, he saw some soot falling out of the chimney and into the fireplace.

"Aha!" says he. "I'm gon' light a fire in the fireplace and smoke you out, Brer Rabbit." He started stacking wood in the fireplace.

Brer Rabbit laughed.

"What's so funny?"

"Ain't gon' tell, Brer Fox."

"What you laughing at, I said."

"Well, nothing, except I just found a box of money hid up here behind a loose brick."

Brer Fox wasn't gon' get fooled this time. "That's a lie, and you know it." He commenced to stacking the wood again.

"Don't have to take my word for it," Brer Rabbit said, just as calmly as he could be. "Look up here and see for yourself."

Brer Fox peered up the chimney. Brer Rabbit dropped a brick square on his head. If somebody dropped a brick on your head, that would pretty well take care of things, now wouldn't it?

Brer Wolf Tries to Catch Brer Rabbit

After Brer Rabbit dropped the brick on Brer Fox's head, Brer Fox was laid up in the hospital for a week or so. The day he got out he commenced to scheming again.

He was walking down the road and ran into his cousin, Brer Wolf. They hadn't seen each other since the big family barbecue last Juvember, so they hugged and exchanged news about their kin, and then Brer Fox brought his cousin up to date on all that Brer Rabbit had been doing.

"This has got to stop," says Brer Wolf. "We got to get that rabbit."

"Easier said than done."

"Well, I got a plan, but for it to work, we got to get him inside your house, Brer Fox."

"He wouldn't come in my house if you promised him free lettuce and yogurt for a year."

"Don't you worry about that. I can get him there," says Brer Wolf.

"How?"

"You go home, Brer Fox, get in bed and make like you dead. And don't say nothing until Brer Rabbit puts his hands on you. When he does, grab him, and we got us a good supper!"

Brer Wolf went over to Brer Rabbit's house and knocked on the door. *Bam! Bam! Bam!* Nobody answered. Brer Wolf commenced to banging and kicking on the door like he didn't have no manners, which he didn't. BLAMMITY BLAM BLAM BLAM BLAMMITY!

Finally a teenichy voice came from inside. "Who's there?"

"A friend."

"All them what say friend ain't friend," Brer Rabbit answered. "Who's there?"

"I got bad news."

Bad news will get folks to listen when good news won't. Brer Rabbit cracked the door and peeked half-a-eyeball out.

"Brer Fox died this morning," Brer Wolf said real mournfullike.

Brer Rabbit raised half-a-eyebrow. "That so?"

"He never recuperated from that lick on the head when you dropped the brick on him. I just thought you'd want to know."

This was bad news that was sho' nuf' good news. But it wasn't news to be accepted on somebody else's say-so. He decided to sneak over to Brer Fox's and verify it.

When he got there, everything was quiet and still. He peeped through the open window, and there, lying on the bed, hands folded across his chest, eyes closed, was Brer Fox.

"Po' Brer Fox," said Brer Rabbit. "He sho' is dead. Leastwise he look dead. Of course, I always heard that when folks was dead and somebody came to see'em, dead folks would raise up a leg and holler 'Wahoo!' "

Brer Fox raised up his leg and hollered, "Wahoo!"

Brer Rabbit didn't waste no time getting away from there.

Brer Rabbit Finally Gets Beaten

You know, it ain't possible to go through life without meeting your match some time or other. Brer Rabbit was no exception.

One day he and Brer Turtle were having a good laugh, remembering the time Brer Turtle conked Brer Fox on the head.

Brer Turtle said, "If Brer Fox had chased me instead of you, I would've been caught just as sure as you're born."

Brer Rabbit chuckled. "Brer Turtle, I could've caught you myself."

Brer Turtle looked incredulous. "You must be joking, Brer Rabbit. You couldn't have caught me if your feet had turned to wheels and your tail to a motor."

"Hold on a minute!" Brer Rabbit couldn't believe his big ears. "You so slow that when you moving you look like you standing still."

"I ain't got time to beat my lips with you over it. I got fifty dollars say I'm the fastest."

"And I got fifty say you been shaving the hair off your legs or something, but I know you done lost your mind."

"Brer Rabbit, I hate to take your money, but if that's what you want, that's what you got."

Brer Rabbit laughed. "I'll leave you so far behind that I can plant greens at the beginning of the race and by the time you cross the finish line, them greens will be ready to pick."

"I hope your feet as fast as your mouth."

They got Brer Buzzard to be the race judge and hold the bet money. It was to be a five-mile race, with posts set a mile apart. Brer Turtle claimed he could race faster going through the woods. Everybody told him he was out of his mind. How could he expect to beat Brer Rabbit, who would be running on the road! Brer Turtle said, "Watch me."

Brer Rabbit went into training. He bought a red jogging suit, a green sweatband, and some yellow Adidas sneakers, and he jogged ten miles every day. Then he'd come home and do a whole mess of push-ups, sit-ups, and skip rope to his records. Some folks wondered if he was training for a race or "Soul Train."

Brer Turtle didn't do a thing. You see, it's a strange thing about the Turtle family. There were six of 'em, including Brer Turtle, and they all looked alike. The only way to tell them apart was to put'em under a magnifying glass, and even then you could make a mistake.

On the day of the race, folks was there from all over. Even the TV networks were there, so the folks on the Moon could see it. Miz Meadows and the girls brought lunch baskets and lots of Dr Pepper to drink. Brer Rabbit showed up in his shades, wearing a gold jogging suit with a tan stripe, and when he took that off, he had on emerald-green racing shorts. Everybody ooohed and aaahed and rushed to get his autograph.

Meanwhile, Brer Turtle and his family had been up with the sun. He had put his wife in the woods at the starting line, and he stationed each of his children near the other posts. Brer Turtle hid himself in the woods at the finish line.

Race time came and Brer Rabbit hollered, "You ready, Brer Turtle?"

Miz Turtle was off a little ways in the woods and, disguising her voice, hollered, "Let's go!"

Brer Turkey Buzzard fired the gun and the race was on. Brer Rabbit took off like a 747 jet. Miz Turtle went home.

Brer Rabbit came to the one-mile post. "Where you at, Brer Turtle?"

Brer Turtle's young'un crawled on the road and said, "Right with you, Brer Rabbit."

Brer Rabbit started running a little faster. He came to the two-mile post. "Where you at, Brer Turtle?"

"Right with you," came the answer.

Brer Rabbit ran a little faster. He passed the three-mile post, the four-mile post, and every time he hollered for Brer Turtle, the answer came back, "Right with you!"

The finish line was in sight now, a quarter mile away.

Brer Rabbit could see Brer Buzzard with the checkered flag, but he didn't see Brer Turtle come out of the woods and hide behind the post marking the finish line.

"Give me the money, Brer Buzzard! Give me the money!" Brer Rabbit started hollering, and Miz Meadows and the girls started cheering like they'd lost their senses.

Brer Rabbit was a hundred yards from the finish line when Brer Turtle came from behind the post and crossed the line. "Soon as I catch my breath, I be pleased to take that fifty dollars, Brer Buzzard."

Brer Buzzard handed over the money, and Brer Turtle went home.

Mr. Jack Sparrow Meets His End

Brer Rabbit was mad after he lost the race to Brer Turtle. The neighbors could hear him cussing and carrying on so bad that they almost called the police. Brer Rabbit had to get even with Brer Turtle. But as hard as he thought, as long as he thought, as wide and high as he thought, he didn't have a thought.

That just made him more mad. He decided finally, "If I can't get even with Brer Turtle, then I'll show Miz Meadows and the girls that I'm still the boss of Brer Fox!"

Unfortunately, Brer Rabbit did his deciding out loud. Mr. Jack Sparrow was sitting in a nearby tree, and he heard every word. The period on Brer Rabbit's sentence was hardly dry before Mr. Jack Sparrow started chirping:

"I'm gon' to tell Brer Fox! I'm gon' to tell Brer Fox! Just as sho' as you born, I'm gon' to tell Brer Fox!" And he flew off.

Brer Rabbit got a little worried. To tell the truth, he was downright scared, and he lit out for home. His eyes were on the ground and his feet were in the air and consequently he didn't see Brer Fox until he'd bumped into him and almost knocked him over.

"What's the matter, Brer Rabbit? You in an awful hurry today."

"Brer Fox! I been looking all over for you! What's this I hear about you going to beat me up, beat my wife up, beat my children up, and tear my house down?" He looked mad enough to chew concrete.

"What are you talking about?" Brer Fox wanted to know.

"You heard me! What did I do to make you want to do all that to me and mine?"

"Brer Rabbit, I don't know who told you that, but it's a lie!" Brer Fox started to get a little heated. "Who been telling lies on me?"

Brer Rabbit hemmed and hawed and pretended like he didn't want to say, but finally: "It was Mr. Jack Sparrow. I couldn't believe my ears, but he swore up, down, and sideways that it was the truth."

Brer Fox didn't say another word. He took off down the road looking for Mr. Jack Sparrow. Brer Rabbit smiled and went on home.

Brer Fox hadn't gone far when he heard somebody call his name. "Brer Fox!"

It was Mr. Jack Sparrow, but Brer Fox kept walking like he hadn't heard.

"Brer Fox! Brer Fox!" Mr. Jack Sparrow called, flying around his head.

Brer Fox make like he still ain't heard. Then he came to a tree stump and sat down like he was tired.

"Brer Fox!" said Mr. Jack Sparrow, lighting on the ground beside him. "I got something to tell you."

"Get on my tail, Mr. Jack Sparrow. You know, I'm deaf in one ear and can't hear out of the other."

Mr. Jack Sparrow hopped on his tail.

"Believe you better get on my back, Mr. Jack Sparrow. I'm deaf in one ear and can't hear out the other."

Mr. Jack Sparrow hopped on his back.

"Naw, that won't do either. Still can't hear. Hop on my head."

Mr. Jack Sparrow hopped on his head.

"Doggone it. Believe you better hop on my tooth. I'm deaf in one ear and can't hear out the other, but I got a little hearing in my eyetooth."

Mr. Jack Sparrow hopped on Brer Fox's tooth, and Brer Fox opened his mouth real wide and—GULP!

Tattletales never do come to a good end.

Brer Rabbit Gets Caught One More Time

When Brer Rabbit wasn't getting in and out of trouble, he was courting. Miz Meadows had a sister, Miz Motts, and she moved down from Philly-Me-York. Brer Rabbit decided to court both of them. Now don't come asking me about Brer Rabbit's family arrangements. How folks arranges their families is their business. Ain't yours and it definitely ain't mine.

Courting back in them days ain't like it is now. Well, wait a minute. Come to think of it, I don't know how it is now, being a married man. But back in my time, you took a girl to a restaurant and spent some money; then you took her to a movie show or something like that and spent some more money. She goes home happy and you go home broke. In Brer Rabbit's time, it was the way it's supposed to be: You went to the girl's house before breakfast and stayed until after dinner.

One morning about breakfast time Brer Rabbit went over to see Miz Motts, but she wasn't home. Somebody else might have spent the whole day waiting, or wore themselves out hunting all over the community for her. Not Brer Rabbit. She wasn't home? That was her tough luck! He went on over to Miz Meadows's house, and who should be there but Miz Motts.

Well, they all had a good time that day laughing and talking and carrying on. Long about nightfall Brer Rabbit said he had to go. The ladies asked him to stay for supper. Brer Rabbit was tempted, but it wasn't safe for him to be out after dark, what with the other animals always scheming against him. So he excused himself and headed for home.

He hadn't gone far when he saw a big basket sitting by the side of the road. He looked up the road and didn't see nobody. He looked down the road and didn't see nobody. He looked before and behind and all around. He didn't see nobody. He listened and he listened some more. He didn't hear nothing. He waited and he waited, but nobody came.

Brer Rabbit tipped over to the basket and peeked inside. It was full of grass. He reached in, got a little, and chewed on it for a while, his eyes closed. "Well, it looks like sparrow grass. It feels like sparrow grass. It tastes like sparrow grass, and it seems to me that that's what it is!"

Having reached that scientific conclusion, he jumped up in the air, clicked his heels together, and dived headfirst into all that sweet sparrow grass, and landed right on top of Brer Wolf, who was hiding underneath.

Brer Rabbit knew he was caught this time, but he laughed. "I knew you were in here, Brer Wolf. I knew you by the smell. I was just trying to scare you."

Brer Wolf grinned and licked his lips real slow. "Glad you knowed me, Brer Rabbit, 'cause I knew you the minute you jumped in. I told Brer Fox yesterday that this was the way to catch you, and catch you I did!"

Brer Rabbit got seriously scared and he started begging Brer Wolf to let him go. Brer Wolf's grin got bigger and Brer Rabbit could see the saliva sliding down his big teeth. Brer Wolf climbed out of the basket holding Brer Rabbit by the neck.

"Where you taking me, Brer Wolf?"

"Down to the creek."

"What you taking me down there for?"

"So I can wash my hands after I skin you."

"Oh, Brer Wolf! Please let me go!"

"You make me laugh."

"You don't understand. That sparrow grass made me sick."

"You don't know about sick, Brer Rabbit, until I get done with you."

"Where I come from, nobody eats sick folk."

"Where I come from, them's the only ones we eat."

They got down to the creek and Brer Rabbit was desperate now. He begged and he pleaded and he pleaded and he begged and Brer Wolf grinned and grinned.

Brer Wolf squeezed Brer Rabbit's neck a little harder while he decided what to do.

Brer Rabbit started crying and boo-hooing. "Ber—ber—Brer Wooly—ooly—oolf, if you gon' kill me and eat me, you got to do it right," he blubbered.

"What you mean?"

"I want you to be polite, Brer Wooly—ooly—oolf!"

"And how am I supposed to do that?"

"I want you to say grace, Brer Wolf, and say it quick, please, because I'm getting weak."

"And how I say grace, Brer Rabbit?"

"You fold your hands under your chin, close your eyes, and say, 'Bless us and put us in the crack where Ole Boy can't find us.' Say it quick, 'cause I'm going fast."

Brer Wolf folded his hands under his chin, shut his eyes, and said, "Bless us and—" He didn't get any further, because the minute he folded his hands, Brer Rabbit jumped up off the ground. He took off from there so fast it took his shadow a week to catch him.

The Death of Brer Wolf

Brer Rabbit had tricked Brer Wolf and he was four times seven times eleven mad.

One day Brer Rabbit left his house to go to town, and Brer Wolf tore it down and took off one of his children.

Brer Rabbit built a straw house and Brer Wolf tore that down. Then he made one out of pine tops. Brer Wolf tore that one down. He made one out of bark, and that didn't last too much longer than it takes to drink a milk shake. Finally, Brer Rabbit hired some carpenters and built him a house with a stone foundation, two-car garage, and a picture window. After that, he had a little peace and quiet and wasn't scared to leave home and visit his neighbors every now and then.

One afternoon he was at home when he heard a lot of racket outside. Before he could get up to see what was going on, Brer Wolf bust through the front door. "Save me! Save me! Some hunters with dogs are after me. Hide me somewhere so the dogs won't get me."

"Jump in that chest over there," Brer Rabbit said, pointing toward the fireplace.

Brer Wolf jumped in. He figured that when night came,

he'd get out and take care of Brer Rabbit once and for all. He was so busy thinking about what he was going to do, he didn't hear what Brer Rabbit did. Brer Rabbit locked the trunk!

Brer Rabbit sat back down in his rocking chair and stuck a big wad of chewing tobacco in his jaw. This here was rabbit-chewing tobacco. From what I hear, it's supposed to be pretty good. So he sat there just rocking, chewing, and spitting.

"Is the dogs gone yet, Brer Rabbit?" Brer Wolf asked after a while.

"No. I think I hear one sniffing around the chimney."

Brer Rabbit got up and filled a great big pot with water and put it on the fire.

Brer Wolf was listening and said, "What you doing, Brer Rabbit?"

"Just fixing to make you a nice cup of elderberry tea."

Brer Rabbit went to his tool chest, got out a drill, and started boring holes in the chest.

"What you doing now, Brer Rabbit?"

"Just making some holes so you can get some air."

Brer Rabbit put some more wood on the fire.

"Now what you doing?"

"Building the fire up so you won't get cold."

The water was boiling now. Brer Rabbit took the kettle off the fire and started pouring it on the chest.

"What's that I hear, Brer Rabbit?"

"Just the wind blowing."

The water started splattering through the holes.

"What's that I feel, Brer Rabbit?"

"Must be fleas biting you."

"They biting mighty hard."

"Turn over," suggested Brer Rabbit.

Brer Wolf turned over and Brer Rabbit kept pouring.

"What's that I feel now, Brer Rabbit?"

"Must be more fleas."

"They eating me up, Brer Rabbit." And them was the last words Brer Wolf said, 'cause that scalding water did what it was supposed to.

Next winter all the neighbors admired the nice wolfskin mittens Brer Rabbit and his family had.

Brer Fox and Brer Rabbit Go Hunting

After Brer Rabbit took care of Brer Wolf, Brer Fox decided it was time him and Brer Rabbit became friends. Every time he saw Brer Rabbit you would've thought he was practicing to meet the Queen of England. In a few weeks Brer Fox and Brer Rabbit could be seen sitting on Brer Rabbit's porch in the evening, smoking their cigars and laughing like they was kin.

One morning Brer Fox stopped by and asked Brer Rabbit to go hunting with him. Brer Rabbit didn't feel like doing a thing that day except sitting on the porch and watching his toenails grow, so Brer Fox went off by himself.

He had good hunting that day and caught some pheasant, wild turkey, squab, and a couple of squirrels. By evening his game bag was so full it was busting at the seams.

Well, long about that time Brer Rabbit stretched and thought he'd go and see how Brer Fox had made out. He heard Brer Fox coming along the road, singing loud. "He must've had good hunting," Brer Rabbit muttered to himself.

He hid in the ditch. A few minutes later Brer Fox went by, singing. When Brer Rabbit saw how full his game bag was, his mouth started to water. He ran through the woods until he was some distance ahead of Brer Fox. Then he lay down in the road like he was dead.

A few minutes later Brer Fox came along and saw the rabbit lying in the road. "This rabbit dead," Brer Fox said. "He's fat too." Brer Fox thought for a minute. "Naw, I got plenty game meat," and he went on his way.

Brer Rabbit jumped up, ran through the woods to get ahead of Brer Fox again, and lay down in the road.

When Brer Fox saw what he thought was another dead rabbit, he couldn't believe his eyes. "Here's another one. And this one is just as plump and fat and juicy as the other one." His mouth and nose started to twitch, and his knees trembled just thinking about how good that rabbit would taste. He put down his game bag. "Well, if the Lord wants to provide me with rabbit, ain't no sense in me turning it down. I'll just run back and get that other rabbit, and then come and get this one."

Brer Fox was hardly out of sight before Brer Rabbit grabbed the game bag and went on home.

Next morning Brer Fox came to visit. Brer Rabbit asked him how he had made out hunting.

Brer Fox started foaming at the mouth. "I caught a handful of common sense, Brer Rabbit."

Brer Rabbit smiled. "If I'd knowed that was what you was hunting for, I'd have loaned you some of mine."

Brer Rabbit Tricks Brer Fox Again

When all the animals saw how well Brer Rabbit and Brer Fox were getting along, they decided to patch up their quarrels.

One hot day Brer Rabbit, Brer Fox, Brer Coon, Brer Bear, and a whole lot of the other animals were clearing new ground so they could plant corn and have some roasting ears when autumn came.

Brer Rabbit got tired about three minutes after he started, but he couldn't say anything if he didn't want the other animals calling him lazy. So he kept carrying off the weeds and brambles the others were pulling out of the ground. After a while he screamed real loud and said a briar was stuck in his hand. He wandered off, picking at his hand. As soon as he was out of sight, he started looking for a shady place where he could take a nap.

He saw a well with a bucket in it. That was the very thing he'd been looking for. He climbed, jumped in, and whoops! The bucket went down, down, down until— SPLASH!—it hit the water.

Now, I know you don't know nothing about no well. You probably think that when God made water, He made the faucet too. Well, God don't know nothing about no faucet, and I don't care too much for them myself. When I was coming up, everybody had their own well. Over the well was a pulley with a rope on it. Tied to each end of the rope was a bucket, and when you pulled one bucket up, the other one went down. Brer Rabbit found out about them kind of wells as he looked up at the other bucket.

He didn't know what he was going to do. He couldn't even move around very much or else he'd tip over and land in the water.

Brer Fox and Brer Rabbit might've made up and become friends, but that didn't mean Brer Fox trusted Brer Rabbit. Brer Fox had seen him sneaking off, so he followed. He watched Brer Rabbit get in the bucket and go to the bottom of the well. That was the most astonishing thing he had ever seen. Brer Rabbit had to be up to something.

"I bet you anything that's where Brer Rabbit hides all his money. Or he's probably discovered a gold mine down there!"

Brer Fox peeked down into the well. "Hey, Brer Rabbit! What you doing down there?"

"Who? Me? Fishing. I thought I'd surprise everybody and catch a mess of fish for dinner."

"Many of'em down there?"

"Is there stars in the sky? I'm glad you come, 'cause there's more fish down here than I can haul up. Why don't you come on down and give me a hand?"

"How do I get down there?"

"Jump in the bucket."

Brer Fox did that and started going down. The bucket Brer Rabbit was in started up. As Brer Rabbit passed Brer Fox, he sang out:

Goodbye, Brer Fox, take care of your clothes,
For this is the way the world goes;
Some goes up and some goes down,
You'll get to the bottom all safe and sound.

Just as Brer Fox hit the water—SPLASH!—Brer Rabbit jumped out at the top. He ran and told the other animals that Brer Fox was muddying up the drinking water.

They ran to the well and hauled Brer Fox out, chastising

him for muddying up some good water. Wasn't nothing he could say.

Everybody went back to work, and every now and then Brer Rabbit looked at Brer Fox and laughed. Brer Fox had to give a little dry grin himself.

Brer Rabbit Eats the Butter

The more time the animals spent with each other, the more they liked it. They got to liking each other so much that Brer Rabbit, Brer Fox, and Brer Possum decided to live together. Don't know what their wives and children thought about it. They probably didn't mind since Brer Rabbit, Brer Fox, and Brer Possum was never at home nohow.

Everything was going along fine until the roof sprung a leak. The first sunny day Brer Rabbit, Brer Fox, and Brer Possum got out the ladder, the hammers and nails, and climbed up on the roof. They took their lunch with'em so they wouldn't have to waste time climbing down to eat at lunchtime. But they realized that the butter would melt in the sun, so they went and put it in the well to keep it nice and cool.

They hadn't been working long before Brer Rabbit began thinking about that butter. His stomach started growling like a cat getting ready to fight. He was hammering and nailing when all of a sudden he jumped up and yelled, "Here I am! What you want with me?" Off he went like somebody was calling him.

Brer Fox and Brer Possum watched him go off through the woods and wondered what was wrong. Brer Rabbit hid behind a tree and when he saw them go back to working, he sneaked over to the well, whacked off a pat of butter and ate it. Then he went on back.

"Where you been?" Brer Fox wanted to know.

"Oh, I heard my children calling and I had to go see about them. My wife done took sick."

A half hour passed. The memory of that butter began to work on Brer Rabbit's mind, not to mention his stomach. He raised his head, his ears shot up real straight, and he hollered, "Hold on! I'm coming!" Down the ladder he went.

This time he stayed away a little longer, and when he came back, Brer Fox asked, "How's your wife?"

"Mighty low. Mighty low."

Brer Rabbit didn't work more than fifteen minutes when he was off again. He didn't leave the well this time until the butter was all gone. When he got back to the roof he was feeling mighty good.

"How's your wife?" Brer Possum asked.

"She dead," answered Brer Rabbit, with a sorrowful look.

Brer Possum and Brer Fox felt mighty bad. They decided to stop work, eat lunch, and try to make Brer Rabbit feel better. Brer Fox laid out the food and sent Brer Possum to the well to get the butter.

In a few minutes Brer Possum came back all out of breath. "Hey, y'all! Better come quick! All the butter is gone!"

"Gone where?" Brer Fox wanted to know.

"Just done dried up."

Brer Rabbit grunted. "Dried up in somebody's mouth, I bet."

They went to the well, and sure enough, no butter. Brer Rabbit starts looking at the ground real close, like he's Sherlock Holmes or somebody. "I see tracks. If the two of you go to sleep, I can find out who ate the butter."

Brer Possum and Brer Fox went to sleep. Brer Rabbit took the butter left on his paws and smeared it on Brer Possum's mouth. Then he went back to the roof, ate the lunch, come back and woke Brer Fox.

"There's the butter," he said, pointing to Brer Possum's mouth. "He was the one you sent for the butter, wasn't he? He was the first one down here. Couldn't be nobody else but him."

They woke Brer Possum and Brer Fox accused him of eating up the butter. Naturally, Brer Possum denied everything. But Brer Fox pointed to the evidence around Brer Possum's mouth.

Brer Possum kept pleading his innocence. Finally, he had an idea. "I know how we can catch the one what really did it. Build a fire and everybody try to jump over it. The one that falls in is the one what stole the butter."

They built the fire high and they built the fire wide, and when it was going good, the test began. Brer Rabbit was first, and quite naturally, he leaped over the fire so high he didn't even feel the heat. Next came Brer Fox. He got a good running start and managed to make it over, but it was so close that his tail caught on fire. That's why to this day the underside of a fox's tail is white.

Last to go was Brer Possum. He got a good running start, jumped, and—wham!—landed right in the middle of the fire. That was the end of Brer Possum.

I know it don't seem right, since Brer Possum didn't have a thing to do with the disappearance of the butter. But that's the way of the world. Lots of people suffer for other folks' sins. And I could tell you a thing or two about that if I had a mind to.

Brer Rabbit Saves His Meat

One day Brer Wolf was going home after fishing all day. What's that you say? You say I told you that Brer Rabbit killed Brer Wolf by pouring hot water on him? Well, now, that's true, ain't it? But you got to understand: Back before "once upon a time," dying was different. Just because you died in one story didn't mean you stayed dead for the rest of the stories. That wouldn't be no fun, would it? Of course not.

Now, like I was saying, Brer Wolf was sauntering home with his string of fish when all of a sudden, Miz Partridge came flying out of the bushes at him. He ducked and dodged, wondering what in the dickens was going on.

It finally occurred to him that Miz Partridge must have her nest nearby. Well, Brer Wolf had a lot of fish, but the thought of some nice young partridge was more than he could resist. He dropped his string of fish right there in the road and went to hunt for the nest.

A few minutes passed and along come Brer Rabbit. He stopped when he saw the string of fish lying in the road. He looked at them. The fish looked at him, and that settled that.

When Brer Wolf came back empty-handed, he didn't see nothing in the road but a big wet spot. He looked up the road. No fish. He looked down the road. No fish nowhere.

He sat down and thought the situation over. There was only one explanation, of course: Brer Rabbit!

He went straight there. Brer Rabbit was sitting on the porch.

"You stole my fish," Brer Wolf said without so much as a howdy-do.

"What fish?"

"You know what fish!"

Brer Rabbit said Brer Wolf shouldn't be going around accusing people of crimes they hadn't committed, and Brer Wolf said other folks shouldn't be taking what wasn't theirs, and they went back and forth and forth and back like that until Brer Rabbit said, "If you believe I got your fish, then you can go out back and kill the best cow I got."

Brer Rabbit thought that would put an end to the matter. Nobody would offer his best cow if he was lying. But Brer Wolf knew Brer Rabbit pretty well.

He marched right on back to the pasture, took a close look at all the cows, and being a gentleman of good judgment and discriminating taste, killed the best cow of the lot.

Brer Rabbit couldn't believe his eyes. What was the world coming to when somebody wouldn't believe one of his lies? But that didn't mean Brer Rabbit was whupped.

"Brer Wolf! Brer Wolf! The police is coming! The police is coming! You better run and hide."

Brer Wolf dropped the cow and took off through the underbrush. He was always up to so much no good that it didn't surprise him that the police might be after him.

Brer Wolf wasn't hid good before Brer Rabbit was skinning the cow, cutting it up into pieces and salting it. He called his children and they ran and hid the meat in the smokehouse. When he was finished, Brer Rabbit took the cow's tail and stuck it in the ground.

"Brer Wolf! Hey, Brer Wolf! Come quick! Your cow is going into the ground!"

Brer Wolf came cautiously out of the underbrush and saw Brer Rabbit holding onto the cow's tail like he was

trying to keep it from going into the ground. Brer Wolf grabbed hold. They pulled and—POP!—the tail came out of the ground!

Brer Rabbit shook his head sadly. "We pulled the tail out of the cow and the cow done gone now."

Brer Wolf didn't want to hear nothing like that. He got him a shovel and started digging. Brer Rabbit chuckled and went and sat on his porch. Brer Wolf was shoveling the dirt out so fast you'd a thought he'd turned into a steam shovel. Brer Rabbit just chuckled, and every now and then he sang under his breath:

"He diggy, diggy, diggy, but no meat there. He diggy, diggy, diggy, but no meat there."

Brer Rabbit's Children

Even if Brer Rabbit and Brer Fox had become friends, it didn't mean that Brer Fox had stopped being a fox. When he dropped by to see Brer Rabbit one afternoon and saw the little rabbits all by themselves, well, he couldn't help it that he was a fox. They looked so fat and tender and juicy, he wanted to gobble'em up right then and there, but didn't know how he could without having a good excuse. He still remembered how Brer Rabbit had poured scalding water over his cousin, Brer Wolf.

The little rabbits were huddled in a corner as scared as they could be. Brer Fox sat down in a rocking chair and started rocking back and forth. He saw a stalk of sugar-cane standing by the door. "Break me off a piece of that cane!"

Ain't too many things in this world tougher than sugar-cane. Brer Fox knew they couldn't break it, and when they failed, he'd have an excuse to eat'em.

The little rabbits sweated and they wrestled and they strained and they puffed, but nothing doing.

"You rabbits hurry up! If you don't break me off some of that cane, I'll eat you!"

The little rabbits tried even harder, but they couldn't break it. Then they heard a little bird singing on top of the house:

Take your teeth and gnaw it.
Take your teeth and gnaw it,
Saw it and yoke it,
And then you can break it.

The little rabbits started into gnawing and biting, and

quicker than butter can melt on a hot stove, they had a piece of cane broken off.

Brer Fox wasn't too happy about that. He got up and commenced pacing the floor. He saw a sifter hanging from the wall. "Here! Take this sifter and run down to the creek and get me some fresh water."

The little rabbits ran down there and tried to dip water with the sifter. Naturally the water just kept running out. They didn't know what to do and sat down and cried.

Then, from up in a tree, the little bird started singing:

> *Sifter holds water same as a tray,*
> *If you fill it with moss and daub it with clay;*
> *The Fox gets madder the longer you stay—*
> *Fill it with moss and daub it with clay.*

The little rabbits put moss and clay in the sifter, filled it with water and carried the water to Brer Fox. He was fighting mad now. He pointed to a big log that was setting beside the fireplace. "Put that log on the fire!" he ordered.

The little rabbits tried to lift it. It wouldn't budge. They tried to turn it on end. It wouldn't budge. They tried to roll it. It wouldn't budge. Then they heard the little bird sing:

> *Spit in your hands and tug it and toll it,*
> *Get behind it and push it and pole it;*
> *Spit in your hands and rare back and roll it.*

They set to work and just about time they got the log on the fire, Brer Rabbit and his wife came walking in. Brer

Fox grinned real sheepish like. "Well, Brer Rabbit. Thought you wasn't going to get back before I left."

Brer Rabbit only needed to glance at his children to see that something was wrong, but he pretended like he didn't notice a thing. "Why don't you stay and have supper, Brer Fox? Since Brer Wolf stopped coming to see me, I ain't had much company. Gets mighty lonesome sometime."

Brer Fox allowed as to how Miz Fox was expecting him home for supper, and he tipped on away.

The Death of Brer Fox

One winter the weather got so cold the animals started wondering if the Lord had forgot to send spring. Most of them were all right, since they'd worked hard during the summer, made a good crop, and got all their wood chopped and stacked. All of them, that is, except Brer Rabbit. He hadn't made a crop that year, since he'd been eating out of everybody else's garden, and he hadn't chopped firewood either, figuring that the winter wouldn't be cold.

Brer Rabbit went over to Brer Fox's house one day and he was troubled in his mind. His wife was sick, his children were cold and hungry, and what little fire there was in the fireplace had gone out in the night.

Brer Fox felt bad, and gave him some fire. Brer Rabbit smelled beef cooking and his stomach almost popped out of his belly, it wanted some of that beef so bad. But Brer Rabbit didn't like to beg, so he took the fire and left. He didn't get far before the fire went out. He went back to Brer Fox's house to get some more.

This time the beef smelled even better. "Brer Fox, where you get so much nice beef?"

Brer Fox answered, "Why don't you come over tomorrow? I'll show you where you can get all the beef you want."

Brer Rabbit showed up bright and early the next day.

"There's a man live near Miz Meadows who's got a lot of cattle. He's got one named Bookay. You just go up to her and say *Bookay,* and she'll open her mouth. You jump in and get as much meat as you can carry away."

Brer Rabbit had never heard of such a thing. "Tell you what. Go with me this time and show me how it's done."

They went down to the man's pasture. Brer Fox walked

around among the cattle until he found the one he was looking for. He walked up to her, hollered *Bookay,* and sho' nuf', the cow's mouth swung open like a door. Brer Fox jumped in and Brer Rabbit jumped in after him.

"Now, you can cut almost anything you want, but don't cut near the haslett [heart and liver]."

"I want me a roast," Brer Rabbit hollered back.

"Fine. Just don't cut near the haslett."

"And after I get a roast, going after some London broil and filet mignon and Chateaubriand."

Brer Rabbit was hacking and cutting and sawing and thinking about the hollandaise sauce he was going to make instead of looking where he was cutting and he cut right through the haslett. The cow fell over dead.

Brer Fox said, "Oh, oh. What we gon' do now? When the man come down this evening to look at his cows, we gon' be in a world of trouble."

"You get in the rear of the cow and I'll get in the head," said Brer Rabbit.

That evening the man came and saw his cow was dead. He cut her open to see if he could figure out what killed her. Brer Rabbit crawled out through the cow's mouth and ran up to the man.

"If you want to know who killed your cow, just look in the hind parts and there he is."

The man didn't take time to look. He got a club, beat on the hind part so hard that he killed Brer Fox dead. Brer Rabbit asked the man if he could have Brer Fox's head. The man cut it off and gave it to him.

Brer Rabbit wrapped the head up in old newspaper and took it over to Brer Fox's house. "Miz Fox, I got some nice beef here that your old man sent for supper. But he said not to look at it until you was ready to eat."

Miz Fox took what Brer Rabbit gave her, put it in the pot and set it cooking for supper. Tobe, Brer Fox's oldest boy, was hungry and got tired of waiting to see what was for supper. He looked in the pot. When he saw what it was, he started screaming and yelling. His momma came running in. When she saw that she was cooking her old man's head, she started screaming.

She called the dogs on Brer Rabbit and he took off running like he'd just heard slavery was coming back. The dogs were so close their tongues were lapping his cottontail. He saw a hollow tree and ducked into it just as the dogs was getting ready to jump him.

Miz Fox and Tobe came along a minute later. She told Tobe to guard the tree while she got the shotgun. After she left, Brer Rabbit asked Tobe if he'd be so kind as to go down to the creek and fetch him some cool water. Tobe, being young and not knowing no better, went to get the water, and quite naturally, Brer Rabbit got out.

When Miz Fox come back and found that Brer Rabbit had gotten away, she was fit to be tied. She told Tobe he wasn't going to live to be no grown fox 'cause she was going to kill him right then and there. Tobe was afraid she meant it, so he went through the woods hunting for Brer Rabbit. Since a fox can outrun a rabbit, it wasn't long before he caught him. He brought Brer Rabbit back to his momma. She took Brer Rabbit by the neck and carried him back to the house.

Brer Rabbit said, "Miz Fox, I know my time is up. I just ask one thing of you. Lay me on the grindstone and grind my nose off so I can't smell when I'm dead."

Miz Fox liked that idea, so she carried him out back to

the grindstone. She looked around and realized she needed some water for the grindstone.

"Tobe can turn the handle," said Brer Rabbit, "while you go and get the water."

Well, soon as Miz Fox left to get the water, Brer Rabbit ran off, and this time Tobe didn't catch him.

Brer Rabbit and Brer Lion

Brer Rabbit was in the woods one afternoon when a great wind came up. It blew on the ground and it blew in the tops of the trees. It blew so hard that Brer Rabbit was afraid a tree might fall on him, and he started running.

He was trucking through the woods when he ran smack into Brer Lion. Now, don't come telling me ain't no lions in the United States. Ain't none here now. But back in yonder times, all the animals lived everywhere. The lions and tigers and elephants and foxes and what 'nall run around with each other like they was family. So that's how come wasn't unusual for Brer Rabbit to run up on Brer Lion like he done that day.

"What's your hurry, Brer Rabbit?"

"Run, Brer Lion! There's a hurricane coming."

Brer Lion got scared. "I'm too heavy to run, Brer Rabbit. What am I going to do?"

"Lay down, Brer Lion. Lay down! Get close to the ground!"

Brer Lion shook his head. "The wind might pick me up and blow me away."

"Hug a tree, Brer Lion! Hug a tree!"

"But what if the wind blows all day and into the night?"

"Let me tie you to the tree, Brer Lion. Let me tie you to the tree."

Brer Lion liked that idea. Brer Rabbit tied him to the tree and sat down next to it. After a while, Brer Lion got tired of hugging the tree.

"Brer Rabbit? I don't hear no hurricane."

Brer Rabbit listened. "Neither do I."

"Brer Rabbit? I don't hear no wind."

Brer Rabbit listened. "Neither do I."

"Brer Rabbit? Ain't a leaf moving in the trees."

Brer Rabbit looked up. "Sho' ain't."

"So untie me."

"I'm afraid to, Brer Lion."

Brer Lion began to roar. He roared so loud and so long, the foundations of the Earth started shaking. Least that's what it seemed like, and the other animals came from all over to see what was going on.

When they got close, Brer Rabbit jumped up and began strutting around the tied-up Brer Lion. When the animals saw what Brer Rabbit had done to Brer Lion, you better believe it was the forty-eleventh of Octorerarry before they messed with him again.

Brer Rabbit Takes Care of Brer Tiger

One year Brer Tiger moved into the community. None of the animals wanted to have a thing to do with him. He was so weird-looking with them black and orange stripes. Not only that, he was big, looked like he didn't have no friends and didn't want none. Everybody kept their distance, everybody except Brer Rabbit.

Brer Tiger was hardly moved into his house good when Brer Rabbit invited him to go for a walk so they could get acquainted.

They were strolling along chatting with one another when they came to a creek. Neither one wanted to wade across and get his feet wet. Brer Rabbit saw a vine hanging from a tree and he swung across to the other side. Brer Tiger thought that looked easy enough, so he grabbed the vine and started to swing across. But he's such a heavy creature that the vine broke and he landed smack dab in the middle of the creek—KERSPLASH!

When he drug himself out and saw Brer Rabbit sitting on the bank laughing, he growled. Brer Rabbit laughed again.

"How come you ain't scared of me like all the other animals?" Brer Tiger wanted to know. "Everybody else run when my shadow hits the ground."

"How come the fleas ain't scared of you?" Brer Rabbit asked. "They littler than me."

Brer Tiger didn't like that kind of sass. "You best be glad I had my breakfast, 'cause if I was hungry you'd be in my stomach now."

Brer Rabbit looked at him. "Brer Tiger, I'm gon' tell you something. If you'd done that, you'd have more sense in you than you got now."

Brer Tiger growled louder. "I'm going to let you off this time, but next time I see you, you mine."

Brer Rabbit laughed. "If you so much as dream about messing with me, I want you to get up the next morning and come apologize."

Brer Rabbit hopped away. Brer Tiger got so mad he grabbed a tree and clawed all the bark off it.

Brer Rabbit was angry too. He shook his fist at the tree stumps and carried on like he was quarreling with his shadow because it was following after him.

He hadn't gone far when he heard a terrible noise. It was Brer Elephant tromping through the woods, eating off the tops of the trees. Brer Rabbit marched up to him.

"Brer Elephant, how would you like to help me run Brer Tiger back where he came from?"

"Well, having him in the community sho' done lowered property values, Brer Rabbit, but I don't know. If I help you, I won't get hurt, will I?"

"What can hurt something as big as you?"

"Brer Tiger got sharp claws and big teeth. He might bite and scratch me."

Brer Rabbit said, "Don't worry about that. Just do what I say and we'll run Brer Tiger away from here."

Early the next morning Brer Rabbit was up and moving about. When he saw Brer Tiger coming, he ran to where he'd told Brer Elephant to wait. Brer Rabbit tied a long vine around one of Brer Elephant's hind legs and tied the other end to a big tree. Then Brer Elephant kneeled down and Brer Rabbit hopped on.

A couple of minutes later Brer Tiger came up and saw Brer Rabbit on Brer Elephant's back. He smiled. He thought Brer Rabbit was caught up there and couldn't get down. Brer Elephant started swinging backward and forward and rocking from side to side.

"Well, Brer Rabbit. I ain't had my breakfast this morning and I sho' am hungry," said Brer Tiger.

"That so?" Brer Rabbit returned. "Well, you just wait till I get through skinning this here Elephant I caught this morning and I'll be down to take care of you."

Brer Rabbit whispered in Brer Elephant's ear: "When I put my nose on your neck, scream loud as you can. Don't be scared. Just scream!"

Brer Elephant screamed so loud he knocked over a couple of trees.

"You wait right there, Brer Tiger. I be done skinning this Elephant in a few minutes."

Brer Rabbit bent over and made like he was nibbling

behind Brer Elephant's ear. Brer Elephant screamed again. A couple of more trees fell.

Brer Tiger started inching backward.

"Where you going, Brer Tiger? I'm almost done. Be down to get you shortly. Just hold on."

Brer Rabbit bent over; Brer Elephant screamed; some more trees fell, and Brer Tiger began putting himself into serious reverse.

"I'm all done now. Elephant blood is all right, but ain't as good as Tiger blood from what I hear."

Brer Rabbit made like he was about to get off the Elephant, but Brer Tiger wasn't around to see if he did or not. He lit off from there and before noontime had moved out of his house and left the community.

Brer Lion Meets the Creature

After Brer Rabbit ran Brer Tiger out of the community, Brer Lion decided he better do something before he got run out. He sent word to the other animals that he was going to eat one member of every family.

Well, there was all kinds of crying and grieving going on in the community, but wasn't nothing the animals could do about it. After a month or so, Brer Lion had eaten his way through every family except Brer Rabbit's. He sent word to Brer Rabbit that it was his turn now.

Miz Rabbit and all the little Rabbits started crying and sniffling and carrying on. Brer Rabbit smoked a cigar like wasn't nothing wrong.

He left the house and went on down the road toward Brer Lion's house. He was almost there when he stopped beside a deep lake. He mussed up his hair and drawed himself in until he was hardly big as a bar of soap that everybody in the family had taken a shower with. Then he looked at himself in the water. He looked like he had one foot in the grave.

He limped and wheezed up to Brer Lion's house. Brer Lion looked at him and shook his head.

"Brer Rabbit, you won't make more than a mouthful. I be hungrier when I get through eating you than I was before."

"I know I ain't fat, Brer Lion, and I probably got a lot of fleas on me. I got a bad cough, and my feets smell, and I got earwax in my navel. But I'm willing. I just want you to know that."

Brer Lion stared hard at him, shaking his head. "I'm gon' have to eat your whole family to get one decent meal if they all look like you."

"Well, Brer Lion, when I was coming over here just now I saw a creature that was as big and fat as you. I said to myself that I wished I was that fat so Brer Lion could have a *good* dinner on me."

"Who was that you saw?" Brer Lion wanted to know.

"Didn't ask his name. I said my how-do's to him and he don't say nothing back. I decided I'd best get on away from him."

"Show me where he is."

"I be glad to, Brer Lion, but I'm afraid of what he might do to you."

"Do to who?" Brer Lion roared. "Show me where he is. We'll see who be doing what to who!"

Brer Rabbit shook his head. "I don't want your death on my conscience."

"TAKE ME TO HIM!"

Brer Rabbit shrugged. "All right. But I be there to back you up. Can't no one animal deal with this creature. He gon' break your legs, Brer Lion!"

Brer Lion was so mad he was trembling. He followed Brer Rabbit to the lake. Brer Rabbit looked around like he was afraid. "He was around here somewhere, and he still around. I can feel it in my bones."

Brer Rabbit creeped forward and looked in the lake. He screamed and jumped back. "He's in there, Brer Lion! Let's get out of here!"

Brer Lion walked up to the lake and peered in. Sure enough, there was a creature looking back at him. Brer Lion hollered at him. Creature in the lake don't say a word. Brer Lion shook his mane; creature shook his. Brer Lion showed his teeth; creature showed his. Brer Lion got so mad that he jumped into the lake head first.

Of course, Brer Lion don't know nothing about swimming and he thrashed around in the lake like he was fighting some creature. He was fighting all right—fighting Ole Boy.

Don't nobody win fights with Ole Boy.

The Talking House

When the animals heard of how Brer Rabbit had gotten rid of Brer Lion, they showed him a new respect. All of them except Brer Wolf. He went over to Brer Rabbit's house one day when everybody was out and sneaked inside.

In the middle of the afternoon Brer Rabbit came home and noticed that everything was mighty still. The door to the house was open a crack. His wife always shut the door tight. He peeped in the windows but didn't see nothing. He listened at the chimney. Didn't hear nothing.

He said to himself, "The pot knows what's going up the chimney. The rafters know who's in the loft. The mattress knows who's under the bed. But I ain't a pot. I ain't the rafters, and I ain't the mattress. But that don't matter. I'm going to find out if anybody's in that house and I ain't going inside to do it either. There're more ways to find out who fell in the pond without falling in yourself."

He went off a ways from the house and hollered, *"Hey, house! How you doing today?"*

House didn't answer.

"HEY, HOUSE! HOW YOU DOING TODAY?"

House still don't answer.

Inside, behind the door, Brer Wolf starts to get a little bit nervous. He ain't never heard of no such goings on as this. He peeped through the crack in the door, but can't see a thing.

"Hey, House! What's the matter? You done forgot your manners?"

Brer Wolf is getting nervous sho' nuf' now.

"Hey, House! You feeling sick today? You ain't never failed to greet me before when I holler."

Brer Wolf decided he better holler back, except he don't know what a house sound like when it hollers. He made his voice as hoarse as he could and hollered, *"Hey, yourself!"*

"You sound like you got a bad cold, House!"

Brer Wolf hollered this time in his own voice. *"Hey, yourself!"*

Brer Rabbit laughed and laughed and then he shouted, *"Brer Wolf! You got to do some practicing if you want to talk like a house!"*

Brer Wolf slunk on away and decided he'd better let Brer Rabbit be for a while.

Brer Rabbit Gets Beaten Again

Brer Rabbit and Brer Buzzard decided to grow a crop together and divide it up at the end of the season.

Come harvest time Brer Rabbit looked at his garden. He had carrots big as fence posts. And cabbage! He had cabbage so big he couldn't fit even one into a wheelbarrow. The lettuce leaves were so wide they looked like shade trees. It was the best crop Brer Rabbit had ever made and he wasn't about to divide nothing with nobody.

He went to see Brer Buzzard. "I don't know how to tell you this, but my garden didn't do well this year. Must've been that dry spell we had a while back. Didn't a thing come up, so I ain't got nothing to divide with you."

"Some years are like that, Brer Rabbit. You just go ahead and take half of what I got, 'cause a deal is a deal."

Brer Rabbit looked around Brer Buzzard's garden and saw peanuts as big as footballs, and ears of corn with such big, juicy kernels they popped open with juice if you looked at'em too hard. Brer Rabbit loaded up and went home, thinking about the good eating he would have all winter.

Brer Buzzard knew Brer Rabbit was lying. All summer he had made daily reconnaissance flights over Brer Rabbit's garden. A few days later Brer Buzzard stopped by to see him. "I just found a gold mine on the other side of the river. But it's too much for me to handle by myself. Give me a hand and I'll divide it with you."

Brer Rabbit didn't need to hear another word. "Lead the way!"

When they got to the river, Brer Rabbit stopped.

"How am I going to get across, Brer Buzzard?"

Brer Buzzard allowed as to how he didn't know.

Brer Rabbit thought for a minute. "How about I get on your back and you fly me over?"

Brer Buzzard was agreeable. They'd been flying for a while when Brer Buzzard lit in the top of a tall pine tree. Brer Rabbit looked down. The pine tree was stuck in the middle of an island and the island was stuck in the middle of the river. Brer Rabbit understood immediately that he had a serious problem.

"I'm sure glad you stopped to rest, Brer Buzzard. Don't see how you do it, but flying makes me dizzy. But, you know, I just remembered something. There's a gold mine near my house. Why don't we go back and dig that one first and then come and dig yours?"

Brer Buzzard thought that was the funniest thing he'd ever heard. He laughed and laughed and laughed until the tree started shaking.

"Wait a minute!" hollered Brer Rabbit. "Hold on! You keep on shaking this tree and I'll fall right in the river."

"That so?" said Brer Buzzard, and started laughing again. "I'll stop laughing if you give me half of your crop what belong to me."

Wasn't a thing Brer Rabbit could do. He divided up his crop and that was that, except he was weak in the knees for a month.

Brer Rabbit Tricks Brer Bear

Brer Rabbit decided gardening was too much hard work. So he went back to his old ways—eating from everybody else's garden. He made a tour through the community to see what everybody was planting and his eye was caught by Brer Fox's peanut patch.

Soon as the peanuts were ready, Brer Rabbit decided to make his acquaintance with them. Every night he ate his fill and started bringing his family, including some second and third cousins of his great-aunt on his daddy's uncle's side of the house.

Brer Fox had a good idea who was eating his peanuts, but he couldn't catch him. He inspected his fence and finally found a small hole on the north side. Brer Fox tied a rope with a loop knot and put it inside the hole. If anybody stepped in it, the rope would grab his leg and hoist'im right up in the air.

That night Brer Rabbit came down to the peanut patch. He climbed through the hole and WHOOSH! Next thing he knew he was hanging in the air upside down.

There wasn't a thing he could do, so he tried to make himself comfortable and catch a little sleep. He'd worry about Brer Fox when Brer Fox showed up the next morning.

Long about daybreak Brer Rabbit woke up, because he heard somebody coming. It was Brer Bear.

"Good morning, Brer Bear," he sang out, merry as Santa Claus.

Brer Bear looked all around.

"Up here!"

Brer Bear looked up and saw Brer Rabbit hanging upside down. "Brer Rabbit. How you do this morning?"

"Just fine, Brer Bear. Couldn't be better."

"Don't look like it to me. What you doing up there?"

"Making a dollar a minute," said Brer Rabbit.

"How?"

"I'm keeping the crows out of Brer Fox's peanut patch."

Brer Bear was overjoyed. He'd been on his way down to the welfare office, 'cause his family had gotten too big for him to support. "Say, Brer Rabbit. Could you let me take over for a while? I need the work and I promise I won't

work too long, but it sure would be a help to me and my family."

Brer Rabbit didn't want to appear too anxious, so he hemmed and hawed before agreeing. Brer Bear let Brer Rabbit down, and Brer Rabbit helped Brer Bear get the rope around his foot and swung him up in the air.

No sooner was Brer Bear swinging in the breeze than Brer Rabbit ran to Brer Fox's house. "Brer Fox! Brer Fox! Come quick! Come quick if you want to see who's been stealing your peanuts."

Brer Fox ran down to the garden and there was Brer Bear.

Before Brer Bear could thank Brer Fox for the chance to make a little money, Brer Fox grabbed a stick and was beating on Brer Bear like he was a drum in a marching band.

Brer Rabbit got away from there as quick as he could.

The End of Brer Bear

A few days later Brer Rabbit happened on Brer Bear, which he hadn't planned on. But he greeted him like they were the best of friends.

"Howdy, Brer Bear. Haven't seen you in a while. How's Miz Brune and Miz Brindle?" Miz Brune was Brer Bear's wife and Miz Brindle was his girlfriend. Don't come asking me how they worked the thing out with each other. From what I hear, folks be doing the same thing now. The animals was doing it long before deodorant, that's all.

Brer Bear said everybody was doing just fine. Brer Rabbit noticed Brer Bear inching close to him.

"Say, Brer Bear," he said quickly. "I got business with you, come to think of it."

"What's that, Brer Rabbit?" Brer Bear said, suspicious-like.

"I was out in the woods back of my house day before yesterday, and I came across one of them old-time honey trees. You know the kind I mean? Them old trees what are hollow from bottom to top and filled with honey?"

Brer Bear smiled. "My granddaddy told me about trees like that, but I ain't never found one."

"Well, why don't you come along with me? Honey ain't

no use to my family. If you don't get it, it's just going to go to waste."

When they got to the woods, Brer Bear said, "I can smell the honey."

Brer Rabbit nodded. "I can hear the bees zooming."

They looked at the tree, wondering how to get the honey.

Finally Brer Rabbit says, "Tell you what. You climb to the top. See that hole up there?" Brer Bear nodded.

"Stick your head in there. I'll get a tree limb and push the honeycomb up to you."

Brer Bear spit on his hands, rubbed 'em together, and shinnied up the tree. Brer Rabbit got a limb and went in the bottom of the tree and started pushing. But he wasn't pushing honeycomb. It was a beehive swarming with bees. He pushed it very gently until the hive was right under Brer Bear's chin.

It's a crying shame the way them bees got on Brer Bear's head. It swelled up so much that Brer Bear couldn't get his head out of the hole. For all anybody know, them bees are stinging him still.

Brer Fox Gets Tricked Again

One time Mr. Man caught Brer Rabbit in his collard green patch. Now don't come asking me what Mr. Man's name was. That ain't in the story. Just Mr. Man. Might have been Slip-Shot Sam. Then again, it could've been One-Eyed Riley. Of course, it might as easily been Freddie Eddie, Freddy Teddy, or Stagolee, 'cepting he never did no work far as I knows. I don't know what Mr. Man's name was, and don't care. Mr. Man is good enough for the story so it's good enough for you.

Like I was saying, Mr. Man caught Brer Rabbit in his collard green patch. Mr. Man had been trying to catch him for a long time and he was overjoyed.

"Got you now! Got you now! I can't get all my greens out of your stomach, but I sure can take some hair off your hide."

He tied Brer Rabbit to a tree alongside the road and went to get a stick. He was going to beat the Devil out of Brer Rabbit and whup some Jesus in. That's the truth!

Brer Rabbit wasn't none too pleased about this turn of events and he was doing some serious scheming when along comes Brer Fox. He saw Brer Rabbit all tied up and stopped to enjoy the sight.

"Somebody finally got you, huh? Fancy that!" He laughed and laughed.

He was laughing so hard it was a moment or two before he realized that Brer Rabbit was laughing right along with him. And laughing harder! "What you laughing at?"

"Just thinking about all the fun I'm going to have when Miz Meadows comes back."

"What're you talking about?"

"Miz Meadows is having a wedding at her house today. She say I got to come, but I don't know as I can. I got to go get the doctor for my children. They sick with the hee-beejitis. Miz Meadows say she don't care. Say if I ain't at the wedding, won't be no fun. She went to town to get the preacher and tied me up to make sure I'd be here when she come back by."

"I ain't heard about no wedding," Brer Fox said, his feelings hurt.

"This is a special wedding and party. She don't invite

just anybody. But I can't go, Brer Fox. I got to go get the doctor. Now I know that if you took my place at the party, Miz Meadows would find that you just as much of a fun man as me and she might stop all her hard feelings about you."

Wasn't nothing Brer Fox wanted more than to be on good terms with Miz Meadows, so he untied Brer Rabbit and let Brer Rabbit tie him to the tree.

"Miz Meadows should be along with the preacher any minute. I sho' nuf' appreciate what you doing for me, Brer Fox." Brer Rabbit hopped into the woods and hid to see what was going to happen.

When Mr. Man came back with a stick big enough to build a house on, he exclaimed, "What! The one what stole my greens has been replaced by the one what's been in my hen house. That's even better." He started in on Brer Fox with the stick. *Blammity-blam-blam-blam.* He beat Brer Fox

until the stick wasn't even good for toothpicks, and went off to get another one.

Brer Rabbit come sauntering out of the woods like he hadn't seen a thing. "That's strange," he said. "Miz Meadows and the preacher should've been here by now. I done been to the doctor's, gone to my house and back, and they still ain't come. That's mighty strange."

"Brer Rabbit!" cried Brer Fox. "Turn me loose from here. Maybe Miz Meadows went the back way." He was trying to pretend like nothing had happened to him.

"Could be," said Brer Rabbit. "Say, Brer Fox? How come your hair is all messed up and your head is all bashed in? Something been bothering you?"

Brer Fox didn't say a word.

Brer Rabbit smiled. "Remember that time you was after my children?" He chuckled. "If there ain't no hard feelings, I reckon I could untie you."

Brer Fox didn't have no choice. He apologized for trying to get Brer Rabbit's children and Brer Rabbit untied him. Just then Mr. Man reappeared with his buggy whip, and Brer Fox and Brer Rabbit didn't waste no time getting away from there.

Brer Rabbit and the Little Girl

If there was one thing in the world Brer Rabbit liked, it was lettuce. He would do anything for lettuce. One day he was going down a road and passed by a field of lettuce, more lettuce than he had seen in all his life! As far as he could see there were rows and rows and rows and rows and rows of lettuce. But between Brer Rabbit and all that lettuce was a wire fence.

Just as he started putting his mind to how he was going to get it, a little girl walked across the road, opened the gate, went in, picked a head of lettuce, and left.

Next morning, bright and early, Brer Rabbit was back. When the little girl came down the road, Brer Rabbit went to meet her.

"Good morning, young lady," he said.

"How you this morning, Brer Rabbit?"

"Just fine. Just fine. Say, you not Mr. Man's little girl, are you?"

"I am," she said proudly.

"Sho' nuf'!" he exclaimed, looking at her admiringly. "He told me about you, but I didn't expect to meet such a pretty young lady."

She blushed. "Why, thank you very much."

"He said he had a daughter who would let me in that field of lettuce over yonder, but I sho' didn't expect nobody as pretty as you."

The little girl just grinned and blushed and giggled. "Well, come on and I'll open the gate for you."

"Obliged," said Brer Rabbit.

He went to a far corner of the field and started eating. And he ate, and he ate, and he ate. The next morning he was back. The little girl let him in again and Brer Rabbit took up where he'd left off. This went on for about a week before Mr. Man noticed he was missing a whole lot of lettuce. He was right angry about it, too, and accused the folks what worked on his place of stealing it. He was about to fire all of them when the little girl said, "Daddy, you must've forgot. You told Brer Rabbit he could have all the lettuce he wanted."

Mr. Man wanted to know what she was talking about, and the little girl told him. Mr. Man nodded. "I see. Well, if Brer Rabbit comes tomorrow, you let him in the field, then come and tell me. There's something I want to talk to him about."

Next morning after the little girl let Brer Rabbit in the field, she went and told her daddy. Mr. Man rushed down to the field with a fishing line and slipped in the gate. Brer Rabbit was eyeball deep in the lettuce, going at it like the statute of limitations on eating was about to expire. Suddenly Mr. Man grabbed him around the neck and Brer Rabbit found himself dangling in the air, staring Mr. Man in the face.

Mr. Man tied Brer Rabbit up tight. "You know what I'm going to do to you?"

"No, but I got a feeling it ain't gon' be to my liking. In fact, I know it ain't."

"It's gon' be to mine. First I'm going to give you a whupping. And for that I got a red cowhide whip. Then I'm going to skin you. Then I'm going to nail your hide to the barn door, and then I just might start all over again from the beginning." Mr. Man told his little girl to watch Brer Rabbit while he went up to the house to get his whip.

No sooner had Mr. Man left than Brer Rabbit began to sing, and he could sing. Women had been known to faint when Brer Rabbit sang. So he started, and this is what he sang:

The Jaybird hunts the sparrow's nest,
The bee-martin sails all around;
The squirrel hollers from the top of the tree,
Mr. Mole, he stay in the ground;
He hide and he stay til the dark drops down—
Mr. Mole, he hide in the ground.

The little girl thought that was the prettiest song she'd ever heard and she laughed and clapped her hands and asked him to sing another one. Brer Rabbit said he couldn't. His throat was hurting from where Mr. Man had been holding him. But the little girl begged and pleaded. Brer Rabbit said, "If you think I can sing, you ought to see me dance!"

"Would you dance for me? Please, Brer Rabbit? Please?"

"How can I dance all tied up like this?"

"I'll untie you," said the little girl.

"You do and I'll show you some dancing."

The little girl untied him, and he danced all right. Danced all the way home. Made up some new steps getting there too!

Brer Rabbit Goes Back to Mr. Man's Garden

Mr. Man's garden was too delicious-looking for Brer Rabbit to leave alone. And anyway, it wasn't right for Mr. Man to have all them pretty vegetables to himself. Obviously, he didn't believe in sharing. Being worried about Mr. Man's soul, Brer Rabbit decided he'd *make* Mr. Man share.

A few mornings later Mr. Man went to town. As he was leaving he hollered to his daughter, "Janey! Don't you let Brer Rabbit get in my green peas. You hear me?"

"Yes, Daddy," she said.

Brer Rabbit was hiding in the bushes, listening. Soon as Mr. Man left, Brer Rabbit walked up to the little girl as bold as day.

"Ain't you Janey?" he asked.

"My daddy call me Janey. What your daddy call you?"

"Well, my daddy dead, but when he was living he called me Billy Malone." He smiled. "I passed your daddy in the road and he said for me to come tell you to give me some sparrow grass."

Janey had been warned against Brer Rabbit, but not Billy Malone, so she opened the gate and let Brer Rabbit into the garden. Brer Rabbit got as much sparrow grass as he could carry and left.

Mr. Man came back and saw that somebody had been in his garden. He asked Janey about it. She told him that Billy Malone said it was all right for him to go in and get some sparrow grass. Mr. Man knew something was up but didn't say anything.

Next morning when he got ready to go, he told Janey to keep an eye out for Brer Rabbit and not let *anybody* get any sparrow grass.

When Mr. Man was out of sight, Brer Rabbit come walking down the road and greeted the little girl, bowing low like a real gentleman. "I saw your daddy just now. He said I couldn't have no sparrow grass today, but it would be all right if I helped myself to the English peas."

The little girl opened the gate and Brer Rabbit made off with enough English peas to feed all of England.

When Mr. Man came back, his pea vines looked like a storm had hit'em, and he was hot! "Who been in my peas?" he asked his daughter.

"Mr. Billy Malone," she said.

"What this Billy Malone look like?"

"He got a split lip, pop eyes, big ears, and a bobtail, Daddy."

Mr. Man didn't have a bit of trouble recognizing that description. He fixed a box trap and set it in the garden among the peanuts. The next morning he told Janey, "Now, whatever you do today, don't let nobody have any sparrow grass, and don't let'em get any more English peas, the few I got left."

Soon as Mr. Man was out of sight, here come Brer Rabbit. He bowed low and said, "Good morning, Miz Janey. I met your daddy down the road there and he said I can't have no more sparrow grass or English peas, but to help myself to the peanuts."

Janey let him in the garden. Brer Rabbit headed straight for the peanut patch, where he tripped the string and the box fell right on top of him. He was caught and he knew it.

Wasn't long before Mr. Man came back. He went to the peanut patch and saw the overturned box. He stooped down, peered through the slats, and saw Brer Rabbit inside, quivering.

Mr. Man whooped. "Yes, sir! I got you this time, you devil! I got you! And when I get through with you, ain' gon' be nothing left. I'm gon' carry your foot in my pocket, put your meat in the pot, and wear your fur on my head."

Words like that always put a chill up and down Brer Rabbit's spine. "Mr. Man, I know I done wrong. And if

you let me go, I promise I'll stay away from your garden."

Mr. Man chuckled. "You gon' stay away from my garden if I don't let you go too. I got to go to the house to get my butcher knife."

Mr. Man went to the house, but he forgot to close the garden gate behind him. Brer Fox came down the road, and seeing the open gate, took it as an invitation and walked on in. He heard something hollering and making a lot of racket. He wandered around until he found the noise coming from underneath a box. "What the dickens is that?" he asked.

Brer Rabbit would've known that voice anywhere. "Run, Brer Fox! Run! Get out of here right now if you care about your life!"

"What's wrong, Brer Rabbit?"

"Mr. Man trapped me in here and is making me eat lamb. I'm about to bust wide open I done ate so much lamb. Run, Brer Fox, before he catch you."

Brer Fox wasn't thinking about running. "How's the lamb?"

"It tastes good at first, but enough is enough and too much is plenty. You better get out of here before he catches you."

Brer Fox wasn't running anywhere. "I like lamb, Brer Rabbit." He took the box off Brer Rabbit. "Put the box over me." Brer Rabbit did so gladly and decided not to wait around for the next chapter.

The story don't say what happened to Brer Fox. Brer Rabbit took care of himself. Now it's up to Brer Fox to take care of himself. That's the name of that tune.

Brer Possum Hears the Singing

Brer Rabbit stayed away from Mr. Man's garden for about a month, but he kept having dreams about all those pretty vegetables, and dream-food don't make a meal. No, indeed!

Mr. Man figured that Brer Rabbit would be back and he left the garden gate wide open. He told his daughter, "Janey, I want you to watch careful. If Brer Rabbit or Mr. Billy Malone, or whatever he calls himself, goes in the garden, I want you to run quick and close the gate tight."

"Yes, Daddy."

When Brer Rabbit came and saw the gate open, he thought luck was with him. He ducked in the garden and got down to some serious eating. When he got ready to go, he found the gate closed. He shook it, but it didn't open. He pushed it; it still didn't open. He grunted and pulled on it; the gate didn't budge.

Brer Rabbit hollered, "Hey, Janey! Come open the gate! It hurts my feelings to find the gate shut like this."

Janey came, but she didn't say a word.

"Come on, Janey! Open the gate! It hurts my feelings to see the gate shut like this. If you don't open the gate, I'll tear it off its hinges."

"Daddy told me not to open the gate."

Brer Rabbit opened his mouth wide. "See my long sharp teeth? If you don't open this gate, I'll bite you through and through."

That scared Janey and she opened the gate right quick.

When Mr. Man came back and asked about Brer Rabbit, Janey said, "He was here, Daddy, but I let him out. He said he was going to bite me through and through with his long sharp teeth."

Mr. Man said, "Janey, how is he going to bite you with him on one side of the gate and you the other?"

Janey hadn't thought about that.

Next morning Brer Rabbit went to the garden, found the gate open, went in and proceeded to make friends with Mr. Man's mustard greens. He ate until he was near 'bout green himself. He got ready to go, and lo and behold the gate was shut. He pushed; the gate didn't open. He kicked; gate still didn't open. He butted the gate with his head; nothing doing.

"Hey, Janey!" he hollered. "Come and open this gate! It's bad to mess with a man like me. Very bad! Open the gate."

Janey don't say a word.

"Shame on you," Brer Rabbit told her. "Shame on you doing me like this. You hurting my feelings. Open this gate before I tear it down."

"My daddy told me not to."

Brer Rabbit opened his eyes wide. "See my big eyes? I'll pop one of these eyes at you and kill you dead if you don't open this gate. Open the gate before my eye pops."

Janey hurried right now to get that gate open.

When Mr. Man came back, he asked where Brer Rabbit was. Janey told her daddy he was gone because he was going to pop one of his eyes and kill her.

"Brer Rabbit told a big tale, Janey. He can't do nothing like that."

Next morning Brer Rabbit came, went in the garden, and commenced on the artichokes. He ate artichokes until he was choking. When he got ready to go he figured the gate would be shut, and it was. He pulled it; he shook it; he kicked it; and he cussed it. Gate didn't open.

"Hey, Janey! Come open this gate! It's very bad to treat your own kinfolks like this. It makes me feel so sad when you do me like this."

Janey didn't say a word.

"You ain't supposed to treat kinfolks like this, Janey. Didn't your daddy teach you anything?"

"How you kin to me?" Janey asked.

"Your granddaddy chased my uncle with a dog once. That makes us kin. Now open the gate."

Janey didn't say a word.

"See my long sharp teeth. I'll bite you through and through."

"Not as long as you on that side of the gate and I stay over here."

"See my big eye. I'll pop it at you and shoot you dead!"

"No, you won't. Can't nobody do nothing like that."

Brer Rabbit was hot now. "See my horns!" He made his ears stand up stiff and straight. "I'll run you through."

She ran and opened the gate, and Brer Rabbit got on away from there.

When Mr. Man came back and Janey told him what happened, he said, "Tomorrow when Brer Rabbit comes, you shut the gate and go over to your girlfriend's house and play."

That suited Janey just fine.

Next day Brer Rabbit came and did away with the radishes. When he was ready to go, the gate was shut and he couldn't get it open. He called for Janey, but she didn't come. He tried to find a crack in the fence. No cracks. He looked for a hole. No holes. He tried to jump over. Fence was too high.

Mr. Man came, went in the garden, and grabbed Brer

Rabbit. He tied him in a sack, tied the sack high up on a tree limb, and went off to get his cane.

While he was gone, Brer Possum wandered into the garden. He looked up and saw the bag hanging from the tree limb.

"What's that bag hanging up there for?"

Brer Rabbit said, "Hush, Brer Possum! I'm listening to the singing in the clouds."

"I don't hear no singing, Brer Rabbit."

"Hush, I said! How can I hear if you keep flapping your mouth?"

There was a long pause. "I hear it now!" exclaimed Brer Rabbit. "I wish you could hear the singing in the clouds, Brer Possum."

"So do I."

"Tell you what. I'll let you sit in the bag and listen if you promise not to stay too long."

Brer Possum promised. He climbed the tree, untied the bag, and let it down real slow. Brer Rabbit crawled out and Brer Possum crawled in. Brer Rabbit tied the mouth of the sack real tight and started to pull the rope up to the tree limb.

"I don't hear them singing, Brer Rabbit."

"You will soon enough."

Brer Rabbit tied the sack on the limb.

"I don't hear them singing, Brer Rabbit."

"You'll hear them, Brer Possum. You'll hear them."

Brer Rabbit ran and hid in the bushes.

Just about the time Mr. Man came back, Brer Possum called out, "I don't hear them singing."

Mr. Man said, "I'll make you hear singing!"

Mr. Man took the bag down from the tree, grabbed his cane, and beat on that sack until his arms were tired. Mr.

Man figured Brer Rabbit had to be dead by now. Just as he started to open the sack, Brer Rabbit came out of the bushes and hollered, "I ate your artichokes! I ate your radishes! I ate your peas! I ate your greens, and I'm going to be eating out of your garden until you die!"

Brer Rabbit's Riddle

Mr. Man had almost caught Brer Rabbit, so Brer Rabbit decided it was time to settle down and do some honest work. Maybe he was getting old, or going through a midlife change.

He cleared a piece of ground back of his house and planted the nicest sweet potato patch anybody had ever seen. Brer Fox saw him sweating out there every day and couldn't believe his eyes! Something must've scared Brer Rabbit for him to be putting in a hard day's work. And if Brer Rabbit was living scared, Brer Fox saw his chance to get even for some of the misery he'd suffered.

Brer Fox decided to test Brer Rabbit, and one night he knocked down part of his fence. Next morning Brer Rabbit put it back up. That wasn't the Brer Rabbit that Brer Fox knew. Next night Brer Fox knocked it *all* down. Brer Rabbit patiently put the fence back up and went on to work in his potato patch. Brer Fox made ready to move in for the kill.

Next day he went over to Brer Rabbit's house. "I got a proposition for you. Let's take a walk and talk it over."

"Walk where?" Brer Rabbit wanted to know.

"Right over yonder."

"Where is over yonder?"

"Don't be so suspicious. What I wants to talk to you about is these fine peaches I found. I need your help getting them down."

This was something Brer Rabbit could understand. Before long they came to the peach orchard. Brer Rabbit picked a tree so heavy with peaches it was about to break, and he climbed up. Brer Fox sat at the base of the tree, figuring he would grab Brer Rabbit when he climbed down.

Brer Rabbit knew that, so when Brer Fox told him to throw down the peaches, Brer Rabbit hollered, "Can't! If you miss, the peaches will get squashed on the ground. I'm going to throw them over there in the soft grass."

When Brer Fox went to pick the peaches up, Brer Rabbit hurried out of the tree and ran into the weeds. "Say, Brer Fox! I got a riddle for you."

"What is it?"

"It go like this," and then Brer Rabbit sang:

Big bird rob and little bird sing,
The big bee zoom and the little bee sting,
The little man lead and the big horse follows—
Can you tell what's good for a head in a hollow?

Brer Fox scratched his head and squinched up his face. He scratched his armpit and squinched some more. He scratched his rear and the more he scratched and the more he squinched, the more mixed up he got. Finally, he admitted, "That's a good riddle, Brer Rabbit. What's the answer?"

Brer Rabbit shook his head. "Can't tell you. But I'll give you some help. This is one of them riddles you can't figure out unless you eat some honey. And I know where we can get plenty honey."

Brer Fox followed Brer Rabbit until they came to Brer Bear's backyard, where there were a lot of bee-gums. For all you city folks what ain't been properly educated, a bee-gum is a beehive what's in a gum tree.

Well, Brer Fox didn't have much of a sweet tooth, but he sho' did want to figure out the riddle. He watched while Brer Rabbit walked around among the bee-gums, tapping on them with a stick until he found one that sounded full of honey.

"This is a good one, Brer Fox. Now, put your head in and get some honey."

Brer Rabbit tilted the bee-gum and Brer Fox stuck his

head in. No sooner was it in than Brer Rabbit turned that bee-gum loose and down it came—*ker-swoosh!*—right tight on Brer Fox's neck.

Brer Fox kicked; he squealed; he jumped; he squalled; he danced; he pranced; he begged; he even prayed, but nothing doing. He called out for Brer Rabbit to help him, but shoots! By that time Brer Rabbit was sitting on his front porch smoking a cigar.

After a while Brer Rabbit looked up to see Brer Fox's granddaddy, who folks called Gran'sir' Gray Fox.

"How you today, Gran'sir' Gray Fox?" Brer Rabbit greeted him.

"Not doing too well," Gran'sir' Gray Fox said. "I got the old age in my teeths."

"Sorry to hear that," Brer Rabbit replied. "What brings you over to these parts?"

"You ain't seen that good-for-nothing, triflin' grandson of mine, have you?"

Brer Rabbit chuckled. "I seen him. Me and him been doing riddles. He's off somewhere right now trying to figure out one I gave him. Why don't I tell it to you? If you figure it out, it'll take you right to him."

"All right, Brer Rabbit. Lay it on me."

The big bird rob and the little bird sing,
The big bee zoom and the little bee sting,
The little man lead and the big horse follows—
Can you tell what's good for a head in a hollow?

Gran'sir' Gray Fox put a pinch of snuff in his lip, scratched his head, and coughed a couple of times. He thought and thought and thought and scratched some more, but he couldn't make it out either.

Brer Rabbit laughed and then sang:

Bee-gum mighty big to make a Fox collar,
Can you tell what's good for a head in a hollow?

Gran'sir' Gray Fox put some more snuff in his lip, scratched some more, thought some more, scratched again. Then he smiled, nodded, and headed for Brer Bear's bee-gum trees.

He got there just in time to see Brer Bear catch Brer Fox with the bee-gum on his head. Yes, he got there just in time to see Brer Bear lay into Brer Fox with a hickory stick like Sister Goose battling clothes. Gran'sir' Gray Fox enjoyed the sight too.

The Moon in the Pond

Brer Rabbit went to see Brer Turtle one evening. Brer Turtle could tell by his sweet smile that he had some trick in mind, and if anybody was born to be a partner in trickery, Brer Turtle was the man. He was a man among men!

"I got an idea, Brer Turtle."

"Tell me something I don't know."

Brer Rabbit grinned. "I'm going to tell Brer Fox, Brer Wolf, and Brer Bear that I'm having a fishing party down at the pond tomorrow night. I need you to back me up no matter what I say. You understand?"

Brer Turtle said he sho' did. "And if I ain't there tomorrow night, then you know the grasshopper flew away with me," and he laughed.

Brer Rabbit and Brer Turtle shook hands and Brer Rabbit went home and went to bed. Brer Turtle knew that if he was going to be at the pond by tomorrow night he best get started now.

Next day Brer Rabbit sent word to all the animals about the fishing frolic. Brer Fox invited Miz Meadows and Miz Motts as his guests.

That night Brer Bear brought a hook and line. Brer Wolf brought a hook and line too. Brer Fox brought a dip net, and Brer Turtle brought the bait. Miz Meadows and Miz Motts brought themselves dressed up all pretty.

Brer Bear said he was going to fish for mud-cats. Brer Wolf said he was going to fish for horneyheads. Brer Fox wanted to catch some perch for the ladies. Brer Turtle said he'd fish for minnows, and Brer Rabbit looked at Brer Turtle and said he was going to fish for suckers.

They got their fishing poles and what-all ready and Brer

Rabbit went to the edge of the pond to cast first. He drew back his arm to throw his fishing line in the water and suddenly stopped. He stared. The pole dropped from his hand. He leaned forward. He stared. He scratched his head and stared some more. "I don't believe it," he said finally, in a hushed voice.

Miz Meadows thought he might have seen a snake and she hollered out, "Brer Rabbit, what in the name of goodness is the matter?"

Brer Rabbit didn't say nothing, and scratched his head some more. Then he turned around and said, "Ladies and gentlemen, we might as well pack up our gear and go on down to the fish store and buy some fish. Ain't gon' be no fishing at the pond this night."

Brer Turtle said, "That's the truth! That's sho' nuf' the truth."

"Now, ladies, don't be scared. All us brave gentlemen here will take care of y'all. Accidents do happen, but I don't have any idea how this one took place."

"What's the matter?" Miz Meadows asked, exasperated now.

"Why, look for yourselves. The Moon done fell in the water."

Brer Fox looked in and said, "Well, well, well!"

Brer Bear looked in. "Mighty bad, mighty bad!"

Miz Meadows stared at it and squalled out, "Ain't that too much?"

Brer Rabbit shrugged his shoulders. "You can say what you want. But unless we get that Moon out of the water, ain't gon' be no fishing party tonight. You can ask Brer Turtle. He know more about water than anybody here. He'll tell you."

"That's the truth," piped up Brer Turtle.

"How we gon' get the Moon out?" Miz Motts asked Brer Turtle.

"We best leave that to Brer Rabbit."

Brer Rabbit stared up in the sky like he was thinking hard. After a while he said, "Well, if we could borrow Brer Mud Turtle's seine net, we could drag the Moon out."

"Brer Mud Turtle's my first cousin," Brer Turtle said. "I calls him Unk Mud, we so close. He wouldn't mind your borrowing his net."

Brer Rabbit went to borrow the net. While he was gone, Brer Turtle said his grandparents had told him that whoever took the Moon out of the water would find a great pot of money underneath. Brer Fox, Brer Wolf, and Brer Bear got real interested. They said they wouldn't be gentlemen if they let Brer Rabbit do all the work of getting the Moon out of the pond after he done all the work to get the seine net.

When Brer Rabbit got back, they told him they'd take the net and get the Moon out. Brer Turtle winked at Brer Rabbit, and after an appropriate number of protests, Brer Rabbit turned the net over to them.

Brer Fox grabbed hold of one end, Brer Wolf grabbed the other, and Brer Bear came along behind to unsnag the net if it got caught on any logs or debris.

They made one haul—no Moon. They hauled again— no Moon. They went farther out in the pond. The water was getting in their ears. Brer Fox and Brer Wolf and Brer Bear shook their heads to get it out and while they were shaking their heads they got to where the bottom of the pond dropped away, and that's just what they did—dropped off the edge of the shelf right into the deep water. Have mercy! They kicked and sputtered, went under and came up coughing and snorting and went under and came up again.

Finally they dragged themselves out, dripping water like waterfalls.

Brer Rabbit looked at them. "I guess you gentlemen best go home and get into some dry clothes. Next time we'll have better luck. I heard that the Moon will always bite at a hook if you use fools for bait."

Brer Fox, Brer Bear, and Brer Wolf sloshed away, and Brer Rabbit and Brer Turtle went home with Miz Meadows and Miz Motts.

Why Brer Bear Has No Tail

After the trick Brer Rabbit and Brer Turtle played at the pond, they decided to go into business together.

Brer Rabbit went to see Brer Turtle one morning. Miz Turtle said Brer Turtle had gone to visit Brer Mud Turtle. Brer Rabbit went over there and the three of them had a good time sitting around talking and telling jokes.

Way up in the heat of the day they decided to go to the pond and cool off. There was a big slippery rock there that Brer Turtle and Brer Mud Turtle loved to slide down and into the water.

Brer Rabbit sat off to one side and got a kick out of all the fun Brer Turtle and Brer Mud Turtle were having. After a while Brer Bear came along.

"What's going on, folks? I see Brer Rabbit is here, and Brer Turtle and Unk Tommy Mud Turtle is here too."

"Sit down, Brer Bear, and take a load off your feet. We just enjoying the day like there ain't no hard times."

"How come you ain't joining in the fun, Brer Rabbit?" Brer Bear wanted to know.

Brer Rabbit winked at Brer Turtle and Unk Tommy Mud Turtle. "Goodness gracious, Brer Bear! I done had my fun. I was just sitting here letting my clothes dry."

"Maybe Brer Bear might like to join us," suggested Brer Turtle, who was floating on his back in the middle of the pond.

Brer Rabbit laughed real loud. "Who? Brer Bear? You must be joking! His feets are too big. Anyway, his tail is too long for him to be sliding down that rock."

Back in them days Brer Bear had a long pretty tail and it swished angrily. "Who you talking about, Brer Rabbit? You think I'm scared to slide down that rock, don't you?"

Without another word he climbed up on it, squatted, tucked his tail under him, and started down. First he went kinna slow. He was grinning, 'cause this was fun. All of a sudden he got to the slick part of that rock and ZOOM! He was flying sho' nuf' now. Brer Bear swallowed that grin and started screaming. When he hit the water it was like a mountain falling in. So much water went out of the pond, it took until the next summer for it to get filled up again.

Brer Bear walked out of the pond, a sheepish grin on his face. He went back up to where Brer Rabbit was sitting. "Told you I wasn't scared."

Brer Rabbit had his hand behind his back. "You forgot something." He handed Brer Bear his tail.

Brer Bear felt his hind parts and sho' nuf', his tail was gone. It had come off when he hit the slick part of that rock.

"I got some chicken grease at home. It's good for sore places," Brer Rabbit laughed.

Brer Bear was sore all right, but whether he was more sore in his hindparts or his feelings, I just don't know.

Wiley Wolf and Riley Rabbit

There was one period when the animals were getting along so well together, things were almost boring. Brer Rabbit seemed like he'd forgotten how to play tricks. And his best friend was Brer Wolf!

Every Sunday either Brer Rabbit went over to Brer Wolf's or Brer Wolf went to Brer Rabbit's. They were as friendly with each other as the fleas on a dog's back, and they'd sit on the porch and chew tobacco or smoke cigars and talk about all the things they used to do to each other.

While they reminisced, their two oldest boys, Wiley Wolf and Riley Rabbit, played in the yard. Wiley and Riley would jump and run and hide and slide and just have a good time with each other.

"It does my heart good to see our young'uns playing together like they do," said Brer Wolf. "That's how we should've been with each other all these years. I'm just glad our young'uns got better manners than we had."

When it came time for Brer Rabbit to go, Brer Wolf said, "Brer Rabbit, why don't you let Riley Rabbit come over during the week and play with Wiley? I think we ought to do all we can to encourage them to get along."

Brer Rabbit agreed.

Brer Wolf and Wiley walked part of the way home with Brer Rabbit and Riley. When they got to the crossroads, everybody shook hands and Brer Rabbit said Riley would be over to play with Wiley during the week.

Brer Wolf had done a lot of talking about what good friends him and Brer Rabbit had become. But that don't mean his wolf nature wouldn't come on him when he wasn't even looking for it. As he was walking back home with Wiley, he said, "When Riley comes to play with you this week, I think y'all might have fun playing Riding in the Bag."

"What's that, Poppa?"

Brer Wolf was amazed. "You mean I ain't told you about Riding in the Bag? I must not be much of a daddy if I ain't told you about that game. You get in a bag and let Riley pull you around the yard. Then he gets in the bag and you pull him around for a while. That's all there is to it."

When Riley came to visit, him and Wiley played the game and had a good time. But it seemed like Riley didn't have no more sense than to drag Wiley over big rocks and stumps and roots sticking up out of the ground. And when Wiley complained that he was getting hurt, Riley said he wasn't going to do it no more and went right back to doing it.

When Riley went home that night he told Brer Rabbit about the fun game he'd played with Wiley. Brer Rabbit listened and looked thoughtful, but he didn't say anything.

When Wiley told Brer Wolf about how much fun they'd had, Brer Wolf shut his eyes like he was dreaming and began licking his chops.

"There's two parts to the game, Wiley. The second part is called Tying the Bag." He smiled.

Next time Riley came over to play with Wiley, they played Riding in the Bag until they were wore out. Then Wiley suggested they play tying each other up in the bag.

What neither of 'em knowed was that Brer Rabbit was hiding nearby. When he heard Wiley's suggestion, he walked in the yard and called Riley to him.

"It's almost time for you to come home. When Wiley's turn to get tied in the bag comes, tie it as tight as you can. Then run on home. Your momma's got some chores for you."

Brer Rabbit left and Riley and Wiley played tying each other up in the bag for a while. When it was Wiley's turn to get in the bag, Riley tied it as tight as he could.

Brer Rabbit to the Rescue

Brer Fox was coming from town one evening when he saw Brer Turtle. He thought this was as good a time as any to grab Brer Rabbit's best friend.

He was close to home so he ran, got a sack, and ran back, knowing Brer Turtle wouldn't have covered more than two or three feet of ground.

Brer Fox didn't even say how-do like the animals usually did, but just reached down, grabbed Brer Turtle, and flung him in the sack. Brer Turtle squalled and kicked and screamed. Brer Fox tied a knot in the sack and headed for home.

Brer Rabbit was lurking around Brer Fox's watermelon patch, wondering how he was going to get one, when he heard Brer Fox coming, singing like he'd just discovered happiness. Brer Rabbit jumped into a ditch and hid.

"I wonder what's in that sack Brer Fox got slung over his shoulder?" Brer Rabbit wondered. He wondered and he wondered, and the more he wondered, the more he didn't know. He knew this much: Brer Fox had absolutely no business walking up the road singing and carrying something which nobody but him knew what it was.

Brer Rabbit went up to his house and yelled, "Hey, Brer Fox! Brer Fox! Come quick! There's a whole crowd of folks down in your watermelon patch. They carrying off watermelons and tromping on your vines like it's a holiday or something! I tried to get'em out, but they ain't gon' pay a little man like me no mind. You better hurry!"

Brer Fox dashed out. Brer Rabbit chuckled and went inside.

He looked around until he saw the sack in the corner. He picked it up and felt it.

"Let me alone!" came a voice from inside. "Turn me loose! You hear me?"

Brer Rabbit dropped the sack and jumped back. Then he laughed. "Only one man in the world can make a fuss like that and that's Brer Turtle."

"Brer Rabbit? That you?"

"It was when I got up this morning."

"Get me out of here. I got dust in my throat and grit in my eye and I can't breathe none too good either. Get me out, Brer Rabbit."

"Tell me one thing, Brer Turtle. I can figure out how you got in the sack, but I can't for the life of me figure how you managed to tie a knot in it after you was inside."

Brer Turtle wasn't in the mood for none of Brer Rabbit's joking. "If you don't get me out of this sack, I'll tell your wife about all the time you spend with Miz Meadows and the girls."

Brer Rabbit untied the sack in a hurry. He carried Brer Turtle out to the woods and looked around for a while.

"What you looking for, Brer Rabbit?"

"There it is!" Brer Rabbit exclaimed.

He took a hornet's nest down from a tree and stuffed the opening with leaves. Then he took the nest to Brer Fox's house and put it in the sack. He tied the sack tightly, then picked it up, flung it at the wall, dropped it on the floor, and swung it over his head a couple of times to get the hornets stirred up good. Then he put the sack back in the corner and ran to the woods where Brer Turtle was hiding.

A few minutes later Brer Fox came up the road, and he was angry! He stormed in the house. Brer Rabbit and Brer Turtle waited. All of a sudden they heard chairs falling, dishes breaking, the table turning over. It sounded like a

bunch of cows was loose in the house.

Brer Fox came tearing through the door—and he hadn't even stopped to open it. The hornets were on him like a second skin.

Yes, that was one day Brer Fox found out what pain and suffering is all about.

———————————

The Noise in the Woods

Brer Rabbit was meandering through the woods one day when he heard Mr. Man chopping down a tree. Brer Rabbit stopped to listen. All of a sudden—KUBBER-LANG-BANG-BLAM!

Brer Rabbit jumped up in the air and took off running. Now, Brer Rabbit might try to claim he wasn't scared, but it's just like lightning and thunder. Folks know that thunder can't hurt'em, but when a loud clap of it come, they get scared and want to run anyhow. Well, that's the way it was with Brer Rabbit that morning.

He ran and he ran and he ran some more, until he was almost out of breath. And about then, Brer Coon came along.

"What's your hurry, Brer Rabbit?"

"Ain't got no time to tarry."

"Is your folks sick?"

"No, thank God. Ain't got no time to tarry!"

"Well, what's the matter?"

"Mighty big racket back there in the woods. Ain't got no time to tarry!"

Brer Coon got kinna skittish, because he was a long ways away from home. He took off running and hadn't gone far when he run smack dab into Brer Fox.

"Brer Coon! Where you going?"

"Ain't got no time to tarry!"

"Is your folks sick?"

"No, thank God. Ain't got no time to tarry!"

"Well, what's the matter, Brer Coon?"

"Mighty queer noise back there in the woods. Ain't got no time to tarry!"

And Brer Fox split the wind. He hadn't gone far when he run smack dab into Brer Wolf.

"Brer Fox! Stop and rest yourself!"

"Ain't got no time to tarry!"

"Is your folks sick?"

"No, thank God. Ain't got no time to tarry!"

"Well, good or bad, Brer Fox. Tell me the news!"

"There's a mighty noise back there in the woods. Ain't got no time to tarry!"

Brer Wolf scratched earth getting away from there. He hadn't gone far before he ran into Brer Bear. Brer Bear asked him what was wrong and Brer Wolf told him about the mighty noise. Brer Bear might have been big but he wasn't slow and he shook the earth getting away. Before long every animal in the community was running like Ole Boy was after them.

They ran and they ran until they came to Brer Turtle's house. Being about out of breath by this time, they stopped to rest. Brer Turtle wanted to know what all the excitement was.

"Mighty noise back there in the woods," Brer Fox said.

"What it sound like?"

None of them knew.

"Who heard the racket?" Brer Turtle asked.

They asked one another and found out that none of them had.

Brer Turtle chuckled. "Excuse me, gentlemen. Believe it's time for me to go eat my breakfast." And he left.

The animals inquired among each other. They weren't surprised to discover that Brer Rabbit was the one what started the news about the noise.

They went over to his house one sunny afternoon and

he was sitting on the porch, getting a tan.

"What you trying to make a fool of me for?" Brer Bear spoke up.

"Fool of who, Brer Bear?"

"Me, Brer Rabbit! That's who."

"This is the first time I've seen you today, Brer Bear."

Brer Coon spoke up. "Well, you seen me today, and you made a fool of me."

"How I fool you?"

"You pretended like there was a big racket in the woods, Brer Rabbit."

"Wasn't no pretend. There was a big racket in the woods."

"What kind?" Brer Coon asked.

Brer Rabbit chuckled. "You ought to ask me that first, Brer Coon. Wasn't nothing but Mr. Man cutting down a tree. If you'd asked me, I would've told you. Sho' would have." And he turned his face up to the sun, closed his eyes, a big smile on his face.

Brer Rabbit Gets the Meat Again

Brer Rabbit was hungry for some meat, Brer Wolf was hungry for some meat, so off they went and killed somebody's cow.

When it was time to divide the meat, Brer Wolf, wary of Brer Rabbit's tricks, said, "I'm the biggest and I should have the most!" He pulled out his butcher knife and started cutting up the cow. Brer Rabbit didn't like that one bit, especially because Brer Wolf was going to take all of it.

Brer Rabbit walked around the cow slowly. He stooped down and sniffed at it. "Brer Wolf? That meat smell all right to you?"

Brer Wolf was steady cutting and carving. He knew what Brer Rabbit was up to. "Smells right fresh. Right fresh."

Brer Rabbit walked around the carcass one more time, squeezing and patting the meat. "It feels flabby to me. How does it feel to you?"

Brer Wolf was steady cutting and carving. "Feels right fresh. Right fresh."

Brer Rabbit got indignant. "I'm trying to be your friend and tell you a thing or two so's you won't die, but you ain't got sense enough to pay me no mind." He stomped off.

A little while later he came back with some fire and a dish of salt.

"What you up to, Brer Rabbit?" Brer Wolf asked suspiciously.

"I ain't taking my share home until I know what's wrong with it."

Brer Rabbit built a fire and carved himself a nice steak. He put it over the fire until it was cooked the way he liked it—medium rare. He nibbled at it; he tasted it; and finally he started chewing. "Maybe I was wrong about this here meat," he said, smacking his lips. He ate the whole thing. "I guess I was wrong, Brer Wolf," he said when he finished, patting his stomach.

Brer Wolf was steady carving and cutting, but kept one eye on Brer Rabbit. Brer Rabbit was sitting on a stump like a judge on a bench.

Suddenly, he threw up his hands and groaned. He swayed backward and forward, groaning. He clutched at his stomach and rocked from side to side. "Oh, Lord! Oh, Lord!"

Brer Wolf stopped cutting. Brer Rabbit's eyes began rolling around in his head. He screamed, fell on the ground, and began thrashing around. "I been poisoned! I been poisoned! Oh, Lordy! Run quick and get the doctor, Brer Wolf! Run quick!"

Brer Wolf got scared and ran for the doctor. But by the time he got back with the doctor, Brer Rabbit was gone. So was the meat. The only thing left was the bill, which the doctor slapped in his hand for wasting his time.

Brer Wolf Gets in More Trouble

Wasn't more than two, three days later when Brer Rabbit met up with Brer Wolf on the road to town. Brer Wolf acted like nothing was wrong.

"Say there, Brer Rabbit! How you be this morning?" Brer Wolf chuckled. "You ought to be 'shamed about the way you tricked me the other day."

Brer Rabbit allowed as to how that was probably true. "How you be, Brer Wolf? How's your folk?"

"Just fine." Then he snarled, "And a whole lot better than you gon' be before this day is over!"

Brer Wolf grabbed for Brer Rabbit. He ducked and off they went through the woods. Brer Wolf was pushing Brer Rabbit for all he was worth. Brer Rabbit began to feel the saliva from Brer Wolf's teeth dropping on his back. He headed for a hollow log he'd picked out for times just like this, a log with holes at both ends.

Brer Wolf saw Brer Rabbit go in, but didn't see him go out. But Brer Rabbit didn't stop to say good-bye either.

Brer Wolf sat down in front of the log to do some profound thinking about what to do to Brer Rabbit, and happened to see Brer Bear clearing new ground.

"Brer Bear! I got Brer Rabbit trapped. Go fetch me some fire!"

When Brer Bear came back with a firebrand, they put it to the log. After a while, it was nothing but ashes. Brer Wolf and Brer Bear smiled, slapped hands, and went home. Had the best sleep they'd had in years that night.

Next day, Brer Wolf went to visit Miz Meadows and the girls. When he got there, Brer Rabbit was sitting on the porch with his arms around them. Brer Wolf almost fainted.

Brer Rabbit wished him how-do and grinned like nothing had ever happened. "Come set a spell, Brer Wolf. Always good to see a good friend like you. Fact is, you a better friend than I ever realized."

"How so?" Brer Wolf wanted to know, still not sure if he was talking to a ghost or if he had lost his mind.

"I was thinking about when you burned me up in that hollow log. When you get the time, I sho' wish you'd do it again."

"Brer Rabbit? One of us is crazy, and it ain't me. What are you talking about?"

Brer Rabbit lowered his voice. "I don't know if I can tell you. I don't want the news to get out."

"I won't tell a soul on the top side of the world."

Brer Rabbit thought for a minute. "All right." He lowered his voice almost to a whisper. "When you get in a hollow log and somebody sets it on fire, honey oozes out all over you. That's what keeps you from getting burned

up. And then you got the job of licking all that honey off."
He chuckled. "That's some job, ain't it? So, please. When
you get time, I got a nice hollow log picked out and it
would be a favor to me if you'd burn me up again."

"I got time right now," said Brer Wolf.

"I knowed you was the kind of man I was looking for."

Off they went. When they got there, Brer Wolf said Brer
Rabbit owed him a favor.

"How so?"

"I burnt you up so you could get the honey. Now it's
your turn to burn me up."

"That ain't fair!" Brer Rabbit exclaimed. "I been looking
forward to getting burned up in this log for days."

They argued the matter back and over until Brer Rabbit
relented. Brer Wolf crawled in the log. (This log wasn't
hollow at both ends.) Brer Rabbit got a pile of leaves and
twigs, stuffed them in the log and put a match to them.
Then he piled up rocks in the opening.

"Getting kinna warm in here, Brer Rabbit, and I don't
see no honey."

"Don't be in a hurry."

The fire got to burning good and the wood was popping like a gun going off.

"Getting hot now, Brer Rabbit. I still don't see no honey."

"It'll come, Brer Wolf. It'll come."

"I need some air! I'm choking!"

"Fresh air make honey sour. Don't be in such a hurry."

"It's hot in here, Brer Rabbit!"

"That means it's almost time for the honey to come."

"*Ow-Ow!* I'm burning up, Brer Rabbit!"

"Wait for the honey, Brer Wolf!"

"*Ow-ow!* I can't take it no more, Brer Rabbit!"

Brer Rabbit piled on some more leaves and wood. "I'll give you honey. Same kind you wanted to give me."

Brer Rabbit Tells on Brer Wolf

The animals were divided up into two big groups. There were the ones with claws and long teeth, like Brer Rabbit, Brer Fox, Brer Wolf, and all them. Then there were the animals with horns—folks like Brer Bull, Brer Steer, Sister Cow, Mr. Benjamin Ram, Brer Billy Goat, Brer Rhinossyhoss, and can't leave out Miz Unicorn. There were a lots more, but I can't recollect their names right this minute.

Well, it was late over in the summer one year when the horned animals decided to have a convention and decide what to do about the animals with claws and teeth always chasing them. They went way back out in the woods close to Lost Forty and started their meeting.

Brer Wolf got news of the meeting and sneaked out there to see what was going on. He got a couple of sticks, tied them on his head, and walked up to where a group of horned animals were talking.

"Who you?" Brer Bull demanded to know, eyeing him suspiciously.

"Baaa! I'm little Sook Calf."

Brer Bull wasn't convinced, but he didn't say anything.

Brer Wolf listened to the animals complaining about how he and Brer Rabbit and Brer Fox treated them. He started getting a little nervous. About that time a great big horsefly zoomed by and without thinking Brer Wolf snapped at it.

Somebody laughed loudly.

"Who's making all that racket and showing they ain't got no manners?" Brer Bull bellowed.

Nobody said anything, and after a minute they went back to talking.

Brer Wolf knew that laugh. He ought to, as many times as he had heard it coming at him. Yes, Brer Rabbit had sneaked out to the convention too, and he was hiding in the bushes. When he saw Brer Wolf with them sticks tied on his head and snapping at the horsefly, he couldn't help laughing. Then he sang:

> *O kittle-cattle, kittle-cattle, where are your eyes?*
> *Whoever saw a Sook Calf snapping at flies?*

The horned animals looked around, wondering what that was all about. They went back to talking, but before Brer Wolf could get his ear back in the conversation good, a flea bit him on his neck. Without thinking, he scratched at it with his hind foot.

Brer Rabbit laughed and sang:

> *Scritchum-scratchum, lawsy, my laws!*
> *Look at that Sook Calf scratching with claws!*

Brer Wolf got scared, but none of the horned animals paid him any attention. A few minutes later Brer Rabbit sang out again:

Rinktum-tinktum, ride him on a rail!
That Sook Calf got a long bushy tail!

Brer Wolf was scared sho' nuf' now, especially when he
saw Brer Bull looking at him right hard. Brer Rabbit knew
this wasn't the time to stop:

One and one never can make six,
Sticks ain't horns, and horns ain't sticks.

Brer Bull and Brer Wolf moved at the same time—Brer
Bull at Brer Wolf and Brer Wolf at getting away from there.
Brer Wolf had to keep out of sight for a week or so after
that, 'cause Brer Rabbit told everybody that Brer Wolf had
been walking in the woods with a chair on his head trying
to court Sister Moose.

Brer Rabbit and the Mosquitoes

Brer Wolf had a daughter who was sho' nuf' good-looking. Now, before I go any further I can hear you thinking
that Brer Wolf been killed off twice. What that got to do
with anything? Am I the tale? Is the tale me? Or is the tale
the tale? Well, you can figure that out. If I ain't the tale,
and the tale ain't me, it don't make one bit of difference if
Brer Wolf was dead or alive. Ain't that so?

Dead or dead, Brer Wolf had a daughter and she was a
fine young thing. All the animals was hitting on her! First
one was Brer Fox. He was sitting on the porch talking his
stuff to her, and everybody know that Brer Fox could talk

stuff sho' nuf'. All of a sudden the mosquitoes started coming around. The mosquitoes at Brer Wolf's house was near 'bout big as airplanes and just as loud. Brer Fox started hitting and slapping at them. Brer Wolf came out of the house and told Brer Fox to go. "Any man what can't put up with a few mosquitoes can't court my daughter."

Next was Brer Coon. He hardly got one foot on the porch before he was slapping and biting at the mosquitoes. Brer Wolf showed him how the road run the same both ways.

Next was Brer Mink and he declared war on them mosquitoes. Brer Wolf told him to fight his war somewhere else.

It went on this way until all the animals had eliminated themselves except Brer Rabbit. He sent word that he was coming courting. Brer Wolf's daughter, who had always thought Brer Rabbit was kind of cute, put on her mascara and eyeliner and whatever else it is that the women put on their face. She squeezed herself into a pair of jeans four sizes too small. Have mercy! And she put on a pink halter top! When Brer Rabbit saw her, he thought he'd died and gone to heaven.

When Brer Wolf saw what his daughter was looking like, he said there was no way in this lifetime she was gon' sit there in the porch swing by herself with Brer Rabbit. Not with all he knowed about Brer Rabbit! So he pulled his rocking chair out and sat with them.

They hadn't been there long before Brer Rabbit heard the mosquitoes coming. *Zoom, zoom, zoom.*

"Mighty nice place you got here, Brer Wolf."

Zoom, zoom, zoom.

"Some say it's too low in the swamps," Brer Wolf answered.

Zoom, zoom, zoom.

The mosquitoes were *zooming* so fierce that Brer Rabbit started getting scared, and when Brer Rabbit gets scared, his mind works like a brand-new car motor.

"I was in town today, Brer Wolf, and I saw a spotted horse. Never seen a spotted horse in my life."

Zoom, zoom, zoom.

"Do tell! I ain't never seen one of them myself."

"You're wonderful," said the girl. She figured wouldn't nobody else in the world could've seen a spotted horse. Shows you how far gone she was.

Zoom, zoom, zoom.

"My granddaddy was spotted, Brer Wolf."

"Do tell!"

Zoom, zoom, zoom.

"That's the naked truth I'm telling you. He was spotted all over. He had one spot right here." Brer Rabbit slapped his face and killed one of the mosquitoes.

"I don't want nobody to laugh, but my granddaddy had spots all over. Had that one on the side of his face which I just showed you. Had another one right here on his leg."

Slap!

Another mosquito gone.

"Even had one right here in between his shoulder blades."

Blip!

"And one down here at his hipbone."

Phap!

Brer Rabbit kept on talking about his granddaddy's spots until near 'bout every mosquito in the county was dead. Brer Wolf was so tired of hearing about Brer Rabbit's granddaddy's spots he fell asleep.

At which point, Brer Wolf's daughter dragged Brer Rabbit off to the woods, and the story don't go no further.

How Brer Rabbit Became a Scary Monster

Brer Rabbit was sitting around his house one day with nothing to do, so he decided to pay a call on Brer Bear. Well, not exactly on Brer Bear. On Brer Bear's house!

He sneaked over there and hid in the woods. After a while, Brer Bear, Miz Brune, and Miz Brindle came out and went off down the road like they were going on a picnic. Miz Brune and Miz Brindle had their parasols and Brer Bear was toting a picnic basket. Brer Rabbit waited until they were out of sight and then went in the house.

Brer Rabbit didn't have anything in mind. He was just curious how other folks lived and every now and then went in somebody's house when nobody was home. He peeked in here and poked in there, opened this and rubbed his paws over that. While he was peeking and poking and opening and rubbing, he bumped up against a shelf in the kitchen, and a bucket of honey what Brer Bear kept there tipped over. Before Brer Rabbit knowed it, he was covered with honey, and I mean covered! If you'd seen him, you'd a thought he was a big piece of saltwater taffy. Brer Rabbit couldn't do a thing until the honey dripped off his eyes and he could open'em up to get a good look at the mess he'd gotten himself in this time.

"What am I gon' do?" He was scared to go outside, because he might attract every fly and bee in four counties. But if he stayed in the house, Brer Bear would find him and that would be worst.

So he tipped out of the house and made it to the woods. He commenced to rolling around on the ground, trying to get the honey off. But instead of getting it off, all the dead leaves and twigs and trash what was on the ground stuck to him. He rolled, and the leaves stuck. He rolled the other way, and more leaves stuck. He started jumping up and down and whirling around trying to get the leaves off. He shook and he shivered. He quivered and he quavered. He did a front flip and he did a back flip. He spun around like he was a baton in a majorette's hand. But the leaves and twigs stuck to him like they'd growed there.

"What am I gon' do now?" he wanted to know. Things had just gone from worse to worser. He had to get home and get himself in the bathtub.

He set off through the woods and every step he took, the leaves went *swishy-swushy, splushy-splishy, swishy-swushy, splushy-splishy*. If Sister Ocean had had legs and gone for a walk, I reckon that's what she would've sounded like.

Brer Rabbit was afraid that if anybody saw him, they'd laugh him out of the community, and Miz Meadows and the girls wouldn't allow him to sit on the porch ever again.

He was hurrying across the pasture when he ran into Sister Cow. Sister Cow took one look, raised her tail and took off running like she'd just seen the butcher. Brer Rabbit smiled.

Next person Brer Rabbit run into was a man taking some shoats to market. The man looked at Brer Rabbit. The shoats looked at Brer Rabbit, and I expect the man and them shoats are still running.

Brer Rabbit laughed, but his laugh caught in his throat when he saw Brer Bear, Miz Brune, and Miz Brindle coming back from their picnic. But he squared his shoulders, stood up straight, and walked right at'em. Brer Bear stopped. Miz Brindle, she stopped. Miz Brune, she stopped. Brer Rabbit kept coming. *Swishy-swushy. Splushy-splishy.* Miz Brune throwed down her parasol and ran. *Swishy-swushy. Splushy-splishy.* Miz Brindle throwed down her parasol and ran. Brer Bear stood his ground. Takes more than some swishy-swushy to scare him.

Brer Rabbit jumped up in the air and shook himself real hard. The sound of them leaves scraping on one another sounded like graveyard dirt on dry bones. Brer Rabbit hollered out:

I'm Megog de Roy,
The Devil's baby boy,
My body odor is stronger than you.

That took care of Brer Bear. He dropped the picnic basket, and some farmer lost a whole fence that day 'cause Brer
Bear tore it down getting away from there.

Brer Rabbit strutted on down the road and came on Brer
Wolf and Brer Fox, who were plotting on how they were
going to get him. They was so deep into their plotting that
they didn't see him until he was standing right in front of
them, excepting they looked up and saw the most awfulest
looking creature the world has ever seen.

Brer Wolf wanted to show Brer Fox how big and bad

he was. He looked at the creature and growled, "Who you?"
Brer Rabbit jumped up in the air, shook himself and said:

I'm Megog de Roy,
The Devil's baby boy.
My body odor is stronger than you.

He jumped up in the air again and then charged. Brer Wolf
and Brer Fox got away from there so fast they didn't even
leave tracks behind.

Brer Rabbit went home, got cleaned up, and then went
to see Miz Meadows and the girls. He told them he'd heard
that some creature called Megog de Roy had put a scare
into Brer Fox. For weeks after, every time Brer Fox showed
his face, Miz Meadows and the girls asked him if he wasn't
afraid that Megog de Roy might get him.

Brer Fox, Brer Rabbit, and King Deer's Daughter

Miz Meadows and the girls might have been good-looking
and pleasant to be around, but there wasn't nobody as pretty
as King Deer's daughter. Miz Meadows and the girls
couldn't hold a candle to her. She had long black hair and
a complexion the color of nutmeg. I won't go into no more
details 'cause you too young to be hearing too much.

Both Brer Fox and Brer Rabbit wanted to marry her and
they set to courting. One of them was always at her house,
and most of the time they were both there. After observ-
ing the two of them for a while, King Deer started to fa-

vor Brer Fox. He seemed more serious and responsible than Brer Rabbit. Brer Rabbit didn't like that one bit and knew he had to change King Deer's mind.

He was going through King Deer's pasture one day and threw some rocks at two of King Deer's goats and killed them. When he got to King Deer's house, Brer Rabbit asked him, "When is the wedding going to be?"

"What wedding?" King Deer wanted to know.

"The one between your daughter and Brer Fox."

King Deer hadn't put out any news about a wedding. "What you talking about, Brer Rabbit?"

"I thought there was going to be a wedding. I saw Brer Fox down in your pasture throwing rocks at the chickens and killing your goats. I knew he wouldn't be making free with your animals like that if he wasn't going to be a member of your family."

King Deer shook his head. "Brer Rabbit, you don't expect me to believe a tale like that, do you?"

Brer Rabbit shrugged. "Go down to the pasture and see for yourself."

King Deer did, and when he came back he was mad.

Brer Rabbit said, "Now hold on, King Deer. A man shouldn't be too hasty. Don't do nothing to Brer Fox before you sure he the one. Let me talk to him. We're good friends. If he killed your goats, I know I can get him to tell it."

King Deer said, "If you man enough to do something like that, you can marry my daughter."

Brer Rabbit didn't need to hear another word and he set off to find Brer Fox. He didn't go far, because Brer Fox was coming up the road on his way to King Deer's house. He had on his best Sears suit and was looking sharp.

"Where you going?" Brer Rabbit wanted to know.

"Out of my way, Rabbit. I'm going to see my girl."

"That's nice. King Deer told me you were going to marry his daughter."

Brer Fox swelled up so with pride that he popped one of the buttons on his fly.

Brer Rabbit smiled. "King Deer asked me to come around tonight and serenade his daughter as part of the celebration. I told him that you was a music man, too, and how it would be good if I could get you to help with the serenading."

So Brer Rabbit and Brer Fox went off in the woods to practice. Brer Rabbit played the quills, which is what they called pipes back in them times, and Brer Fox played the triangle. Brer Rabbit made up a song for him and Brer Fox to sing. They practiced all through the day, and when night came they went to King Deer's house.

King Deer and his daughter were setting on the porch. Brer Rabbit looked at Brer Fox, counted off the beat, and they started into playing. After they played a tune or two, it was time for the song. Brer Rabbit began singing:

> *Some folks pile up more than they can tote,*
> *And that's what the matter with King Deer's goat.*

Brer Fox sang out:

> *That's so, that's so, and I'm glad that it's so.*

Then Brer Rabbit blew on the quills and Brer Fox played the triangle and Brer Rabbit sang the next verse:

Some kill sheep and some kill shoats,
But Brer Fox kill King Deer's goats.

King Deer didn't need to hear another word. He came off the porch and went upside Brer Fox's head with his walking stick, and Brer Fox took off down the road.

King Deer's daughter invited Brer Rabbit to sit a while with her. Now, some say they got married. Some say they didn't. I don't know, and to tell the truth, don't much care, 'cause that ain't what the story was about. If you worried about it, make up your own story.

Brer Rabbit Breaks Up the Party

Like I said at the beginning, if there was one thing the animals agreed on, it was partying. If the sun came up on time, they had a party! If the rain was wet, they partied! If the grass was green, they partied!

One day Brer Fox decided to have a party because it was Tuesday. He invited Brer Bear, Brer Wolf, Brer Coon, and some of the other animals, but he didn't invite Brer Rabbit.

The animals got to Brer Fox's and he poured the liquor, turned on the radio, and the animals got to dancing and drinking and telling jokes and just having a good time.

Quite naturally, Brer Rabbit heard about the party and decided to invite himself. He went up to the attic of his house and got an old drum he had and headed to Brer Fox's.

The animals had just started partying good when all of

a sudden they heard this noise like thunder mixed with hail—*Diddybum, diddybum, diddybum-bum-bum-bum—diddybum!*

Brer Coon, who always had one ear out the window, said, "Turn down that radio, y'all!"

Diddybum, diddybum, diddybum-bum-bum—diddybum!

"What's that?" Brer Coon wanted to know.

Diddybum, diddybum, diddybum-bum-bum—diddybum!

Brer Coon reached under his chair for his hat. "Well, gentlemen, I believe it's time I headed for home. I told the ole lady that I wouldn't be gone more than a minute and here it is getting on toward moon-up." He started toward the door, walking slow, like he was cool. By the time he reached the back gate, here come the other animals with Brer Fox in the lead. Them animals kicked up a small dust storm getting into the woods.

Brer Rabbit came on toward the house—*Diddybum, diddybum, diddybum-bum-bum—diddybum!* When he got there, everybody was gone. Brer Rabbit kicked open the door, walked in and hollered, "Brer Fox! Where you at?"

Wasn't no answer and Brer Rabbit laughed. He sat down in Brer Fox's easy chair, spit on the floor, and laughed some more.

He looked around and saw the liquor sitting on the sideboard. He poured himself a drink. Then he poured himself another one. Before long Brer Rabbit was feeling mighty good.

Meanwhile the animals was down there in the woods listening for the *diddy-bum.* They didn't hear it for a long while, and Brer Fox, feeling kind of foolish now, said, "Come on. Let's get back to the party. Brer Coon come scaring us for nothing."

They headed back to the house real slowlike. Fact of the matter is, they creeped back. If somebody had shook a bush, them animals would've jumped out of their skins.

They peeped in the windows and saw Brer Rabbit standing by the sideboard drinking like liquor was about to be outlawed. By now he wasn't none too steady on his legs and Brer Fox saw his chance.

He bust in the door. "I got you now, Brer Rabbit! I got you now!" Him and the other animals surrounded Brer Rabbit.

Brer Rabbit was a long way from being drunk, but he pretended he was drunker than he was. He staggered around the room the way a butterfly go through the air. He looked at Brer Fox kinna cross-eyed, slapped him on the back, and hollered, "How's your mama?" And he giggled.

Brer Fox was ready to get down to business, the business being what they were going to do with Brer Rabbit. Brer Bear was the judge among all the animals, so he put on his glasses and cleared his throat.

"According to the law, the best way to deal with a creature that has been a pest in the community like Brer Rabbit is to drown him." And saying that, he took off his glasses.

Brer Fox, who was the jury foreman, clapped his hands and say he sho' nuf' like the law. So it was agreed to drown Brer Rabbit in the creek.

Brer Rabbit didn't like that idea at all. He started trembling and hollered out in a pitiful voice, "In the name of goodness, please don't fling me in the creek! Y'all know I can't swim. If you gon' throw me in the creek, then have some pity on me and let me have a walking stick so's I can have something to hold onto while I drown."

Brer Fox looked at Brer Bear. Brer Bear put his glasses back on, scratched his head, mumbled to himself, and said, finally, "Well, I don't remember nothing in the law that would be against it." And he took his glasses off.

They gave Brer Rabbit a walking stick, carried him down to the creek and threw him in. Brer Rabbit landed on his feet, and using the stick, walked across. It wasn't no more than knee-deep to begin with.

When Brer Rabbit got to the other side, he hollered back, "I sho' wish you'd stop buying that cheap liquor, Brer Fox!" And with that, he was gone!

Brer Rabbit Outwits Mr. Man

You remember how Brer Rabbit tricked Brer Bear into getting tied in the tree? Well, after that, Brer Bear decided to find a job. He finally got one as the ferryman on the big river. Before long all the animals agreed that Brer Bear had natural talent for the job. He could take the ferry back and forth across the river so smooth you didn't even know you were moving.

Once Mr. Man came down to the ferry with a mare and a colt. Brer Bear let down the plank for the mare and the colt to come aboard. That was where the trouble started.

Mr. Man got in front to lead the mare on. She went halfway and balked. Mr. Man pulled and the mare dug in her hind legs. Mr. Man pushed and the mare dug in her front legs. Mr. Man tried to ride her on board. She dug in both legs and you'd of thought she'd suddenly turned to stone. The colt thought Mr. Man was trying to do something to its mama, and it started running around like a pig with hot dishwater on its back.

Mr. Man decided to study on the situation for a while. He studied. Brer Bear sat down next to him and he studied. Between the two of them they didn't get one idea.

Finally Brer Bear decided to give up thinking. It had never been one of his virtues anyway. He looked around and saw Brer Rabbit sitting on a stump, laughing and holding his sides.

Brer Bear went over to him. "What's so funny?"

"You and Mr. Man," Brer Rabbit said.

"Instead of sitting here laughing at us, why don't you help us get that mare and colt on the ferry? With three of us working at it, we could get 'em on."

Brer Rabbit shook his head. "How come I want to do

that? I wouldn't have nothing to laugh at." And Brer Rabbit broke up again.

Brer Bear gave a dry grin and started to walk away.

"Hold up there, Brer Bear!" Brer Rabbit called to him. "I guess I done laughed enough. Getting that mare and that colt on the ferry is easy as going to sleep in a swing."

Brer Bear said, "If you help us get that colt on the ferry, I'll do anything you want me to."

Brer Rabbit shrugged. "All you got to do is pick up the colt and put it on. Its mama will just naturally follow."

Brer Bear went wobbling back to the ferry, picked up the colt and put it on. Just like Brer Rabbit had said, the mare walked on the ferryboat like she'd been born there.

Mr. Man wanted to know how he'd figured that out. Brer Bear told him that Brer Rabbit had done the figuring. "Brer Rabbit is something else!" Brer Bear exclaimed proudly. "He's not only the smartest one of all us animals. He's even smarter than people. Can't nobody fool him and can't nobody outdo him."

Mr. Man didn't like that. "We'll see about that. I be back in a day or two and I bet you a pot of honey against a dish of cream that I can outdo Brer Rabbit."

Brer Bear smiled. "That's a bet!"

A couple of days later Mr. Man came back and he had two mares with him. Them two mares looked exactly alike. They were the same color, same size, and even had the same gait.

After Brer Bear had ferried Mr. Man across, Mr. Man said, "One of these mares is the mama and the other one is the daughter. Now, go get Brer Rabbit and ask him to tell me which is which."

Brer Bear looked at the two mares and he was sorry he

had made the bet. Wasn't no way Brer Rabbit was going to be able to tell which was which. He shook his head.

Mr. Man laughed. "Give me my dish of cream!"

But Brer Bear could smell the pot of honey Mr. Man had in his saddlebags.

"Give me my dish of cream!" Mr. Man repeated.

Brer Bear wasn't going to give up a dish of cream just like that. He went up on the hill and called Brer Rabbit. Brer Rabbit had been staying in the vicinity, waiting for Mr. Man to come back, so he came running.

"I apologize, Brer Rabbit, for getting you into all this. I just hope you won't be too mad at me." He explained the puzzle to Brer Rabbit. Brer Rabbit chuckled.

"Brer Bear, tell you what you do. Get two bunches of grass and put them in front of the mares."

Brer Bear did as Brer Rabbit told him. Brer Rabbit watched as the mares started eating. One mare ate all her grass first and started to eating the other mare's grass. That mare held up her head so the first mare could eat that grass too.

"The one holding up her head is the mama," said Brer Rabbit.

Mr. Man's mouth fell open. "That's right! How did you know?"

"Easy. The youngest one eats the fastest, being young and all. Being the youngest, she's also the hungriest. And the mama stopped eating hers so that the youngest could have that too."

Mr. Man was astonished, but he still wasn't satisfied that a rabbit could be smarter than a person. He gave Brer Bear the pot of honey.

"I bet you another pot of honey that I can fool Brer Rabbit!"

"Bet!" said Brer Bear, licking at the honey pot. "Y'all wait right here."

Mr. Man went off. In a little while he was back carrying a basket. He held the basket up high so Brer Rabbit couldn't see inside and then hung it in a tree limb.

"Now! Tell me what's in the basket, Brer Rabbit." Mr. Man knowed he had him this time.

Brer Rabbit looked at the basket for a long time, and finally said, "The sparrow can tell you."

Mr. Man like to have fainted. "What kind of creature are you?" he wanted to know. "You must be a hoodoo man." He took the basket out of the tree and there was a gray sparrow inside. He gave Brer Bear another pot of honey and shook his head at Brer Rabbit. "You one of these graveyard rabbits. I'm gon' stay away from you."

After Mr. Man was gone, Brer Bear turned to Brer Rabbit. "Tell me, sho' nuf' Brer Rabbit. How did you know there was a sparrow in there?"

Brer Rabbit laughed. "I didn't. What I said was that only a sparrow could tell, because only a sparrow could fly high enough to see down in the basket."

Brer Rabbit laughed and Brer Bear laughed and they both agreed that the honey was sho' nuf' good.

Brer Wolf, Brer Fox, and the Little Rabbits

Brer Wolf and Brer Fox went to see Brer Rabbit one day. Wasn't nobody home except the little Rabbits playing in the yard. Brer Wolf looked at them. They looked so plump and fat he was licking his chops without knowing he was doing it. Brer Wolf looked at Brer Fox and licked his chops again. Brer Fox looked at Brer Wolf and licked his.

"They mighty fat, ain't they?" said Brer Wolf.

Brer Fox grinned. "Man, hush your mouth!"

The little Rabbits kept on playing but began easing out of the yard. They kept their ears sharp, though.

"Ain't they slick and pretty?" said Brer Wolf.

Brer Fox started drooling. "I wish you'd shut up," he grinned.

The little Rabbits kept playing and inching their way out of the yard and they kept listening.

Brer Wolf smacked his mouth. "Ain't they juicy and tender?"

Brer Fox's eyes started to roll around in his head. "Man, if you don't hush up, I'm going to start twitching, and when I start twitching, I can't help myself."

The little Rabbits kept playing and easing out of the yard and they kept listening.

"Let's eat'em!" Brer Wolf said suddenly!

"Let's eat'em!" exclaimed Brer Fox, twitching all over.

The little Rabbits were still playing, but they knew everything that was going on.

Brer Wolf and Brer Fox decided that when Brer Rabbit got home, one of them would get him in a dispute about something or other and the other one would catch the little Rabbits.

"You best at talking, Brer Wolf. I'll coax the little Rabbits. I got a way with children, you know."

Brer Wolf snorted. "You can't make a gourd out of a pumpkin. You know I ain't never been too good at talking, but your tongue's as slick as glass. I can bite a whole lot better than I can talk. Them little Rabbits don't need coaxing; they need grabbing, and I'm the man for that. You keep Brer Rabbit busy. *I'll* grab the little Rabbits."

They knew that whichever one grabbed the little Rabbits first wasn't gon' leave even a shadow for the other one. While they were arguing back and forth, the little Rabbits took off down the road—*blickety-blickety*—looking for their daddy.

They hadn't gone far when they ran into him coming from town with a jug over his shoulder.

"What you got, Daddy?" they cried.

"A jug of molasses."

"Can we have some?" they wanted to know.

Brer Rabbit pulled the stopper out and let them lick the molasses off the bottom of it. After they'd gotten their breath, they told him all about Brer Fox and Brer Wolf. Brer Rabbit chuckled to himself.

He picked up the jug and he and the little Rabbits started home. When they were almost there, Brer Rabbit said, "Now y'all stay out of sight until I call you."

The little Rabbits were happy to get out of sight, because they had seen Brer Wolf's sharp teeth and Brer Fox's red red tongue. They got down in the weeds and were as still as a mouse in a barrel of flour.

Brer Rabbit sauntered on home. Brer Fox and Brer Wolf were sitting on his front-porch step, smiling smiley smiles. They how-do'd with Brer Rabbit and he how-do'd with them.

"What you got in that jug there, Brer Rabbit?" Brer Wolf wanted to know.

Brer Rabbit hemmed and hawed and made like he didn't want to tell. That made Brer Wolf more curious.

"What you got in that jug, Brer Rabbit?"

Brer Rabbit shook his head and looked real serious. He started talking to Brer Wolf about the weather or whatever and Brer Fox took this chance to sneak off and grab the little Rabbits.

Brer Rabbit unstoppered the jug and handed it to Brer Wolf. "Take a little taste of this."

Brer Wolf took a hit on the jug and smacked his lips. "That's all right, Brer Rabbit! What is it?"

Brer Rabbit leaned close to Brer Wolf. "Don't tell nobody. It's Fox blood."

Brer Wolf's eyes got big. "How you know?"

"I knows what I knows."

"Let me have another hit on that, Brer Rabbit."

Brer Rabbit shook his head. "Don't know how come you want to drink up what little I got when you can get some more for yourself. And the fresher it is, the better."

"How you know?"

"I knows what I knows."

Brer Wolf jumped up and started off after Brer Fox. When he got close, he made a grab for him. Brer Fox ducked and dodged and headed for the woods with Brer Wolf's hot breath on his tail.

When Brer Rabbit got through laughing, he called his young'uns out of the weeds.

Now don't come asking me if Brer Wolf caught Brer Fox. It's all I can do to follow the tale when it's on the big road. Ain't no way I can keep up with them animals when they get to running through the woods. I don't know about you, but when I go in the woods, I got to know where I'm going.

Brer Rabbit's Luck

The time came when the animals made catching Brer Rabbit a full-time job. They didn't even take off holidays or weekends. But no matter what they tried, Brer Rabbit got out of it. They decided Brer Rabbit must have something he conjured with—a John the Conqueror root, a black cat bone, tuna fish casserole, or something!

Brer Bear allowed as to how he thought Brer Rabbit was a natural-born witch. Brer Wolf said he didn't know about that, but it sure wouldn't surprise him if Brer Rabbit was in cahoots with one. Brer Fox said it had to be something like that because Brer Rabbit had more luck than smarts.

That set them to worrying about where Brer Rabbit got his luck when they couldn't buy none with a truckload of money. They worried and fretted so much they couldn't get to sleep at night. Some of them even started getting a little gray over it.

While they were doing all this worrying, one of Brer Bear's children took sick. He asked Miz Rabbit if she would mind setting up a while with Miz Bear to keep her company. Naturally, Miz Rabbit went.

Miz Bear was rocking the baby to keep it from fretting, when all of a sudden Miz Rabbit dropped her knitting. "Oh, my goodness!" she exclaimed.

"What's the matter, Sister Rabbit?"

"I just remembered that I left my ole man's money purse on the mantel. Anybody could walk in and take it. I don't know what he got in there, but whatever it is, he done told me to guard it with my life. What am I going to do, Sister Bear?"

"Oh, don't worry about it none. I'm sure everything will be all right."

Miz Rabbit said she hoped so, because it was a long way to her house and she wasn't about to go back in the middle of the night.

It just so happened that Brer Wolf was doing his worrying that night on Brer Bear's back porch. He heard every word and took off for Brer Rabbit's.

He sneaked in the house quietly and there on the mantelpiece was Brer Rabbit's purse. Brer Wolf opened it. Inside he found some collard seeds, a calamus root, and a great big rabbit foot! He chuckled and ran home with the purse, as pleased as a man who'd found a gold mine.

Brer Rabbit didn't miss the purse for a few days, but when he did, he tore up the house looking for it. He asked his wife about it. She said she'd given it to him more than a week and a half ago and if he had lost it, don't come blaming her, 'cause it was his purse, and if he didn't have sense enough to keep up with his own things it wasn't her fault, 'cause she had enough to do with taking care of the house and all the children, and speaking of children, when was he going to get them those high-heel sneakers they'd been wanting, 'cause she was tired of hearing about 'em— and Brer Rabbit just sneaked on out.

He was troubled deep in his mind now. "I know where I put that purse, but I don't know where I left it."

All of sudden it seemed like Brer Wolf had all the luck and Brer Rabbit didn't have a lick. Brer Wolf got fat and Brer Rabbit got lean. Brer Wolf could run fast; Brer Rabbit couldn't move as fast as Sister Cow. Brer Wolf felt healthy and Brer Rabbit felt sick all the time. After a month or so, Brer Rabbit knew there was only one thing to do.

He had to talk to Aunt Mammy-Bammy Big-Money.

She was the Witch-Rabbit and lived way off in a deep, dark, dank, smelly, slimey swamp. To get there you had to ride some, slide some; jump some, hump some; hop some, flop some; walk some, balk some; creep some, sleep some; fly some, cry some; follow some, holler some; wade some, spade some; and if you weren't careful, you still wouldn't get there. Brer Rabbit made it, but he was plumb wore out when he did.

He sat down to rest, and in a little while he saw black smoke coming out of a hole in the ground. That was where Aunt Mammy-Bammy Big-Money lived. The smoke got blacker and blacker. Brer Rabbit knew the time had come to say what was on his mind.

"Mammy-Bammy Big-Money, I need your help."

"Son Riley Rabbit, why so? Son Riley Rabbit, why so?"

"Mammy-Bammy Big-Money, I lost that foot you gave me."

"Oh, Riley Rabbit, why so? Son Riley Rabbit, why so?"

"Mammy-Bammy Big Money, my luck done gone. I don't know where that foot is."

"The Wolf took and stole your luck, Son Riley Rabbit, Riley. Go find the track, go get it back, Son Riley Rabbit, Riley."

Aunt Mammy-Bammy Big-Money sucked all the black smoke back in the hole. Brer Rabbit headed for home, wondering how he was going to get the foot back from Brer Wolf. He didn't know, so he hid out near Brer Wolf's house and waited his chance. He waited a day. He waited a week. He waited near 'bout a month.

Finally, one night Brer Wolf came home from a big party. Brer Rabbit knew his waiting was over. After Brer Wolf was good and asleep, Brer Rabbit sneaked in the house. He saw Brer Wolf's coat on the back of a rocking chair. Brer Rabbit searched through the pockets, and in the inside pocket was his purse. He took it and was gone.

Even though he had his purse back and the rabbit's foot was still in it, Brer Rabbit didn't feel like he had his luck back. It seemed that he wasn't getting out of trouble as easily as he used to. Maybe old age was setting in on him.

He decided to go talk things over with Aunt Mammy-Bammy Big-Money again. His wife packed him a lunch of bacon and cornbread.

When he got there, he hollered out, "Mammy-Bammy Big-Money! O Mammy-Bammy Big-Money! I journeyed far, I journeyed fast; I'm glad I found the place at last!"

Great big black smoke rose up out of the ground and Mammy-Bammy Big-Money said, "Where for, Son Riley Rabbit, Riley? Son Riley Rabbit, Riley, where for?"

"Mammy-Bammy Big-Money, I'm afraid I'm losing my mind. Don't seem like I can fool the other animals good as I used to. They done come nigh to catching me here recently and doing away with me for good."

Mammy-Bammy Big-Money sat there sucking in black smoke and belching it out until you couldn't see nothing except her great big eyeballs and her great big ears. Finally, she said, "There's a squirrel up in that tree over yonder, Son Riley. Go catch it and bring it to me, Son Riley Rabbit, Riley."

"I ain't got much sense left," Brer Rabbit said, "but if I can't get that squirrel out of that tree, I'm in worse shape than I thought I was."

Brer Rabbit went over to the tree, took the bacon and cornbread out of the bag, found two rocks, and put the bag over his hands. He waited a little while, then he banged the two rocks together—*blip!*

Squirrel hollered, "Hey!"

Brer Rabbit waited a little longer and then slapped the rocks together again—*blap!*

Squirrel ran down the tree a little ways and hollered, "Heyo!"

Brer Rabbit don't say a word, but pops the rocks together—*blop!*

Squirrel came down the tree trunk a little bit farther. "Who that?"

"Biggidy Dicky Big-Bag," said Brer Rabbit.

"What you doing?"

"Cracking hickory nuts."

"Can I crack some?"

"Come get in the bag," Brer Rabbit said.

Squirrel hesitated, then scampered down the tree and right into the bag. Brer Rabbit closed it tight, tied it, and gave it to Mammy-Bammy Big-Money.

The ole Witch-Rabbit turned the squirrel loose and said, "There's a snake lying over there in the grass, Son Riley. Bring him here and be fast about it, Son Riley Rabbit, Riley."

Brer Rabbit looked around and saw the biggest rattlesnake he'd ever seen. He was wrapped around himself five or six times and looked like he was ready to do business with anybody come down the pike.

Brer Rabbit studied the situation for a few minutes, then went off in the bushes, cut a young grapevine, and made a slipknot in it.

"How you today, Mr. Snake?"

Snake don't say a word. He just coiled up a little tighter,

flicking his tongue in and out of his mouth quicker than a lamb can shake its tail.

Brer Rabbit don't pay it no never mind. "I'm glad I ran into you today. Me and Brer Bear was arguing a few weeks ago about how long you are. We both agree that you the prettiest thing ever swished across the earth. You even prettier when you curled up in the sun like you are now. Brer Bear say that when you stretch out you about three feet long. I told him he better get his eyes examined, 'cause I know you five feet long if you an inch. Well, we got to arguing back and forth so much, I come close to going upside Brer Bear's head with my walking stick."

Mr. Snake don't say a word, but seemed to relax a little bit.

"I told Brer Bear that the next time I saw you I was going to take your measurements. So that's why I'm glad I run into you today. Would you be so good as to uncoil yourself?"

Mr. Snake was feeling mighty proud now, and he stretched himself out like he was being judged in a contest.

"That's one foot," Brer Rabbit said, as he started measuring from the tail forward. "Two feet. There's Brer Bear's three feet and I still got a ways to go. Four feet."

Brer Rabbit was at the head now and just as he said, "Five feet! That's what I told Brer Bear," he dropped the slipknot over Mr. Snake's head and pulled it tight. He dragged the Snake over to Mammy-Bammy Big-Money, but when he got there, she had disappeared.

Then he heard a voice from far off: "If you get any more sense, Son Riley, you gon' be the death of us all, Son Riley Rabbit, Riley."

Brer Rabbit felt all right now. He took the snake home, made snake stew, and used the snake oil as an ointment for his limbs. He didn't need no oil for his brain. Fact was, Brer Rabbit thought he just might be better than ever.

Julius Lester is the critically acclaimed author of books for both children and adults. His six Dial books include *To Be a Slave*, the first Newbery Medal Honor Book by a black author; *Long Journey Home: Stories from Black History*, a National Book Award finalist; *Who I Am; Two Love Stories; This Strange New Feeling;* and *The Knee-High Man and Other Tales*, an American Library Association Notable Book and Lewis Carroll Shelf Award Winner. His adult books include *Search for the New Land; The Seventh Son: The Thought and Writings of W.E.B. Du Bois;* and *Do Lord Remember Me*. The son of a Methodist minister, Mr. Lester was born in St. Louis. At fourteen he moved to Nashville, where he was later to receive his Bachelor of Arts from Fisk University. The father of four children, Mr. Lester now lives in Amherst, where he teaches at the University of Massachusetts.

Jerry Pinkney received the Coretta Scott King Award for Illustration and the Christopher Award for his latest book for Dial, *The Patchwork Quilt*, written by Valerie Flournoy. Mr. Pinkney's artwork has been shown at the 1986 International Children's Book Exhibition at the Bologna Book Fair and in museums around the country. He studied at the Philadelphia Museum College of Art. He and his wife, who have four grown children, live in Croton-on-Hudson, New York.

More Tales of Uncle Remus

FURTHER ADVENTURES OF BRER RABBIT,
HIS FRIENDS, ENEMIES, AND OTHERS

More Tales of Uncle Remus
Further Adventures of Brer Rabbit,
His Friends, Enemies, and Others

as told by JULIUS LESTER

illustrated by Jerry Pinkney

DIAL BOOKS

New York

Published by Dial Books
375 Hudson Street
New York, New York 10014

Design by Jane Byers Bierhorst
First Edition

Library of Congress Cataloging in Publication Data

Lester, Julius.
More tales of Uncle Remus. Further adventures of
Brer Rabbit, his friends, enemies, and others.

Summary : The author retells the classic Afro-American tales.
1. Afro-Americans—Folklore. 2. Tales—United States.
[1. Folklore, Afro-American. 2. Animals—Folklore.]
I. Pinkney, Jerry, ill. II. Title. III. Title: Further
adventures of Brer Rabbit, his friends, enemies, and others.
PZ8.1.L434Tal 1988   398.2'08996073   86-32890
ISBN 0-8037-0419-4 : ISBN 0-8037-0420-8 (lib. bdg.)

The publisher wishes to express its sincere thanks to the estate
of Joel Chandler Harris for its gracious support during the
publication of this new version of The Tales of Uncle Remus.

Each black-and-white drawing is made of pencil and graphite; and
each full-color picture consists of a pencil, graphite, and watercolor
painting that is color-separated and reproduced in full color.

To the memory of my father
J. L.

For my brothers and sisters,
Edward, William, Joan, Claudia, and Helen
J. P.

Who is Brer Rabbit? From where does he come? And why are these tales important? Since the publication of the first volume in this series, *The Tales of Uncle Remus: The Adventures of Brer Rabbit,* these are among the questions I've been asked most often.

These are important questions, reflecting both a curiosity about the mystery of folktales and our attraction to them, and a sense that these tales, as entertaining as they are, are more than entertainment.

Answering the questions entails dispelling some widely held and entrenched assumptions:

(1) Brer Rabbit is a symbol of how black people responded to slavery. Unable to resist physically, black resistance to slavery found sublimated expression through the figure of the wily Rabbit who outsmarted those seeking to oppress him. This is the interpretation offered by Joel Chandler Harris, who wrote that "the negro [sic] selects as his hero the weakest and most harmless of all animals and brings him out victorious." This view was reiterated by folklorists well into the present century.

(2) The Brer Rabbit tales were transplanted from Africa and are merely variants of the tales about Anansi the Spider, still current in West Africa.

(3) The tales are important because they chronicle the survival techniques used by slaves.

Such assumptions appear to answer the questions, but the appearance is deceiving. To accept these answers is to reduce the tales to imaginative political tracts. Such a view fails to recognize or appreciate the complexity and richness of Brer Rabbit. To see the tales only as the response of powerless slaves to slavery raises more questions than are answered. For example, if the Brer Rabbit tales are only a form of compensation necessitated by slavery, why have the tales always enjoyed a wide audience among whites? Most important, what is it in the tales that compels us to delight in the adventures of Brer Rabbit today?

The answer is simple: Whether we are black or white, slave or free, child or adult, Brer Rabbit is us.

2

Brer Rabbit cannot be explained by looking at his sociopolitical origins. If this were so, we might reasonably expect to find similar tales among many groups of oppressed people throughout time. What we find instead is similar tales among practically every people, regardless of the political circumstances of their lives.

Among North American Indian groups similar tales are found with the hero taking the form of Raven, Mink, Bluejay, Coyote, Rabbit, Hare, and Spider. Among blacks of the Bahamas and West Indies the figure is known as Compé Anansi, as Ti Malice in Haiti, and as Reynard the Fox in Europe. Whatever name a particular culture gives to this creature, he is the Trickster, or as the Winnebago Indians called him, "the cunning one."

How do we explain the similarities between Trickster tales? The famous tale of the "Tortoise and the Hare" is found in Aesop's Fables as well as the Uncle Remus Tales. It stretches credibility to believe that after a hard day's work in the fields, slaves sat around the hearth and read Aesop, especially since most were illiterate.

The universality of Trickster tales is not the result of cultural borrowings, but of the universality in what it is to be human. The emotions we live and the emotions which live us are culturally unbounded and are the same, whether enacted in a slave's cabin or in a king's palace.

The Brer Rabbit tales as collected by Joel Chandler Harris are rather tame for Trickster tales. They are even tame for Brer Rabbit tales collected by others, because Trickster tales are noted for their obscenity. ("Signifying Monkey" is a notable example in Afro-American folklore and is told today in many urban black

communities.) Whether Harris never collected any of the ob-
scene Brer Rabbit tales, suppressed them, or simply was un-
aware of them, we do not know. (In the famous "Brer Rabbit
and the Tar Baby" story, there is only the minimal allusion in
the Harris version that the tar baby is female. One can easily
imagine a far more salacious rendition of the story in which the
femaleness of the tar baby becomes central.) Despite the absence of the all-important element of obscenity in the Brer Rabbit tales as collected by Joel Chandler Harris, these tales share
the essential characteristics of Trickster tales.

(1) Trickster tales do not have any feeling of "And they lived
happily ever after." Instead we finish hearing or reading a Brer
Rabbit tale fully aware that another tale has to follow. Indeed,
we look forward to the continuation of what we sense to be
and hope is an endless story.

(2) Trickster tales are not moral. Uncle Remus said, "Creatures don't know nothing at all about that's good and that's
bad. They don't know right from wrong. They see what they
want and they get it if they can, by hook or crook." The mor-
alist in us may be outraged and offended by Brer Rabbit or any
Trickster, because Trickster lies, cheats, deceives, and the reward for his trickery is not punishment but, generally, victory.
We can enter the stories only by suspending "moral conscience," as Roger Abrahams, the eminent scholar of Afro-
American folklore, phrased it. It is precisely in this suspension
of moral conscience that Trickster is the avatar of a higher morality.

(3) Those who interpret the Brer Rabbit tales from a sociopolitical perspective point to the ingenious ways Brer Rabbit
has of escaping the many plots of Brer Fox and Brer Wolf, who,

in this analysis, would represent white people. This analysis overlooks the fact that there are as many Brer Rabbit stories in which Brer Rabbit is the instigator of trouble, violence, and even murder. One notable example in this volume is "Being Fashionable Ain't Always Healthy."

While one might want to see Brer Rabbit as Victim, he is not. Neither is he Victor, because he is defeated more often than our image of him might want to admit. Trickster is beyond such a simplistic dichotomy, either pole of which would transform him into a cute bunny.

The outcome of Trickster's escapades is not crucial to the tales, nor important even. What is central is the spirit he brings to them. It is this spirit that both attracts and repels us. We envy it even as we shudder at the thought of emulating it. Regardless, we value Brer Rabbit's spirit, because, as Roger Abrahams wrote: "Trickster's vitality and inventiveness are valued for their own sake . . . the principle of vitality seems more important than that of right and wrong." What we value in Brer Rabbit and any Trickster is not only the amorality, but especially the raw energy of Life and Nature dramatized by the tales.

(4) The essence of Trickster tales is "patterned disordering," to use Roger Abraham's wonderful phrase. This is not the disorder which leads to chaos and destruction. Quite the contrary. It is disorder that is integral to the ordered pattern of life, that disorder without which life's ordered pattern would become rigid and sterile. It is the Trickster in us who knocks over the glass of water at a formal dinner. It is Trickster who makes so-called "Freudian slips," who laughs at the most inappropriate times.

Teachers and parents know Trickster well, because there is one in every classroom and every large family. Trickster is the class clown, the child who seems to have a genius for walking a thin line between fun and trouble, the child who is always "up to something," but you can never punish him or her because what he or she does is disruptive but never rebellious or serious enough to merit severe punishment. And it is always entertaining because Trickster is charming and likeable, surrounded as he or she is by an aura of innocence and vulnerabilty.

That Trickster tales should appear all over the world should not surprise us then, because Trickster existed before the tales. As the classical philologist Károly Kerényi put it, "The hero is stronger than the stories told about him. . . . [Trickster] comes before the expression in words. We must also grant him the greater consistency, an unchanging, indestructible core that not only antedates all the stories told about him, *but has survived in spite of them*." (Italics added.)

Trickster would exist even if there were no tales. Fortunately there are tales, because "In mythology, we hear the world telling its own story to itself" (Kerényi). That is why we love Brer Rabbit. Through him we hear a portion of our story. It is not a story we could hear in any other way, perhaps because Trickster's amorality shames us. But "shameless untruthfulness is . . . a property of the world" (Kerényi), and therefore, a property belonging to each of us because we are human. To be moral about it does not always tell us how to live with it. Through the tales we live with, laugh with, and love, something of ourselves which is beyond our powers to redeem.

Trickster keeps us in reality. And this is where Trickster's amoral morality is superior to our moral posturing, our certitude that we know, absolutely, what is right and what is wrong. The more we are alienated from Trickster, the more likely we are to believe the inflated ideas we have about ourselves. Notice in the Brer Rabbit stories how often he exploits the other animals' images of themselves. Brer Rabbit appeals to their vanity, their pride, their posturing egos, and invariably they believe him. The instant they do, they are in Brer Rabbit's power and lost to themselves.

Trickster's function is to keep Order from taking itself too seriously. In Kerényi's words, "Disorder belongs to the totality of life, and the spirit of this disorder is the trickster. His function . . . is to add disorder to order and so make a whole, to render possible, within the fixed bounds of what is permitted, an experience of what is not permitted."

That is the charisma of Brer Rabbit, his undeniable appeal. Through him we experience "what is not permitted," and thereby we are made whole. Not perfect, but whole. The ideal of human perfection is one of the most dangerous of human delusions. To be human is to be whole. To be human is to love our irredeemable imperfections with the same passion as our virtues.

Károly Kerényi quotes W. F. Otto, who, in *Homeric Gods*, wrote that Trickster is the "spirit of a [lifestyle] which recurs under the most diverse conditions and which embraces loss as well as gain, mischief as well as kindliness. Though much of this must seem questionable from a moral point of view, nevertheless it is a configuration which belongs to the fundamental aspects of living reality, and hence, according to Greek feeling, demands reverence, if not for all its individual expressions, at least for the totality of its meaning and being."

Where others find it logical that the Brer Rabbit tales arose under the conditions of slavery, I think it is remarkable that they did so. The tales were not psychological compensation for the obvious lack of power in the slaves' lives. Rather, they represented an extraordinary effort to balance the totalitarian order of the slave system with archetypal disorder and thereby become whole.

We are not slaves, and yet the need for wholeness remains. I am awed that these tales about Brer Rabbit, created by slaves, speak so directly and with such clarity to us who are not slaves—that in these tales created by slaves is the vital voice of our humanity.

Julius Lester

Amherst, Massachusetts
16 September 1987

Contents

More Tales of Uncle Remus
FURTHER ADVENTURES OF BRER RABBIT,
HIS FRIENDS, ENEMIES, AND OTHERS

Brer Rabbit Gets Brer Fox's Dinner

If you ain't never heard about Brer Rabbit and Brer Fox, you might get the idea from these stories that they are enemies. Well, that ain't the way it is. On the other hand they weren't friends either. Brer Rabbit was Brer Rabbit, which meant he couldn't help it if he woke up some mornings and the first thing he thought about was creating devilment. And Brer Fox was Brer Fox. Wasn't his fault if he woke up thinking about the same thing. So they weren't enemies and they weren't friends. They were who they were. Another way of putting it is: They ain't who they wasn't. Now that that's all clear, let's get on with the story.

Not having anything better or worse to do one day, Brer Rabbit decided to see what Brer Fox was up to. As he got close to Brer Fox's house, he heard a lot of hammering. When he got there, he saw Brer Fox on the roof nailing shingles as fast as he could.

Well, Brer Rabbit treated work like he did his mamma, and he wouldn't hit his mamma a lick. So he looked around to see what else he could see, and there by the fence post was Brer Fox's dinner pail. Brer Rabbit knew there was more food in it than there was in his stomach. That didn't seem right. How was he going to get Brer Fox's dinner from where it wasn't doing no good to where it would do a whole lot of good?

"Brer Fox! How you doing today?" Brer Rabbit called up.

"Busy. Ain't got time to be flapping gums with you."

"What you doing up there?"

"Putting on a new roof before winter come."

"You need some help?"

"I do, but where am I going to get it at?"

"I'm a powerful man with a hammer, Brer Fox. I'll give you a hand."

Brer Rabbit climbed up to the roof and set to work. Pretty soon he was out-hammering Brer Fox. He was putting roofing on like winter was on the outskirts of town. He nailed and nailed and nailed until he was right up to Brer Fox's tail.

Brer Rabbit pushed the tail to one side, but, a tail being a tail, it just swished right back.

"Don't know how come some folks got to have such long tails," Brer Rabbit mumbled to himself.

He brushed the tail aside again and resumed nailing. He nailed under Brer Fox. He nailed around Brer Fox. He nailed beside Brer Fox. He nailed and he nailed until all of a sudden Brer Fox dropped his hammer and let out a yell, "Ow! Brer Rabbit! You done nailed my tail!"

Brer Rabbit looked at him, eyes big. "I done what? You got to be joking, Brer Fox. Don't be accusing me of something I ain't done."

Brer Fox hollered and squalled and kicked and squealed. "Have mercy, Brer Rabbit! Unnail my tail! Unnail my tail!"

Brer Rabbit started down the ladder, shaking his head. "I must be losing my aim, my stroke, or something. Maybe my eyes is getting weak. I ain't never nailed nobody's tail before. Doing something like that upsets me. Doing something like that upsets me so much, it makes me hungry."

All the while Brer Fox is hollering and screaming and squalling.

Brer Rabbit climbed down the ladder, still muttering to himself about how getting upset made him hungry. He opened up Brer Fox's dinner pail and helped himself to the fried chicken, corn, and biscuits inside. When he finished, he wiped his mouth on his coattail, belched a time or two, and went on down the road, hoping he hadn't done no permanent damage to Brer Fox's long, pretty tail.

Brer Rabbit and Brer Fox Kill a Cow

Brer Fox didn't have any hard feelings about getting his tail nailed, since no damage was done. So, a few days later, he and Brer Rabbit met up with each other, and after talking about first one thing and then the other they found out they had something in common: Their taste buds were crying out for some beef.

They went out to Mr. Man's field and killed his cow. I think it was Mr. Man's cow. Could've been Brer Porcupine's cow. Then again, it could've been Brer Snake's cow.

Then again . . . well, never mind. I know one thing: Brer Rabbit wasn't going to kill his own cow, and Brer Fox wasn't going to kill his.

They killed the cow, and Brer Rabbit told Brer Fox to run home and get a pan, tray, or something if he wanted the haslet. That's the liver, the heart, and innards. Some folks think there's nothing better. I don't happen to be one of them, but then again, I ain't in the story.

Brer Fox was crazy about the haslet, so off he went to get a pan. He couldn't get over the fact that Brer Rabbit would offer it to him. Maybe he wasn't such a bad fella after all.

As Brer Fox was thinking that very thought, Brer Rabbit was busy cutting out the haslet and hiding it in the woods. When Brer Fox came back, Brer Rabbit was sitting on the ground crying and boohooing.

"What happened, Brer Rabbit? What's the matter?"

"I wish you'd stayed, Brer Fox. I sho' wish you'd stayed."

"How come? What happened?"

"A man came and stole the haslet. I ran after him, but it must've been Fast-Foot Freddy. That sucker could run."

"Which way did he go?"

"Off down the road."

Brer Fox took off after him. Soon as he was out of sight, Brer Rabbit cut off the right hindquarter and hid it in the woods.

When Brer Fox came back, he was huffing and puffing and his tail was dragging the ground. He'd run almost to Los Francisco looking for Fast-Foot Freddy.

"You just a minute too late, Brer Fox!"

"What's the matter now?"

"Well, another man came along and took the right hindquarter. He went off through the woods over yonder. I know you can catch him 'cause he ain't got much of a start and he probably can't travel too fast carrying a hindquarter."

Brer Fox took off again. Brer Rabbit cut off the left hindquarter and hid it in the woods. When Brer Fox came back empty-handed, Brer Rabbit told him that another man had come and taken the left hindquarter.

Brer Fox might be dumb, but even he had a limit. He looked kinna suspicious at Brer Rabbit but didn't say nothing. He pretended like he was going to look for this man but circled back and hid in the woods where he could see what Brer Rabbit was up to.

Brer Rabbit got busy butchering the forequarters and started carrying it off to his hiding place.

"Where you going with that beef?" Brer Fox demanded, jumping out at Brer Rabbit.

Brer Rabbit put the meat down, looked at Brer Fox, and shook his head in dismay. "Where you think I'm going with it? With all these men coming around stealing our beef I decided to hide this piece so we'd end up with a little something."

Brer Fox had had too many doings with Brer Rabbit to believe that. He grabbed at him, but Brer Rabbit ducked and took off running. They went through the woods, streaking like lizards going for a hole. Brer Fox was gaining on Brer Rabbit, but Brer Rabbit ran into a hollow tree.

"I got you now!" Brer Fox said.

About that time Brer Buzzard came along, and Brer Fox asked him to watch the hole while he went and got his carving knife.

"Brer Buzzard?" called Brer Rabbit. "There's a nice fat gray squirrel in here, and it's as dead as anything can be. It's just starting to stink, and I know you don't eat nothing that don't stink."

Brer Buzzard chuckled. "I don't believe you."

"That's all right, Brer Buzzard. I still got the advantage over you 'cause I can see you and you can't see me."

Brer Buzzard didn't think that was a good idea at all. No telling what Brer Rabbit would be up to if nobody was watching him. Brer Buzzard stuck his head inside the tree, and Brer Rabbit threw a handful of dirt in his eyes and ran out.

You think he ran home? Why would he do that? He ran back and got the beef he'd hid. Then he went home!

Brer Fox and the Grapes

Way back before "Once upon a time" and "In the beginning," there wasn't much difference between people and animals. That's the truth! You can see it on the face of a dog or cat to this very day. You know how a dog or cat looks at you sometime like it wants to say something? Well, somewhere along the way the animals forgot all the English they knew. So, when a dog or cat look at you like it wants to speak, it's trying to remember English, but it can't.

Reason I mention all that is because the animals went courting Miz Meadows and the girls, and I don't want to hear a whole bunch of nonsense about animals couldn't court ladies. What you learn in school is facts. What I talk is truth!

Brer Rabbit and Brer Fox were as crazy as they could be about Miz Meadows and the girls. If one wasn't sitting on the porch with 'em, the other one was. When Brer Fox came and found Brer Rabbit was already there, he would be so mad that he'd go down the road and bite off a sticker bush. Or when Brer Rabbit found that Brer Fox had beat him there, he'd go down the road a piece and paw up so much dirt, he'd find himself in a hole.

Brer Rabbit wasn't one to tolerate a situation like this for long, so he set himself to thinking about rectifying it. He was sitting alongside the road thinking and rectifying when Brer Fox come along looking as slick and shiny as if somebody had just taken him out of the box. Brer Rabbit hailed him, and Brer Fox stopped.

"Glad you come along, Brer Fox, 'cause I got some mighty good news."

"Tell it and be quick, 'cause Miz Meadows done invited me to dinner."

"Well, yesterday I came across the biggest and fattest bunch of grapes I ever seen. They were so big and fat that the juice was just oozing out."

Brer Fox's mouth started to water, and he forgot all about Miz Meadows and the girls. "Show me where they at!"

"I thought you said Miz Meadows put your name in the pot."

"Well, I can go see her and the girls later. Where them grapes at?"

Brer Rabbit squinched up his face. "Well, you know where you went to get sweet gum for Miz Meadows and the girls the other day?"

Brer Fox allowed as to how he did.

"Well, they ain't there. You go to the sweet gum, and then you go up the creek until you get to a patch of bamboo brier, but the grapes ain't there. Then you follow your left hand across the hill until you come to that big red-oak root—but the grapes ain't there. Then you go down the hill until you come to that other stream, the one with the dogwood tree leaning over it, and near the dogwood there's a vine. On that vine is the grapes. They so ripe they look like they melted together. You'll probably find them full of bugs, but you can take your fine bushy tail and brush them off."

Brer Fox thanked Brer Rabbit and he took off running. When he was out of sight, Brer Rabbit followed. Brer Fox didn't look to the right or the left, and he didn't look behind. He ran until he came to the sweet gum tree, and then he turned up the creek until he came to the bamboo brier and went to the left until he came to the big red-oak root and then down the hill to the stream where the dogwood was. He saw the vine. Way up on the vine were the grapes, and they were all covered with bugs, just like Brer Rabbit had said.

Brer Fox climbed up the vine and swatted at the grapes with his fine bushy tail. *Have mercy!* Brer Fox gave a yell that Miz Meadows and the girls said they heard all the way to their house. He yelled and—*kerblim!*—down he came.

Brer Fox learned a little too late that he was so busy looking at the grapes he'd pictured in his mind, his eyes forgot what a wasp's nest looks like. When Brer Fox fell off the vine, the wasp nest came too. Them wasps didn't like having their house knocked down, and they told Brer Fox a thing or two about it. He run and he kick and he scratch and he bite and he scramble and he holler and he howl, but the wasps wasn't through expressing their opinions on the situation.

Brer Rabbit was hid over in some weeds watching with great interest until the wasps made like they wanted to express their opinion to him, and he lit out and headed straight for Miz Meadows's.

When he got there, Miz Meadows asked him where was Brer Fox.

"He gone grape hunting."

Miz Meadows couldn't believe her ears. "Grape hunting? Me and the girls been in the kitchen all day cooking a nice supper for him. That's the last time he'll ever set foot on this porch."

Miz Meadows and the girls asked Brer Rabbit if he'd like to take supper with them, and he allowed as to how he would be pleased. He had just sat down at the table and tucked his bib in when he looked through the window and saw Brer Fox limping by. He was swollen up like a balloon about to bust. Brer Rabbit told Miz Meadows to look out the window.

Miz Meadows put her head out and hollered, "Brer Fox, you look like you ate *all* the grapes!"

Wasn't a thing he could do except slink on home.

Brer Rabbit Falls in Love

One spring it was so pretty that folks who had never heard of love, didn't want to be in love, or had given up on it fell in love like it was a hole in the ground. Them kind of springs are dangerous. I reckon you too young to know what I'm talking about, but you will one day, and the Lord help you then.

It was one of them kind of springs when the breezes were so soft you wanted to grab one and put it on your bed to use for a sheet. It was one of them springs when the little leaves coming out on the trees looked better than money. Tell me that wasn't a dangerous spring! It was one of them springs when Brer Rabbit couldn't even think about causing no devilment. There ought to be a law against a spring like that!

Yes, Brer Rabbit had fallen in love, and it was with one of Miz Meadows's girls. Don't nobody know why, 'cause he'd been knowing the girl longer than black folks have known hard times, but that's the way love is. One day you fine and the next day you in love.

Brer Rabbit would go over to Miz Meadows and the girls in the morning, but instead of being full of stories and jokes like always he'd just sit there and sigh. Miz Meadows thought he had some dread disease like the rutabago or the Winnebago, especially when he started to lose weight.

Finally she asked, "Brer Rabbit? What's the matter with you? You sick?"

He hemmed and hawed and finally admitted that he was in love with one of the girls. He couldn't sleep, couldn't eat, couldn't steal, couldn't scheme, and was even beginning to feel sorry about some of the tricks he'd played on Brer Wolf.

"You sho' 'nuf in bad shape," Miz Meadows told him. "Have you told the girl you in love with her?"

Brer Rabbit shook his head. "I'm ashamed to."

Miz Meadows couldn't believe her ears. "Brer Rabbit, you *might've* felt something akin to shame before hens had their teeth pulled, but not since then. I done seen you do too many things to too many folks to be sitting here believing you feeling like you feeling. You can't convince me that there's a girl on the topside of the earth that could faze you."

"I'm ashamed to say it, Miz Meadows, but I'm afraid the girl won't have me."

"Just hush up your mouth and get on away from here. You ain't Brer Rabbit. You somebody look like him what's parading around low-rating his name. The Brer Rabbit I know wouldn't be carrying on like this."

Brer Rabbit couldn't help himself, and he went on off down the road until he came to a shade tree by the creek.

He hadn't been sitting there long before the girl he was in love with came up from the creek with a pail of water on her head, singing:

Oh, says the woodpecker, pecking on the tree,
Once I courted Miz Kitty Killdee,
But she proved fickle and from me fled,
And since that time my head's been red.

Brer Rabbit's heart started going pitty-pat, his ears jumped straight up in the air like attennae on a TV set, and he slicked down his hair real flat. When she finished singing, he sang back to her:

Katy, Katy! Won't you marry?
Katy, Katy! Choose me then!
Mamma says if you will marry,
She will kill the turkey hen;
Then we'll have a new convention,
Then we'll know the rights of men.

Now, don't be asking me what the last part of the song is about, 'cause I don't know. It was in the story when I got it, so I keep it. You can chunk it out for all I care.

By the time Brer Rabbit finished singing his song, the girl was standing there in front of him. She was a right pretty little thing, and she put down her pail and giggled at Brer Rabbit's song.

"How you this morning?" Brer Rabbit asked.

"I'm fine. How you?"

"Weak as water," Brer Rabbit said. "I ain't been feeling too well."

"So's I noticed. You got all the signs of somebody what come down with love. That's worse than the double pneumonia, TB, and terminal ugliness put together. The only cure is for you to go off somewhere and get a wife."

It was clear from the way she talked that she hadn't been

eyeballing him like he'd been eyeballing her, and that made him feel worse. He scrapped at the dirt with his foot, drawing little pictures in it. Folks do the foolishest things when they fall in love. Drawing dirt pictures with your foot! Finally he asked, "How come you don't get married?"

The girl bust out laughing. "I got too much sense than to do something like that without no sign or no dream."

"What kind of sign you want?" Brer Rabbit asked eagerly.

"Any kind! Don't make no difference to me. But I done tried all the spells, and I ain't seen no sign yet."

"What kind of spells have you tried?"

"So many I can't remember them all," the girl admitted. "I flung a ball of yarn out the window at midnight, and nobody came and wound it up. I took a looking glass and looked down the well. That was supposed to show me my future husband's face, but all I seen was water. I took a hard-boiled egg, scooped all the yellow out, and filled it up with salt and ate it without drinking any water. Then I went to bed, but I didn't dream about a blessed soul. I went out between sunset and dark and flung hempseed over my left shoulder, but my future husband didn't appear. Looks to me like I ain't gon' get no sign, and if I don't get a sign, I ain't gon' marry."

"If you'd told me about it, I bet you anything you would've seen your future husband."

The girl giggled. "Hush up, Brer Rabbit! If you don't get away from here, I'm gon' hit you! You too funny for words! Just who do you think I would've seen?"

Brer Rabbit drew another picture in the dirt with his foot, blushed, and finally said in a low voice, "You would've seen me."

The girl was shocked and hurt. "You ought to be ashamed

of yourself, making fun of me like that. I got better things to do than stand here and let you hurt my feelings." And she flounced on up the path.

Brer Rabbit sat down and thought that if that's how women were, maybe love wasn't all it was cracked up to be. But he was too far in love to know what good sense he was thinking.

He sat there for a long time, scratching his fleas, pulling on his moustache, and sighing. Suddenly he jumped up, cracked his heels together, and laughed so hard that he started choking.

"You want a sign, huh? Well, I'm going to give you one, girl! I'll give you a hundred!"

He went down to the canebrake and cut a long reed like the kind folks used to use for fishing poles. He hollowed it out and, when dark came, went up to Miz Meadows and the girls' house. He could hear them sitting around the table, laughing and talking.

"I saw Brer Rabbit down at the creek today," he heard the girl say.

"What was he doing there?" the other girl asked.

"I don't know, but his hair was slicked down and shining like glass."

Miz Meadows sighed. "I don't care nothin' about Brer Rabbit. I wish somebody would come and wash all these dishes."

The girls didn't want to hear nothing about no dishes. "Brer Rabbit said he wanted to be my husband. But I told him I wasn't marrying nobody until I got a sign. That's the only way I can be sure."

When Brer Rabbit heard that, he took one end of the hollow reed and stuck it in a crack on the outside of the chimney and then ran to the other end, which was laying in the weeds. He held it to his ear, and he could hear almost as good as if he was in the room.

Miz Meadows was saying, "Well, what kind of sign do you want?"

"I don't care," the girl answered. "Just so it's a sign."

Brer Rabbit put his mouth to the end of the reed and sang in a hoarse voice:

> *Some like cake and some like pie,*
> *Some love to laugh and some love to cry,*
> *But the girl that stays single will die, die, die.*

"Who's that out there?" said Miz Meadows.

She and the girls jumped up and hunted all over the house, all around the house, and all under the house but didn't see a soul. They went back in, and just as they sat down again, Brer Rabbit sang out:

> *The drought ain't wet and the rain ain't dry,*
> *Where you sow your wheat you can't cut rye,*
> *But the girl that stays single will die, die, die.*

Miz Meadows and the girls didn't know what to do this time, so they just sat there. Brer Rabbit sang out again:

> *I want the girl that's after a sign,*
> *I want the girl and she must be mine—*
> *She'll see her lover down by the big pine.*

Next morning, bright and early, the girl went down to the big pine. There was Brer Rabbit looking as lifelike as he did in his pictures. The girl tried to pretend like she was out taking a walk and happened to come that way. Brer Rabbit knowed better, and she did too. Pretty soon they was arguing and disputing with one another like they was already married. I suspect that was the real sign the girl had been looking for.

The Ol' African Helps Out

A new girl moved to town. Her name was Melody Mellif-ulous, and she was sho' 'nuf pretty. To tell the truth, she was fine! Brer Rabbit took one look, and his heart turned a double backflip and went *thumpty-thumpty, thump-thump.* He was weak in the knees, started trembling all over, and got light in the head. Some folks call that love. I calls it foolishness, which don't mean I ain't been foolish a time or two in my day. But that ain't part of the story, praise goodness!

Melody didn't care nothing about Brer Rabbit. He sent her flowers. She sent 'em back. He sent her greeting cards. She sent 'em back. He sent her a box of Swiss chocolates. She ate that. (Ain't no woman in the world gon' send back a box of chocolates.) No matter what he did, she didn't pay him no mind. If it had been raining and Melody had had the only umbrella in the world, Brer Rabbit would've drowned.

He was getting desperate, which meant there was only one thing to do. He went to see the Ol' African. The Ol' African was a conjure man. Folks nowadays don't believe in conjuring, and I feel sorry for 'em. Back in my time if you had a problem, you went to somebody who could conjure. The Ol' African was the best conjure person there's ever been. That man could get Kool-Aid out of a rock. One time he planted a garden, and while the rest of us was growing onions, tomatoes, and all like that, the Ol' African grew fried chicken, mashed potatoes, and gravy. If you was in trouble, that was definitely the man to see.

Brer Rabbit explained the situation to him. The Ol' African said, "You need a charm bag."

"Tell me what to do," Brer Rabbit exclaimed.

"You bring me one elephant tusk, an alligator tooth, and the bill of that bird called the ricebud."

"Be back in a little while," said Brer Rabbit.

He went way back out in the woods, and after a while here come Brer Elephant, busting through the trees big as Mt. Everest.

Brer Rabbit looked up at him. "You sho' are big. Something big as you can't be strong."

"Watch this," Brer Elephant said.

He grabbed a thirty-foot pine tree with his trunk, pulled it out of the ground, and flung it over his shoulder into the next county.

Brer Rabbit shook his head. "That tree was weak in the roots. I could see that before you pulled it up."

"Watch this!"

He ran through the woods and knocked over all the trees in his path.

Brer Rabbit shook his head. "Them was nothing but saplings. See that big oak tree? If you can destroy it, you strong."

Brer Rabbit pointed to a tree so big around, it looked like it had been growing since the Lord stuck it in the

ground. Brer Elephant ran into the tree and bounced off like a ball. He backed up, got a running start, and hit the tree again. He didn't bounce off this time 'cause one of his tusks was stuck. Brer Elephant pulled and he strained. After a while he realized that the only way to get free was to pull himself out of his tusk. That's what he did, and he sho' was a funny sight with only one tusk.

Brer Rabbit pried the tusk from the tree and took it back to the Ol' African. Ol' African said, "Elephant too big to be smart. Now I need that alligator tooth."

Brer Rabbit headed toward the creek, but before he got

there, he found Brer Alligator laying in the road, sunning himself.

"Ain't this road kinna inconvenient, Brer Alligator?" said Brer Rabbit. "You need a road what run right next to the creek. That way you wouldn't have to go so far to get in the water when you wanted to take a swim."

Brer Alligator liked that idea, so he and Brer Rabbit set to work. Brer Alligator was beating down the grass with his tail, and Brer Rabbit was knocking the bushes down with his cane. He hit left; he hit right; he hit up and he hit down and he hit all around. He hit and hit and he hit Brer Alligator in the mouth and knocked a tooth out. He grabbed the tooth and ran back to the Ol' African.

"Now I need the bill of the ricebud."

It took him a while to find a ricebud. It ain't one of your everyday birds, like a sparrow or a robin.

When he finally found one, he asked, "Can you fly?"

"Watch this!"

Ricebud flew up in the air, did a few loop-the-loops, and came back.

"That's pretty good," allowed Brer Rabbit. "But the wind have to be blowing when you fly. I know you can't fly when there ain't no wind."

They waited until the wind died down, and the ricebud flew around in circles, flew upside down, and did a couple of figure eights.

"You something else!" Brer Rabbit exclaimed when the ricebud came back. "But I bet you can't fly in the house when there ain't no wind."

Ricebud flew straight into the house, and Brer Rabbit shut the door. He caught him, pulled off his bill, and hurried back with it to the Ol' African.

Ol' African took the tusk, the alligator tooth, and the

ricebud bill and put 'em in a little bag. He put the bag around Brer Rabbit's neck.

"Melody Mellifulous won't be able to let you alone now."

That was sho' 'nuf the truth. She started sending Brer Rabbit flowers and cards and chocolate and begging him to marry her. But after doing all that work to get her Brer Rabbit wasn't interested no more. He finally threw the charm bag in the creek and Melody stopped pestering him.

The Courting Contest

I don't know what got into the animals, but they all fell in love with Miz Meadows and the girls at the same time. Now don't come telling me that a couple of stories ago you thought Brer Rabbit got married. That don't have nothing to do with nothing, 'cause animals ain't people and people ain't bananas. So, like I said, all the animals fell in love with Miz Meadows and the girls. Maybe somebody put something in the water, or Sister Moon turned up her lights too bright.

From sunup 'til moondown somebody was at the house. Especially around suppertime. It got so bad that Miz Meadows and the girls had to lock themselves in the bathroom to get a minute's worth of peace.

Miz Meadows got sick and tired of it! Seemed like the only way she was going to get rid of the animals was if she or one of the girls said "I do!" They weren't about to be that foolish. But they had to do something if they weren't going to spend the rest of their lives in the bathroom.

One Saturday morning Miz Meadows woke up, looked out the window, and Brer Rabbit, Brer Coon, Brer Possum, Brer Turtle, Brer Wolf, Brer Fox, and Brer Bear were sitting on the porch. Why, Brer Sun hadn't even finished his morning cup of coffee and there they were! And if that wasn't bad enough, she almost fainted from the smell of all the different colognes they were wearing. Enough was enough!

She stuck her head out the window and said, "Gentlemen, I have an announcement! Next Saturday I'd like y'all to meet me and the girls at the big granite rock down the road. The one who can take a sledgehammer and knock the dust out of it can choose which one of us he wants to marry. And until then I don't want none of y'all to darken my door."

Well, you ain't seen such excitement since us was freed from slavery. All the animals commenced to getting ready for the contest. They spent the whole week doing push-ups, sit-ups, chin-ups, and hiccups. They ran and jogged and skipped rope and lifted weights. All of them, that is, except Brer Rabbit.

He knew it was easier to get the wet out of water than dust out of granite. There had to be another way to skin this cat.

The night before the contest Brer Rabbit went over to Brer Coon's house and borrowed a pair of bedroom slippers. Next morning he filled the slippers with ashes from his fireplace, put 'em on, and went to the contest.

Well, when the animals looked around and saw Brer Rabbit strolling up with slippers on, they laughed. Brer Fox yelled out, "Say, Brer Rabbit! You forget to wash your feet?"

"Get out of my way," Brer Rabbit said, pushing the animals back. "I'm going to raise so much dust up out of this rock, Brer Sun won't be able to see nothing down here for a week!"

"Hold on, Brer Rabbit!" cried Brer Fox. "I was here first." He snatched the sledgehammer, reared back, and lammed the rock. Didn't knock a chip off it. He took two more turns and nothing. He was out of the contest.

Brer Wolf was next. He pounded on the rock three times real quick with all his might. He didn't get the time of day.

Next was Brer Possum. Didn't nobody expect much from him, and he didn't disappoint them.

Now came Brer Coon. Brer Coon made that ol' hammer ring, but he didn't raise no dust.

Brer Turtle's turn was next, but he said he had a crick in his neck.

Finally came Brer Bear. Miz Meadows and the girls got kinna nervous 'cause everybody knew if there was dust in that rock, Brer Bear would get it out. Brer Bear brought the hammer down; the ground shook. But no dust. He swung again; the trees shook. But no dust. The third time he hit the rock so hard the Lord looked down from heaven and hollered, "What you trying to do? Destroy the world?" Still, no dust.

Everybody got ready to go 'cause if Brer Bear couldn't do it, it couldn't be done. Miz Meadows and the girls breathed a sigh of relief. But they'd forgotten about Brer Rabbit.

"Hold on! Where y'all going? If y'all had let me go first, you wouldn't have had to embarrass yourselves."

He grabbed the sledgehammer, hit the rock, jumped in the air, kicked his heels together, and the dust from the ashes flew out of his slippers.

"Stand back, ladies!" He hit the rock again, kicked his heels, and dust flew everywhere.

"One more once!" he hollered. He hit the rock, kicked his heels, and there was so much dust in the air folks started coughing.

That was that. Brer Rabbit chose one of the girls for his wife, and they had a big wedding. I don't remember off-hand which one of the girls he married, but I think it was Molly Cottontail. Then again, it could've been Yolanda Yogurt. Ain't neither one a proper name for a lady if you ask me, but I guess in them days folks didn't know much about naming.

Brer Rabbit, Brer Coon, and the Frogs

Among the animals Brer Rabbit was the best at trickifying, but he had to share the title of best fisherman with Brer Coon. Brer Rabbit liked to set his line for fish, and Brer Coon liked to set his for frogs.

One summer, though, Brer Rabbit was having all the luck. He pulled in a mess of fish everyday, while Brer Coon couldn't catch a frog to save his soul.

"Brer Rabbit? How come you catching so many fish?"

Brer Rabbit shrugged. "I don't know. I just bait my hook, drop it in, and, before I can blink, I got a fish."

"I bait my hook, and I can't even catch a cold."

Brer Rabbit scratched his fleas. "You must've forgot about that time you made all the frogs mad."

"Me? What did I do?"

"You remember once during the dark of the moon when you caught King Frog?"

Brer Coon smiled. "He sho' was some good eating too."

"Maybe so. But ever since then everytime you show your face at the creek, I hear the frogs sing, *'Here he come! There he goes! Hit him in the eye! Hit him in the eye! Mash him and smash him! Smash him and mash him!'* That's what they say to one another."

"Well, if that's what's going on, how am I going to catch any of them? My family is getting so skinny, they navels are having long conversations with their backbones."

Brer Rabbit smiled. "Well, you and me been friends for a long time. You ain't never bared your sharp teeth at me, so I believe I'll help you out."

"Appreciate it, Brer Rabbit. I sho' do that."

"Tell you what you do. Get on that sandbar out there between the creek and the river. When you get out there, stagger around like you sick. Then whirl around and around and fall down like you dead. After you fall down, jerk your legs once or twice and lie still. And I mean still! If a fly lights on your nose, let him stay there. Don't blink your eyes; don't twitch your tail. Just lie there until you hear from me, and when I say move, you move!"

Brer Coon did just like Brer Rabbit told him. After Brer Coon had been lying there for a while, Brer Rabbit called out, "Coon dead! Coon dead!"

Frogs popped up from everywhere!

"Coon dead!" Brer Rabbit repeated. "Coon dead!"

One frog said: *"Don't believe it! Don't believe it!"*

Another frog said: *"Yes, he is! Yes, he is!"*

And a little bitty frog said: *"No, he ain't! No, he ain't!"*

The frogs got to croaking back and forth, disputing the matter. Brer Rabbit sat there on the bank scratching his fleas like he don't care what the frogs think.

The frogs decided to investigate and hopped over to Brer Coon. He looked dead. That he did. There was a fly crawling up inside his nose and he didn't even twitch.

Brer Rabbit called out, "Y'all been wanting to get rid of Brer Coon. This is your time, Cousin Frogs. Just bury him deep in the sand."

The Big Frog said, *"How we going to do it? How we going to do it?"*

"Dig the sand out from under him and let him down in the hole."

There must've been a hundred of them that went to digging. Sand flew out of so fast, it looked like a storm in the Saharry Desert. Brer Coon didn't twitch. The frogs kept digging until Brer Coon was in a nice hole.

"This deep enough?" Big Frog wanted to know. *"This deep enough?"*

"Can you jump out?" Brer Rabbit asked.

"Yes, I can. Yes, I can."

"Then it ain't deep enough."

The frogs made some more sand fly.

"This deep enough? This deep enough?"

"Can you jump out?"

Big Frog said, *"Yes, I can. Yes, I can."*

"Dig it deeper."

The frogs dug and dug and dug.

"This deep enough? This deep enough?"

"Can you jump out?"

"No, I can't. No, I can't. Come help me. Come help me."
Brer Rabbit laughed and hollered out, "RISE UP, BRER
COON! RISE UP, AND GET YOUR MEAT!"

Brer Rabbit's Laughing Place

Just like all the frogs got to disputing among themselves
about whether Brer Coon was dead, the animals would
get into disputes from time to time.

This particular day they got to arguing about who could
laugh the loudest. Naturally each animal thought it could
laugh louder than all the rest put together. Before you knew
it, they were mad enough to fight.

Brer Bull broke in and said, "Tell you what we do! Let
us have a laughing convention."

The animals liked that idea and said they didn't know
Brer Bull had so much sense.

Brer Rabbit said, "Brer Bull ain't got no more sense
than he ever had, and that was never much. Anybody with
sense know that Brer Monkey is the laughingest thing on
the top side of the earth."

The animals were embarrassed. The truth of that was so
obvious they wondered why they hadn't thought of it.

"Anyway," Brer Rabbit continued, "what you need is a
laughing place."

"What's that?" they wanted to know.

"A place that don't belong to nobody but you, a place
where you can go anytime you want and laugh yourself silly."

"You got one?"

"Sho'."

"Well, how you know how to find a laughing place?" Brer Buzzard asked. "And how you know it's a laughing place when you get there?"

"Don't nobody have to tell you. You know."

"Can we see your laughing place, Brer Rabbit?" asked Brer Lion.

Brer Rabbit thought for a minute. "I can't be taking everybody to my laughing place. By the time y'all got through tromping around and laughing, wouldn't be no laughter left for me. But I tell you what. Y'all pick one body and I'll take him. He can come back and tell you what it's like."

The animals got to discussing it among themselves. Since each one of them wanted to go, everybody voted for himself, and another fight almost broke out. They figured the only way to solve it was to have Brer Rabbit choose.

"I pick Brer Fox," said Brer Rabbit. "He's highly thought of in the community, and I ain't never heard nobody breathe a breath against him."

The animals said that was a fine idea, and to tell the truth, they'd had Brer Fox in mind all the while.

Brer Rabbit told Brer Fox to meet him at Lucy's Crossroad that afternoon.

When Brer Fox got there, he looked around. "Don't look funny to me."

"Keep your shirt on, Brer Fox."

Brer Rabbit led him east-northeast-southwest until they came to a place where there were bamboo briars, blackberry bushes, and honeysuckles all tangled up together in a pine thicket.

"Now, what you got to do is run back and forth and

forth and back through the thicket."

Brer Fox didn't want to do it, especially since his wife had told him to watch out for Brer Rabbit. But Brer Fox knew if he didn't, Brer Rabbit would go back and tell all the other animals he was afraid.

So Brer Fox took a running start and went through the bushes and the vines like he was running a race. He ran around in circles; he ran around in squares; on one of them runs he made a trapezoid-triangle-square. He was having such a good time running that he didn't see the hornet's nest until his head knocked it off a low-hanging tree limb.

Them hornets jumped on Brer Fox with all their feet. He was running sho' 'nuf now and hollering yap, yap, yap, and ouch, ouch, ouch, and yow, yow, yow, and Brer Rabbit was laughing, laughing, laughing. Brer Fox rolled and wallowed and hollered and squalled and fell, and Brer Rabbit laughed and laughed and laughed.

After the hornets had enough fox meat to last 'em a while, they left Brer Fox sitting there in the thicket. He was so mad, he thought he was going to bust.

Brer Rabbit looked at him. "I'm sho' glad you had such a good time. I'll have to get you to come back again real soon. You looked like you was having a good time."

Brer Fox bared his teeth. "You said this was a laughing place."

"What you think I been doing, Brer Fox? Didn't you hear me laughing? I reckon you must not heard me right. I said this was *my* laughing place. Didn't say nothing about it being yours. And anyway, who ever heard of a fox and a rabbit having the same laughing place? Everybody know foxes don't have a sense of humor."

Brer Rabbit Gets the House to Himself

One time the animals were getting on so well together that they decided to build a house where they could all live. Brer Bear was there, and Brer Fox, Brer Wolf, Brer Coon, and Brer Possum. They were all there, even, as I remember, Brer Mink. They drew up the plans and set to work.

Brer Rabbit claimed that standing on a ladder made him dizzy, and if he stayed in the sun too long, he'd get a heatstroke. So he stuck a pencil behind his ear and walked around, marking this and that, measuring thems and thoses with a yardstick. Folks walking by saw Brer Rabbit and said he was doing more work than all the other animals put together. Of course, Brer Rabbit wasn't doing a thing and would've been more help if he'd just laid down under a shade tree and gone to sleep.

In no time at all, the animals had put up the finest house you've ever seen. It was two stories with a big curving staircase, forty-'leven bedrooms, seventeen-'leven bathrooms, a TV room, a room for video games, a sauna, a hot tub, central air conditioning, a Cuisinart in the kitchen, and a bidet for Miz Brindle and Miz Brune.

The animals moved in, and naturally Brer Rabbit took the biggest bedroom for himself. While the others were admiring the house and getting settled, Brer Rabbit went out and got a gun, a great big gun that would make a lot of noise, and sneaked it to his room. Then he sneaked in an old cannon, and finally a tub of nasty slop water.

The next day the animals were sitting in the TV room watching a soap opera. After a while Brer Rabbit excused himself and said he was going to go take a nap. The other animals didn't pay him no mind.

After a while they heard Brer Rabbit shout, "When a big man like me want to sit down, where he going to sit?"

The animals laughed and hollered back, "If a big man like you can't sit in a chair, he better sit on the floor."

Brer Rabbit hollered back, "You better look out then, 'cause I'm gon' sit down."

BANG! Off went Brer Rabbit's gun.

The animals got quiet. When they didn't hear nothing else, they went back to watching the soap opera.

After a while Brer Rabbit hollered out again, "When a big man like me want to sneeze, where he going to sneeze at?"

The animals laughed and hollered back, "If you such a big man, sneeze where you want to!"

"All right!" Brer Rabbit hollered back. "You better watch out, 'cause I'm gon' sneeze!"

And KABLUM! BLUM! BLUM! He set off the cannon. The windows rattled, and the house shook, and Brer Bear fell off his rocking chair—*kerblump!* Brer Mink and Brer Possum said that Brer Rabbit sho' must have an awful cold.

After a while Brer Rabbit called out again, "When a big man like me takes a chaw of chewing tobacco, where he gon' spit?"

The other animals were getting tired of this nonsense, and they hollered back, "Big man or little man, spit where you want to!"

Brer Rabbit hollered, "Well, this is the way a big man spit!" And with that he turned over the tub of slop water.

When the other animals heard it come sloshing down the stairs, they didn't get old and they didn't get gray getting out of that house. Brer Fox and Brer Wolf went through the front door. Brer Bear, Miz Brindle, and Miz Brune all tried to go through the back door at once, and that was a sight to see. Brer Otter and Brer Mink went through the windows. And the other animals went up and out through the chimney.

Soon as all the animals were gone, Brer Rabbit locked the doors and windows and went to bed, where he slept the sleep of the just.

Miz Partridge Tricks Brer Rabbit

You might be getting the impression that Brer Rabbit was the smartest thing that ever shined his shoes. He was smart all right, and sometimes when a person thinks he's so smart that he can outthink God, that'll be the time he finds out he ain't so smart after all.

One day Brer Rabbit had a yearning for bird's eggs. He got a basket, hung it on his arm, and set out. He was going through the woods, singing and humming to himself, when he saw Miz Partridge sitting in a hole in the ground.

"Where you going with that basket on your arm?" she wanted to know.

"Hunting bird eggs."

"Ain't that bad manners to be robbing a bird's nest?"

"When a man is hungry, he can't stand on manners."

"Well, if you want bird eggs, I'll show you some."

Miz Partridge took him to a nest with two big eggs in it.

Brer Rabbit looked and shook his head. "That's a hen's nest."

They went a little further, and Miz Partridge showed him a guinea nest. "Now, this is a sho' 'nuf bird nest."

"Ain't you got no sense, woman? This is a potrack nest. Let me do the leading this time. I'll find a bird nest."

Brer Rabbit headed straight for Miz Partridge's nest. She started getting nervous but thought her nest was hidden deep enough in the tall grasses that Brer Rabbit wouldn't find it.

Brer Rabbit stopped and sniffed the air. "I smell bird eggs."

Miz Partridge laughed nervously. "Can't nobody smell bird eggs."

"What you want to bet?" He charged through the grass, pushing it out of his way, until he found her nest piled high with eggs.

Miz Partridge pretended to be astonished. "My goodness! Who'd ever thought a body could smell eggs?"

Brer Rabbit started putting the eggs in his basket.

"Wait a minute, Brer Rabbit. You better let me examine them eggs. I done forgot more about eggs than you ever knowed."

Brer Rabbit couldn't argue with that. Miz Partridge broke one of the eggs open and tasted it. She hardly got it to her mouth before she fell over backward and started flopping and fluttering and twisting and turning. She flew up in the air; she fell down; she fluttered and jumped up again.

Brer Rabbit got scared. Miz Partridge was doing as good of a job of acting as Brer Rabbit had ever done.

"Run, Brer Rabbit! Run! These are snake eggs and they're poison."

Brer Rabbit ran away from there like Brer Dog was after him, and from that day to this a rabbit won't go near an egg.

The Famine

One year famine came to the community. The animals put their seed in the ground to make a crop, but the sky turned to iron and not a drop of rain fell. The leaves on the trees looked like they was going to turn to powder, and the ground was like it had been cooked. Old Man Hungriness had taken off his clothes and was parading around everywhere.

One day when the animals' stomachs were growling so loud they could barely hear themselves think, Brer Fox went to see Brer Rabbit.

"Where our bread gon' come from, Brer Rabbit?"

"Look like it might be coming from nowhere."

"I'm serious, Brer Rabbit. What we gon' do?"

They talked about the situation for a while until Brer Rabbit said, "Looks to me like we ain' got no choice but to sell our families."

Brer Fox nodded. "I think you right."

The next morning Brer Fox tied up his wife and put her in the back of his wagon and went over to Brer Rabbit's. He had his wife and all seven of his children tied up, and put them in the back of the wagon.

"I believe I'll set back here with my folks, Brer Fox, until they get used to the surroundings."

Brer Fox cracked the whip, and the wagon moved off toward town.

"No nodding back there," Brer Fox called out every now and then.

"You miss the ruts and the rocks, and I'll miss the nodding," Brer Rabbit would reply.

Brer Fox would chuckle. All the while, though, Brer Rabbit was untying his family. When he finished, he climbed on the seat next to Brer Fox, and they began talking about all the food they were going to get for selling their families.

After a while one of Brer Rabbit's children hopped out of the wagon, and Miz Fox sang out:

One from seven
Don't leave eleven.

Brer Fox turned around, kicked her, and told her to shut up that racket. Another of Brer Rabbit's children hopped out, and Miz Fox sang:

One from six
Leaves me less kicks.

Brer Fox didn't pay her no mind this time and went on talking with Brer Rabbit about all the food they were going to get. Miz Fox kept singing as the children kept jumping out of the wagon:

One from five
Leaves four alive;
One from four
Leaves three and no more;
One from three
Leaves two to go free;
One from one,
and all done gone.

When they got close to town, Brer Fox looked back in the wagon to make sure everybody was all right and saw that Brer Rabbit's family was gone. "Good grief! Where's your family, Brer Rabbit?"

Brer Rabbit looked and he began moaning and crying and screaming and wailing. "That's what I was afraid of," he hollered. "I knowed if I put them back there, Miz Fox would eat them up. I knowed it!"

Miz Fox swore up and down that she hadn't eaten them, but Brer Fox wasn't about to believe her. So when they got to town, he sold her, and he and Brer Rabbit went to the store and bought a lot of food.

They were on their way home when Brer Fox remembered that he'd forgotten to get some chewing tobacco. He asked Brer Rabbit to stay with the wagon while he hurried back to town. Brer Rabbit said he couldn't think of anything he'd rather do.

As soon as Brer Fox was out of sight, Brer Rabbit slapped the horses with the whip and took the wagon home. He put the horses in his stable, all the food in his smokehouse, the wagon in the barn, and some corn in his pocket. Then he cut the horses' tails off, went out to the road, and stuck the tails in the mud.

After a while Brer Fox came charging up the road. He was so angry the saliva was dripping off his teeth. Brer Rabbit saw him coming and started pulling on the horses' tails.

"Brer Fox! Run here! Quick! Brer Fox! You just in time if you ain't too late. Come here! Quick!"

Brer Fox ran to Brer Rabbit and shoved him away. "Looks like my horses done got caught in the quicksand. Get out of the way, Brer Rabbit. You too little and weak to do a man's job."

Brer Fox pulled hard on one of the tails. It came out, and Brer Fox went flying across the road. He jumped up and pulled on the other horse's tail. It came out, and he turned a somersault and went flying across the road again. While he was turning all these somersaults and flying across the road, Brer Rabbit sprinkled a little corn in the holes where the horses' tails had been.

When Brer Fox saw that corn, he started digging and grabbling in the mud and dug a hole deep enough to be his grave. And that's what it turned out to be too, because Brer Fox was digging so hard and so furious that he just plumb wore himself out and keeled over dead right there in the hole.

I tell you this much: It took Brer Rabbit and his family a lot less time to put the dirt back in the hole than it had taken Brer Fox to get it out.

Brer Rabbit, Brer Bear, and the Honey

All the animals—horn, claw, and wing—lived there in the community together, and they all shared the same fate. When times was good, they all prospered. And when times were bad, they all suffered.

When the famine came, it was one of the suffering times. Wasn't no food to be had, no money, and no jobs. It was all the animals could do to scuffle along and make the buckle and tongue meet. Most of them went to bed hungry every night.

All of them, that is, except Brer Bear. The skinnier they got, the fatter he got. He was just wallowing in fat. Shoots! Brer Bear was so fat, he couldn't keep the flies off himself.

Everyday the animals talked among themselves about how come Brer Bear was so fat and they were so skinny. Brer Rabbit was tired of talking and decided to keep an eye on Brer Bear.

Before long he noticed that Brer Bear was acting mighty strange. Instead of staying up at night talking politics and watching television, he was going to bed same time as the chickens and was up and gone by first light. It wasn't natural to go to bed with the sun and get up with it. If God had meant for folks to live like that, he wouldn't have invented electricity.

One night Brer Rabbit went over to Brer Bear's house. He scrapped his foot on the porch and cleared his throat. Miz Brune, and then again, it could've been Miz Brindle (I never could tell 'em apart)—one of 'em came to the door, and when she saw it was Brer Rabbit, she invited him in out of the evening chill.

Miz Brune pulled him a chair up close to the fireplace,

and Brer Rabbit crossed his legs and allowed as to how he hadn't seen Brer Bear in a coon's age.

"Times is so hard," Miz Brune said, "that my ol' man been working soon and late just to make both ends meet." She got up and said she had to fix a bag of ashes for Brer Bear to take to work with him in the morning.

"What in the world Brer Bear do with a bag of ashes, Miz Brune?"

She laughed and said she didn't know. "But I got to get a bag together every night and leave it for him in the corner by the chimney."

"Where is Brer Bear?"

"You sit here long enough, you won't have to ask where he at 'cause you be hearing him." She laughed. "I ain't never heard nobody snore like he do."

They chatted on for a while longer, and then Brer Rabbit said it was time for him to be getting on down the road. But he didn't go no farther than it took to find a place where he could hide and watch the house. He spent the night there, chasing lightning bugs and getting the frogs all confused by making frog sounds.

Long about the time the chickens started crowing up the sun, Brer Bear came out of the house, the bag of ashes over his shoulders, and made for the woods. Brer Rabbit followed along behind, but not wanting to get caught, he was scared to follow too close. First thing he knew, Brer Bear was out of sight, and for the life of him Brer Rabbit couldn't figure out which way he'd gone.

Brer Rabbit went home, worrying about what Brer Bear could be doing with a bag of ashes.

That night he went back to Brer Bear's house. After he was sure Miz Brune was good and asleep, he sneaked in and found the bag of ashes next to the chimney. He picked it up. It was sho' 'nuf heavy. He set the bag down and tore a tiny hole in one corner. Some of the ashes got up his nose, and he was about to sneeze. He held his breath and ran out of the house, and when that sneeze came out— goodness gracious!—the chickens started cackling and Sister Moon swayed for a minute like she wasn't sure she was going to be able to hang on to her perch. Brer Rabbit decided to get on out of there.

When morning came, he went back along the way Brer Bear had gone the day before until he saw a little trail of ashes. That was the reason he'd put the hole in the sack. Everytime Brer Bear took a step, he jolted the ashes out. Brer Rabbit followed the ashes, uphill and downhill, through bushes and through briars, until he came on Brer Bear.

Now, what you think Brer Bear was doing? If you said he was in a tree eating honey off a honeycomb, you would be right. He was eating the good stuff, the natural, stark-naked bee juice.

When Brer Rabbit saw him, though, he liked to have fainted, because Brer Bear had poured the sack of ashes over himself, and he was a horrible-looking sight. I reckon he'd covered himself with ashes so the bees wouldn't sting him. Brer Bear was way up in the tree, eating honey by the handful, with the bees zooming all around him. Brer Rabbit looked around, and everywhere were hollow poplar trees, and every one was so full of honeycombs that the honey was dripping down the sides.

Brer Rabbit watched Brer Bear eat honey until his stomach started saying *Want some! Want some!*

Brer Rabbit shouted up, "Please, Brer Bear! I'm awful

hungry! I sho' would be pleased if you'd hand me down a handful of honey."

"You better get away from here, you trifling, good-for-nothing cottontail nuisance."

"Please, Brer Bear! Just a handful."

"Get on away from here before I come down and make you into a pair of gloves for one of my children."

The next day Brer Rabbit got all the animals together—horn, claw, and wing—and told 'em how come Brer Bear was rolling in fat.

"Don't understand how he could do that to us," Brer Possum said.

"He could've at least let us smell some of that honey even if we couldn't taste it," said Brer Rat.

"Speak for yourself. I want me some of that honey!" said Brer Fox.

"And we gon' feast on honey before the sun start running from the moon," said Brer Rabbit.

"How?" all the animals asked at once.

"We gon' start a hurricane!"

If the animals hadn't known Brer Rabbit so well, they would've thought he'd lost his mind. But if Brer Rabbit said he was going to start a hurricane, a hurricane was coming.

Brer Rabbit led them quietly out to the honey orchard. He put all the big animals behind big trees and the little animals behind the little trees.

"Now, when I holler, y'all rub and shake these trees."

He told all the ones with wings and could fly to get up in the trees. "When I holler, you beat your wings as hard as you can."

All the ones with wings who could run but not fly high he put in the weeds. "When I holler, run through the grass as hard as you can."

When everybody was in place, Brer Rabbit took a long rope, and he went way back in the woods. Then he ran toward the honey orchard, dragging the rope and yelling and hollering.

Brer Bear looked down from the top of the tree. "What's wrong, Brer Rabbit?"

"Hurricane coming! Hurricane coming! I got to go somewhere and tie myself to a tree before I get blown all the way to Jamoca Junction. Can't you hear it, Brer Bear?" Brer Rabbit hollered real loud.

The animals behind the trees started shaking them, and the birds in the weeds started running back and forth, and the birds in the trees started fluttering, and it sounded like the world was coming to an end.

Brer Bear scrambled out of that tree and hit the ground—*kerbiff!* "Brer Rabbit! Tie me to the tree with you! Tie me, too!"

The animals were into it now, and they were shaking the trees and fluttering and running back and forth and creating such a commotion that even Brer Rabbit started to get a little scared. He hurried and tied Brer Bear real tight to the tree, and when he tied the last knot, he called to the animals, "Come and look at Brer Bear!"

All the animals came and laughed at Brer Bear, and then they went to work on that honey orchard. They ate their fill and then took a lot of honey home for their wives and children. I expect that somebody came along eventually and untied Brer Bear.

Brer Snake Catches Brer Wolf

The honey was good while it lasted, but it didn't last forever, and it seemed like the famine was going to.

Brer Wolf and Brer Rabbit were talking one day.

"How is this here recession treating you, Brer Rabbit?"

"Not too good. Can't find a job. Ain't got no money, and I'm hungry all the time."

"Me too. Me too," agreed Brer Wolf. "What can we do?"

Brer Rabbit shook his head. "I don't know, but something funny is going on. I saw Brer Snake yesterday. He was looking fat and sleek, while the rest of us are going around with our ribs showing. Seems to me that the country is in a bad way when our stomachs are growling so loud you'd think it was a thunderstorm, and the snakes are laying up in the sun like the economy was prospering."

"We ought to run all the snakes out of the country."

Brer Rabbit shook his head. "I'd rather find out where they getting their food from."

"Me too," agreed Brer Wolf. "Me too."

They decided to see what they could find out.

Next day Brer Rabbit was going through the countryside when he heard a noise in the woods. He jumped into a ditch and hid. A minute later Brer Black Snake come swishing by like he was greased. He swished on across the road and into the woods on the other side. Brer Rabbit followed at a distance and saw Brer Black Snake swish right up to a great big ol' poplar tree.

Brer Black Snake circled the tree one time, stopped, and sang out:

> *Watsilla, watsilla,*
> *Consario wo!*
> *Watsilla, watsilla,*
> *Consario wo!*

Before Brer Rabbit could blink an eye, a door in the tree flew open and Brer Black Snake swished in.

"I'll be!" exclaimed Brer Rabbit. "So that's where your food is."

Brer Rabbit went up to the tree to see if he could hear anything, but he couldn't. After a while he heard the same song:

Watsilla, watsilla,
Consario wo!
Watsilla, watsilla,
Consario wo!

Brer Rabbit leaped a leaping leap into the weeds, and as he did, the door in the tree flew open, and out swished Brer Black Snake. He looked around and then slid on his way. Brer Rabbit came out of hiding and went up to the tree.

He walked around the tree looking for the door but couldn't find it. Finally it came to him that maybe he had to sing the song.

Watsilla, watsilla,
Bandario, wo-haw!

As he sang the first part, the door opened a little ways, but when he sang the last part, it slammed shut. Brer Rabbit tried again:

Watsilla, watsilla,
Bandario, wo-haw!

Same thing happened. Door opened a little and then slammed shut.

"Must not have the song right," Brer Rabbit said.

Brer Rabbit went back and hid. That evening along came

Brer Black Snake again. Brer Rabbit crept closer as Brer Black Snake sang:

> *Watsilla, watsilla,*
> *Consario wo!*
> *Watsilla, watsilla,*
> *Consario wo!*

The door opened and Brer Black Snake swished on in. Brer Rabbit sang the song over and over to himself. Soon as Brer Black Snake came out and went his way, Brer Rabbit went up to the tree and sang the song. The door flung open and Brer Rabbit went in.

My goodness! He thought he'd died and gone to heaven. There was ham, pork chops, mince pie, fried chicken, hamburgers, and french fries stacked up in there hot, like they'd just been cooked. Brer Rabbit didn't wonder how and how come and all that. He just sat down and went to eating. When he'd had his fill, he went to tell Brer Wolf what he'd found.

Brer Wolf came back to the tree with Brer Rabbit. Brer Rabbit sang the song, the door opened, and he went inside, leaving Brer Wolf outside. After Brer Rabbit had eaten all he wanted, he came out.

"What'd you leave me out here for?" Brer Wolf wanted to know.

"You was standing watch. Now I'll sing the song and stand watch for you."

Brer Rabbit sang the song, the door flew open, and in went Brer Wolf. Brer Rabbit was standing watch until he heard Brer Black Snake coming, at which point he decided to keep watch from the bushes.

Brer Black Snake sang the song, the door flew open, and in he went. For a minute Brer Rabbit didn't hear nothing. Then there came all this noise, like a fight going on. The door flew open and out came Brer Wolf all tied up.

Brer Black Snake tied Brer Wolf to a tree limb and started wearing him out with his tail. And everytime Brer Black Snake hit Brer Wolf, Brer Rabbit hollered, "Serves him right! Serves him right!"

Brer Rabbit Gets the Meat

One day Brer Rabbit met up with Brer Fox. Now, don't come telling me about Brer Fox died a couple of stories back. What makes you think this is the same Brer Fox? Back in them times all the foxes was named Brer, and on top of that they all looked like one another too, which is how come they was all named Brer, 'cepting the ladies, of course. So, just because Brer Fox was dead don't mean he wasn't alive. Now, let me get back to the story before it melts and ain't worth telling.

"How you today?" Brer Rabbit wanted to know.

"Ain't doing too good. You?"

"Ain't doing too good myself. What's your problem?"

"Well, to tell the truth, I'm hungry. I can't remember the last time I had me a piece of meat. What's troubling you?"

"I'm hungry too. My stomach been having a long conversation with my backbone. I can't even remember what meat looks like, not to mention taste like."

They walked on together, commiserating and disputing about which one's stomach growled the loudest, when they saw Mr. Man coming toward them with a big piece of meat under his arm.

"Brer Fox! You see what I see?"

"Sho' do, Brer Rabbit! I wouldn't mind having a taste of that."

"We gon' get some of that meat. In fact, we gon' get all that meat."

"How, Brer Rabbit?"

"You just follow along behind me and Mr. Man at a distance."

Brer Rabbit hailed Mr. Man, asked after his health and the health of his family as he fell in step beside him. Mr. Man said that everybody was doing just fine.

"Glad to hear it, Mr. Man."

Brer Rabbit started sniffing the air like he smell smoke somewhere. After a while Mr. Man wanted to know if he had a cold.

"I smell something, and it don't smell like ripe peaches either," Brer Rabbit said.

Mr. Man said he don't smell a thing.

"Rabbits got better noses than people." Brer Rabbit kept sniffing the air until finally he grabbed his nose. "Peeuuu! Something just downright stinks!" Brer Rabbit looked around. "It's that meat you got, Mr. Man. Where'd you get that meat at? The dump?"

Mr. Man looked kind of ashamed, especially when he noticed some big green flies circling his meat. Brer Rabbit moved over to the other side of the road, still holding his nose. Mr. Man put the meat down.

"What can I do about it, Brer Rabbit?"

"Well, I heard that if you drag a piece of meat through the dirt, it'll get fresh again. I ain't had no experience with nothing like that myself, but my granddaddy said he tried it once and it worked."

"But I ain't got no string, Brer Rabbit."

Brer Rabbit chuckled. "You ought to spend more time in the woods and less in town. String ain't no problem." Brer Rabbit went off in the woods and, a few minutes later, came back with a long bamboo vine.

"That's mighty long, ain't it?"

"It got to be long," Brer Rabbit told him. "You want the wind to get between you and the meat."

Mr. Man tied the bamboo vine around the meat. Brer Rabbit broke off a branch from a bush and said he'd stay behind to fan the meat and keep the flies off.

Soon as Mr. Man started pulling the meat, Brer Rabbit got a big rock, untied the meat, and tied the rock on. Then he signaled Brer Fox, and they picked up the meat and ran into the woods.

Brer Fox suggested they sample it. Brer Rabbit couldn't have agreed more.

Brer Fox gnawed off a hunk, shut both eyes, and chewed and tasted, tasted and chewed, a silly smile spreading across his face. When he finished, he smacked his mouth, licked his lips, and sighed with satisfaction.

"That sho' is some mighty good lamb!"

"That ain't lamb," protested Brer Rabbit. "Any fool can see that that ain't lamb."

"It's lamb!"

"It ain't!"

Brer Rabbit gnawed off a hunk. He closed his eyes and

chewed and tasted, tasted and chewed, and then chewed and tasted some more. Then he smacked his lips, licked 'em real slow, and sighed with satisfaction.

"It's pork!" Brer Rabbit announced.

"Pork! Brer Rabbit, what's the matter with you? You ain't had meat in so long, you can't tell the difference between pork and lamb no more."

"It's pork!"

"It ain't!"

"Is!"

"Ain't!"

They argued and they tasted. They tasted and they argued.

"Well," Brer Rabbit began, "ain't no point in us arguing about it 'cause we can agree on one thing, I bet."

"What's that?"

"It's good!"

Brer Fox laughed. "That's sho' 'nuf the truth."

Brer Rabbit started walking away.

"Where you going?"

"To get a drink of water."

A few minutes later Brer Rabbit came back, wiping his mouth and clearing his throat.

"Where the stream at, Brer Rabbit?"

"Across the road, down the hill, and up the big gully."

Brer Fox went across the road and down the hill, but he didn't see a big gully. He kept going until he came to a big gully, but after looking all around he didn't see any stream.

While he was looking for the stream, which didn't exist, of course, Brer Rabbit dug a hole and he shoved the meat in and covered it up. Then he cut a long hickory switch and went and hid in a clump of bushes.

When he heard Brer Fox coming back, he took the hickory switch and hit a tree. *Pow! Pow!*

"Oh, please, Mr. Man!" he hollered.

Pow! Pow!

"Ow! Oh! Ooo! Don't hit me no more!"

Pow! Chippy-row-pow!

"Don't hit me no more, Mr. Man! Please don't hit me no more!"

Brer Fox was enjoying what he was hearing. It was about time somebody caught up to Brer Rabbit and gave him a taste of his own medicine.

After a while the racket died down, and Brer Rabbit hollered out, "Run, Brer Fox! Run! Mr. Man say he coming looking for you now!"

Brer Fox lit out from there. Brer Rabbit came out, dug up the meat, and let me tell you, he sho' did eat good that night.

Brer Rabbit Scares Everybody

The famine finally ended, and the next year Brer Rabbit made a good crop of peanuts. He sold it and was going to buy a red truck he'd had his eye on.

When he told Miz Rabbit what he was planning, she got righteous: "Truck, my foot! What you want a truck for? Where you gon' get the money to keep gas in it? Now you listen here to me, Brer Rabbit! The children need some tin cups to drink out of and some tin plates to eat off.

And I need a new coffeepot, 'cause you know how much I likes a good cup of coffee first thing in the morning. If you buy that truck, you best prepare yourself to eat, sleep, and go to the bathroom in it!"

Brer Rabbit had sense enough to know that he best back off on the truck. He smiled real nice, kissed his wife on the cheek, and told her he'd go to town Wednesday and buy up a whole lot of stuff for her and the kids.

Miz Rabbit didn't waste no time running across the road to tell Miz Mink that Brer Rabbit was going to town Wednesday to buy some nice things for her and the kids.

What she want to say that for? When Brer Mink got home that evening, Miz Mink told him what Brer Rabbit was going to do for his family, and she wanted to know when was Brer Mink going to do something nice for her? Miz Mink carried the word to Miz Fox, who proceeded to low-rate Brer Fox, and Miz Fox told it to Miz Wolf, who wanted to know from Brer Wolf how come he couldn't treat his family as good as Brer Rabbit treated his, and it didn't take no time at all for Brer Mink, Brer Fox, Brer Wolf, Brer Bear, and all the other animals to get together and declare that Brer Rabbit had gone a little too far this time. Playing tricks on folks was one thing, but buying your wife and children presents, well, that was something else again. They agreed very quickly to lay hold to Brer Rabbit on his way back from town that Wednesday and do away with him.

Wednesday came and Brer Rabbit went to town. He bought some soda pop, a plug of chewing tobacco, and a pocket handkerchief for himself. He bought his wife the coffeepot and a copy of Paris *Vogue,* and he got the children the tin plates, tin cups, and some *Star Wars* under-wear.

Toward sundown he headed home feeling mighty proud of himself. After a while he got tired from carrying all the packages and sat down under a tree to rest. He was sitting there fanning with one of the tin plates when a teenichy sapsucker started flying around his head chirping and carrying on. Brer Rabbit tried to shoo the bird away. The bird made more racket and finally lit right on top of Brer Rabbit's head and started singing:

> *Pilly-pee, pilly-wee!*
> *I see what he don't see!*
> *I see, pilly-pee,*
> *I see what he don't see.*

He sang it over and over until Brer Rabbit started looking around. Finally he saw marks on the ground where it looked like somebody had been sitting. He examined the marks a little closer.

"Well, well, well. There's the print of Brer Fox's tail. And there's the print of Brer Wolf's foot. And right there is the print of Brer Bear's bottom. They all been here, and I bet you anything they hiding out in the big gully down there in the hollow."

Brer Rabbit hid his packages in the bushes and slipped around through the woods to see what he could see. It was just like he figured. Brer Fox, Brer Wolf, and Brer Bear were hiding in the gully.

Brer Rabbit hurried back to where he'd hid his packages. He took out the coffeepot, turned it upside down, and put it on his head. Then he put the tin cups on his

suspenders and on his pants. Next he took the tin plates
in his hands and sneaked back through the woods until he
came to the hill overlooking the gully.

He ran down the hill—*rickety, rackety, slambang!* When
the animals heard all the racket, they turned around. Never
in their lives had they seen a creature with a coffeepot for
a head and cups rattling all over his body.

Brer Bear jumped up, knocked Brer Wolf down, stepped
on Brer Fox, and got away from there. Brer Wolf and Brer
Fox was scrambling and trying to get up so they could get
away, but before they could, Brer Rabbit was right on
'em.

"Gimme room! Turn me loose! I'm Ol' Man Spewter-Splutter with long claws, and scales on my back! I'm snaggletoothed and double-jointed! Gimme room!" And he jumped up—*rickety, rackety, slambang!*

Them animals tore up some trees getting away from there. Next morning Brer Rabbit went back to the spot, and he and his children picked up enough kindling wood to last through the winter.

Grinny Granny Wolf

Brer Rabbit went over to Brer Wolf's house one day and knocked on the door—*bim, bim, bim.* No answer.

"I know you there, Brer Wolf! How come you don't want to answer the door for me?"

Bam, bam, bam. Still no answer.

Brer Rabbit was insulted. "You better open this door before I knock it in." No answer.

Blammity-blam-blam-blam. No answer.

Brer Rabbit knocked the door down and went in. There was a fire burning in the fireplace, a pot sitting on the fire, and an old woman sitting by the pot. The fire was burning, the pot was boiling, and the old woman was taking a nap.

The old woman was Grinny Granny Wolf. She was cripple in one leg, blind in one eye, couldn't see out of the other, and deaf in one ear. But with her good ear she had heard Brer Rabbit banging on the door, and when he came in, she said, "Come and see your old grandma, Grandson.

The fire is burning; the pot is boiling. Come fix your grandma some food, Grandson."

She thought he was Brer Wolf.

Brer Rabbit made himself comfortable by the fire. "Hi, Granny! I'm crippled myself. I'm blind in one eye. I want you to boil me in the water. If you do, my leg will be well and I'll be able to see."

Brer Rabbit took a root and dropped it in the pot. "I feel all right now, Granny. My leg is getting strong and I can see out of my blind eye."

Grinny Granny Wolf cried out, "I'm cripple in one leg and blind in both eyes. Why don't you put me in the pot and make me well?"

Brer Rabbit laughed. "Why not, Granny? I'll make you all well again." He picked up Grinny Granny Wolf and put her in the pot of boiling water.

"Ow! Take me out of here!"

"Too soon. Too soon."

"I'm about to boil away. Ow! Take me out of here!"

"Too soon. Too soon!"

After a while she was dead. Brer Rabbit took the bones out of her body and left the meat in the pot. He took Grinny Granny Wolf's clothes and put them on. He took her cap and put it on. And then he sat in the chair she'd been sitting in.

After a while Brer Wolf came home. "I'm hungry, Grinny Granny. I've been working hard."

"Your dinner is ready, Grin'son Gran'son," said Brer Rabbit in Grinny Granny Wolf's voice.

Brer Wolf looked in the pot and smelled. He filled his plate and ate a big helping. When he was done, he patted his belly. "That was good."

Brer Wolf called his children to come have supper. The children said, "We can't eat our grandmama."

Brer Rabbit jumped out of the chair. "Brer Wolf, you ate your grandmama!" He laughed and ran on away from there before Brer Wolf could grab him.

Now, I tell you the truth: That ain't one of my favorite stories, but the way I look on it is like this: Brer Wolf must've done something sho' 'nuf terrible to Brer Rabbit for him to carry on like that. Something mighty terrible. Of course, if I sits here and thinks about some of the things been done to me and mine, I begin to understand that story more and more. I sho' do.

The Fire Test

Brer Rabbit had to go to town one day. He told his children not to open the door for anybody. Brer Wolf had been creeping around the house with big eyes and a angry belly, wanting revenge for what Brer Rabbit had done to Grinny Granny Wolf.

"When I come back, I'll knock on the door and sing:

> *I'll stay when you away,*
> *'Cause no gold will pay toll!*"

The little rabbits promised, and Brer Rabbit went on his way.

Brer Wolf had been hiding under the house and had heard every word. Soon as Brer Rabbit was out of sight,

Brer Wolf knocked on the door—*blip, blip, blip.*

"Who that?" the little rabbits called out.

Brer Wolf sang:

> *I'll stay when you away,*
> *'Cause no gold will pay toll!*

The little rabbits liked to have died laughing. "Go away, Brer Wolf! Go away! You ain't our daddy!"

Brer Wolf slunk off, but everytime he got to thinking about them tender young rabbits, his stomach growled. He went back to the door—*blap, blap, blap!*

"Who that?"

Brer Wolf sang:

> *I'll stay when you away,*
> *'Cause no gold will pay toll!*

The little rabbits thought that was the funniest thing they'd ever heard, even funnier than the last time Brer Wolf had come to the door. "Go away, Brer Wolf! Go away! Our daddy don't sing like he got a bad cold."

Brer Wolf slunk away, but a little while later he was back—*blam, blam, blam!*

"Who that?"

This time Brer Wolf sang as pretty as he could:

> *I'll stay when you away,*
> *'Cause no gold will pay toll!*

"Go away, Brer Wolf! Go away! Our daddy can sing pretty! Go away! Go away!"

Brer Wolf slunk off one more time. This time he went back out in the woods and practiced and practiced until he could sing almost as good as one of God's angels, which was almost as good as Brer Rabbit. He went back to the house, knocked on the door, and when the little rabbits asked who it was, he sang out so pretty that they opened the door. Brer Wolf rushed in and gobbled them up.

Toward sundown Brer Rabbit got home and found the door open. He went in slowly and looked around. He didn't see his children anywhere. He searched all over the house. Finally, over in the corner by the fireplace, he saw a pile of tiny bones.

Next morning he went to all the animals' houses and asked if they knew who had eaten his children. None of them did, especially Brer Wolf. Finally Brer Rabbit went and asked his best friend, Brer Turtle, what he should do.

Brer Turtle called a meeting of all the animals and made a proposal. "Now, somebody done gone and ate all of Brer Rabbit's children, and we got to find out who done it. If we don't, he might eat our children next, and before long won't be no children left in the community."

All the animals agreed with that, especially Brer Wolf.

"What we gon' do?" Brer Bear wanted to know.

"Let's dig a deep pit," Brer Turtle said.

"I'll dig the pit!" Brer Wolf offered.

"Let's fill the pit full of kindling and brush."

"I'll fill the pit!" Brer Wolf said.

"And then set it afire."

"I'll light the fire!" Brer Wolf offered.

"And when the fire is blazing hot, all the animals must jump over it. The one what destroyed Brer Rabbit's children will drop in and get burnt up."

Brer Wolf suddenly looked like he had business at the other end of the county. But since he'd been the one with the most mouth, the animals gave him the shovel, and he started digging.

After a while the pit was dug, and it was deep. The kindling and brush were piled high, and the fire was blazing hot. The animals stared at it, their eyes big, waiting to see who would go first.

Finally Brer Mink allowed that he never did have an interest in Brer Rabbit's children. To tell the truth, he didn't care too much for his own. He got a running start and jumped on over. Brer Coon was next, and he sailed over without even getting singed. Brer Bear said he felt heavier

than he had in weeks, but he hadn't seen Brer Rabbit's children since the town carnival. He leaped over. All the animals jumped over high and clear, except Brer Turtle, and nobody expected him to jump 'cause it was well known he didn't like rabbit meat.

So it was Brer Wolf's turn. He was trembling and was most sorry now he'd dug the pit so deep and the fire so high. He took a great long running start. By the time he got to where he was supposed to jump, he'd worn himself out. He jumped and landed right smack in the middle of the fire. All the animals knew then who'd done the deed, and not a tear was shed.

Brer Rabbit Catches Wattle Weasel

The animals were working on some project or other—building a Frisbee factory or something like that. Everyday when they came to work, they put their butter in the springhouse. And everyday when lunchtime came, they found that somebody had eaten their butter. They hid it every place in the springhouse they could think of. Didn't matter. Everyday the butter came up missing.

They did a little detective work and discovered Wattle Weasel's tracks around the springhouse. So they decided to take turns keeping watch.

Brer Mink had the first turn. He watched and he listened. He listened and he watched. He didn't see nothing. He didn't hear nothing. But he kept listening and watching because the animals had decided that if Wattle Weasel ate the butter while one of them was supposed to be watching, that animal couldn't have any butter for the rest of the year.

Brer Mink watched and waited. He watched, waited, and listened so long that he started getting cramps in his legs and the rheumeritis in his ears, and that was just about the time Wattle Weasel popped his head in the door.

"Hey, Brer Mink! What's happening? You look lonesome. Why don't you come out and play hide-and-go-seek with me?"

Brer Mink knew Wattle Weasel couldn't steal the butter if they were playing. They played until Brer Mink was totally exhausted, not to mention just plain tired. He flopped down on the ground, and Wattle Weasel dashed in the springhouse and ate all the butter. When the animals came to get their butter and found it gone, Brer Mink's butter-eating days had come to an end.

Next to stand guard was Brer Possum. He hadn't been there long before Wattle Weasel sneaked in. Wattle Weasel knew that the one thing Brer Possum couldn't stand was being tickled. He walked up to Brer Possum and started tickling him in the short ribs. Brer Possum giggled. Wattle Weasel kept tickling him, and Brer Possum kept laughing until he was lying on the floor panting for air. Wattle Weasel ate all the butter in peace. That was the end of Brer Possum's butter-licking days.

It was Brer Coon's turn next. Wattle Weasel came in the door and challenged him to a footrace. Brer Coon loved to run, and off they went. They ran and ran until Brer Coon was so tired he couldn't twitch a toe. But Wattle

Weasel could. Back to the springhouse he went and ate up the butter. Brer Coon sho' was going to miss eating butter.

Brer Fox was next in line to watch. Wattle Weasel was afraid of him, and it took a while to figure out how to handle him. He went down to Mr. Man's chicken coop, let all the chickens out, and drove them up to the springhouse. When Brer Fox saw all them nice fat hens, he couldn't help himself, and he dashed out to grab as many as he could. Wattle Weasel went in and ate the butter. Brer Fox joined them that were going to be eating dry toast.

Brer Wolf announced that he was the man for the job. He was setting in the springhouse when he heard some talking outside.

"I wonder who put that lamb down there by the chinkapin tree, and I'd sho' like to know where Brer Wolf is," Brer Wolf heard somebody say.

Brer Wolf tore out the door and headed for the chinkapin tree. When he got there, no lamb was in sight, and when he got back to the springhouse, neither was the butter. So he got marked down.

The next day Brer Bear had hardly taken his seat before Wattle Weasel sauntered in. "Thought I heard you snorting in here, Brer Bear. How you today?"

Brer Bear didn't say a word but kept a close eye on Wattle Weasel.

"You got any ticks on you, Brer Bear?" Before Brer Bear could answer, Wattle Weasel began to rub Brer Bear's back and scratch his sides. When it comes to back rubs, Brer Bear is kinna like my wife. Give that woman a back rub and you can near 'bout get anything you want. Brer Bear just relaxed, grinned, and before long his snoring sounded like a bunch of airplanes going off to war. Wattle Weasel ate the butter. When Brer Bear woke up, he knew his butter-eating days were a thing of the past.

The animals didn't know what to do. They talked about it for a while and decided there was only one thing to do: Send for Brer Rabbit.

A delegation went over to pay a call on him. They laid out the problem, and it took some talking before he was convinced that this wasn't some trick to catch him. Finally he agreed.

Brer Rabbit got a long piece of string, went to the springhouse, and hid up in the rafters. He hadn't been there long before Wattle Weasel came creeping in. He looked around, didn't see anybody, and just as he started to nibble the butter, Brer Rabbit hollered, "Let that butter alone!"

Wattle Weasel jumped back like the butter had burnt his tongue. "Brer Rabbit?"

"Who else? You let that butter alone!"

"Let me get one little teenichy taste, Brer Rabbit."

"Let that butter alone, I said."

Wattle Weasel pretended like he didn't want the butter anyway and suggested that he and Brer Rabbit run a race.

"I'm tired."

"Let's play hide-and-go-seek, then," Wattle Weasel said eagerly.

"I'm too old for that."

They talked back and forth for a while about what they could do, and finally Brer Rabbit had a suggestion. "Let's tie our tails together, and then we'll see whose is strongest."

Wattle Weasel had never played that game before, so he was agreeable. They tied each other's tails to the ends of a string, with Wattle Weasel inside the springhouse and Brer Rabbit outside. Soon as Wattle Weasel started to pull, Brer Rabbit slipped the string off his tail and tied it around a tree. Wattle Weasel pulled and pulled and strained and strained. Finally he hollered out, "Come and untie me, Brer Rabbit. Looks like our match is a draw. I can't outpull you and you can't outpull me."

Brer Rabbit pretended like he didn't hear him. After a while all the animals came because they were afraid Brer Rabbit had gone into cahoots with Wattle Weasel, and they would have to worry about two folks taking their butter. When they got there, Brer Rabbit was sitting outside filing his nails with an emery board, and Wattle Weasel was inside, tied by his tail.

That was one time the animals appreciated Brer Rabbit for being smarter than they were.

Brer Rabbit and Mr. Man's Chickens

Mr. Man had the nicest chickens anybody had ever seen. They looked ready for the frying pan without even taking their feathers off.

When the animals saw Mr. Man's chickens, they got friendly with him in a hurry. Every Sunday they came over, and Mr. Man didn't have no more sense than to show off his chickens. He took the animals into the chicken yard, and it was all they could do to control themselves. Brer Wolf's jaw trembled like he had the palsy. Brer Fox drooled like a teething baby. Brer Rabbit laughed like he had the hysterics and ought to be locked up somewhere.

One night when the moon wasn't shining, Brer Rabbit decided to call on Mr. Man. When he got there, all the lights were out. The dog was curled up under the house snoring almost as loud as Mr. Man.

"Something's wrong," Brer Rabbit said softly to himself. "Everytime I come over here, Mr. Man takes me in the chicken yard and shows me his chickens. Wonder is something wrong with him. I bet something done happened and nobody told me about it 'cause they knew how sorry I would be. If I could get in, I could see if everything was all right."

Brer Rabbit walked around the house and peeped in all the windows but didn't see anybody. "I bet if Mr. Man knew I was here, he'd come out and show me his chickens. So I might as well go make sure that they're all right."

He went to the chicken house, and lo and behold the door was unlocked. Brer Rabbit grinned. "Mr. Man must've known I was coming and left the chicken house unlocked so I could go in and admire his chickens."

He went inside. "It's on the chilly side tonight, and I'm worried that these chickens might get cold and freeze to death. If I'd been thinking, I would've brought a bag with me, and they could've used it for an overcoat." Then he looked down at his hands. "I don't know what's the matter with me! I got a bag right here in my hands and forgot that I had it. The chickens are lucky that I brought it. They would've frozen to death out here tonight."

Brer Rabbit proceeded to fill his sack with chickens. He was amazed that the sack didn't get full until every one of Mr. Man's chickens was inside. He took the chickens home, and him, Miz Rabbit, and the little rabbits spent the rest of that night cleaning them.

"Let's burn these feathers in the fire," Miz Rabbit said when they were finally done.

Brer Rabbit shook his head. "Whole neighborhood would smell them. I got a better idea."

He put all the feathers in the sack and, the next morning, went off down the road to Brer Fox's house.

Brer Fox was sitting on the porch. They exchanged how-do's and all the pertinent news about their families.

"Where you going, Brer Rabbit?"

"If I had enough wind, I'd be going to the mill, but this sack is so heavy, I ain't sure I'm going to make it. I ain't strong in the back and limber in the knees like I used to be. To tell the truth, I'm on the downgrade." Brer Rabbit let the sack drop to the ground.

"What you got? Corn or wheat?"

"Neither," Brer Rabbit said like he didn't want to tell. "Just some stuff to sell to the miller."

"Well, what is it?"

Brer Rabbit looked around as if he wanted to be sure nobody could overhear him. "Promise you won't tell a soul?"

"Promise," said Brer Fox.

"I got a sack full of winniannimus grass. They paying nine dollars a pound at the mill."

If Brer Fox hadn't been awake before, he was now. He came down and lifted the bag. "Feels light to me."

"Of course it feels light to a big strong man like you. To a little fella like me that's a heavy load."

Brer Fox swelled up with pride. "Well, I'll tote the bag to the mill for you if you want, Brer Rabbit."

"I sho' do appreciate it, Brer Fox."

Off they went down the road.

"Tell me, Brer Rabbit. What do they do with winnian-nimus grass after it's ground up?"

"Rich folks buys it to make whipmewhopme pudding."

After they'd been traveling for a while, Brer Rabbit looked back and saw Mr. Man coming and he was coming fast! "Brer Fox? You 'bout the movingest man I know. You done plumb wore me out, and I needs a little rest. You go on and I'll catch up with you. If I don't, wait for me at the mill."

"You take all the rest you need, Brer Rabbit."

Brer Fox went on, and Brer Rabbit sat down beside the road.

Not too many minutes passed before Mr. Man came up. "Who's that up ahead with that sack on his back?" he wanted to know, and he didn't ask too politely either.

"Brer Fox."

"What's he got in that bag?"

Brer Rabbit shrugged. "He said it was some kind of grass he was taking to the mill to get ground. But I saw some chicken feathers sticking through the bag, so I ain't sure what's in there."

"That's the man I'm looking for," said Mr. Man. "I'm going to make him sorry that he even knows what a chicken is."

Mr. Man went after Brer Fox, and Brer Rabbit ducked around through the woods and followed.

"What you got in the bag, Brer Fox?" Mr. Man asked when he caught up to him.

"Winniannimus grass. I'm taking it to the mill to get it ground. The rich folks make whipmewhopme pudding from it."

"I ain't never seen no winniannimus grass. What does it look like?"

Brer Fox put the sack on the ground, opened it up. Just then a little gust of wind come up and blew chicken feathers so high in the air, it looked like snow was coming down.

Mr. Man yelled, "Whipmewhopme pudding! I'm going to whip you and whop you and make pudding out of you!"

He grabbed Brer Fox and whipped him and whopped
him until Brother Sun was running over to the other side
of the world to get away from Sister Moon, who was intent on marrying him. And Brer Rabbit just laughed and
laughed and laughed.

The Barbecue

Mr. Man not only had some nice chickens, but he also had
the prettiest garden you'd ever want to see. Everybody came
to see it. Some looked over the fence and admired it. Some

peeped through the cracks in the fence and ooohed and aaahed. Then, there was Brer Rabbit. He preferred starlight, moonlight, cloudlight, and nightlight.

So there was Mr. Man; there was Mr. Man's garden; there was Brer Rabbit; and finally there was nightlight. That's a powerful combination, and there was only one thing that could happen.

One morning Mr. Man went to admire his garden, and wasn't too much to admire. All the cabbage was gone. All the turnips were gone, the carrots and the mustard greens too. He was so mad that he almost didn't see the rabbit tracks in the dust. That was about the only thing Brer Rabbit didn't take with him.

Mr. Man called up his hunting dogs and set 'em out hunting for Brer Rabbit. Brer Rabbit hadn't made it home yet, and he heard the dogs yipping and barking, and he started running. He ran around in circles and triangles and trapezoids and got them dogs so confused they didn't know where they were.

Brer Rabbit flopped under a shade tree and started fanning himself, and before long Brer Fox came by.

"What's going on, Brer Rabbit? I thought I heard a lot of dogs barking."

Brer Rabbit shrugged. "Mr. Man is having a big barbecue down to the creek. I told him I didn't want to come, but he says I gotta and set the dogs to running me there." He shook his head. "It's a problem being so popular. If you want to go to the barbecue, just get out there in the road and start running, and the dogs'll run you right to it."

Brer Fox started dribbling at the mouth and took off down the road. He was hardly out of sight before Brer

Wolf came up. Brer Rabbit told him the news about the barbecue, and off he went. The dust from his feet hadn't settled before Brer Bear came along. Well, when he heard about Mr. Man's special barbecue sauce and the juice oozing out of the meat, he took off. Brer Rabbit was watching him wobbling down the road when here come Brer Coon, and Brer Rabbit told him about the barbecue, and he was off and running too.

Well, when the dogs saw all the animals running along the road, they forgot all about Brer Rabbit and took off chasing the animals, and who knows where everybody ended up.

And that just goes to show you: When you get invited to a barbecue, you better find out when and where it's at and who's doing the barbecuing!

Brer Alligator Learns About Trouble

One day Brer Dog was after Brer Rabbit. I don't know what the trouble was, but Brer Dog ran through the woods, down the gully, up the other side, and over the gully, over the hill, and down to the creek, where Brer Rabbit ducked into a hole in the creek bank. Brer Dog came to a screeching halt. He sniffed around for a while but couldn't find him. Finally Brer Dog gave up and left, feeling pretty good. He'd given Brer Rabbit a run he wouldn't forget for a long time.

After Brer Dog left, Brer Rabbit crawled out of the hole and flopped down on the bank. He was huffing and blowing, trying to get his breath back, when Brer Alligator swam over.

"What's happening, Brer Rabbit? How come you huffing and puffing so hard?"

Brer Rabbit sat up and shook his head. "I been having trouble, Brer Alligator. Brer Dog was running me."

Brer Alligator chuckled. "I done got fat on trouble like that. I be glad to hear Brer Dog bark if he bring me that kind of trouble." He crawled out of the creek and lay down next to Brer Rabbit.

"Hold on there, Brer Alligator. When trouble come visiting, he makes your sides puff, and your breath come so fast you can't keep up with it."

Brer Alligator twitched his tail, stretched, and laughed. "Nothing don't bother me. I catch shrimp. I catch crab. I make my bed when the sun is shining hot. Yes, Brer Rabbit, I enjoy myself! I be proud to see trouble."

"I wouldn't be too sure about that if I was you. Trouble come upon you when you have your eyes shut; he come on you from the side you can't see. He don't come on you in the creek, he come on you in the broom grass."

"If he do, I'll shake his hand and tell him howdy."

Brer Rabbit was getting a little angry. "You can laugh at me, but you won't laugh when trouble comes."

Brer Alligator began to get sleepy. He nodded off, and his head dropped down, down, down until the grass began tickling his nose. He woke up, coughing and sneezing so hard that he almost blew all the water out of the creek.

This was obviously not a good spot for a nap, so he crawled to a nice open place of broom grass. He stretched out, closed his eyes, opened his mouth, and was asleep, just like that.

Brer Alligator slept. Brer Rabbit watched. In a few minutes Brer Alligator started snoring, and Brer Rabbit was sorry he hadn't thought to bring his earmuffs. After a while Brer Alligator started twitching in his sleep, and Brer Rabbit knew he was dreaming.

"This day I'm going to make you know trouble," Brer Rabbit said to himself. *"I'm going to make you know trouble very, very well, Brer Alligator."*

And with that Brer Rabbit proceeded to set the broom grass on fire.

Brer Alligator was dreaming hard now. His tail was flopping, and his body was twitching, and the broom grass was burning, burning, burning. Brer Alligator started dreaming that the sun was very, very hot, that it was warming his back, warming his stomach, warming his feet. Brer Alligator twitched and squirmed. Suddenly his eyes opened, and all around him was fire, fire, fire.

He ran to the north. Fire! He ran to the south. Fire! He ran to the east and to the west. Fire and more fire! "Trouble, trouble, trouble! *Trouble, trouble!*"

Brer Rabbit yelled, "Hey, Brer Alligator! What you mean, trouble?"

Brer Alligator lashed his tail. "Oh, my Lord! Trouble! *Trouble, trouble, trouble!*"

"Shake his hand, Brer Alligator! Tell him how do!"

"Oh, my Lord! *Trouble, trouble, trouble!*"

"Laugh with him, Brer Alligator! Laugh with him! Ask him how his health has been! You said you wanted to make his acquaintance. Now you got to get to know him."

Brer Alligator got so mad that he dashed through the burning broom grass and scattered the fire, which got all on his back. He dove into the creek, and the water hissed 'cause he was so hot. His tail shriveled up, and his back shriveled up. And they've stayed shriveled up to this very day. That's the reason the alligator has bumps on his back and his tail.

Of course, I reckon it goes without saying that any possibility of friendship between Brer Alligator and Brer Rabbit ended that day.

Brer Fox Gets Tricked Again

Brer Fox and Brer Rabbit were walking down the road one afternoon when Brer Fox saw some tracks in the dirt.

"Hold up, Brer Rabbit! Looks to me like Brer Dog been along here and not too long ago."

Brer Rabbit looked at the tracks. "That track ain't fit Brer Dog no time in world history. If I ain't mistaken, these tracks belong to Cousin Wildcat. I ain't seen him since I was a little cottontail."

"How big is he, Brer Rabbit?"

"He's about your size, I reckon. I remember when I was just a young'un, I saw my granddaddy beat up on Cousin Wildcat so bad, it made me feel sorry for him." Brer Rabbit chuckled. "If you want to have some fun, Brer Fox, that's some fun!"

Brer Fox wanted to know what kind of fun Brer Rabbit was talking about.

"Simple. Just go tackle Cousin Wildcat and knock him around some."

Brer Fox scratched his ear. "I don't know. His tracks are too much like Brer Dog for me. And I ain' never had no fun with Brer Dog, and he done had a lot with me."

Brer Rabbit looked disgusted. "Brer Fox? I'd never have thought a man like you would've been scared."

Brer Fox couldn't admit he was scared, so he went with Brer Rabbit to find Cousin Wildcat. They followed the tracks up the road, down the lane, across the turnip patch, and down a dreen. Don't come asking me what a dreen is. It's in the story that they went down a dreen, so that's what they did. And after they went down the dreen, they went up a big gully.

Finally they found Cousin Wildcat.

"Hey!" Brer Rabbit called out. "What you doing?"

Cousin Wildcat looked at him but didn't say a word.

"Ain't you got no manners? We'll teach you some manners if you not careful. Now, answer my question. What you doing?"

Cousin Wildcat rubbed himself against a tree just like a house cat rubs against the leg of a chair. He still don't say nothing.

"Why you want to pester us when we ain't been pestering you? I know you! You the same Cousin Wildcat what my granddaddy used to kick and beat. I got somebody here who's a better man than my granddaddy ever dreamed of being! I bet he'll make you talk."

Cousin Wildcat bristled up, but he still don't say a word.

"Go on, Brer Fox! Slap him down! That's what my granddaddy would've done. If he tries to run, I'll grab him."

Brer Fox wasn't none too eager, but he started toward the creature. Cousin Wildcat walked around the tree, rubbing himself, but he still don't say nothing.

"Slap him down, Brer Fox! Slap him down! If he tries to run, I'll catch him."

Brer Fox moved a little closer, and Cousin Wildcat stood up on his hind legs, his paws in the air. But he still don't say nothing.

"Don't you try that old trick, Cousin Wildcat! You fooled my granddaddy that way one time, but you can't fool us. Begging ain't going to help you. Pop him one, Brer Fox! If he runs, I'll catch him."

Brer Fox saw the creature looking humble, sitting up like he was begging for mercy, and he took heart. He marched up to Cousin Wildcat, and just as he was getting ready to pop him one, Cousin Wildcat hit Brer Fox in the stomach.

Brer Fox hollered so loud, four trees fell down, and the pictures on everybody's TV sets got fuzzy and stayed that way for a week. Brer Fox hit the ground, his arms wrapped around his stomach.

"Hit him again, Brer Fox! Hit him again! I'm backing you up! If he tries to get past me, I'll cripple him! Hit him again!"

But Brer Fox just lay there and moaned. Cousin Wildcat turned and walked away like he was the king of the mountain.

Brer Rabbit ran over to Brer Fox. "You had him and you let him get away!" And he ran on home, laughing all the way.

Brer Rabbit and Brer Bullfrog

Brer Bullfrog was the biggest nuisance in the whole community. He is the man what invented staying up late and carrying on. All night long and every night long Brer Bullfrog and his kin were up talking and arguing and singing and carrying on something outrageous. All the animals moved out of the neighborhood to get away from him. Next thing they knew, here come Brer Bullfrog saying he was lonesome.

Every night when folks had just got sleep good, Brer Bullfrog would start up: *"Here I is! Here I is! Where is you? Where is you? Come along! Come along!"*

The only one who didn't care was Brer Rabbit. Anything that upset the other animals was fine with him. And to tell the truth, Brer Rabbit liked to be out and about at night. So between Brer Bullfrog bellowing all night long and Brer Rabbit laughing all night long, the animals gave up and learned to sleep as best they could.

Well, this particular time Brer Rabbit noticed that he was just about out of calamus root, and the only place where it grew was down near where Brer Bullfrog lived.

Brer Rabbit hadn't been gathering the root long when Brer Bullfrog started up. Brer Rabbit had never heard Brer Bullfrog close up before, and he decided right quick that a little bit of Brer Bullfrog's music would last a lifetime.

"Where you going? Where you going? Don't go too far! Don't go too far! Come back soon! Come back soon!"

Brer Rabbit didn't have no intention of coming back. He'd have to see how cooking tasted without calamus root.

"Be my friend! Be my friend!"

Brer Rabbit tried to ignore Brer Frog.

"Jug of rum! Jug of rum! Wade in here and I'll give you some!"

That got Brer Rabbit's attention. He liked a little taste of rum every now and then, so he went down to the edge of the pond to look and see if there was a jug of rum setting on the bottom. The water looked mighty cold and very deep. It was going *lap-lap,* and Brer Rabbit had about decided to leave the jug where it was when, suddenly, he was in the water! He never knew if he slipped, fell, or got pushed. But he did know that he was in the water. He splashed and kicked and spluttered and finally hauled himself out. Day-old dishwater looked better than he did.

He sneezed and he snozed and snozed and sneezed, and so much water was pouring off him, he looked like a rainstorm.

If that wasn't bad enough, he had to listen to Brer Bullfrog laughing. Brer Rabbit drug himself home to dry off.

The next morning Brer Rabbit went to work, and I don't

mean no job. He went to work keeping an eye on Brer Bullfrog. He knew that when winter came, Brer Bullfrog had to move out of the pond before it froze over. And the day Brer Bullfrog moved would be the day he wished he hadn't.

Every day, all day, Brer Rabbit followed Brer Bullfrog around. Finally, one chilly morning, Brer Bullfrog come walking along the path in his Sunday best. He had on a little soldier hat with green and white speckles all over it, a long green coat, white satin britches, a white silk vest, and shoes with silver buckles. He was carrying a green umbrella, and he put the umbrella cover on his tail to keep it from dragging on the ground and getting dirty.

Now, just a minute! Don't be telling me that frogs ain't got tails. They ain't got tails *now,* which is how come we got this story. Back before my great-granddaddy's great-granddaddy's mamma's time frogs had tails, and you're about to find out how come they ain't got 'em no more.

Well, like I was saying, Brer Bullfrog was coming along the path going to his winter place when Brer Rabbit jumped out in front of him. Brer Rabbit looked at Brer Bullfrog, trembled like he was scared, and scurried off in the bushes.

Brer Bullfrog laughed and decided to have a little fun. He shook his umbrella at Brer Rabbit and hollered, "Where's my gun?"

Brer Rabbit came out of the bushes with both hands up in the air. Then he turned and ran.

"Come here, you rascal! Let me give you the whupping you deserve!"

Brer Bullfrog chased after him, and Brer Rabbit led him to a hollow tree where he had hidden an ax. Brer Rabbit grabbed the ax and ducked out the other side. Brer Bull-

frog ran into the tree. Brer Rabbit went around the tree, and when he saw Brer Bullfrog's tail sticking out of the hole—*whack! whack! whack!*

Well, that just took all the starch out of Brer Bullfrog. He ain't been himself from that day to this. And from that day to this frogs ain't had tails.

Brer Rabbit Meets Up with Cousin Wildcat

About a week later Brer Rabbit was galloping down the road—*clickety-clickety, clickety-lickety*—when something dropped out of the sky and grabbed him. It only took his mind a twitch to realize that it was Cousin Wildcat, who had been sitting up in a tree when he heard Brer Rabbit lickety-clickety down the road.

Cousin Wildcat hugged Brer Rabbit right close. Brer Rabbit started to kick and squall. Cousin Wildcat rubbed his wet nose in Brer Rabbit's ear. A cold chill went up and down Brer Rabbit's spine.

"Brer Rabbit, I just naturally love you," he whispered in his ear. "You been fooling with me. Your granddaddy fooled with me. And it wasn't so long ago that you tried to put Brer Fox on me." He chuckled way down deep in his throat. "Brer Rabbit, I just naturally love you." He laughed again, and his long teeth grazed Brer Rabbit's ears.

"Look here, Cousin Wildcat. I didn't put Brer Fox on you. I thought you'd want him for supper. If you can't understand that, ain't no point in you and me being friends."

Cousin Wildcat wiped his nose on Brer Rabbit's ear, but Brer Rabbit kept talking.

"Tell the truth, Cousin Wildcat. During all these years have I personally ever pestered you?"

Cousin Wildcat thought for a minute. "Can't say that you have."

"I know I ain't, and what's more, I have done my best down through the years to help you out. Now, even though you jumped down out of that tree on me and scared me so much that I was afraid my cottontail was going to drop off, I'm willing to do you another favor."

"What's that?"

"There's some wild turkeys not too far from here. Let's go over there, and I'll shoo them in your direction. You lay down on the ground like you dead, and when the turkeys come to investigate, you can jump up and catch a whole slew of them."

When they got to the place, Cousin Wildcat lay down in the clearing and pretended he was dead. Brer Rabbit went and found the turkeys. It was Brer Gibley Gobbler and all his kin. Brer Rabbit got in behind them and ran 'em toward Cousin Wildcat.

The turkeys stopped when they saw Cousin Wildcat. They stretched their necks and looked at him. Some said he was dead. Others said he wasn't. They gobbled back and forth, but they didn't get too close.

Cousin Wildcat lay there like he was dead. The wind ruffled his hair, but he didn't move. The sun shone down on him, but he didn't move. The turkeys gobbled and gobbled and stretched their necks. Then they gobbled some more. They stood on one foot and then the other, but they kept their distance.

It was too much for Cousin Wildcat. He jumped at one of the turkeys. The turkey flew up in the air, and Cousin Wildcat ran under him. He ran at another turkey. It rose up in the air, and Cousin Wildcat ran under him. He kept running and leaping, and the turkeys kept flying up in the air until Cousin Wildcat was stiff in his joints, out of breath, and just plain humiliated. He fell over on the ground, and Brer Gibley Gobbler got his kin away from there.

And to this day when you hear turkeys gobbling, they be talking about what happened way back there in the ancient times when Cousin Wildcat tried to catch them.

Brer Rabbit Gets a Little Comeuppance

Once a year all the animals got together for their political convention. This was when they went over all their laws to see if any needed to be thrown out, or if they should make some new ones. They made highfaluting speeches and generally enjoyed piling words on top of words like they was afraid language was going out of fashion.

This particular year Brer Rabbit was sitting next to Brer Dog. Everytime Brer Dog opened his mouth to make a speech, Brer Rabbit couldn't help noticing how strong his teeth looked and how bright and white they shone. It made him kind of nervous.

Everytime Brer Dog said something, Brer Rabbit jumped and twitched. All the animals noticed and started laughing at Brer Rabbit.

Brer Dog thought they were laughing at him. He started

growling and snapping. Brer Rabbit ducked under the chair. This made the animals laugh even more, and that made Brer Dog madder. He started howling, and Brer Rabbit shook like he'd caught a chill.

After a while Brer Dog quieted down, and Brer Rabbit eased out from under the chair. He got around among the other animals and began to do some politicking. "We ought to pass a law to make all the animals what eat with their teeth eat with their claws."

Brer Wolf, Brer Fox, and Brer Dog didn't like that idea one bit. So the law didn't pass. Next day Brer Rabbit started politicking again.

"Have you seen them teeth on Brer Dog? He got teeth like knives. We got to have a law to sew Brer Dog's mouth up. There's no telling what he might do with them teeth."

Now, that was a law Brer Wolf and Brer Fox could go along with. Brer Dog had chased them from can to can't on more than one occasion.

The law was passed. The day came for Brer Dog's mouth to be sewed up. Brer Lion was chairing the meeting, and he wanted to know who was going to sew up Brer Dog's mouth.

Brer Fox said, "The man what proposed the law ought to be the man to do the deed."

Brer Dog was laying over in the corner sharpening his teeth on a dinosaur bone. The animals looked at him and knew they weren't getting anywheres near him. They looked at Brer Rabbit.

He gave a little dry grin. "I'd sho' do it, but I ain't got a needle."

Brer Fox reached in the flap of his coat collar. "I got a big one right here, Brer Rabbit!"

Brer Rabbit gave another little grin. "Needle ain't no good without thread."

Brer Bear pulled a loose thread from his big ol' coat. "Here's some thread, Brer Rabbit."

Brer Rabbit said, "Thank you. I'd sho' appreciate it if you gentlemen would hold on to that needle and thread for me. I'm just sorry this matter didn't come up sooner 'cause this is the time of day I always take my walk."

And he tipped on out. The animals laughed at Brer Rabbit a long time about that one.

Brer Rabbit Advises Brer Lion

Brer Rabbit happened to see Brer Lion a week or so later. After they exchanged news about their families and what all, Brer Rabbit said, "Brer Lion, the times is changing."

"What you mean?"

"I'm moving back up in the hills, where it won't be so easy to find me."

"How come, Brer Rabbit? Something terrible must be happening for you to leave out of here."

Brer Rabbit nodded. "I've got to get away from Mr. Man."

Brer Lion laughed. "Mr. Man? You scared of Mr. Man? You got to be joking with me."

Brer Rabbit shook his head. "I'm not joking, Brer Lion."

Brer Lion roared. "I'm not scared of Mr. Man. I'll have Mr. Man for dinner if I come across him."

"Don't be too sure about that. Mr. Man got something

called a gun. It's like a stick, excepting he raises it up to his eye, points it at you, and goes *bang!* one time, and you get hit in the head. He go *bang!* a second time, and you get cripple in the leg."

Brer Lion laughed. "I'll take Mr. Man's gun, throw it away, and have Mr. Man for breakfast."

"Well, I tell you the truth. I'm scared."

Brer Lion said, "I can understand how you feel 'cause I'm scared of Miz Partridge."

Brer Rabbit couldn't believe his ears. "You scared of the wrong one, Brer Lion. Miz Partridge flies away if you wink at her. I'm not scared of Miz Partridge."

"Well, once I was walking along the road, and just as I went past some bushes, Miz Partridge flew up—*fud-d-d-d-d-e-c!* It liked to scared me to death."

Brer Rabbit shook his head. "Don't know about you, Brer Lion. You scared of what can't hurt you, and ain't scared of what can."

A few weeks went by, and Brer Rabbit was out walking one day when he heard a loud moaning sound. He went to investigate and found Brer Lion laying on the ground, moaning and groaning and crying. He had a hole in his head and three holes in his side.

Brer Rabbit looked at him. "Look like Miz Partridge done hurt you very bad, Brer Lion."

Brer Lion moaned and groaned and cried. "It wasn't Miz Partridge. It was Mr. Man with his gun."

Brer Rabbit nodded sadly. "That's what I tried to tell you, Brer Lion. Miz Partridge could *scare* you, but she couldn't hurt you. That's just what I was trying to tell you."

But it was too late for Brer Lion to learn that lesson.

Brer Rabbit's Money Mint

Brer Fox and Brer Rabbit were standing by the road talking about much of nothing. Brer Rabbit said that he was feeling between *My gracious!* and *Thank gracious!* Brer Fox say he know what he mean.

Brer Fox heard something rattling in Brer Rabbit's pocket. "Ain't that money I hear you rattling?"

Brer Rabbit shrugged. "Just small change." He took out a big handful of money. It was shining so bright that Brer Sun had to put on his sunglasses to keep from going blind.

"Where did you get it?"

"From where they make it at. The mint."

"Where's that at, Brer Rabbit?"

"In this place and that place. Over yonder and over here. You got to learn to keep your eyes open, Brer Fox."

"Learn me, Brer Rabbit! Please learn me!"

Brer Rabbit shook his head. "If I learn you, the next thing I know, word be spread all over the community, and I can't have that."

"I swear to you that I won't breathe a word to a soul."

Brer Rabbit thought about it for a minute, then shrugged. "All right. Ain't nothing to it. You just watch the road until you see a wagon come along. If it's the right kind of wagon, it's got two wheels in the front and two wheels in the back. And if you look real close, you'll notice that the wheels in the front are smaller than the ones in the back. Now, when you see that, what does it make you think of?"

Brer Fox thought and thought, but being as how he was kinna poor in the thinking department, he finally said, "I don't know, Brer Rabbit."

Brer Rabbit looked at Brer Fox like he was dumb as hog slop. "It's simple. After the wagon goes on for a ways, them big back wheels has got to catch up with them little front wheels. Common sense ought to tell you that."

Brer Fox nodded. "That's sho' the truth, ain't it?"

"Well, when the big back wheels catch up to the little front wheels, them wheels going to grind together. When that happens, all that brand-new money is going to fall out of the wagon."

Brer Fox clapped his hands. "And that's all there is to it?"

"That's it, Brer Fox. Next time you see a wagon going by, you call me if you don't want to follow along with it. I don't mind taking the money what drops down."

Well, along about then what do you think they heard? That's right! A wagon!

"I'll take this wagon, Brer Rabbit."

Brer Rabbit shrugged. "Help yourself. I got to be getting on home anyway."

Brer Rabbit left, but he circled back to watch Brer Fox. Sure enough, when the wagon passed, Brer Fox started galloping alongside, waiting for the back wheels to catch up to the front wheels. Some folks say he's galloping still.

Brer Rabbit Makes a Deal with Mr. Man

Mr. Man was going around his farm one day when he noticed that a pig was missing. Day after that a duck was missing. The day after that a chicken was gone.

Mr. Man might not have been the smartest person on the top side of the earth, but he knew something was going on. He made a trap and put a chicken in it.

First thing next morning Mr. Man went to see about his trap. In it was Brer Fox and a whole bunch of chicken feathers.

Brer Fox gave one of his little dry grins. "You probably won't believe this, but I was passing by on my way home last night and heard a chicken hollering and fluttering. I came in to see what was the matter. As I came in, the chicken went out and shut the door, leaving all these feathers behind."

Mr. Man gave a little grunt. "If that chicken hollered right now, I bet she would scare you."

"How so?"

" 'Cause she so close to you."

Mr. Man got a rope, tied Brer Fox tightly, and then took him home and hung him on a nail on the wall. "Keep your eye on him until I get back," Mr. Man told his wife.

Mr. Man's wife was shelling peas.

"That's a lot of peas you got to shell," Brer Fox offered.

"You said a mouthful."

Brer Fox had been tricked by Brer Rabbit so many times that he was bound to learn something about scheming. "If you'll untie me and take me down from here, I'll shell them peas for you, and you can be fixing the rest of the dinner. And when I'm done, you can tie me again and hang me back on the wall."

The woman shook her head. Brer Fox kept on talking and he talked sweet and he talked low and he talked so much stuff that Mr. Man's wife decided that he couldn't be as bad as her husband thought. So she took him down and untied him.

Brer Fox started shelling peas. The woman stirred her stew. Brer Fox kept one eye on her. She kept one eye on him. They kept eyeing each other until suddenly Brer Fox made a break for the door. The woman was just a little quicker. She slammed the door shut, grabbed a stick, and started chasing Brer Fox around the room. Brer Fox dashed up the chimney, and as he did so, he turned over the pot of stew, which put out the fire and scalded the woman's foot. She screamed, and Brer Fox got away from there.

When Mr. Man came home, he wasn't none too happy when he found out what had happened. He yelled at the woman, and she started crying. He kept on yelling until she got mad: "What you mean calling me an airhead for letting Brer Fox get away? You the one got more holes in your head than Swiss cheese. If you'd had any sense, you would've killed that fox when you had him. Now you want to blame it on me, and I ain't taking the heavy for this one!"

Mr. Man had to admit that his wife had a point. He apologized and took a walk in the field. He was feeling mighty bad about everything.

Brer Rabbit was taking his evening stroll when he saw Mr. Man sitting on a fence like he didn't have a friend in the world. Brer Rabbit went over and asked what was the matter. Mr. Man told him. Brer Rabbit chuckled.

"Looks like Brer Fox done learned a thing or two from me. If I ain't careful, he gon' start thinking he's smart as me." He thought for a minute. "Mr. Man? How much will you give me if I make Brer Fox sorry for what he done to you and your wife?"

"Brer Rabbit, you can eat all the peanuts and all the cabbage in my garden that you want."

"And you won't set your dogs on me?"

"No, sir."

Brer Rabbit stuck out his hand, and they shook. "We got a deal."

He thought for a while longer. "I'm going to need some chicken gizzards."

Mr. Man got them and came back. "Anything else?"

"This is just fine. I be back in the morning to start in on your peanut patch."

Brer Rabbit put the chicken gizzards in a sack and started toward Brer Fox's house. He hadn't gone far when he came upon him. They exchanged all the news about their kin, but while they were doing this, Brer Fox was sniffing the air.

"Brer Rabbit, I believe I smell chicken gizzards."

"I reckon that's so, Brer Fox. I got some right here in this sack."

Brer Fox started licking his lips. "How many you got?"

"Somewhere between seven and eleven."

"What you planning on doing with 'em?"

"I'm going to give 'em to the man who helps me with my hay."

"Show me the hay!" Brer Fox exclaimed, jumping up in the air. "Show me the hay! I'll carry that hay anywheres you want."

So Brer Rabbit and Brer Fox went over to the hayfield. Brer Rabbit started loading hay on Brer Fox's back until he looked like a haystack with fox feet.

They started up the hill. Brer Rabbit took out his flint and steel and struck it on the hay.

"What's that noise?" Brer Fox wanted to know.

"Cricket."

The hay started to crackle and blaze.

"What's *that* noise?"

"Grasshopper singing."

The hay started to burn good.

"I smell smoke."

"Somebody's burning new ground."

"I sho' do feel hot."

"You working hard."

Before long the hay burned down on Brer Fox. He yelled and scooted out from under. He jumped; he twisted; he turned; he rolled, but that fire was just burning him. He ran to the creek and jumped in. When he came out, the hair was burned off his back and his hide was full of blisters.

That's just what he gets for not being patient and waiting until he could get away clean without scalding Mr. Man's wife.

Brer Rabbit Doctors Brer Fox's Burns

Brer Rabbit decided he wasn't done with Brer Fox. He got a string of red pepper, stewed it down with some hog fat and mutton suet. He picked out the pepper and let the fat and suet get cold and thick, spread it on a piece of rag, and set off for Brer Fox's house.

When he got close, he saw Brer Fox sitting on the porch looking miserable. Brer Rabbit started yelling, "Ointment! Salve for burns and blisters!" He walked past Brer Fox's house like he didn't see him.

"Brer Rabbit!" called Brer Fox.

Brer Rabbit kept walking.

"BRER RABBIT!"

Brer Rabbit turned around and looked at Brer Fox. Then he went on down the road like he hadn't seen him.

Brer Fox caught up with him. "Didn't you hear me calling you?"

Brer Rabbit whirled around, and he was angry! "What you want and make it quick! I ain't got time for the likes of you!"

Brer Fox was confused. "What you mad at me about?"

"What am I mad at you about? My hay, that's what! You said you was going to carry it up the hill for me."

"But, Brer Rabbit! You saw with your own eyes why I couldn't! The sun set the hay on fire. I was lucky to escape with my life."

Brer Rabbit thought for a minute. "Well, you sho' got the marks on your back. I thought you were playing one of your tricks on me. To tell the truth, my feelings were hurt."

Brer Fox was in so much misery, he didn't have time to be worrying about hurt feelings. "I heard you hollering that you got some salve for burns and blisters."

Brer Rabbit pulled out the rag. "This'll do the trick. Get your wife to spread it all over you as soon as you can."

Brer Fox took it and went home. Brer Rabbit hid in the bushes to watch. Hardly a minute passed before Brer Fox gave out with a scream that curdled all the milk for miles around. He bust through the door and in seven jumps was in the creek, and the creek was almost a mile away.

Brer Rabbit followed, and it was all he could do to keep from busting out laughing.

Brer Fox looked like a dolphin the way he was jumping up and down in the water.

"My goodness, Brer Fox! Is that a new style of fishing you doing?"

"Brer Rabbit! You done ruined me! That stuff you gave me was poison!"

Brer Rabbit looked astonished. "Did I gave you the wrong salve?" He looked in his pouch. "I'm so sorry, Brer Fox! Instead of giving you the n'yam-n'yam plaster, I gave you the n'yip-n'yip plaster. I must be losing all my seventy senses."

And he fell back in the weeds and laughed until he was sick.

Brer Fox Sets a Fire

Brer Fox decided he'd better let Brer Rabbit alone for a while. He was still mad, though, and if he couldn't get the best of Brer Rabbit, he'd do something to one of the other animals.

As he was walking down the road thinking these very thoughts, who should he see but Brer Turtle. If he could whup anybody, it had to be Brer Turtle.

"How you today, Brer Turtle?"

"Slow, Brer Fox. Mighty slow. Day in and day out I'm slow, and looks like I'm getting slower. How you today?"

"Fine, just fine. Say, Brer Turtle? Your eyes are red. How come?"

"It's on account of all the trouble I see. Trouble come and pile up on trouble."

Brer Fox laughed. "Listen here, Brer Turtle. You don't know what trouble is! If you want to see some trouble, you ought to come with me. I'll show you trouble!"

"Well, if you can show me worst trouble, I'm the one wants to glimpse it."

Brer Fox asked him if he had ever seen Ol' Boy. Brer Turtle said he hadn't, but he'd heard of him. Brer Fox said that Ol' Boy was the kind of trouble he was talking about.

"Let me see him," said Brer Turtle. "It'll make me feel better to see worse trouble than what I got."

"All right! Tell you what you do. Go lay down in that sagebrush field yonder, and before long you'll catch a glimpse of Ol' Boy."

When Brer Turtle had been sitting in the middle of the field for a while, Brer Fox set the field on fire. Fire was blazing up everywhere, and right there in the middle of it was po' Brer Turtle.

He started moving fast as he could to get away, and you know about how fast that was. But he was doing his best, and he stumbled across Brer Rabbit, who was asleep behind a log. Brer Rabbit woke up, looked around, and knew that they were going to be shaking hands with Ol' Boy if he didn't do something.

"What we gon' do, Brer Rabbit?"

"There's a big hollow stump right over here. Come on!"

Brer Rabbit carried him over to the stump, and they crawled in. Brer Rabbit went back to sleep so's he could finish his nap.

When the fire died down, Brer Turtle stuck his head up out of the stump. Brer Fox was at the edge of the field, craning his neck trying to see through the smoke. Brer

Rabbit woke up, saw Brer Fox, and hollered out like he was Brer Turtle: "Brer Fox! Oh, Brer Fox! Come here! Quick! I done caught Brer Rabbit!"

Without thinking Brer Fox started running across the field. It was still hot from the fire, and his feet were burnt almost to ashes. He hopped and screamed and jumped and ouched and rolled on the ground, which only made it worse. Finally he managed to get back on cool ground and started making his way home, hopping first on one foot and then the other. Brer Rabbit and Brer Turtle followed him all the way, laughing every step he took.

Brer Rabbit Builds a Tower

Well, the animals decided something had to be done about Brer Rabbit. They talked it over among themselves and agreed that from then on Brer Rabbit couldn't drink out of the same creek with them, walk the same road, or go washing in the same wash hole.

When Brer Rabbit saw the animals holding secret meetings, he knew that something was up, so he reinforced his house, put in some Plexiglass windows, new locks on the doors, and started building a steeple on top.

Folks wondered what he was up to, and some thought he was building his own church.

Brer Rabbit didn't pay 'em no mind. He hammered; he nailed; he knocked; he lammed! Folks hollered at him, but he wouldn't look up. He just worked from sunup to moonrise.

When he finished, he took a deep breath, wiped his brow, and went in the house. He got a long piece of thick rope and told his wife, "Put a kettle of water on the fire and stay close by. I'm going up to the steeple, and everything you hear me tell you not to do, you do!"

He went back up to his steeple, sat down in his rocking chair, and looked out over the landscape.

Wasn't long before the animals came to see what he was going to do next. He didn't do a thing except smoke his cigar and rock in his rocking chair.

Brer Turtle came along. "Hey, Brer Rabbit!" he hollered up. "What you doing way up in the elements like that?"

"Resting myself. Why don't you come up and visit, Brer Turtle?"

Brer Turtle shook his head. "Too far in the air for me. Why don't you come down? I'm afraid to shake hands with you that far up in the elements."

"Not so, Brer Turtle. Not so. Come on up." Brer Rabbit let down the rope. "Just grab on, and up you'll come, *linktum sinktum blinktum boo!*"

So Brer Turtle grabbed the rope in his mouth, and Brer Rabbit pulled him up. That was a sight to see, his little tail sticking out, his legs wiggling, and him spinning around in the air half-scared to death.

But he made it safe and sound, and Brer Rabbit offered him some lunch. When the other animals saw Brer Turtle and Brer Rabbit up there chewing and smacking their lips, they wanted to come up.

"Hey, Brer Rabbit!" called out Brer Wolf. "How you doing?"

"Not too good," responded Brer Rabbit. "But I thank the Lord that I'm still able to chew my food. Why don't you come on up, Brer Wolf?"

"Don't mind if I do."

Brer Rabbit let down the rope. Brer Wolf caught hold, and Brer Rabbit started to haul him up.

"Stir 'round, ol' woman, and set the table. But before you do that, get the kettle to make the coffee."

Brer Wolf wondered what Brer Rabbit was talking about.

Brer Rabbit pulled on the rope until Brer Wolf was just opposite the upstairs bedroom window of the house.

"Watch out there, ol' woman! Don't spill all that hot

boiling water on Brer Wolf!"

Brer Wolf didn't hear another word because Miz Rabbit threw the kettle of boiling water out the window on him. Brer Wolf hollered and fell to the ground—*ka-boom*!

Brer Rabbit looked down from the steeple and apologized, but all the apologies in the world wasn't going to make hair grow back on Brer Wolf.

Brer Rabbit Saves Brer Wolf—Maybe

Brer Wolf had to go away to get himself a wolf wig, so Brer Rabbit decided it was safe to come out of his steeple. He was so happy to be out that he got dressed up and strutted down the road like he'd just discovered where the lights go when you turn 'em out.

He hadn't gone far when he heard somebody hollering: "Oh, Lordy! Won't somebody help me!"

Brer Rabbit turned this way and that trying to figure out where it was coming from.

"Help! Please help me, somebody!"

"Where you at?" Brer Rabbit called back.

"Help! Please help me! I'm down here in the gully underneath a great big rock!"

Brer Rabbit ran down to the gully, and there, under a great big rock, was none other than Brer Wolf! The sweat was pouring off him, and he looked pitiful. Not liking to see somebody in trouble that he hadn't put 'em in, Brer Rabbit felt sorry for Brer Wolf.

It took him a while, but he finally managed to roll the

rock off. Brer Wolf was hurt more in his feelings than any place else, and it occurred to him that he probably wouldn't ever have a better chance to grab Brer Rabbit. So that was what he did!

Brer Rabbit kicked and squealed, and the more he kicked, the tighter Brer Wolf squeezed his neck.

"Is this the way you thank a body for saving your life?"

Brer Wolf grinned. "I'll thank you, and then I'll make fresh meat out of you."

"If you talk that way, I'll never do you another good turn as long as I live."

Brer Wolf grinned some more. "You spoke truth that time, Brer Rabbit. You won't do me another good turn until you're dead."

Brer Rabbit shook his head. "There's a law in this community what say you can't kill folks who've done you a favor."

"I ain't never heard of no such law," Brer Wolf responded, confused now.

"Well, let's go see Brer Turtle. He know the law."

So off they went to Brer Turtle's house, where Brer Wolf explained his side, and Brer Rabbit explained his.

Brer Turtle put on his glasses and cleared his throat. "This is a mixed-up case. Ain't no doubt about that. Before I can see which side the law come down on, I got to see the place where the incident took place."

They carried Brer Turtle down to the gully and showed him where Brer Wolf had been trapped under the rock. Brer Turtle walked around and poked at the spot with his cane. Then he shook his head. "I hate to put y'all to so much trouble, but I have to see how the rock was lying on Brer Wolf."

Brer Wolf lay down, and Brer Rabbit rolled the rock back on top of him. Brer Turtle walked around and around. He made some marks on the ground, stared at them, and walked around some more.

"Say, Brer Turtle. This rock is getting kinna heavy."

Brer Turtle made some more marks on the ground and did some more walking around, deep in thought.

"Brer Turtle! This rock is squeezing the breath out of me."

Brer Turtle took his glasses off and cleared his throat. "I have reached my decision. Brer Rabbit! You were in the wrong. You didn't have no business coming along and bothering Brer Wolf when he wasn't bothering you. He was minding his business, and you ought to have been minding yours."

Brer Rabbit looked ashamed.

"When you were going down the road yonder, I know you were going somewhere. If you were going somewhere, you should've gone on. Brer Wolf wasn't going nowhere then, and he ain't going nowhere now. You found him under that rock, and under that rock you should've left him."

Brer Rabbit thanked Brer Turtle for his legal wisdom. They gave each other high fives and went on to town talking about what a smart man Brer Turtle was.

Mammy-Bammy Big-Money Takes Care of Brer Wolf

Aunt Mammy-Bammy Big-Money got sick and tired of Brer Wolf taking up space in the world. And when Mammy-Bammy Big-Money said your time had come, you best make your reservation with the gravedigger.

Mammy-Bammy Big-Money was the witch rabbit, and she knew everything that was going on. She sent word to Brer Rabbit that she wanted to see him.

She lived way off in a deep, dark swamp between Lost Forty and the outskirts of Hell, and to get there, you had to ride some, slide some; jump some, hump some; hop some, flop some; walk some, balk some; creep some, sleep some; fly some, cry some; follow some, holler some; wade some, spade some; and if you weren't careful, you still might miss the turnoff. Brer Rabbit got there, but he was plumb wore out when he did.

He and Mammy-Bammy Big-Money talked for a long while about how they were going to rid the world of Brer Wolf. They finally got their plan all fixed up, and Brer Rabbit went on back.

A few days later Brer Rabbit ran into Brer Wolf's house all out of breath. "Brer Wolf! Brer Wolf! I just came from the river, and Mammy-Bammy Big-Money is lying there dead! Let's go eat her up!"

"You lying, Brer Rabbit."

"I ain't telling no tale, Brer Wolf. Come on! Let's go!"

"You sure she's dead?"

"Brer Wolf, she dead, I'm telling you! A body can't get no more dead. Let's go!"

They got all the other animals together, and by the time they got down to the river, so many folks were there, you would've thought it was a rock concert. Everybody could see with their own eyes that Brer Rabbit hadn't lied. Mammy-Bammy Big-Money was deader than death. Brer Wolf jumped up in the air, clicked his heels, and let out a holler!

The problem now was how to divide up her carcass. He asked Brer Mink, Brer Coon, Brer Possum, Brer Turtle, and Brer Rabbit what part they wanted. They all agreed that since he was the biggest and had the biggest appetite, he should get first choice.

Brer Wolf nodded, pleased. He turned to Brer Coon and said, "You and me been friends since Ol' Boy was in diapers. How much of this meat you think an old feeble man like me ought to take?"

"Why don't you take one of the forequarters?"

Brer Wolf was astonished. "Have mercy, Brer Coon! I thought you was my friend. From the way you talk, I can tell you ain't got no feeling for me. What you say leaves me feeling on the lonely side. Brer Mink! You and me been knowing each other since before Santa Claus had a beard. How much of this meat you think ought to be my share?"

"I reckon you should get one of the forequarters and a big chunk off the bulge of the neck."

"Get away from here, Brer Mink! I don't want to know you if you talk like that. Brer Possum! I been knowing you since before rainwater found out it could turn to snowflakes. Look at me, look at my family, and then tell me how much of this meat should be my share."

Brer Possum thought for a minute. "Take half, Brer Wolf! Take half!"

Brer Wolf shook his head in dismay. "And I thought you knew something about friendship. I can't believe what I'm hearing."

Brer Wolf asked Brer Turtle, who told him to take everything except one of the hindquarters. Brer Wolf shook his head. "I never did think that folks who said they were my friends would want to starve me like this."

Then Brer Wolf asked Brer Rabbit for his opinion.

Brer Rabbit stood up. "Gentlemen, take a look at Brer Wolf's family. Just by looking at 'em you can tell that they're hungry, and you know Brer Wolf is monstrously hungry. Takes a lot of meat to keep a family of wolves going. So I'm going to put it to you straight: Brer Wolf should have first chance at Big-Money. I say we tie him on and let him eat as much as he wants, and we can have whatever's left."

Brer Wolf laughed. "I knowed you was my partner, Brer Rabbit! You my honey partner!"

They tied Brer Wolf on to Mammy-Bammy Big-Money.

Brer Wolf bit her on the neck. Mammy-Bammy Big-Money twitched and jumped up. Brer Wolf hollered, "Come here, somebody! Get me off here! She ain't dead!"

Brer Rabbit yelled back, "Never mind that, Brer Wolf! She dead! Sho' 'nuf. She dead! Bite her again!"

Brer Wolf bent over and bit her again, and Mammy-Bammy Big-Money started running. Brer Wolf was hollering like the world had caught fire: "Help! Get me off here! Help, somebody! Untie me, Brer Rabbit! Untie me!"

Brer Rabbit shouted back, "She dead, Brer Wolf! She dead! Nail her, Brer Wolf! Bite her! Gnaw her!"

Brer Wolf went back to biting, and Mammy-Bammy Big-Money kept running along the riverbank until she came to the deepest part of the river. She picked up speed, leaped, and landed—*cumberjoom!*—right smack in the middle of the river. She turned over on her back and stayed that way until Brer Wolf was drowned dead.

Brer Rabbit and the Gizzard Eater

Among the animals nobody could out-party Brer Rabbit. He knew all the dances from the waltz to the tango to the twist, and way I hear it, he invented discoing and break-dancing. But don't quote me on that.

One time, however, Brer Rabbit partied too much, 'cause a big rainstorm came up, and when Brer Rabbit put out for home, the streams had become creeks and the creeks rivers and the rivers—well, if I told you what the rivers had become, you'd accuse me of having told truth good-bye.

Brer Rabbit had to backtrack and go 'round this way and that before he got as far as the creek close to his house. Many times he'd walked across that creek on a log, but the log had washed away. The creek was big and wide now, and it made him feel like he'd been lost so long that his family had forgotten him. And it was the wettest wet water Brer Rabbit had ever seen.

Brer Rabbit thought if he could holler loud enough, maybe somebody would come fetch him a boat. So he set in to hollering: "HEY, SOMEBODY! HEEEEEY! HEEEEYOOOOOOO!"

All that racket woke up Brer Alligator, who was sleeping at the bottom of the creek. *Who's that trying to holler the bottom out of the creek?* he wondered.

He rose to the top like he wasn't nothing more than a cork. He looked around with his two eyes like two bullets floating on the water. Then he saw Brer Rabbit.

"What's happening, Brer Rabbit? How's your daughter?"

Brer Alligator had had eyes for Brer Rabbit's daughter for a long time.

"She ain't doing too well, Brer 'Gator. When I left home, her head was all swole up. Some of the neighbor's children been flinging rocks at her, and one hit right smack on top of her head, and I had to run for the doctor."

Brer Alligator shook his head. "Don't know what the world's coming to, Brer Rabbit. Pretty soon won't be no peace nowhere except in my bed at the bottom of the creek."

"Ain't that the truth! And no sooner than I go for the doctor than this storm come along, and all the streams rose up like they mad at somebody. I'm over here, and my daughter is over there, waiting for me to bring the medicine the doctor gave me. I would try to swim across, but I'm afraid that these pills in my pocket might melt. And I might get poisoned then, since the doctor say the pills supposed to go *in* you, not *on* you."

Brer Alligator floated on top of the water like he didn't weigh more than a postage stamp, and he looked like he was about to cry. "Well, Brer Rabbit, if there ever was a rover, you the one. Up you come and off you go, and there ain't no more keeping up with you than if you had wings. If you think you can stay put in one place long enough, I'll take you across the creek."

Brer Rabbit rubbed his chin. "Brer 'Gator, how deep is that water?"

"Well, if I stood up straight in the water, there'd be enough room beneath my tail for my wife and my children to stand up straight and still not touch bottom."

Brer Rabbit moved back from the edge and looked like he was going to faint. "That makes me feel farther from home than them what's done lost for good! How in the world you going to get me across this slippery water?"

"Take you across on my back, but don't go around telling folks that I decided to be a water horse."

"I wouldn't say nothing to nobody about it, Brer 'Gator, but listen here. I heard that your tail is mighty limber. I heard you can knock a chip from the back of your head with the tip end of your tail and not even be half-trying."

"That's true, Brer Rabbit, but don't hold it against me. That's the way Ol' Maker put me together, so that's the way I be."

Brer Rabbit thought for a while and finally said, "Well, that sounds like it's somewhere in the neighborhood of the truth, so I reckon I'll let you carry me across."

Brer Alligator floated over to the bank, smiling as he came. His teeth looked like they more properly belonged in a sawmill than in a creature's mouth, and Brer Rabbit started shaking like he'd caught a chill.

"Brer 'Gator, your back is mighty rough. How am I going to ride on it?"

"The roughness will help you hold on. You can fit your feet on the bumps and be as comfortable as if you were at home in your rocking chair."

Brer Rabbit got on and immediately wished he was off, but Brer Alligator slid off through the water like he was greased.

Brer Rabbit was scared, especially when he noticed that Brer Alligator wasn't headed for the landing place on the other side of the creek. "Brer 'Gator? If I ain't mistaken, you ain't heading for the landing."

Brer Alligator grinned a toothy grin. "You sho' got good eyes, Brer Rabbit. I been waiting a long, long time for

you. You probably done forgot that day when you said you was going to show me Ol' Man Trouble. Well, you not only showed him to me; you had me shake hands with him when you set that dry grass on fire and near 'bout burned me up. That's the reason my back is so rough now and my hide is so tough. Well, I've been waiting for you since then, and here you are."

Brer Alligator laughed. Brer Rabbit didn't see what was funny. He just sat there, shaking and quivering. Finally he asked in a weak voice, "What you gon' do with me, Brer 'Gator?"

"Well, ever since that fire I ain't been myself. I went to the doctor, and he say my condition is getting worse. All the smoke from that fire done something to my insides, and there's only one thing can cure me."

"What's that?" Brer Rabbit wasn't sure he wanted to know.

"Rabbit gizzard," Brer Alligator said, grinning a toothy grin.

Brer Rabbit laughed then. "Well, this is both our lucky day, Brer 'Gator."

"I know it's mine, but how is it yours?"

"Well, I've been feeling kinna po'ly myself. The doctor told me my problem was that I had a double gizzard, and one of my gizzards had to be took out, but he don't know how to do it. Say it's a job for the gizzard eater. Well, I asked him where I could find the gizzard eater. He say he don't know, but when I meet up with him, I'd know it."

Brer Alligator kept slipping through the water, but he don't say nothing.

"What I'm telling you is the fatal truth," Brer Rabbit continued. "Doctor told me that the worst thing a man with a double gizzard could do would be to cross the water with that double gizzard in him. If that gizzard smell water, I'll swell up so bad my skin couldn't hold me. So that's why last night, when I came to cross this creek, I took out my double gizzard and hid it in a hollow hickory log. Now, since you obviously a gizzard eater, you can help me get shed of the thing. If you in the mood, I'll take you right to the stump and show you where I hid it. Or, if you want to be lonesome about it, I'll let you go by yourself, and I'll stay here."

"Where you say you'll stay?"

"Anywhere you want me to, Brer 'Gator. I don't care where I stay just so long as I get rid of that double gizzard. It probably be best if you go by yourself, because as much trouble as that double gizzard gives me, I feel kind of sentimental about it. If I see you gobble it up, I just might start boohooing, and that wouldn't be no good for your digestion. If you go by yourself, just rap on the stump and say 'If you are ready, *I'm* ready and a little more so.' The gizzard won't give you no trouble then. I hid it right there in them woods yonder."

Brer Alligator had about as much sense as the man who tried to climb a fence after somebody knocked it down. He went on through the water to the landing, and Brer Rabbit took a big leap onto solid ground. He turned around and sang out:

> *You po' ol' 'gator, if you knew A from izzard,*
> *You'd know mighty well that I'd keep my gizzard.*

And with that he was gone!

Why Dogs Are Always Sniffing

Before Brer Lion was Brer Lion, he was King Lion, and he was king of all the animals. There wasn't much to kinging back in them days. All he did was sit on his throne chair every day and hold his crown on his head.

He had been sitting there holding his crown on his head for seventy-eleven years and one day decided to go out and have some fun, like them he'd been kinging it over. He called his advisors together and told them what he had in mind and wanted to know what he should do.

They talked it over and decided that the best thing would be for the king to go fishing. He liked that idea. So all the folks what worked in the palace ran around getting together everything the king would need—pole and line and hooks and bait, a chair to sit on, and a lot of fish. It wouldn't do for the king to go fishing and not catch nothing.

When the king was ready to go, Brer Rabbit started giggling.

"What's so funny?" the king wanted to know.

"Ain't none of my business, but seems to me that you done forgot something."

"What's that, Brer Rabbit?"

"Who gon' do the kinging while you fishing?"

The king threw up his hands and shook his head. "I don't know what's the matter with me. How could I forget something like that?"

Brer Rabbit shrugged. "It probably don't matter 'cause don't nothing ever happen nohow."

"That ain't the point," the king insisted. "Here I was about to go out and have some fun and leave everything to look after itself. I tell you the truth, there ain't no fun in being king. Your time ain't your own, and everytime you turn around, you hurt your knee running into some bylaw. Somebody got to be king today." The king sat down and thought for a long time. Finally he said, "Brer Rabbit, what about you? I'll pay you a dollar, and you can sit in my throne chair and hold the crown on your head."

That sounded all right to Brer Rabbit. The ol' woman had been on him about buying her some flowers so she would know he loved her. The dollar would come in handy.

The king went fishing, and Brer Rabbit sat down on the throne chair. Of course, he wasn't about to sit there and hold a crown on his head all day. He sent one of the servants for some string and tied the crown on his head and made a little bow under his chin.

Wasn't long before he heard a lot of howling and growling and whining outside.

"What's going on?" Brer Rabbit wanted to know.

One of the advisors said, "Well, if the king was here, he wouldn't pay no attention to all that noise. The king would wait until somebody came and told somebody what the racket was about, and that somebody would tell somebody else, and maybe, about dinnertime, the word might or might not get to the king."

Brer Rabbit said, "If the king would get up and look out the window, he'd know what the racket was."

"That ain't kinging," said the advisor.

Brer Rabbit said, "Oh," and sat back down in the throne chair and went to sleep. Long about dinnertime one of the advisors came in and said Brer Dog had to see the king. Brer Rabbit rubbed the sleep out of his eyes and said to show Brer Dog in.

Brer Dog came in, and he was a pathetic-looking thing.

He looked so hungry that you could count all the ribs in his body. He was so skinny, he didn't even cast a shadow. He had his head down and was shivering all over like he was cold.

Brer Rabbit looked at him closely to see if he knew this dog. Sure enough, it was the very same dog that had been chasing him all over the countryside for more years than Brer Rabbit could count.

Brer Dog stood there with his head hanging down and his tail between his legs. He didn't look like he had the strength to jump on a broken-down truck full of raw hamburger meat.

"What's your business with the king?" one of the advisors asked.

Brer Dog started moaning. "I'm having the worse time anybody on the top side of the world has ever had. We used to get meat. Now we get bones and not too many of them. We used to be able to run all through the countryside. Now Mr. Man wants to lock us up in the house and call us Fido or Spot. Used to be a time when a dog was respected. But it ain't like that no more. Anything the king could do to help us sho' would be appreciated."

Brer Rabbit studied over the situation. Finally he turned to one of his advisors and asked if there was any turpentine around. The advisor said he thought they could find some.

"Mix together a pound of red peppers with the turpentine and bring it to me."

The advisor had it done, and it was brought to Brer Rabbit. He grabbed Brer Dog and rubbed the turpentine and red peppers all over his body. Brer Dog howled and ran out of the palace as fast as he could.

Day followed day just the same way they do now, and Brer Dog didn't come back home. His kinfolk got worried. They waited a few weeks more, and still no sign of Brer Dog. So they went to see the king to ask him if he knew where Brer Dog was.

Naturally they didn't get to see the king, but they saw one of the advisors, who told them that Brer Dog had been there and had seen the king and that the king had given him what he'd come after.

The dogs looked at each other. "He ain't come back home," said one of 'em.

"You'd better hunt him up, then, and find out what he did with what the king gave him."

"But how we going to know him when we find him?" the dogs wanted to know.

"You'll be able to tell him by the smell of the turpentine and red pepper the king put on him to kill his fleas and cure his bites."

Well, from that day to this the dogs have been hunting for Brer Dog. They been smelling along the ground; they smell the trees and the stumps and the bushes, and when they see a dog they don't know, they smell him. Sometimes they smell a bush or a stump or something and start growling and scratching the ground, practicing what they're going to do when they catch up to Brer Dog. So when you see a dog come sniffing along, you let him go on his way 'cause one of these days I believe they just might catch up to Brer Dog.

Being Fashionable Ain't Always Healthy

One Septerarry an awful storm hit the part of the country where the animals lived. The animals were afraid they were going to be blown to the other side of the world if they stayed on the top side. They managed to come through the storm all right, but an animal that lived way far away didn't make out too good.

That was ol' Craney Crow. Folks call 'em herons now, but back in them times he had a name what somebody could say, and it sounded like English.

The storm was even worse down in Craney Crow's country. That wind got a hold of Craney Crow and turned him around and around in the air. When it set him down, he was up in the animals' part of the world.

Craney Crow didn't know where he was. He wasn't even too sure that he was. He'd been whirled around so much that he leaned against a tree like a drunk man for an hour or so before he thought about trying to walk.

When he was feeling more like himself, he looked around to see where he was. He couldn't see a thing because it was the middle of the night. All he knew was that he was a long way from home. There was water halfway up his legs, and that felt familiar 'cause Craney Crow had always lived where he could wade in the water.

What Craney Crow didn't know was that the wind had set him down in the Long Cane Swamp. After a while the Sun started to rise and shine his lamp into the Swamp, and Craney Crow could see. But seeing didn't tell him any more than not seeing had.

The Swamp knew somebody was in it who didn't belong there, and it was disturbed. But the Sun was coming up, so the Swamp went to sleep, 'cause that's when it slept. The Swamp had the worst sleep that day it had ever had, before or since. It had nothing but bad dreams and daymares.

After a while the Sun stood right above the Swamp. Even it knew something was wrong. He wanted to see in and shone as much of his light into the dark Swamp as he could but couldn't see nothing. Bright as the lamp of the Sun is, it can't light up the Swamp. So it went on its way to the other side of the world.

While the Sun was arching over the Swamp trying to find out what the trouble was, Craney Crow was wading around in the water, looking for a frog or a fish to take the edge off his appetite. But there wasn't a frog or fish to be seen. The Swamp had gone to sleep.

Ol' Craney Crow walked around, his eyes as wide open as a fresh-dug grave. He'd never seen anything like the Swamp in his life. He was used to grass and water. There was nothing here but vines, and reeds, and trees with moss on them that made 'em look like Gransir Graybeard. The vines and creepers looked like they were reaching out for him.

He walked around like the ground was hot. He didn't know how in the world he was going to make his home in such a strange place.

Toward evening Craney Crow walked out of the water onto the muddy bank. The Swamp yawned and stretched itself. Brer Mud Turtle opened his eyes and sneezed so hard that he rolled off the bank into the water—*kersplash!* Craney Crow jumped back and almost stepped on Brer Billy Black Snake. That scared him so much that he jumped back again and near 'bout landed on a frog, which is what he'd been looking for all day.

Craney Crow was so scared by all the creatures coming to life that he didn't even think about eating the frog. Jack-o-lanterns were flying around, their lights blinking on and off like they were looking for him. The frogs hollered at him, *"What're you doing here? What're you doing here?"* The coon ran by and laughed at him. Mr. Billy Gray Fox peeped out of a clump of bushes and barked at him. Mr. Mink peeped his green eyes at him, and the whipperwill scolded him.

After a while all the creatures left him alone and went about their business. Ol' Craney Crow started moving around again. He noticed that the birds that flew around in the daytime were going to bed without their heads. He looked into a lot of bushes, and sure enough, all the day birds had all gone to sleep without their heads.

Craney Crow had never seen such a thing. That must be the custom of the day birds in this part of the country. Craney Crow wanted so much to be a part of this new community the wind had placed him down in. But how could he if he went to sleep with his head on? Of course, if Craney Crow had looked real close, or if his eyes had been more accustomed to the night, he would've seen that the birds had simply tucked their heads under their wings. But Craney Crow didn't see that.

It was long past Craney Crow's bedtime. He looked around and saw Brer Pop-Eye staring at him. That was what Brer Rabbit called himself when he went down to the low country.

"How do, Mr. Craney Crow," said Brer Pop-Eye.

"How do, Brer Pop-Eye. You might be just the man I'm looking for. Would you be good enough to tell me something?"

"If I know it, I'll tell it to you."

"I'd sho' appreciate it. What I want to know is this: How do all the flying birds take their heads off when they go to bed? I just can't figure out how they do it."

"I ain't surprised, Mr. Craney Crow. You a stranger in these parts. The mosquitoes in this Swamp are so awful that the only way the birds can get some sleep is to take their heads off and put 'em someplace where the mosquitoes can't get them."

"But how in the world do they do it, Brer Pop-Eye?"

Brer Pop-Eye laughed. "They don't do it by themselves. No, indeed! They hired someone to do it for them."

"Where can I find him? I sho' would like to get some sleep."

"You stay right here. He be around soon. He's probably checking to make sure he ain't missed nobody."

Mr. Craney Crow thought for a moment. "Tell me this. How do they get their heads back on?"

Brer Pop-Eye shook his head. "Can't tell you. I'm a night person myself. About the time they be getting their heads back on is about the time I go to sleep. But if you want me to, I'll hunt up the man in charge of taking their heads off."

Ol' Craney Crow thanked him. Brer Pop-Eye took off and came back in a little while with Brer Wolf. Brer Wolf's tongue was hanging out of his mouth and dripping so much wet it made a puddle at his feet.

"This is Dock Wolf. Dock, this is Mr. Craney Crow."

Craney Crow told Dock Wolf how much he wanted to go to sleep like the other birds so maybe they'd be friends with him in the morning.

Dock Wolf put his thumb in his vest holes and looked like a sho' 'nuf doctor. "I don't know as I can help you,

Mr. Craney Crow. To tell the truth, I ain't never seen a creature with such a long neck as yours."

He felt Craney Crow's neck tenderly, running his hands up and down it. "Hold your head lower, Mr. Craney Crow." Mr. Craney Crow did and—*snap*—that was the last of Mr. Craney Crow. Brer Wolf slung him over his back and trotted on home. But that was after him and Brer Rabbit gave each other high fives.

Brer Rabbit decided it was time for him to get on home too. It took longer than it should have because he couldn't walk for laughing about Mr. Craney Crow. He'd walk a little ways, then have to sit down beside the road 'cause he was laughing so hard. Finally he made it as far as Brer Fox's house.

Brer Fox was working in his pea patch. When he heard somebody laughing, he looked over the fence to see who it was. And there was Brer Rabbit rolling around in the grass, holding his sides and laughing.

"Hey, Brer Rabbit! What's the matter with you?"

Brer Rabbit was laughing so hard, he couldn't do nothing but shake his head.

Miz Fox stuck her head out the window. "Sandy, what's all that racket? Don't you know that the baby just went to sleep?"

"It ain't nobody but Brer Rabbit, and it look to me like he got the hysterics."

"Well, I don't care what he got. He better take his racket away from here before he wakes the baby and scares the life out of them what ain't asleep."

Brer Rabbit caught his breath and walked up to the house to pass the time of day with Brer Fox and his wife. "I apologize for all my carrying on," he told them, "but I can't help it. Maybe it ain't right to laugh at them who ain't got the sense they ought to have been born with, but I can't help myself. To tell the truth, I should've been home hours ago, and I would've been if not for something I saw last night." He started laughing again.

"What did you see, Brer Rabbit?" Miz Fox wanted to know. "It sho' sounds like it was funny, and I ain't never turned a good laugh away from my door."

So Brer Rabbit told them all about ol' Craney Crow coming into the Swamp and not knowing how to go to bed. "And the funny thing was that Craney Crow didn't know that when you go to bed, you're supposed to take your head off." Brer Rabbit started laughing again.

Miz Fox looked at Brer Fox. He looked at her, and they didn't know what to say or how to say it.

Brer Rabbit saw how they were looking at each other but didn't let on. "Craney Crow looked like a man who's been around and knows what the fashion is. But when he got to the Swamp and saw all the creatures sleeping with their heads off, he looked like somebody who just came out of the country and seen neon lights for the first time. He stood there with his mouth open like he ain't got no more sense than a crocker sack." Brer Rabbit laughed again. "Well, I been trying to get home all this time to tell my wife about how Craney Crow looked when he seen what the new fashion is."

Brer Rabbit commenced to laughing again. Brer Fox and Miz Fox laughed too. They didn't want Brer Rabbit to think that they were as dumb as Craney Crow.

"Where Craney Crow come from that he don't know the fashion?" Miz Fox asked.

Brer Rabbit shook his head. "He must be from so far back in the country that the Sun don't shine there yet."

Brer Fox said that he didn't much care about fashion, to tell the truth.

Brer Rabbit agreed. "I like the old ways myself. But when something new comes along that makes sense, I ain't gon' turn my back on it just because it's new. No, sir! Before I got in the habit of sleeping with my head off, I wouldn't have believed that it could be so comfortable. The first time I tried it, well, I don't mind telling you I was a little nervous. But I got used to it pretty quick, and now, if it was to go out of fashion, I'd keep right on with it and wouldn't care what nobody thought."

Brer Rabbit looked up at the Sun, which was steadily climbing the arch of heaven, made his farewells, and went on his way.

"Well, that's something, ain't it?" Brer Fox said to his wife. "Sleeping with your head off. I ain't never heard of such a thing."

Miz Fox grunted. "The world ain't big enough to hold all the things you ain't heard of. Here I am scrimping and working my eyeballs out to be as good as the neighbors, and you don't give a hoot if your family is in fashion or not."

"Sleeping with your head off is a fashion I ain't got much interest in trying."

"No, and you ain't got no interest in what folks say about me and the children neither. No wonder Brer Rabbit was laughing so hard. You ought to seen the way your mouth was hanging open when he was telling us about it. I bet he's setting up right now telling his wife about how tacky the Fox family is."

Miz Fox went back in the house. After a while Brer Fox came in to eat breakfast, but the stove looked as cold as a snowball in February. "Ain't you fixing my breakfast this morning?"

"Fixing and eating breakfast is one of the fashions. If you ain't gon' follow the fashions, I don't see how come I should."

Brer Fox went out back of the house and sat down to do some thinking and scratch his fleas. That night when it was time to go to bed, Brer Fox came in. "I reckon I'm ready to get my head taken off so's I can sleep."

Miz Fox was so happy. "I knowed you loved me," she said.

Brer Fox grinned. "But I don't know nothing about how to do it. I reckon you gon' have to help me."

Miz Fox didn't know no more than Brer Fox did, so they sat on the edge of the bed and talked about it for a while.

"You could twist my head off."

"Ticklish as you is, that ain't gon' work."

"What about the ax?"

"That give me the heebie-jeebies."

They sat in silence for a long while until Miz Fox said, "The ax scares me. But on the other hand, we know that if something is the fashion, it ain't gon' hurt."

She went to the woodshed and came back with the ax. "You ready, honey?"

"Ready as I'll ever be," Brer Fox responded.

Whack! Off came his head at the neck. Brer Fox squirmed and twitched and kicked. Miz Fox smiled and said, "That's a sign he's dreaming."

After a while Brer Fox was still. "He look like he having the best sleep he's ever had."

Miz Fox got ready to go to bed and then realized that she still had her head on. She bent over and shook Brer Fox, trying to wake him up so he could help get her head off. She shook him; she hollered at him, but he didn't stir. So she had to go to bed with her head on.

She couldn't sleep for worrying about what the neighbors would think if they knew she was lying in bed with her head on. When she finally got to sleep, she had awful dreams. In one of them Brer Rabbit was laughing at her, and when she made a grab for him, dogs started chasing her. She was glad when morning came.

She went to wake up Brer Fox, but he just lay there. She shook him and yelled at him and pushed him and pulled him. But he just lay there. She started hollering so loud that Brer Rabbit, who was going by on the road, thought she was calling him. He went to the door to see what she wanted.

"Brer Rabbit!" she exclaimed. "I'm sho' glad to see you. I been trying to wake up Brer Fox, and he's lazier this morning than I've ever seen him, and that's saying a lot."

"He'll get up in good time," Brer Rabbit assured her.

"I don't know what you call good time," she insisted. "The Sun's already way up the sky, and he's still asleep. If I'd known that taking your head off would make you sleep like that, I might not have done it."

"What did you say?" Brer Rabbit asked.

"Brer Fox had me take his head off before he went to bed last night."

"What did you take it off with?"

"The ax."

Brer Rabbit covered his mouth with his hands and walked away. It looked like he was crying. But he wasn't. When he got down the road a piece, he started laughing. He laughed so hard, he fell over in the ditch. Like he'd said, some folks didn't have the sense they should've been born with.

The Race

Brer Rabbit went to the Rainmaker's house, which was between Thunder and Lightning and Dark Clouds. Don't nobody know how to get there no more. Folks nowadays need a map to get from one place to another, and where Ol' Rainmaker live at on no map. Where he lived wasn't far and it wasn't near, and if Brer Rabbit had known where he was going, he wouldn't have gotten there.

Rainmaker was storing up water for all the storms he was going to make that year, and he was glad to take a break when Brer Rabbit walked up.

"How you doing, Ol' Rainmaker?"

Ol' Rainmaker allowed as to how he was doing all right. They chatted back and forth for a while, which was the way folks did things back in them days. Finally Brer Rabbit got down to business.

"I was wondering, Ol' Rainmaker, if you could fix up a race between Brer Dust and Cousin Rain to see which one can run the fastest."

Ol' Rainmaker didn't like the idea, and he flashed some lightning and rumbled some thunder while he thought it over. "If anybody but you had come and asked me, Brer Rabbit, I wouldn't do it. Seeing as how it's you, I'll fix it up for you."

Brer Rabbit sent news to all the animals that next Sunday, in the middle of the big road, there was going to be a race.

Sunday came, and all the animals were there. They spread out along the road so they could see the race from start to finish. Brer Bear was at the bend in the road. Brer Fox was at the crossroads. Brer Wolf was at the starting line, and Brer Possum was at the finish line, and the rest were scattered in between.

They waited and waited, and after a while a cloud came floating over. It wasn't a big cloud, but Brer Rabbit knew that Cousin Rain and Uncle Wind were in it. The cloud dropped down slowly until it was right over the road, and then it settled slowly to the ground. Cousin Rain and Uncle Wind got out and went to the starting line. Of course, Brer Dust was already there.

Brer Rabbit fired the starting gun, and they were off! Uncle Wind didn't mean to, but he was as much help to Brer Dust as he was to Cousin Rain 'cause he blew and blew, and Brer Dust whirled up, and before any of the animals knew anything, there was dust everywhere. Brer Coon was holding on to Brer Bear to keep from getting blowed away, but Miz Partridge was blown halfway to Mr. Sun's summer place on Lake Gimme a Break. All the animals were covered with so much dust, they looked like sand dunes.

Then Cousin Rain got going. If the animals were miserable being turned into sand dunes, they had the double misery when Cousin Rain made 'em into mud dunes. Of course Brer Rabbit had had a raincoat and umbrella hidden away and put 'em on when the race started. He was dry as a rock in the desert.

The animals got so mad they forgot all about the race and set out after Brer Rabbit, and he outran Brer Dust and Cousin Rain and he wasn't even supposed to be in the race.

As for who won the real race, well, it turned out this way: Cousin Rain thought she had lost. Brer Dust had put so much dust in the air that she hadn't been able to see a thing.

"Where you at, Brer Dust? You done crossed the finish line?"

Brer Dust hollered back, "I fell down in the mud and can't run no more."

So Cousin Rain was the winner.

APPENDIX

Appendix for *The Tales of Uncle Remus: The Adventures of Brer Rabbit* (Vol. I) and *More Tales of Uncle Remus: Further Adventures of Brer Rabbit, His Friends, Enemies, and Others* (Vol. II)

The following separate stories were combined into single stories:

"The Wonderful Tar-Baby Story" and "How Mr. Rabbit Was Too Sharp for Mr. Fox" became "Brer Rabbit and the Tar Baby" (Vol. I).

"Mr. Rabbit Grossly Deceives Mr. Fox," "Mr. Fox Is Again Victimized," and "Mr. Fox Is Outdone by Mr. Buzzard" became "Brer Rabbit Gets Even" (Vol. I).

"Brother Rabbit and His Famous Foot" and "Brother Rabbit Submits to a Test" became "Brer Rabbit's Luck" (Vol. I).

"Mr. Man Has Some Meat" and "Brother Rabbit Gets the Meat" became "Brer Rabbit Gets the Meat" (Vol. II).

"How Craney-Crow Lost His Head" and "Brother Fox Follows the Fashion" became "Being Fashionable Ain't Always Healthy" (Vol. II).

The following Brer Rabbit stories of Joel Chandler Harris were omitted from these two volumes (See Introduction, Vol. I):

"Brother Rabbit Gets the Provisions"
"Cutta Cord-La!"
"Brother Fox and the White Muscadines"
"Mr. Hawk and Brother Rabbit"
"Brother Fox Makes a Narrow Escape"
"Brother Fox's Fish Trap"
"Brother Rabbit and the Gingercakes"
"Brother Rabbit and Miss Nancy"
"Brer Rabbit's Frolic"
"Brer Rabbit and the Gold Mine"
"How Brer Rabbit Saved Brer B'ar's Life"
"Brother Rabbit's Bear Hunt"
"Taily-Po"
"Brother Rabbit, Brother Fox, and Two Fat Pullets"
"How Brother Rabbit Brought Family Trouble on Brother Fox"

BIBLIOGRAPHY

Afro-American Folktales: Stories from Black Traditions in the New World. Selected and edited by Roger D. Abrahams. Pantheon Books, New York, 1985.
This is an important collection of black folktales from an important folklorist.

"The Trickster in Relation to Greek Mythology," by Károly Kerényi in *The Trickster: A Study in American Indian Mythology,* by Paul Radin. Philosophical Library. New York, 1956.

"On the Psychology of the Trickster Figure," by C. G. Jung in the work cited above.

The Zande Trickster, edited by E. E. Evans-Pritchard. Oxford University Press, London, 1967.

ABOUT THE AUTHOR

Julius Lester is the critically acclaimed author of books for both children and adults. His latest book for Dial, *The Tales of Uncle Remus: The Adventures of Brer Rabbit*, is an *American Bookseller* Pick of the Lists. Other books for Dial include *To Be a Slave*, a Newbery Medal Honor Book; *Long Journey Home: Stories from Black History*, a National Book Award finalist; *This Strange New Feeling*; and *The Knee-High Man and Other Tales*, an American Library Association *Notable Book*, *School Library Journal* Best Book of the Year, and Lewis Carroll Shelf Award Winner. His adult books include *Do Lord Remember Me*, a *New York Times* Notable Book, and *Lovesong: Becoming a Jew*.

The son of a Methodist minister, Mr. Lester was born in St. Louis. At fourteen he moved to Nashville, where he later received his Bachelor of Arts from Fisk University. He is married and is the father of four children. He lives in Amherst and teaches at the University of Massachusetts.

ABOUT THE ILLUSTRATOR

Jerry Pinkney has twice received the Coretta Scott King Award for Illustration, first for the Dial book *The Patchwork Quilt*, written by Valerie Flournoy. *The Patchwork Quilt* also won the Christopher Award, was an American Library Association *Notable Book*, a *Booklist* Reviewers' Choice, and a Reading Rainbow selection. Mr. Pinkney has illustrated many other books, including *Song of the Trees* for Dial, written by Mildred D. Taylor. His artwork has been shown at the 1986 Bologna Book Fair, the AIGA Book Show, the Society of Illustrators Annual Show, and in museums around the country.

Mr. Pinkney studied at the Philadelphia Museum College of Art. He and his wife, who have four grown children, live in Croton-on-Hudson, New York.

Further Tales of Uncle Remus
THE MISADVENTURES OF BRER RABBIT, BRER FOX, BRER WOLF, THE DOODANG, AND OTHER CREATURES

Further Tales of Uncle Remus

The Misadventures of Brer Rabbit, Brer Fox,

Brer Wolf, the Doodang, and Other Creatures

as told by JULIUS LESTER

illustrated by Jerry Pinkney

DIAL BOOKS

New York

Published by Dial Books
375 Hudson Street
New York, New York 10014

Library of Congress Cataloging in Publication Data

Lester, Julius.
Further tales of Uncle Remus. The misadventures of
Brer Rabbit, Brer Fox, Brer Wolf, the Doodang,
and other creatures.

Summary : A retelling of the classic Afro-American tales
relating the adventures and misadventures of
Brer Rabbit and his friends and enemies.
1. Afro-Americans—Folklore. 2. Tales—United States.
[1. Folklore, Afro-American. 2. Animals—Folklore.]
I. Pinkney, Jerry, ill. II. Title. III. Title: Further
Adventures of Uncle Remus. IV. Title: Misadventures of
Brer Rabbit, Brer Fox, Brer Wolf, the Doodang, and other creatures.
PZ8.1.L434Fu 1990   398.2'08996073   88-20223
ISBN 0-8037-0610-3 ISBN 0-8037-0611-1 (lib. bdg.)

The publisher wishes to express its sincere thanks to the estate
of Joel Chandler Harris for its gracious support during the
publication of this new version of The Tales of Uncle Remus.

Each black-and-white drawing is made of pencil and graphite; and
each full-color picture consists of a pencil, graphite, and watercolor
painting that is color-separated and reproduced in full color.

To Diana Huss Green
J. L.

For my grandchildren
Gloria, Leon, and Charnelle
J. P.

Contents

Further Tales of Uncle Remus

THE MISADVENTURES OF BRER RABBIT,
BRER FOX, BRER WOLF, THE DOODANG,
AND OTHER CREATURES

Brer Fox and Mr. Man

Many evenings I'll be sitting here thinking about much of nothing and the door will open a crack. I know who it is, so I don't get scared. Instead I close my eyes partways and pretend like I'm napping. After a minute or two I'll see two long ears come around the door followed by two of the biggest eyeballs you've ever seen. I'll give out with a loud snore like I'm sleeping as sound as the Man in the Moon.

Brer Rabbit will look at me real hard, and once he's convinced that I'm asleep, he'll beckon to the other creatures—Brer Fox, Brer Wolf, Brer Turtle, Mr. Benjamin Ram, and all the rest of them—and they'll come in real quiet, pull up chairs, and sit right there in front of the fireplace.

Mr. Benjamin Ram will take out his fiddle and start playing one of them old-time tunes what's been marinated in hard times and high hopes, and them creatures will get to singing and dancing and having a good time. When they're out of breath, they'll go back there in the kitchen and pop some popcorn and make some Kool-Aid and come back in here, and then they'll get to remembering the old times. Brer Fox will remind Brer Rabbit of some trick or other. Then Brer Wolf will remember something else and Brer Turtle will remember his remembrances. When all the popcorn and Kool-Aid is gone, and they've laughed themselves almost into the hospital, they'll wash and dry all the bowls and glasses and everything and go out just as quiet as they come in. I'll open my eyes then and laugh and laugh and laugh about all the things them creatures used to do.

Like Brer Fox, for example. Some folks say Brer Fox was no 'count and good for nothing. Others say he was a schemer and a conniver, and them was his good qualities! Of all the things I heard folks say about him, though, I never did hear nobody say Brer Fox was smart.

One morning Brer Fox was going through the woods when he heard a wagon coming along the road. He hid behind a tree. In a few minutes here come Mr. Man in his wagon, which was loaded down with eggs and butter and chickens. He was on his way to market.

If Brer Fox had his way, Mr. Man might get to market but not with his eggs, butter, and chickens. He was sorry Brer Rabbit wasn't around, because Brer Rabbit would've found a way to get the eggs, butter, and chicken and Mr. Man's horse and wagon too. But Brer Rabbit had won the lottery and was off scuba diving in Jamaica.

Thinking of Brer Rabbit reminded him of the time he went hunting and on his way home with a big bag of game, he came across a dead rabbit lying in the road. About a half mile farther along there was another one. A quarter mile after that he came across still another one. Not being a man to turn down a gift from the Lord, Brer Fox had put down his game bag and gone back to get the rabbits. But when he got back to the place where the first rabbit had been, it wasn't there. What he had thought was a dead rabbit wasn't nothing but Brer Rabbit pretending to be dead. Brer Fox was looking for rabbits what didn't exist, and Brer Rabbit was making off with his game bag.

That was a good trick, and Brer Fox figured that since it had worked on him, it would work on Mr. Man. That tells you right there that Brer Fox's elevator didn't go all the way to the top.

Brer Fox ran through the woods until he got a ways in front of Mr. Man, and he lay down in the road like he was dead. A few minutes later Mr. Man come along, singing to himself. I don't know what he was singing. It was probably the blues, 'cause when a body is feeling good, they got to sing the blues. Then again, when a body is feeling bad they got to sing the blues. Just goes to show how powerful the blues is. No matter how you feeling, singing the blues'll make you feel better.

So Mr. Man is sitting there in his wagon singing the

blues, and all of a sudden his horse whinnied and reared up. Mr. Man took his mind off the blues and put it on the horse and he hollered, "Whoa!" and the horse whoa'd.

Mr. Man saw Brer Fox laying on the ground looking as dead as a New Year's resolution on January second.

Mr. Man laughed. "Well, well, well. There's the one what's been stealing my chickens. Looks like somebody shot him with a gun. Too bad they didn't use two guns."

Mr. Man told the horse to "Giddup," drove around Brer Fox, and went on his way.

Brer Fox got up, ran through the woods until he was a ways in front of Mr. Man, and lay down in the road again.

A few minutes later here come Mr. Man. Mr. Man told his horse to "Whoa!" and the horse whoa'd. "Well, well, well. There's the one what's been stealing my pigs. Looks like somebody killed him. Wished they'd done it when Noah was a little boy."

Mr. Man told the horse to "Giddup!" The wagon wheel came so close to Brer Fox that it rolled over the hairs growing out of his nose.

That didn't bother Brer Fox none. He did the same as before, and when Mr. Man come up on him this time, Mr. Man was perplexed. "How come there are all these dead foxes in the road this morning?"

Deciding that he better investigate, Mr. Man got down from the wagon. He felt Brer Fox's ears; they were right warm. He felt Brer Fox's neck; it was warm too. He examined Brer Fox's short ribs; they were all intact. He investigated Brer Fox's bones; they were solid. He turned Brer Fox over; Brer Fox was as limber as the double-jointed man who was in the carnival which came to town last year.

Mr. Man scratched his head. "What's going on here? This pig-eating chicken-stealer looks like he's dead, but ain't none of his bones broke. I didn't feel no bruises. On top of that, he's warm and limber. Something ain't right! This pig-stealing chicken-eater might be dead. Then again he might not be. I better make sure!"

Mr. Man took his whip, and *pow!* He hit Brer Fox so hard, it hurt me.

Brer Fox didn't need to hear the same message twice. While Mr. Man was drawing back his arm to hit him again, Brer Fox got on away from there. He ran so fast, his shadow had to take the bus home.

King Lion and Mr. Man

When the creatures heard what Mr. Man had done to Brer Fox, they decided to give Mr. Man all the room he wanted. That's what all of 'em decided excepting King Lion. He thought he was the baddest thing to walk the earth since body odor.

Now, I tell you the truth: Folks can come along with their whatchamacallits and they can do what's-his-name. They can walk big, talk big, and feel big. But one day something is going to come down the road that can walk bigger, talk bigger, and feel bigger, and when that day comes, trouble will snatch 'em slonchways and the bigger they are, the worser they get snatched. That's what happened to King Lion.

Everywhere he went, all he could hear was Mr. Man this and Mr. Man the other. King Lion got sick and tired of it. He shook his mane and roared so loud that it broke a couple of windowpanes up in heaven. "Where can I find this Mr. Man?" he wanted to know.

"You don't want to go messing with Mr. Man," Brer Dog told him.

"When I get through with Mr. Man he'll wish he was never born."

"King Lion, don't you start nothing with your mouth that your fists can't finish."

King Lion don't want to hear nothing like that, so he took off down the big road, looking for Mr. Man. The sun rose up and the sun shone hot, but King Lion, he kept on. The wind came up and filled the elements full of dust, but King Lion, he kept on. The rain drifted down and turned the dust into mud, but King Lion, he kept on. And then the sun burned hot once again.

After a while King Lion saw Mr. Steer grazing alongside the road.

"Howdy do, Mr. Steer."

"Howdy do, King Lion."

They exchanged some more pleasantries, inquired about one another's children and kin, and then King Lion got down to business.

"Look-a-here, Mr. Steer. You know anybody around these parts named Mr. Man?"

"Sho' do. Knows him right well."

"Well, that's the one I'm looking for."

"What kind of business you got with Mr. Man?"

King Lion shook his mane and roared. "I'm going to show him who's boss, that's what!"

"You best turn around and point your nose toward home, King Lion. You asking for more trouble than you know exists."

"Don't you know who I am?" King Lion roared. "I'm the King! I'm the baddest thing in the whole world. I'm so bad I know where the lights go when you turn 'em out."

"What difference does that make?" Mr. Steer wanted to know. "You see how big I am, don't you? I got long, sharp horns too. But as big as I am and as sharp as my horns are, Mr. Man caught me and hitched me to a wagon and makes me haul wood and water and drives me anywhere he wants to. You best leave Mr. Man alone or he'll hitch you up to a wagon."

King Lion shook his mane, roared, and went on off down the road. In a little while he saw Mr. Horse eating grass in the field. Him and Mr. Horse exchanged greetings and inquired about one another's family tree, and then King Lion got down to business.

"I know Mr. Man right well," said Mr. Horse when King Lion finished. "Been knowing him a long time. How come you want to make his acquaintance?"

"I'm going to show him who's boss in these parts."

Mr. Horse smiled. "You best leave Mr. Man alone. You see how big I am and how much strength I got and how tough my feet are. Well, Mr. Man come out here and put a saddle on my back and some rope in my mouth. Then he jumped on and now he rides me anywhere he wants to. He makes me run fast when he wants to go fast and walk slow when he wants to go slow. You mess with Mr. Man, he'll put a saddle on your back and a rope in your mouth too."

King Lion looked at Mr. Horse with disgust and went on down the road. He hadn't gone far when he saw Mr. Jack Sparrow sitting in a tree.

"What you doing in this neck of the woods, King Lion?"

King Lion ain't got time now for no pleasantries and family trees. "I'm looking for Mr. Man so I can show him who's the boss."

"He's cutting wood right around the next bend in the road. But if you take my advice, you'll let Mr. Man alone. You see how little I am and you know how high I can fly, but Mr. Man can fetch me out of the sky whenever he wants to. If you not careful, he'll fetch you too."

King Lion was so disgusted that he didn't even say a proper good-bye. He went on down the road and around the bend and there he saw a creature standing on his hindquarters, splitting wood.

King Lion had never seen Mr. Man and didn't know what one looked like. You probably seen Mr. Man, but I bet you ain't never seen one splitting wood and don't know what I'm talking about.

To split wood you need a maul and a wedge. A maul is like a sledgehammer, and a wedge is a heavy piece of iron that's got a sharp edge but is wide and thick in the back. You drive the wedge into the wood with the maul until the wood splits in half. You split the halves in halves and then you can use your ax to split it into kindling wood.

King Lion strutted over. "You know somebody called Mr. Man?"

Mr. Man put down his maul, narrowed his eyes, and looked at King Lion. "I know him as if he was my twin brother."

"I wants to meet him."

"Well," says Mr. Man, "stick your paw right in here and I'll go get him for you."

King Lion stuck his paw in the opening the wedge had

made. Soon as he done that, Mr. Man knocked the wedge out and the log snapped closed like it was the jaws of a shark. *Snap!*

"Ow! OW! OW!" hollered King Lion.

"Don't holler yet. Wait until I give you something good to scream about."

Mr. Man got his whip, same one he'd used on Brer Fox, and he laid into King Lion. He whipped King Lion until his arm was tired and then he let him go.

King Lion was hobbling around through the community on crutches for a long time after that but didn't none of the animals say a word to him about Mr. Man. He might not could whup Mr. Man, but he could still whup them.

Brer Fox and Brer Turtle

While all this was going on between King Lion and Mr. Man, Brer Fox was recuperating from the licking Mr. Man had given him. The weller Brer Fox got, the madder he got.

Don't make sense to me how come he got so mad. Mr. Man had caught him fair and square. Ain't a thing wrong with trying to play a trick on somebody, but if you get caught, take your licks like a man. Or should I say, like a woman? Tell you the truth, with all this here feminicity going around these days, I get scared that some of these feminicitists is going to put their mouth on these stories and next thing you know, we'll be hearing about the Fox-person and the Lionperson. But as long as I'm the one telling the tale, I say Brer Fox should've took his medicine like a man.

When Brer Fox was well enough to move about, he went looking to make somebody pay for what Mr. Man had done to him.

The first somebody he come upon was Brer Turtle. He should've walked past Brer Turtle. Brer Rabbit was the only creature with more smarts than Brer Turtle and sometimes Brer Rabbit had to scramble to keep up with the ol' Hardshell.

"Good morning, Brer Turtle. Where you been this long-come-short?"

"Just lounging around, Brer Fox. Just lounging around."

"You ain't looking too good, if the truth be known."

"I been lounging around and suffering." Brer Turtle sighed.

"What's the matter? Your eyes do look mighty red."

Brer Turtle shook his head. "Brer Fox, you don't know what trouble is."

Brer Fox could've written the book on being in trouble, but he didn't say nothing about that because he was intent on making trouble for Brer Turtle. "What's your problem?"

"I was out walking in the field the other day and Mr. Man come along and set the field on fire. You don't know what trouble is, Brer Fox, until you been caught in a fire."

"How'd you get out of the fire?"

"I had to sit and take it. Smoke sifted into my eyes and the fire scorched my back something terrible."

"And it looks to me, Brer Turtle, like that fire burned your tail off too."

"Naw, thank goodness. Here's my tail." Brer Turtle un-
curled his tail from underneath his shell and as soon as he
did, Brer Fox grabbed it.

"I gotcha, Brer Turtle. I gotcha!"

Brer Turtle begged Brer Fox to let him go, but Brer Fox
act like he deaf. Brer Turtle asked Brer Fox not to drown
him, but Brer Fox don't say nothing. Then Brer Turtle ask
Brer Fox to burn him because he's kinna used to fire. Brer
Fox don't say nothing. Finally Brer Fox carried him down
to the creek and dunked him under the water.

"Brer Fox! Brer Fox! Let go of that stump root you got hold of and catch me."

"I ain't got hold of no stump root! I got hold of your tail!"

"Grab me, Brer Fox! I'm drowning! I'm drowning! Turn loose that stump root and grab me!"

Brer Fox turned loose of Brer Turtle's tail, and Brer Turtle? Shucks, he just slid on down to the bottom of the creek—*kerblunkity-blink*—and went on home.

Brer Fox Gets Tricked by the Frogs

Sometimes I want to feel sorry for Brer Fox. There he was standing on the bank of the creek and wasn't nothing he could do except watch Brer Turtle slowly sink to the bottom.

When Brer Turtle got to his home, he said, *"I-doom-a-ker-kum-mer-ker."* That's Turtle talk. I could tell you what it means 'cause I know creature talk. You been around much as I have, you'll know the language of all the creatures. I even know Cockroach talk but I ain't never thought of nothing to say to a cockroach so I don't talk it none.

Brer Turtle knowed English wasn't good enough to say all that was on his mind and that's how come he switched to Turtle talk. *"I-doom-a-ker-kum-mer-ker."* It's best I don't translate that.

Brer Bullfrog was sitting off in the weeds and when he heard Brer Turtle, he hollered back: *"Jug-a-rum-kum-dum! Jug-a-rum-kum-dum!"*

Another Frog yelled, *"Knee-deep! Knee-deep!"*

Brer Bullfrog said, *"Don't you believe him! Don't you believe him!"*

Then, from way down at the bottom of the creek, Brer Turtle said, *"I-doom-a-ker-kum-mer-ker!"*

The Frog yelled: *"Wade in! Wade in!"*

Brer Bullfrog croaked: *"There you'll find your brother! There you'll find your brother!"*

Brer Fox was listening to all this carrying on and he looked into the water, and sho' 'nuf! There was a Fox looking up at him. Brer Fox leaned over to shake hands with the Fox in the water, and the next thing he knew, he went head over tail and right smack in the water. *Kersplash!*

Brer Bullfrog hollered: *"You found your brother! You found your brother!"*

And from way down at the bottom of the creek Brer Turtle said: *"I-doom-a-ker-kum-mer-ker! I-doom-a-ker-kum-mer-ker!"*

Brer Bear Gets Tricked by Brer Frog

A few days later Brer Fox was telling some of the other creatures about his recent misfortunes. All the other creatures sympathized with him, all of 'em, that is, except Brer Bear.

"You got to be mighty dumb to get fooled by Brer Frog," he said. "If Brer Frog got any brains at all, they in his bass voice."

Brer Fox say, "Let's find out how supple your brains are. Why don't you go on down there to the creek and see if you can get some frog for supper?"

Brer Bear say he didn't think frog was kosher, but then again, he wasn't Jewish so he reckon it don't matter. He went and got his ax and headed for the creek.

Time he got there he saw Brer Bullfrog sitting on the creek bank. Without so much as a "Good morning" or a "How's the family" Brer Bear grabbed him. Then he remembered his manners.

"Good morning, Brer Bullfrog. How's your family? I hope they well and you done took out plenty insurance, 'cause in five minutes you'll be history. Your days of tricking folks have come to an end."

"What did I do?" Brer Bullfrog wanted to know.

"Ain't you the one what tricked Brer Fox into falling into the creek?"

Brer Bullfrog said, "It takes two to make a trick. The tricker and the trickee. Ain't my fault if Brer Fox make such a good trickee."

"I ain't got time for a whole lot of philosophy or psychology. What I'm studying today is frogology." Brer Bear started snapping his jaws and foaming at the mouth.

"Brer Bear! Brer Bear! Please let me off this time. I promise I won't play no more tricks, no matter how good a trickee come along. And not only that. If you let me go, I'll show you a tree that's just oozing with honey."

Brer Bear started gnashing his teeth.

"Please, Brer Bear! Please let me go!"

Brer Bear was too hungry to be thinking about any letting go.

"All right, Brer Bear. I know my time done come. I see

you brought your ax with you too. Just do me this favor. Carry me up to that big flat rock which overlooks the creek. I want to look down and see my family one last time. After I see 'em, you can take your ax and send me to that big lotus pad in the sky."

Well, Brer Bear wasn't a hardhearted man, so he carried Brer Bullfrog to the rock and put him down. Brer Bullfrog creeped to the edge and peered over like he was looking for his kinfolk.

Brer Bear took a deep breath, picked up his ax, and swung it round and round over his head—once, twice, three times—and come down with the ax as hard as he could.

Brer Bear hit that rock so hard it rattled the TV antenna on the Lord's house up in heaven. When he lifted the ax up and looked for a smashed Brer Bullfrog, wasn't a thing

there except a hole. Brer Frog had leaped off the rock, done a back somersault half-double gainer with a twist of lemon, and gone right into the water without so much as a splash.

And just about the time Brer Bear realized that Brer Bullfrog had found another trickee, Brer Bear heard Brer Bullfrog sing out:

> *Ingle-go-jang, my joy, my joy—*
> *Ingle-go-jang, my joy!*
> *I'm right at home, my joy, my joy—*
> *Ingle-go-jang, my joy, my joy!*

To your ears that song might sound funny, 'cause folks don't be using words like that. But to us what knows creature talk, that was a mighty serious song. If folks knew as much about creature talk and Bullfrog language as they used to, they probably wouldn't let me put that song in this story.

Brer Bear, Brer Turtle, and the Rope-Pulling Contest

Brer Bear should've had more sense than to mess with the water creatures. Water creatures got more sense than people, 'cause they done figured out how to live in the water. If it's left to me, we never will figure that out. I stay as far away from water as I can. I don't even speak to my bathtub.

The other reason Brer Bear should've left the water creatures alone was because whenever anybody messed with them, it made Brer Turtle angry, and the last thing anybody wants to do is get Brer Turtle upset.

A week or so later, all the animals were sitting around in Miz Meadows's yard. Well, you know how it is when men get around the ladies. Whenever there's a lady around, men can't think about nothing else but showing off.

Brer Rabbit started flapping his gums about how he was the swiftest of all the animals. Brer Fox said he was the sharpest. Brer Wolf said he was the most vigorous. Brer Bear said he was the strongest.

That was a little too much for Brer Turtle. "Brer Rabbit, everybody know I beat you in the big race, so don't be talking about how fast you are. Brer Fox, I know a thing or two about you but I don't want to embarrass you. Brer Wolf, if the Lord told us to turn in our brains for money, you'd be in debt. And Brer Bear, the only thing strong about you is your breath."

What did Brer Turtle want to say that for? Brer Bear rose up, and he looked big as a mountain and four times stronger. He walked around the circle flexing his muscles and little beads of sweat started popping out on the brows of the creatures, except for Brer Turtle. He was giggling.

"When you through acting like you practicing to be in the Mr. Universe contest, let's find out who's the strongest."

"How we gon' do that?" Brer Bear wanted to know.

"We'll have a rope-pulling contest."

All the creatures agreed that sounded like a good idea. The only problem was, they didn't have a rope. Miz Meadows say she got plenty rope.

"Then, let the good times roll," said Brer Turtle.

There wasn't enough space to have a decent rope-pulling contest in Miz Meadows's yard, so they went down to the creek.

When they got there, Brer Turtle took one end of the rope and gave the other to Brer Bear. "Looks to me like when we get this rope stretched out, Brer Bear, you'll be up there in the woods. When I see the slack go out of the rope, I'll give a holler and you start pulling, and we'll see who's the strongest."

Brer Bear and the other creatures went up in the woods. Then Brer Turtle took his end of the rope and dove into the water. He swam down to the bottom and tied the rope around a great big limb which was stuck in the mud. Then he swam back up to the creek bank.

"I'm ready, Brer Bear! You can start pulling!" he hollered.

Brer Bear wrapped the rope around his hand, gave Miz Meadows a big wink, and started pulling. Nothing happened.

"I said you could start pulling, Brer Bear!"

Brer Bear took both hands and pulled harder. The rope didn't budge.

"Are you pulling yet, Brer Bear?" yelled Brer Turtle.

Brer Bear turned around, put the rope over his shoulder, and pulled. Nothing happened. The rest of the creatures decided to give Brer Bear a hand, and they grabbed hold of the rope and pulled. Nothing happened. Finally Brer Bear decided there wasn't nothing he could do and let the rope go.

As soon as Brer Turtle saw the rope go slack, he dove down in the water, untied the rope from the limb, and swam back up with it. When Brer Bear and the rest of the creatures got down to the creek bank, Brer Turtle was laying there huffing and puffing like he was about to die.

"That last pull you give on the rope was mighty powerful, Brer Bear. Little bit more and I think you would've had me."

Brer Turtle Takes Care of Brer Buzzard

Nothing in the world gets your appetite going like tricking folks, and after tricking Brer Bear, Brer Turtle was hungry.

I don't know about these here modern turtles, but back in my day, the Turtle loved to eat honey. But being so little, even if he found a bee tree, he couldn't get the honey, 'cause he couldn't climb the tree.

Well, after he had shown Brer Bear who was the strongest, he went on off down the road. His mind was wrapping itself around pictures of golden honey when he happened to run into Brer Buzzard.

They shook hands and asked about one another's family and like that. Then it occurred to Brer Turtle that Brer Buzzard might be the man he was looking for.

He explained to Brer Buzzard how he couldn't keep his mind off getting some honey. Brer Buzzard said that *his* mind was just about to land on the very thing Brer Turtle's mind couldn't get off of.

"Then you and me is of one mind, Brer Buzzard. Let's join forces. Two heads are better than one, especially when they on different bodies. You fly around and look for a bee tree and I'll creep and crawl like I always do and hunt down here on the ground."

Brer Buzzard said that sounded like a good idea, and off they went.

Before long Brer Turtle came to a field and found a great big beehive on the ground. He wiggled his head inside and almost drowned in all the honey. He wiggled out and looked to see if Brer Buzzard was around. Brer Buzzard wasn't even a speck in the sky.

Brer Turtle thought for a minute. "Brer Buzzard is used to eating that sweet honey which you can only find in the tops of the trees. This honey what's been on the ground is at least Grade B and might even be Grade Z. What kind of friend would I be to offer honey to Brer Buzzard that ain't as sweet and good as what he's used to? I might as well eat this honey instead of insulting Brer Buzzard with it."

Brer Turtle crawled inside the beehive and proceeded to have himself a honey feast. When he was all done, he wriggled out and licked the honey off his feet so Brer Buzzard wouldn't know he'd found any.

Then it occurred to him that there was probably honey on his back. He stretched out his neck and tried to lick it off, but his neck wouldn't stretch that far. He leaned up against a tree and tried to scrape it off, but nothing doing. He rolled around on his back and tried to get it off, but no luck.

Just as Brer Turtle was deciding that he'd better get away from there before Brer Buzzard come back, he saw him coming in for a landing, his black wings spread out like thunderclouds!

Brer Turtle ran to the beehive, built a fire inside, and ran out shouting "Brer Buzzard! Brer Buzzard! Come here and see how much honey I found. There's so much honey in there, it dripped all over my back like a waterfall. Come quick, Brer Buzzard. You go in and get your half and then I'll get mine."

Brer Buzzard chuckled. "You found that honey just in time, 'cause I got mighty hungry flying around up there."

Brer Buzzard squeezed himself in the beehive. Soon as he was inside, Brer Turtle stopped up the opening with a big rock.

In a few minutes the fire Brer Turtle had built inside got going good. Brer Buzzard hollered out, "Ow! Something is biting me, Brer Turtle!"

"It's the bees biting you, Brer Buzzard. Flop your wings and drive 'em off."

Brer Buzzard started flopping his wings, which didn't do nothing but fan the fire and make it burn bigger and hotter. Before long there wasn't nothing left of Brer Buzzard but the ends of his big wing feathers.

When the ashes cooled down, Brer Turtle took the feathers and made 'em into quill pipes. He played a tune on the quill pipes and sang this song:

> *I fooled you, I fooled you, I fooled you,*
> *Po' Buzzard;*
> *Po' Buzzard I fooled you, I fooled you,*
> *I fooled you.*

If you was to say that wasn't much of a song, I would have to go along with you. But it sho' was the truth.

Brer Fox Wants to Make Music

You probably wondering how Brer Turtle could make music on Buzzard quills. Well, I tell you the truth: I don't know. But 'cause I don't know don't mean that Brer Turtle didn't know, and obviously he did know, 'cause the story say that what he was doing.

Brer Fox didn't know either, but when he heard Brer Turtle playing such pretty music on them quills, he wanted the quills for himself.

He begged and begged Brer Turtle to sell him the quills, but Brer Turtle say, nothing doing. Brer Fox asked Brer Turtle if he could borrow 'em for a week so he could learn how to play pretty music. Brer Turtle just keep on playing.

He asked Brer Turtle to let him look at the quills up close. He had some goose feathers at home and might could make him a set of his own. Brer Turtle thought that was a good idea, 'cause then Brer Fox would stop pestering him.

Brer Turtle held out the quills so Brer Fox could see 'em close up. The minute he did, Brer Fox snatched them quills and ran away.

Brer Turtle hollered, "Thief! Thief!" Everybody wondered how come Brer Turtle was wasting his breath saying the obvious.

Brer Turtle was miserable without his quills. He sat down in the road looking like he needed a dime to call his therapist.

The next morning when Brer Fox come dancing down the road playing on the quills, Brer Turtle was right where Brer Fox had left him. Brer Fox danced around Brer Turtle just a-playing and a-singing:

He fooled po' Brer Buzzard, he did,
But I fooled him. Yes, I fooled him.

The next day Brer Turtle was sitting on a log when Brer Fox came along playing that same song on the quills. Brer Turtle pretend like he ain't heard nothing.

Brer Fox came closer and played louder. Brer Turtle's eyes were closed but his ears was wide open. He listened and listened and when Brer Fox got close, Brer Turtle snapped at Brer Fox's foot.

But he missed. Brer Fox laughed and danced away.

The next morning Brer Turtle went down in a mudhole and smeared himself all over with mud. When he finished he looked like a clod of dirt. Then he crawled under a log where he knew Brer Fox came every morning.

Brer Turtle hadn't been there long before Brer Fox came. He sat down on the log and Brer Turtle stuck his neck out and grabbed Brer Fox's big toe!

They tell me that when a Turtle grabs on to something, it has got to thunder before he'll let go. Brer Fox didn't know nothing about that, 'cause he was in so much pain.

"Let me go, Brer Turtle. Please let me go!"

Brer Turtle talked way down in his throat. "Give me my quills."

"Let me go and I'll get 'em."

"Give me my quills."

"How can I give you the quills with you hanging on my toe?"

"Give me my quills."

Brer Fox wondered if Brer Turtle had gone crazy, 'cause that seemed to be all he could say. Brer Fox hollered for his oldest boy.

"Toby! Toby!"

"What you want, Daddy?"

"Bring Brer Turtle's quills!"

"What'd you say? Bring the fur and the cleaning bills?"

"No, you dummy! Bring Brer Turtle's quills!"

"What you say? Water done spill?"

"No, fool! Bring Brer Turtle's quills."

"What you say, Daddy? Go hurdle the hills?"

Well, it went on this way until Miz Fox began to wonder what all the racket was about. She listened and knew that Brer Fox was hollering for the quills. She took them down there and gave them to Brer Turtle.

Brer Turtle let go of Brer Fox's toe, but for a long time after that everybody could see Brer Turtle's autograph on Brer Fox's foot.

The Pimmerly Plum

Brer Turtle had his quills back, but he was angry. He decided to teach Brer Fox a lesson so that he would stay taught.

You know what Brer Turtle did? Well, he didn't scare him. It was worse than that. He didn't hurt him. It was worse than that. He didn't kill him. It was worse than that. You know what he did? He made a fool out of him.

A few days later Brer Turtle was going down the road. It was one of them hot days and he was huffing and puffing and blowing and sweating, and mostly he was cussing, but I can't put that in the story.

He made his way to the creek, crawled in, and cooled off. After a while he crawled out and settled in the shade of a big tree. Brer Turtle carries his house with him, and when he wants to go to sleep, he just shuts the door and pulls down the shades and he's as snug as a black cat under the couch.

He slept and he slept. He didn't know how long he slept, and since I wasn't there that day, I don't either. But he woke up suddenly, 'cause somebody had picked him up and was shaking him like they were trying to turn him to soup right there in his shell. Brer Turtle kept the door shut tight and listened.

When the shaking stopped, Brer Turtle cracked the door open to see who it was. Wasn't nobody but Brer Fox holding him up in the air.

Brer Turtle opened the door wide and stuck his head out and he was laughing as hard as he could. "Well, well, well. Look who done caught me. Ain't none other than

Brer Fox. You picked a good time to come along, Brer Fox, 'cause I'm so full and feeling so good, I can't do a thing to you."

"How come you so full and feeling so good?" Brer Fox wanted to know.

"I just finished eating Pimmerly Plums."

The Pimmerly Plum was the hardest-to-find fruit there was. Besides Brer Rabbit and Brer Turtle, none of the other creatures had ever even seen it, but they'd sho' 'nuf heard about it. It was supposed to be sweeter than a kiss, more juicy than ripe grapes, and tastier than a plate of waffles dripping with maple syrup.

Just the sound of the words *Pimmerly Plum* sent Brer Fox to daydreaming, and without even knowing he was doing it, he set Brer Turtle down on the ground. Brer Fox's eyes started rolling around in his head and he was dribbling at the mouth.

"Where's the Pimmerly Plum?" he wanted to know.

Brer Turtle laughed a big laugh.

"What you laughing about?"

"Why, Brer Fox! You standing right under the tree."

I got to explain something here. I know practically none of y'all ever seen a sycamore tree. Ain't no sycamore trees in the city and if there was, probably one of them muggers would steal 'em. If you was to ever see a sycamore tree, you'd recognize it immediately, because little round balls hang by a twig from the ends of their branches.

Brer Turtle pointed to the balls and said, "Them's the Pimmerly Plums, Brer Fox."

The balls were too high for Brer Fox to get. What was he going to do?

"That's where being as full of energy as you are don't

work to your advantage, Brer Fox. If you was a Slickum Slow-Come like me, wouldn't be no problem."

"Brer Turtle, what're you talking about?"

"Wouldn't do no good for me to tell you. Nimble heel, restless mind. You ain't got the time to wait and get 'em, Brer Fox."

"Brer Turtle, I got all the time in the world for the Pimmerly Plum."

Brer Turtle shook his head. "Naw, I know you. If I tell you how to get them, you'll start beating your gums and telling all the other creatures. Next thing I know, the Pimmerly Plum will have gone the way of Brer Dodo Bird."

"I wouldn't do that, Brer Turtle. I won't say a word to a living soul. A dead one either."

Brer Turtle closed his eyes like he was thinking. Finally he said, "All right, Brer Fox. I believe you. Whenever I want some of the Pimmerly Plum, this is what I do. I come here to the tree and I get right under it. I put my head back and shut my eyes. Then I open my mouth as wide as I can, and when the Pimmerly Plum is ready to drop, it drops right in my mouth. All you got to do is be patient and don't move."

Brer Fox didn't wait to hear another word. He sat down on his haunches beneath the tree, reared back his head, closed his eyes, and opened his mouth.

Brer Turtle started to laugh but then decided he could laugh louder and longer if he was to do it at home, which is where he went.

You know, it's a curious thing about this story. Ain't nobody ever told me how long Brer Fox sat there with his head reared back, eyes closed and mouth open. For all I know, he might still be there.

Brer Turtle Takes Flying Lessons

Brer Turtle decided to reward himself for having gotten rid of Brer Fox for a while, so he went looking for Brer Buzzard, 'cause he wanted to take flying lessons.

I know. You thought Brer Buzzard got burned up. So what if he did? What makes you think *that* Brer Buzzard was this Brer Buzzard or that this Brer Buzzard was that Brer Buzzard? Sometimes that is that and this is this. Other times this is that and that is the other and everything else is chocolate pudding.

Now, where was I? Oh, yes. Brer Turtle started pestering Brer Buzzard about giving him flying lessons. Brer Buzzard said Brer Turtle couldn't learn to fly because there was too much of him in the same place. But Brer Turtle wasn't about to take no for an answer. Finally Brer Buzzard said he'd do it.

Brer Turtle was ready right then, but Brer Buzzard said he had to go get his pilot's license renewed and it was also his day to get his hair shampooed and nails manicured and he'd see Brer Turtle the next day.

Next morning, just as King Sun was peeking his left eye over the topside of the world, Brer Buzzard sailed in. He squatted down on the grass next to Brer Turtle. Brer Turtle huffed and puffed and finally made it onto Brer Buzzard's back.

Brer Buzzard started off real easy. He caught a nice gentle current of wind under his big wings and soared around for a while over the fields and the river. Brer Turtle said that flying was might nice. A few more lessons and he'd be ready to do it on his own.

Every morning for the next few days Brer Turtle took a ride on Brer Buzzard's back. "Tomorrow morning, Brer

Buzzard, when we get up in the air, I'm gon' do my own flying."

"Whatever you say, Brer Turtle."

Next morning came and Brer Buzzard took Brer Turtle on up. Brer Buzzard got so high in the sky that you could hear the stars yawning as they was going to bed. 'Long about the time King Sun was finishing his first cup of coffee, Brer Buzzard swooped and slid out from under Brer Turtle.

Brer Turtle flapped his feet and wagged his head and shook his tail, but that didn't help him one bit. He turned upside down and right-side up and sideways over sideways

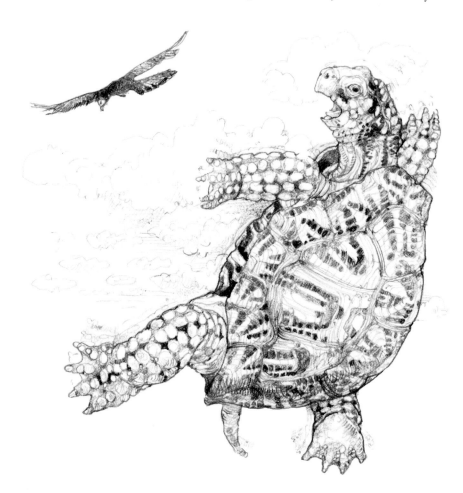

and hit the ground—*ka-blam-a-blam-blam-blam!* If his shell hadn't been so strong, Brer Turtle would've busted wide open.

He lay there huffing and puffing and groaning like the next minute was going to be his last.

Brer Buzzard sailed down and landed next to Brer Turtle. "How you feel?"

"I'm ruined, Brer Buzzard. My back ain't never gon' be the same."

"I tried to tell you that you didn't have the requirements for flying."

"Brer Buzzard, just hush up! I flew as good as you or any of the other winged creatures. But you forgot to teach me how to land! Flying is easy, but landing can be mighty hard on a body."

Brer Buzzard and Brer Hawk

Brer Buzzard is one of the ugliest creatures in nature. If ugly was money, Brer Buzzard would've been the richest thing to ever walk the earth. But if being ugly wasn't bad enough, Brer Buzzard never did score above the single digits on an IQ test. I threw out an empty can of peas the other day what had more sense than Brer Buzzard.

Brer Buzzard could fly high and he could fly low and he could fly around in great big circles. But he didn't have sense enough to stay dry when it rained. On rainy days Brer Buzzard would find a big tall pine tree to sit in. It would rain and the wind would blow and Brer Buzzard would look as raggedy as a mop which has seen a few too many kitchen floors. Brer Buzzard would say, "When the wind stops blowing and the rain stops dripping, I going to build me a house. No doubt about it. And I'm gon' make that house tight to keep the rain and wind out."

The next day when the sky would be all dried out and the wind was curled up again in that big pot the Lord keeps it in and King Sun would turn his light on again, Brer Buzzard would spread his wings, stretch his neck, and dry himself off. "Ain't no point in building a house today," he'd say, " 'cause it ain't raining no more." The only thing Brer Buzzard wasn't dumb about was eating.

One time Brer Hawk was sailing around on his pretty wings looking for something to eat, and he saw Brer Buzzard sitting on a dead limb, looking lazy and lonesome.

Brer Hawk flew down. "What's happening, Brer Buzzard?"

Brer Buzzard shook his head. "Ain't doing too good, Brer Hawk. I'm po' and hungry."

"Well, if you hungry, why don't you go find some food? You ain't got to hunt your food like I do. Ol' Boy do your hunting for you, and Ol' Boy ain't never took a day off from work."

Brer Buzzard shook his head. "That's true, Brer Hawk, but I'm gon' wait on the Lord."

Brer Hawk laughed. "You best go get some breakfast and then come back and wait. It's a lot easier to wait on the Lord when you got something in your stomach."

Brer Buzzard shook his head. "I want to be here so the Lord can provide."

Brer Hawk chuckled. "Whatever you say. You got your ways and I got mine. I see some chickens down there in

Mr. Man's yard. I'm gon' swoop down and get one and then I'll come back and wait with you."

Brer Hawk spread his great wings and took off. Brer Buzzard scrunched his neck down between his shoulders and looked more lonesome than ever. But he kept one eye on Brer Hawk.

Brer Hawk flew way up in the sky. He flew so high that King Sun started to put a For Sale sign in his front yard, 'cause he didn't want to have nothing to do with Brer Hawk's sharp talons and beak. Brer Hawk wasn't thinking about King Sun. He had his sharp eyes on them chickens.

When he had decided on the one that looked the plumpest and juiciest, he tucked in his wings and shot down from the sky like he'd been fired from a gun. He was going so fast that the air turned cold as he flew down through the sky and all the clouds had to put on their winter coats. But Brer Hawk was going too fast for his own good because his aim was a little off and he was too close to the ground to do anything about it.

Po' Brer Hawk. Instead of landing on that chicken he landed on the point of the fence post and that fence post went through him like it was a sword.

Brer Buzzard looked down at Brer Hawk. Brer Hawk don't move. Brer Buzzard wait and watch some more. Brer Hawk still don't move. He was stone dead.

"I knew the Lord would provide," Brer Buzzard said, and he flew on down to where Brer Hawk was waiting for him.

Brer Buzzard Bites the Dust—Again

The second time Brer Buzzard come to an unfortunate end was almost like the first time. But anybody what ain't got enough sense to know how to stay dry when it's raining don't deserve no better.

The way it come about was like this:

One time Brer Wolf and Brer Fox got to arguing about something. Wasn't nothing important, 'cause Brer Wolf and Brer Fox didn't know nothing important. But what ain't important to you and me is earth shaking to somebody else, and that's the way it was with Brer Wolf and Brer Fox.

Brer Wolf said it was so and Brer Fox said it wasn't so. Brer Wolf said was, and Brer Fox said wasn't, and they got to wasing and wasn'ting something fierce until Brer Wolf called Brer Fox dumb and Brer Fox said to Brer Wolf, "Your mama is dumb." Look out! You don't be talking about nobody's mama, not even Brer Wolf's.

Brer Wolf don't say nothing else, leastways not with his mouth. But he had a left jab, a right cross, left uppercut, and right hook that used up a whole lot of words in the dictionary. Brer Fox was scared that Brer Wolf might start using some of them words what's in the encyclopedia, and he took off.

Brer Wolf was right with him, snapping at his tail. Brer Fox knew he had to find someplace to hide. He spied a hollow tree and dove in head first. Brer Wolf snapped at him, but he was just in time to be too late.

Brer Wolf sat down next to the tree and began to think on how to get Brer Fox out. When he couldn't think of nothing, he decided that it would be just as good to keep Brer Fox in.

He gathered up a whole bunch of rocks and filled the hole in the tree until Brer Fox was sealed in as tight as if he was in a grave.

Brer Buzzard was flopping around up in the elements and he saw Brer Wolf sealing up the hole in the tree.

"I believe I better go down and investigate," Brer Buzzard said to himself. "If Brer Wolf is hiding his dinner and planning on coming back for it later, he has put his dinner in the wrong place. But I ain't gon' tell him that."

Brer Buzzard flopped on down. "What you doing, Brer Wolf?"

"Making a tombstone."

Any mention of death brings a smile to Brer Buzzard's face. "Who's dead?" he asked, barely able to contain his joy.

"Brer Fox."

"When did he die?"

"He ain't dead yet, but he won't last long in there. He's all yours, Brer Buzzard." Brer Wolf brushed his hands and clothes off and went on home like a man who'd just finished a good day's work.

Brer Buzzard put his ear close to the tree. He could hear Brer Fox inside crying something awful. Brer Buzzard might not have had sense enough to know how to stay dry, but he knew dead folks don't cry. So he flew on off.

Bright and early the next morning Brer Buzzard came back. He put his ear to the tree. He didn't hear a thing. He waited a while, then listened again. Still don't hear nothing. Then he sang a song:

Boo, boo, book, my filler-ma-loo,
Man out here with news for you.

He put his ear to the tree and listened. Brer Fox sang back:

Go away, go away, my little jug of beer,
The news you bring, I heard last year.

I ain't exactly sure what kind of beer it was, but I know it wasn't Miller Lite or Bud. Seems like I remember somebody telling me it was root beer, but whether it was caffeine free or low cal, I don't know.

When Brer Buzzard heard Brer Fox sing back, he figured that he wasn't dead, which was good figuring. So Brer Buzzard went on about his business.

Bright and early the next morning Brer Buzzard came back. He sang his song and Brer Fox sang his song. Brer Buzzard don't mind. He's a very patient man. Waiting on Ol' Boy had never tired him out.

Brer Fox was not a patient man, especially when he was hungry and his navel and his backbone were carrying on deep philosophical conversations. Brer Fox knew he had to come up with a plan to get out of there.

Bright and early the next morning here come Brer Buzzard. He went up to the tree and stuck his ear against it. Don't hear nothing. Then he sang out:

Boo, boo, boo, my filler-ma-loo,
Man out here with news for you!

He listened at the tree. Don't hear nothing. He listen awhile longer. Still don't hear nothing. A big grin spread over his face.

He started taking the rocks out of the hole. He'd take a few rocks out and listen. Don't hear nothing. He'd take a few more out and listen again. It went on this way until the hole was uncovered.

The minute it was, Brer Fox came charging out like it was Judgment Day and he was gon' be late getting through the Pearly Gates. He grabbed Brer Buzzard by the neck and what he did after that is too horrible to talk about. But I can tell you that by the time Brer Fox got through, there wasn't enough of Brer Buzzard left for a funeral.

The Wise Bird and the Foolish Bird

Once there was a Wise Bird and a Foolish Bird. Both lived in the same country and both used the same forest.

One day the Wise Bird lighted in the tree where the Foolish Bird was sitting.

The Wise Bird looked at the Foolish Bird admiringly. "You are one good-looking bird," he said. "You are long in the leg and deep in the craw. You stand so tall and erect. You look like you're going to live a long time."

The Foolish Bird swelled with pride. "Well, I don't like to brag, but it's always nice when others recognize your good qualities."

"I've always been one to give credit where credit is due," the Wise Bird said. "However, I think there's one area where I can outdo you."

"And what might that be?"

"I can go longer than you can without drinking water."

The Foolish Bird was indignant. "I doubt that very seriously."

"How about we have a little contest, then?" proposed

the Wise Bird. "Let's see who can go the longest without drinking water."

The Foolish Bird stuck out his neck and tossed his head and laughed. "I'll beat you all day every day."

The Wise Bird handed the Foolish Bird a horn. "Here. You take this horn and go up in that tree on the creek side. I'll take this horn and go up in a tree on the hillside. We'll see how long we can go without drinking. When I blow on my horn, you blow on yours and answer me. Me blow, you blow, and then we'll both blow."

The Foolish Bird strutted around on the limb. "I'll beat you all day every day."

The next morning the Wise Bird and the Foolish Bird took their horns and went to their trees.

The Foolish Bird was in the tree by the creek, and before long he discovered that there wasn't a thing to eat in that tree.

The Wise Bird's tree was covered with bark, and the bark was crawling with bugs, ants, and worms. The Wise Bird ate and ate and ate until he thought he was going to burst.

The Foolish Bird was beginning to feel tired from hunger. He sat down and felt more tired. He got up and was still tired. He stood on one leg and then on the other. He tucked his head beneath his wing, but no matter what he did, he was still tired.

The Wise Bird felt so good that he took a little nap, and when he woke up he felt even better. He picked up his horn and tooted it loud and clear:

Tay-tay, tenando wansando waneanzo!

The Foolish Bird was tired but he took his horn and blew:

Tay-tay, tenando wansando waneanzo!

Along about sundown the Wise Bird was hungry again. He ate more bugs and ants and worms, which were crawling all over his tree, and when he was full he felt very, very good. Then he picked up his horn and tooted it loud and clear:

Tay-tay, tenando wansando waneanzo!

The Foolish Bird picked up his horn and answered back, but the sound of his horn was weak.

The next morning when King Sun came up, the Wise Bird ate some more bugs, ants, and worms. Then he drank the dew off the leaves, belched a couple of times, and chuckled. He picked up his horn and started blowing. He blew so good that some of the other birds wondered if Louis Armstrong had come to town.

The Foolish Bird tooted back, but his toot was so faint you could hardly hear it.

When dinnertime came the Wise Bird ate his fill. Then he picked up his horn and did a pretty good imitation of Miles Davis playing "Round about Midnight." The Foolish Bird tooted back but it wasn't as loud as a whisper.

When Sister Moon came up that night, the Wise Bird played a couple of choruses of "Fly Me to the Moon." This time he didn't hear a toot from the Foolish Bird.

The Wise Bird flew over to the tree by the creek, and there was the Foolish Bird as dead as dead can get.

The Wise Bird played "When the Saints Go Marching In" and went on about his business.

The Most-Beautiful-Bird in-the-World Contest

This story is about the most beautiful bird in the whole world. She's gone away now and can't nobody find her.

Some called her the Coogly Bird. Others called her the Cow-Cow Bird. Still others said she was the Coo-Coo Bird. Call her what you please. Call her when you please. It ain't gon' make no difference. If calling would've fetched her back, she would be here now. But the birds been calling for her from that day to this and she ain't come yet. She was the prettiest bird there ever was and ever will be.

Way back yonder when the clouds were thicker than they are now, back when the sun didn't have to go to bed at night to keep from being tired the next day, the creatures didn't have much to do, especially the birds. They flew around and played games; they ate their meals together without getting into squabbles, and spent all their time socializing with one another.

After a while having peace began to get on their nerves and they started getting into squabbles with one another.

One day Miz Red Bird announced that she was the prettiest thing to sit on a limb since apple blossoms. What she want to say that for? Miz Blue Bird said Miz Red Bird better get her mirror checked, 'cause it had started lying to her. Miz Jay Bird said, uh-uh, wasn't nobody more glamorouser than her. Brer Hawk come sticking his lip in the matter and cast a vote for himself. And you might not believe this, but Brer Buzzard say that the other birds didn't know what pretty was until they got a good look at him. The arguing got so bad that war was about to break out.

Miz Wren, Miz Blue Bird, and Miz Robin got together to figure out how to stop all the arguing and fighting. They thought and they thought and they studied and they studied, but they couldn't come up with a solution.

After a while Miz Wren said, "I got an idea. Why don't we go home and ask our menfolk what they think. You know how men are. They know everything except what they know, and that's what they done forgot."

Miz Robin and Miz Blue Bird said that was the smartest thing they'd ever heard.

The next morning Miz Wren, Miz Robin, and Miz Blue Bird got together again. Miz Robin said she'd asked her husband and he said she best help him hunt bugs for the children and stop wasting time on what don't matter. Miz Blue Bird said that when she asked her husband, he said he needed some clean underwear to put on for work the next day. Miz Wren said that when she asked her husband, he wanted to know how come she didn't cook nothing every day but worm casserole with Parmesan cheese. She said she told him that anytime he wanted to try eating in somebody else's kitchen, he was more than welcome. Then he said, "You should have a big gathering of all the lady birds, have everybody parade around and let somebody pick out the prettiest one, and that would be that. If the judge say the Owl was the prettiest, then wasn't no disputing about it. If the judge say the Buzzard was the prettiest, well, that was how it was going to be. Once the

matter is settled, I'll buy you this new cookbook I saw—
Three Hundred and Sixty-five Ways to Cook Worms."

Miz Wren, Miz Robin, and Miz Blue Jay didn't know
about the cookbook, but they thought having a contest
was a good idea. They talked it over with the other birds,
and everybody agreed.

Then they discussed who the judge should be. They
quickly agreed there wasn't nobody better for the job than
Brer Rabbit, 'cause he wasn't a bird eater and his decision
wouldn't be influenced by his stomach.

The day for the contest came. Brer Rabbit was sitting
in a big chair and all the birds started coming in. They
had on their Guccis and Puccis and K mart best and were
wearing high heels and pearls and dangly earrings and smiles
left over from the Miss America contest.

The parade had barely started, though, when Brer Rabbit shook his head.

All the birds stopped. "What's the matter, Brer Rabbit?
How come you shaking your head like something is the
matter?"

Brer Rabbit shook his head again. "Can't be no contest
because one bird is missing." He got up out of his chair
and made a courteous bow. He looked so good that Miz
Swamp Owl's mouth started to water. Rabbit meat was
the tastiest thing in the world to her, but she controlled
herself.

"Wait a minute, Brer Rabbit!" the birds called out.
"Who's missing?"

"Where's Miz Coo-Coo Bird?" he asked.

Didn't nobody know.

Brer Rabbit said, "You gon' have to postpone the contest until somebody can get word to Miz Coo-Coo Bird.

She's got to be in the contest. If she ain't, she might not go along with my decision. If you want all the squabbling to stop, she got to be here. Ain't no two ways about that."

Some of the birds say the contest can go on without Miz Coo-Coo Bird 'cause she wasn't nothing to look at anyway. But they finally agreed there couldn't be no contest if all the birds wasn't there.

Well, time went on just like it does now, except that back in them days mealtime came a whole lot sooner. Some of the birds went looking for Miz Coo-Coo Bird. The rest spent as much time as they could at Brer Rabbit's house trying to get him to see them through their eyes.

It took 'em about a week, but they found Miz Coo-Coo Bird at home, which is where they should've gone first. When the birds saw her, they were surprised. Miz Coo-Coo Bird didn't have on a stitch of clothes. Where there should've been feathers there wasn't nothing but fuzz.

"How come you didn't come to the contest?" the birds asked.

"Look at me! I ain't got nothing to wear."

"Well, we sorry about that, but we got to have all the birds at the contest so it'll be fair."

Miz Coo-Coo Bird shook her head and went on back to cleaning out the oven. The birds persuaded and pleaded and argued. Finally Miz Coo-Coo Bird said, "If y'all will lend me something to wear, I'll come."

The birds went around to all the other birds and asked each one to loan Miz Coo-Coo Bird a feather. Miss Ostrich knew she didn't stand a chance in the contest because of her bony neck and long skinny legs, so she sent Miz Coo-Coo Bird a bunch of the prettiest feathers you ever laid your eyes on.

The day for the contest came and all the birds were there. Miz Coo-Coo Bird was at the head of the parade and wasn't no two ways about it: She was the prettiest of them all. She was dressed in every color there was, and when all them colors blended together they created new colors what nobody had ever seen before and what nobody ain't never seen since.

The parade was scarcely a quarter over before Brer Rabbit stood up and waved his hand. "Stop the contest! Miz Coo-Coo Bird is the prettiest thing ever been put on the topside of the world."

The other birds had to go along with Brer Rabbit, and that was that. The band struck up the music for the dance they were going to have after the contest. Miz Coo-Coo Bird said they would have to excuse her, and she slipped through the bushes and was gone.

And ain't nobody seen her from that day to this. Well, maybe Brer Rabbit know where she is, but if he do, he ain't saying.

The other birds hunted high and low, low and high, sideways to sideways, up and down, and down and up. Everywhere they went, they hollered, "Coo-Coo! Coo-Coo!" That's what the Turtledove is doing when you hear it call. That's what the Pigeon is doing when you hear it. When the Rooster be making racket all through the night and day, he's calling and asking Miz Coo-Coo Bird to bring back the feather what he loaned her.

The old folks told me that when you see birds picking at their feathers and trying to straighten 'em out, what they're really doing is trying to see if the feather they loaned to Miz Coo-coo Bird has grown back.

Brer Fox and Uncle Mud Turtle

Uncle Mud Turtle was the oldest in the Turtle family. Some say he was so old that when the Lord created water and told it to be wet, the water come to Uncle Mud Turtle and asked him how to do that. So why Brer Fox think he could get the best of Uncle Mud Turtle is more than my mind can wrap around.

One day Brer Fox was down at the creek fishing. Maybe the fish heard that Brer Fox was coming, because he couldn't catch a cold.

It was getting over on the hindside of the day and Ol' Man Hungry was becoming good friends with Brer Fox. He put down his fishing pole and stuck his hand in the water. Maybe there was a big ol' catfish tucked in underneath the bank of the creek.

I don't know where the catfish were, but I do know where Uncle Mud Turtle was. He was laying under the bank sound asleep when he felt something fumbling around his head. He moved his head, but that didn't help.

Uncle Mud Turtle opened his mouth and the next time something felt around his head, he shut his mouth on it.

Brer Fox hollered so loud and so awful that folks ten miles away started crying. "Ouch! Turn me loose! Whatever you are, please turn me loose! Help! Help!"

Uncle Mud Turtle shut his mouth tighter until he felt comfortable. He was almost back to sleep when Brer Fox gave a holler so loud and a pull so hard that he jerked Uncle Mud Turtle out of the water.

When Uncle Mud Turtle got up on the bank and saw who he'd caught hold of, he opened his mouth and let Brer Fox go. "Excuse me, Brer Fox. I didn't know that was you. Hope I didn't do your hand no permanent harm. I'm truly sorry."

Brer Fox wasn't in the mood for no apologies. You know how it is. Sometimes we get our feelings hurt so bad that nothing will make 'em feel better until somebody else is hurting bad as we are. That ain't right, but that's just the way we be sometime.

Brer Fox's feelings were hurt because he hadn't been

able to catch nothing and the Hungries were walking back and forth across his stomach with spiked shoes on.

Uncle Mud Turtle saw how angry Brer Fox was, and he acted like he was scared. "Brer Fox, you got to believe me. If I'd known that was you, I would've kept my mouth shut. I know what a dangerous man you are. I knowed your daddy and your granddaddy, and you more dangerous than both of them put together."

"You right about that," answered Brer Fox. "And when I get through with you, the only place your folks will be able to find you will be in their dreams."

Uncle Mud Turtle cried on one side of his face and laughed on the other. "Please, Brer Fox, sir. Let me off this time. I promise I'll be your friend until Sister Moon catches King Sun."

Brer Fox wasn't hearing none of that and made a grab for Uncle Mud Turtle's neck. Uncle Mud Turtle pulled his head and his feet inside his shell.

Brer Fox was so hungry that he picked Uncle Mud Turtle up and started gnawing on the shell. He would've found something softer if he'd chewed on a rock.

From inside the shell Uncle Mud Turtle chuckled and said, "Brer Fox, hard ain't the name for my shell. You'll be jimber jawed before you gnaw through it."

Brer Fox keep on gnawing and gnawing and gouging and gouging.

This went on for a while and Uncle Mud Turtle was getting bored. All he wanted to do was get back under the bank and finish his nap. "Brer Fox, I'll tell you something. Teeth won't get my shell off. Claws won't get it off. But mud and water will." And with that Uncle Mud Turtle went back to sleep.

Brer Fox gnawed and gnawed and gouged and gouged until his mouth was sore and his teeth hurt. Uncle Mud Turtle was snoring so loud it sounded like a chain saw.

Brer Fox put him down on the ground and decided to play a trick on him. "Well, Uncle Mud Turtle, I got to get home and put some bandages on my hand. But you better believe that if it's the last thing I do, I'm gon' pay you back."

Brer Fox made a lot of racket like he was leaving. All he did was go hide behind some bushes. If he'd had any sense he would've known something that simpleminded wasn't gon' fool Uncle Mud Turtle.

Brer Fox's impatience got stirred up, and he came out from behind the bush and grabbed Uncle Mud Turtle. "You better tell me how to get your shell off, 'cause you know you can't outrun me."

"Teeth won't get it off. Claws won't get it off. Mud and water will do the work."

"I ain't got time for no riddles. Tell me how to get this shell off."

Brer Mud Turtle said, "Put me in the mud and rub my back as hard as you can, and the shell will come off."

Brer Fox took Uncle Mud Turtle over to a muddy place next to the creek, shoved him down in it, and started rubbing Uncle Mud Turtle's shell as hard as he could. The harder he rubbed, the deeper Uncle Mud Turtle sank into the mud until—bloop!—Uncle Mud Turtle disappeared.

Brer Fox felt around in the mud. Uncle Mud Turtle was gone. Before it occurred to Brer Fox that Uncle Mud Turtle was at home in the mud, which was how come he was named Uncle *Mud* Turtle, something grabbed Brer Fox's tale and dragged him into the water.

Brer Fox spluttered and kicked and splashed until he got back on dry land. He looked around and there was Uncle Mud Turtle floating in the water and laughing at him. Uncle Mud Turtle had sunk down through the mud and right into the creek.

That was one day Brer Fox would've saved himself a lot of time and trouble if he'd just gone to Wendy's for his dinner.

The Creature with No Claws

Sometimes folks ask me if these tales have any point to 'em, a moral, or something like that. I hope not! Nothing ruins a good story more than a commercial.

But that don't mean you can't learn nothing from these stories. What I've learned is not to believe what I see or what I hear, what I smell or what I taste. I believe only what I can put my hands on and feel. The truth is that folks fool themselves a lot worse than they get fooled by others. If you don't believe it, you ask Brer Wolf the next time you meet him in the big road.

Brer Wolf was going down the big road one day feeling mighty good. I don't know whether he'd just discovered a new mouthwash or what, but he was feeling like he was the boss of everything in the world and that included being able to tell Ol' Man North Wind when to blow, where to blow, and how strong. When somebody feels that good, they dangerous to the very person they want to protect the most—themselves!

Well, Brer Wolf was going down the road when he saw a track in the dirt. He stopped and looked at it.

"What kind of creature is this? Brer Dog didn't make that track. Brer Fox didn't make that track. Looks to me like it's a creature what ain't got no claws. I'm gon' follow him, and when I catch up to him, he'll be my meat!"

The track went up the road and down the road. It went off the road and on the road. It went straight and it went crooked. It zigged and it zagged, but Brer Wolf stayed right with it.

After a while the track started to look fresher and fresher. Brer Wolf stopped and examined it again. He still couldn't see no claw in it. He resumed following the track until, suddenly, he stopped dead still.

Right there in front of his eyes was the creature with no claws. It was the strangest-looking thing Brer Wolf had ever seen. It had a big head, sharp nose, and a bob tail and was walking around and around a big dogwood tree, rubbing his sides against it.

Brer Wolf said, "Looks to me like that creature been in a fight and lost most of his tail. And if that ain't bad enough, looks to me like that creature got some kind of itching disease, 'cause he's about to scratch all the bark off that tree."

Brer Wolf hollered, "Hey! You! What you scratching your hide on my tree for? If you ain't careful you gon' break it down."

The creature don't answer. He just keep on walking around and around the tree, scratching his sides and back.

"Didn't you hear me talking to you? Stop scratching your hide on my tree!"

The creature don't answer. He just keep on walking around and around the tree.

"You better answer me, you molly-dodger! Get out of my woods and leave my tree alone!"

Brer Wolf marched over to the creature like he was going to stomp him into the ground and make dust out of him. The creature kept on rubbing himself against the tree. You know how it is when you get an itch and you scratch and scratch and after a while it feels so good that you can't stop scratching? Well, that's how it was with the creature. He was just scratching and smiling, scratching and smiling. But when Brer Wolf got close, the creature stopped and stood up on his hind legs like a squirrel does when it's eating nuts.

Brer Wolf said, "Uh-huh. You begging, I see. Well, ain't gon' do you no good. I might've let you off if you had minded me when I hollered at you, but I got to teach you a lesson now so that next time I holler, you'll know I mean business."

The creature wrinkled up his face and mouth.

"Ain't no point in you scrunching up your face like you going to cry. Wait till I give you something to cry about."

Brer Wolf drew back his arm to hit the creature. The creature bopped Brer Wolf on the left side of his face, bopped him on the right side, and hit him square in the nose.

About four days later Brer Wolf woke up and wanted to know what had happened. His wife told him, "Fool, don't you know Brer Wildcat when you see him?"

Brer Polecat Finds a Winter Home

Late one year, 'long about the time when old Jack Frost was getting ready to come back from vacation and get to work, Brer Polecat knew it was time to find somewhere to stay for the winter.

He went and knocked on the door where Brer Rattlesnake was hiding from Jack Frost.

"Who's that?" Brer Rattlesnake say.

"It's me. Open the door."

"What you want?"

"It's getting kind of chilly out here," Brer Polecat answered.

"That's what I heard."

"It's too cold to stay out here. I might freeze to death."

"Do tell."

"Let me in there where it's warm."

Brer Rattlesnake say, "Two make a crowd, and I don't like crowds."

"I got a reputation for being a good housekeeper."

"So do I," said Brer Rattlesnake.

Brer Polecat was getting mad. "I'm gon' come in anyhow."

"Ain't room enough in here for both of us."

"I'll make room!" Brer Polecat hollered.

He backed off, got a running start, and slammed into the door. But Brer Rattlesnake had put a bar across the door. Every time Brer Polecat hit the door, it shook but it didn't fall. Wasn't nothing for Brer Polecat to do but go on his way.

Brer Bear had the biggest and warmest house of all the creatures. He had to, 'cause everybody in the Bear family was big and fat. They needed as much room as they could get.

The Bear Family was the happiest family too. There was the boy. His name was Simmon. The girl's name was Sue. And then there was Brer Bear, Miz Brune, and Miz Brindle. They all lived there in the house day after day and night after night. They ate their meals together and segashuated along from day to day, washing their face and hands in the same washpan and wiping on the same towel the way all happy families do.

One day when Jack Frost had put a hard layer of white on everything and Ol' Man North Wind was running around through the community making sure that everybody who wasn't indoors went there, there was a mighty knocking on Brer Bear's door.

"Who's knocking on my door at this time of year?" Brer Bear hollered.

Didn't no answer come, excepting that the banging got louder and bigger.

"Stop trying to tear down my door! Who you and what you want?"

"I'm one and therefore not two. If you are more than one, then who are you and what you doing in there?"

"What's your family name?" Brer Bear wanted to know.

"I'm the knocker and the mover, and if I can't climb over, I'll crawl under. Some call me Brer Polecat. Others call me a big word that ain't worthwhile remembering, but I want to move in. It's cold as the hair in a polar bear's nose out here, and something tells me that it's mighty warm in there where you are."

"It's warm enough for them what stays in here and don't go out there," said Brer Bear. "What do you want?"

"I want a lot of things what I don't get. But I'm a powerful housekeeper."

"I don't need no housekeeper, and there's just enough room for us what's already in here."

Brer Polecat said, "You might think you ain't got no room, but let me in and I'll make room, all the room I want."

Brer Bear opened the door and Brer Polecat came in. When Brer Polecat said he'd make room, he wasn't joking. His breath was so bad that Brer Bear and his whole family had to move out. And far as I know, Brer Polecat is still there.

Brer Bear and Brer Rabbit Take Care of Brer Fox and Brer Wolf

No matter how hard he tried, Brer Rabbit couldn't keep out of trouble. That seemed to be his nature. But when his head bought him trouble deeper than what he'd counted on, he called on his feet, because that's where he kept his lippity-clip and his blickety-blick.

One day Brer Rabbit decided to go bear hunting. You probably want to know how come something as little as Brer Rabbit would go hunting after something as big as Brer Bear. I don't know. But if there's one way to put gray hairs in your head, it's to worry with the ups and downs of Brer Rabbit. Now, maybe he had sense and maybe he didn't. Either way it don't make no difference, because the old times are gone forever, and if it wasn't for these tales, nobody would know that there'd ever been old times.

So, Brer Rabbit was going down the road and happened to meet up with Brer Fox and Brer Wolf. They said their howdy-dos and what all and sat down on the side of the road to tell all they knew and a lot more.

Brer Fox said he was bored. "Ain't nothing happening. No parties, no picnics, no barbecues."

Brer Wolf said he'd given up all that kind of stuff.

Brer Rabbit said, "I don't know what your problem is, Brer Fox. The only time I was bored was when I wasn't born. But even then I was kind of restless."

"Well, what you doing today to keep yourself entertained?"

"I'm getting ready to go bear hunting."

"Bear hunting!" exclaimed Brer Fox and Brer Wolf at

the same time. "You done lost your mind sho' 'nuf this time, Brer Rabbit."

"Them's the very words my wife said just this very morning. She said I'm gon' get myself killed."

Brer Wolf laughed. "She right about that. Something as little as you can't catch no bear. I'm lots bigger than you, but I'd think twice and dream four times before I went out to hunt Brer Bear. Especially now. He just moved into his brand-new house and he's still plenty mad about Brer Polecat."

"That's the very reason why this is the best time to go bear hunting. When a bear is mad, he can't think good."

Brer Fox and Brer Wolf let that roll around in their brains for a minute and agreed that Brer Rabbit was right.

"My grandaddy's grandaddy said he'd had some bear meat once and it was better than fried chicken with cranberry sauce washed down with grape Kool-Aid."

"Do tell!" said Brer Wolf.

"I got a plan, but I need some help. Brer Wolf, if I get Brer Bear on the run, will you and Brer Fox head him off?"

Brer Wolf and Brer Fox looked at each other and nodded. "We'll do it, Brer Rabbit."

Brer Rabbit said he had to go make the arrangements for the barbecue they would have after they caught Brer Bear. "I'll meet y'all here same time tomorrow."

"Hold on, Brer Rabbit," said Brer Wolf. "Exactly what is it that you want us to do? Don't get me wrong. I ain't scared or nothing like that, but I just want to know what the plan is."

"Don't worry about nothing. All you got to do is stand your ground and not get scared when you see Brer Bear coming. He'll be running faster than a locomotive on greased rails, but when he sees you, he'll turn to the side and I'll have him."

After Brer Rabbit left, Brer Wolf and Brer Fox looked at each other. "What you reckon he's really up to?" Brer Wolf wanted to know. "Brer Rabbit got more sense than to go hunting Brer Bear."

Brer Fox shook his head. "Beats me."

Brer Wolf smiled. "I bet I know. He's trying to make fools of us. He thinks we're scared. If we go tomorrow, he'll say that he can't find Brer Bear. If we don't go, he'll laugh and tell everybody that we were too scared."

Brer Fox smiled. "Well, if that's the case, I reckon we be obliged to show up."

While Brer Fox and Brer Wolf were wearing out their brains trying to figure out what Brer Rabbit was up to, Brer Rabbit was on his way to Brer Bear's house.

When he got there he didn't go up on the porch and knock on the door. He'd heard that Brer Bear was sitting behind his door with a shotgun and anybody who knocked on it was going to get blown halfway to Philly-Me-York.

Brer Rabbit stood out in the middle of the road and called out, "Hey! Brer Bear!"

After a few minutes Brer Rabbit heard the locks on the door being unfastened. That took about ten minutes, and then Brer Bear stepped out on the porch. "Come on in, Brer Rabbit!"

Brer Rabbit went in the house and him and Brer Bear sat down in the den. "Why don't we pop some popcorn, Brer Rabbit, and watch some videos. I just got some new ones. You seen the one called *The Brussels Sprout That Ate New York?*"

Brer Rabbit said he hadn't.

"I got another new one too, called *The Day Spinach Disappeared From the Face of the Earth.*"

Seeing as how Brer Rabbit loved all kinds of greens, he said that sounded like a movie too scary for him to watch. "To tell the truth, Brer Bear, this ain't no pleasure visit. I got some important information I feel obliged to pass on to you."

"What's that?" Brer Bear wanted to know.

"I can't testify to the truth of it, you understand, but there's news going around the community that Brer Wolf and Brer Fox found some tracks in their cornfield, suspicious tracks."

"So? If I saw tracks in my field, I'd follow 'em to see where they led."

"Well, from what I hear, Brer Fox and Brer Wolf studied them tracks like detectives and decided that they'd be better off letting them tracks go on off by themselves. They figured that if they followed them tracks, they would end up in more trouble than they could handle."

"Nothing wrong with that. But you don't mean to tell me that Brer Wolf and Brer Fox gon' let the molly-dodger get away with something like that. There's more ways than one to deal with somebody like that."

"That's the truth, Brer Bear. Brer Wolf and Brer Fox done put out the word that they gon' have a big bear hunt. They sent engraved invitations to all the neighbors, at least all them that can read, and the neighbors are supposed to do the driving and they'll do the catching. They asked me if I wouldn't help with the driving, and I told 'em that I'd be more than happy to."

Brer Bear looked at Brer Rabbit real hard. "You told 'em that?"

"Sho' did. Told 'em that I'd help get you started running so they could catch you."

Brer Bear laughed, and his laugh sounded like thunder rolling the way it done when God told Noah to get in the ark. "Tell me something, Brer Rabbit," he asked when he stopped laughing. "How big a family Brer Wolf and Brer Fox got?"

Brer Rabbit shook his head. "Can't say as I know. We ain't been neighbors for a while. I moved off that block, 'cause I don't like them and they don't like me. And that's how come I came and told you what they was planning. Too, it seemed to me that this is something you'd probably like to take part in."

Brer Bear nodded. "I appreciate your thoughtfulness. Seems to me that I ain't got no choice but to be there."

Brer Rabbit and Brer Bear laughed and gave each other high fives and low fives and behind-the-back fives. Then they swapped tales and told jokes and laughed so much until Miz Brune and Miz Brindle came in the den and told Brer Rabbit that he better take his cottontail on home, 'cause all that laughing was keeping the children awake.

Brer Rabbit laughed all the way home and was still laughing when he got in bed.

Miz Rabbit poked her head out from under the covers. "What's wrong with you? What you been up to now?"

Brer Rabbit couldn't talk for laughing. Finally he caught his breath long enough to tell his wife what he was going to do. When she heard it, she didn't laugh one bit.

"You'll keep up with your foolishness until one of these days, somebody is going to catch you in your own trap and then I'll be a widow and have to go on welfare."

Brer Rabbit said, "There's been widows and orphans since the world started turning around." And with that he went to sleep. Miz Rabbit started thinking about filing divorce papers.

Next day Brer Rabbit met up with Brer Fox and Brer Wolf. "Let's go get some bear meat."

Brer Fox and Brer Wolf followed Brer Rabbit down the road and through the woods until they got to the place where the bushes are thick and the shadows are black.

Brer Rabbit stopped. He noticed that Brer Wolf and Brer Fox were hanging back. "You can't be bashful if you gon' help me catch Brer Bear."

Brer Fox and Brer Wolf came closer.

"That's perfect!" exclaimed Brer Rabbit. "Stand right there. I figure I'll have Brer Bear caught before he can get this far and if I do, I'll holler. But if he's too quick for me, I mean, if he gets the idea that I'm after him and starts running, I'll head him in this direction. All you two got to do is stand your ground."

Brer Fox and Brer Wolf stood their ground because they didn't want Brer Rabbit telling nobody afterward that they were afraid.

Brer Rabbit went to Brer Bear's house, which wasn't too far from there. They gave each other a whole bunch of high fives and low fives, and then Brer Bear took off running through the woods with Brer Rabbit close on his tail.

Brer Fox and Brer Wolf heard a loud and awful racket, and all of a sudden Brer Bear was coming straight toward them with Brer Rabbit close behind.

"Head him off!" Brer Rabbit hollered. "Head him off and hold him until I get there!"

Brer Bear was running so fast that blue smoke was rising off his body. Brer Fox and Brer Wolf held their ground

and Brer Bear kept coming. His head was down and his breath was hot and Brer Wolf and Brer Fox reached out to grab him.

Brer Bear hit Brer Wolf with his right hand and Brer Fox with his left. Brer Fox's eyeballs went to Chicago, his tail went to New York, and his hide found itself setting up on the beach in Miami. When Brer Wolf woke up three weeks later, he was speaking French. And Brer Rabbit? Shucks, he laughed so hard that his gray hair turned back to its rightful color.

Brer Fox Gets Away for Once

One summer there was an awful drought. I don't know if Ol' Rainmaker had gone on vacation or if he was on strike or what, but he wasn't on the job.

Every day it seemed like King Sun was angry from the time he got out of bed, 'cause his light was bright and hot. After a while the creeks and the streams started getting low. Pretty soon they dried up. The only water left was in a big lake.

Every day the animals met down at the lake to do their drinking. The big animals drank first, and by the time they finished drinking and stomping around in the water, it was too filthy for the little animals to drink.

They started looking lean and dry—all of them, that is, except Brer Rabbit. Didn't nobody know how he was getting water, but he was.

One day Brer Fox paid him a visit. "I got a problem, Brer Rabbit."

"Tell me about it. Problems are my meat."

"I'm thirsty. The big animals drink so much that by the time us little creatures get to the lake, ain't enough left for us to 'suage our thirst. What am I gon' do?"

Brer Rabbit thought for a little while. "Tell you what you do. Rub syrup all over yourself, and then roll around in some leaves. After that go down to the lake, and when the big animals come to drink, jump up in the air and shake yourself real hard. You'll look as scary as Ol' Boy, and the animals will run away. Then you can drink your fill."

Brer Fox did what Brer Rabbit had told him and went to the lake and hid.

It was close to sundown when the big animals came to drink. They were scuffling and hunching and pushing and scrounging to get as close to the water as they could. Brer Fox jumped out from behind a tree and yelled real loud, "Aaaargh!"

Brer Wolf was so scared he jumped over Brer Bear. Brer Bear was so scared he jumped over Brer Elephant. Brer Elephant decided it would take him too long to do any jumping, so he just started running and all the other creatures followed him.

Brer Fox chuckled and sauntered down to the lake, which he had all to himself. He was drinking his fill and didn't notice when the big creatures sneaked back to take another look at this strange monster. Brer Fox drank and drank, and being filled with all that water made him feel so good that he started playing in the water.

He was splashing around in the water and the syrup started to loosen. Before long all the leaves had washed off.

When the big creatures saw that the strange monster was none other than Brer Fox, Brer Bear yelled, "Let's get him!"

Brer Fox looked at himself and saw all the leaves had washed off, and he didn't waste no time getting away from there.

A day or two after that, Ol' Rainmaker came back from vacation or wherever he'd been, and all the creeks and streams got filled up again and the animals didn't have to worry about water no more.

Taily-po

Mr. Man should've had better sense than to mess with Brer Rabbit. So what if Brer Rabbit tried to eat up everything in Mr. Man's garden? Instead of getting mad Mr. Man should've been happy Brer Rabbit left him with a house to live in. The way Mr. Man acted, you would've thought he was the one who made the seed in his garden grow, and put the orange in the carrots and the red in the tomatoes.

One morning he woke up, looked out the window, and saw Brer Rabbit in his garden having broccoli for breakfast. That did it! Mr. Man called his hunting dogs, Ramboo, Bamboo, and Lamboo. "Go get Brer Rabbit and do away with him!"

When Brer Rabbit heard the dogs coming, he knew they weren't bringing him any hollandaise sauce to put on the broccoli, so he decided to get on away from there.

Round and round and up and down Brer Rabbit went, and round and round and up and down the dogs went. On one of them rounds, or it might've been on the up and down, the dogs started gaining on him.

Brer Rabbit headed for a big hollow tree down by the creek. When he got there, he ran inside, hurried up the stairs, and sat down in a rocking chair to catch his breath.

Now, don't come telling me there can't be stairs and a rocking chair in a hollow tree. Maybe there ain't such things in the hollow trees in your neighborhood. I don't know, 'cause I ain't never investigated the ones where you live. But where Brer Rabbit live, there was a tree with stairs in it and all sorts of other things too. I ain't gon' tell you what else was in the tree, 'cause you wouldn't believe me. I have to admit that I wasn't sure Brer Rabbit was telling the truth when he told me about the swimming pool in that tree, but I seen the rocking chair with my own three eyes.

Brer Rabbit was rocking in the rocking chair and Ramboo, Bamboo, and Lamboo were running around the tree with their noses to the ground trying to figure out which way Brer Rabbit went. They couldn't figure it out, though, and after a while they gave up and went home.

Brer Rabbit knew he had to do something or folks would be reading about him in the obituary column. There was only one thing he could do, and that was to go see Aunt Mammy-Bammy Big-Money.

She was the witch rabbit and she lived way off in a deep, dark, dank, smelly, slimy swamp. To get there you had to ride some, slide some, jump some, hump some, hop some, flop some, walk some, balk some, creep some, sleep some, fly some, cry some, follow some, holler some, wade some, spade some, and if you weren't careful, you still might not get there. Brer Rabbit made it, but he was plumb wore out when he did.

After he caught his breath, he hollered, "Mammy-Bammy Big-Money! Hey! Mammy-Bammy Big-Money! I journeyed far, I journeyed fast; I'm glad I found the place at last."

Big black smoke started belching up out of a hole in the

ground. The smoke got blacker and blacker until Brer Rabbit heard a voice that sounded like graveyard bones rubbing against each other: "Wherefore, Son Riley Rabbit Riley? Wherefore?"

"Mammy-Bammy Big-Money, Mr. Man is out to get me! If I don't do something, he's gon' make rabbit stew out of me."

Mammy-Bammy Big-Money made a terrible sound and sucked in all the black smoke and Brer Rabbit with it. He went tumbling down the hole, tail over head and head over tail, until, *blam!* He landed on the floor in Mammy-Bammy Big-Money's living room.

After his head cleared Brer Rabbit looked around. What he saw scared him so much that his ears lay down flat and didn't come up again for two months.

The walls of Mammy-Bammy Big-Money's house were made from tombstones. The long table she ate off of was made from bones, and at the head of the table was a chair made from skulls. Over in the corner was the bed she slept on and it was made from tiger's claws, and the pillow she laid her head on was a gorilla's skull. Brer Rabbit had never been one to do much praying, but he was praying in Latin and Hebrew and bebop that the Lord would let him get out of there alive!

Mammy-Bammy Big-Money didn't pay no attention to Brer Rabbit. She went over to the wall where an animal skin was hanging. It had a head, feet, and tails, but it wasn't the hide of any creature Brer Rabbit had ever heard about or seen on a *National Geographic* special.

Mammy-Bammy Big-Money took the skin off the wall and laid it on the floor. Then she sprinkled a handful of salt in the fire what was burning in the fireplace and sang:

Rise, skin, rise,
Open your big red eyes—
Sharpen your long black claws,
And work your big strong jaws!

As the salt started snapping and cracking in the fire, the animal skin began moving and stretching itself. Then it started rolling and wallowing around on the floor. When all the salt was burned, the animal skin rose up into a creature with a long tail.

It had been hanging on the wall so long that its hide was hard and stiff and it popped and screeched as the creature worked the wrinkles out. Before long it started feeling supple and was walking around and rubbing itself up against Mammy-Bammy Big-Money like a great big cat.

Mammy-Bammy Big-Money looked at Brer Rabbit and said, "Son Riley Rabbit Riley. Go. Rest in peace. Mr. Man will be taken care of."

Brer Rabbit was more than happy to get away from there. Everybody needs a relative like Mammy-Bammy Big-Money, but they ain't the kind you invite over to watch the Super Bowl with you.

That night, 'long about the time the ghosts in the graveyard were waking up, 'long about the time the full moon was peering in all the dark places and waking up the black cats, 'long about the time the witches were gassing up their brooms, Mr. Man was turning over for the second time and settling down into a deep and dreamless sleep.

Suddenly his eyes opened. "What was that noise?"

He listened.

He heard it again. Something was banging against the pots and pans in the kitchen.

Mr. Man got up and went to investigate.

By the light from the fire in the fireplace he saw a creature with a long tail. The creature saw Mr. Man and ran toward the door. Mr. Man hurried after it, and just as the creature was went out the door, Mr. Man grabbed its tail.

The tail came off in his hand!

Before Mr. Man could wonder about what kind of creature it was whose tail would come off, the tail started wriggling like it was alive. It was wriggling so hard, Mr. Man could hardly hold on to it.

He took it over to the fireplace and laid it on the hearth awhile. He put some wood on the fire to build it up. The tail was still wriggling, and the harder it wriggled, the bigger it got. It reared up and started hitting Mr. Man on his legs. Mr. Man grabbed the tail and threw it in the fire.

The tail started jumping about in the fire. Mr. Man grabbed the tongs and held the tail as tight as he could. It started sizzling like a piece of bacon frying.

After a while the tail stopped shaking and frying. Mr. Man didn't let go, however, until nothing was left but ashes.

Mr. Man went back to bed. He tossed and turned for a long time but finally he dozed off. Just as he got sleep good, there came a scratching and gnawing at the front door.

"Who's there?" he hollered out, sitting up straight.

It was quiet for a long time. Then a voice sang out:

Taily-po! You know and I know
That I want my Taily-po!
Over and under and through the door,
I'm coming to get my Taily-po!

Mr. Man called his dogs. "Here, Ramboo! Here, Bamboo! Lamboo—here, here! Here, dogs, here!"

The dogs came running. Mr. Man told them to go around the house and do away with whatever was scratching at the door. The dogs ran out and they took off running after something. In a minute they were out of hearing.

Mr. Man had just about dropped off to sleep again when there came a scratching and gnawing at the back door.

"Who's that?" he hollered, sitting up in bed.

After a little while a voice sang:

Your name, I know, is Whaley-Joe,
And before I'm going to really go,
I'd like to have my Taily-po;
Give me that and I'll gaily go—
Taily-po! My Taily-po!

Mr. Man went to the front door and called his dogs. The dogs don't answer and the dogs don't come. The gnawing and scratching at the back door is getting louder.

I know you know, and I know I know
That all I want is my Taily-po!

Mr. Man jumped in bed and pulled the covers over his head. He was shivering and quavering and didn't know what he was going to do.

The gnawing and scratching got louder and louder until, all of a sudden, it stopped. Mr. Man couldn't hear nothing. Then there came the sound of a creature's claws walking slowly across the kitchen floor.

The creature started throwing pots and pans around and breaking the dishes. Then it was silent again. Mr. Man was shaking and quavering so much that his bed started trembling.

Then he heard the creature scratching at something. The creature had smelled something in the fireplace and was scratching and pulling at the burning logs.

He scratched and he clawed and flaming coals and burning logs came flying out of the fireplace. They landed on the sofa and the curtains, and wherever they landed, a fire started.

The creature kept clawing and scratching until all the

fire was out of the fireplace and there, at the bottom, it found its tail, safe and sound. The creature grabbed the tail in its mouth and ran out of the house.

Mr. Man smelled smoke. He jumped out of bed and ran to the door of the bedroom and opened it. It seemed like the fire was standing there waiting for him, because as soon as he opened the door, the fire rushed into the bedroom like that was where it had been wanting to go the whole time.

Brer Rabbit was sitting in his rocking chair at home and said, "My goodness, I believe I smell smoke." He smiled.

And way off in the swamp Mammy-Bammy Big-Money raised her head, sniffed the air, and said, "I smell meat frying. I smell Mr. Man's meat frying."

Brer Rabbit, Brer Fox, and the Chickens

Once upon a time all the creatures ate meat. I better stop right here and tell you when "once upon a time" was.

"Once upon a time" was the time before time knew what it was supposed to be doing. Nowadays time has got a lot of flewjus mixed up with it. You think it's standing still, but it's callyhooting and humping and toting the mail. You can't hear the engine, but time has got one and it's a big one too, and time just be steady going. Don't come asking me where it's going. I don't think even time knows where it's going or much care. Its job is just to go and when it gets to where it's going, it just keeps on going. Some folks don't mind going along with time, and they can go right on. Time can let me stay right where I am now. But that's the funny thing about time. It don't leave nobody behind. I reckon that's how come I like these tales so much. They ain't inside time, and as long as I tell 'em, neither am I.

Now, like I was saying, once upon a time the creatures ate meat just like folks do. It was a sad day in the creature world when hay appeared on their dinner plates. Whenever you ever hear a creature howling in the nighttime, it's because that creature is remembering the rib-eye steaks and pork chops and barbecue it used to eat. Brer Rabbit was a filet-mignon-and-bernaise-sauce man and Brer Fox thought there was nothing better than spaghetti and meatballs.

The creatures loved meat so much that they wouldn't eat nothing else. After a while they had just about eaten all the meat in the country.

That wasn't good, especially for King Lion, who ate more meat than anybody. He was having a hard time keeping his big belly full, and if that wasn't bad enough, he got a thorn stuck in his foot and the only thing that could make him feel better was meat. So he issued a decree that all the creatures had to give him a share of their meat.

The meat may have made him feel better, but it didn't get the thorn out of his foot. After a while the pain got so bad that he had to send for the doctor. Guess who the doctor was? None other than Brer Rabbit himself!

Brer Rabbit wasn't like these doctors nowadays who stick needles in your behind and fill you full of pills and powders and pretty-colored liquids. Brer Rabbit got his medicines off the bushes and plants in the fields and woods. He knew that peach leaf was good for the bile and that sheep-sorrel salve was good for sores, and that white turpentine and mutton-suet would heal fresh hurts and cuts. I know y'all don't know what I'm talking about, but I can't be interrupting the story to be giving no medicine lessons. Just take my word for it.

Brer Rabbit wasn't none too happy about doctoring on King Lion. To get a good look at the foot the thorn was in, Brer Rabbit had to get close to King Lion's mouth, and King Lion's mouth was full of blood-red tongue and shiny, sharp teeth.

Every time Brer Rabbit felt King Lion's hot breath blowing on him, he got nervous, 'cause King Lion didn't always know how to control himself when fresh meat was close by. But he got the job done, put a salve on King Lion's foot to draw all the inflammation out, and then got on away from there.

When he walked out of King Lion's house, he noticed all the creatures waiting their turn to go in and give King Lion some meat. All the creatures were there, except Brer Fox.

"Where's Brer Fox?" Brer Rabbit asked.

Didn't nobody know.

"Anybody seen Brer Fox?" Brer Rabbit yelled.

The creatures shook their heads.

Brer Rabbit thought that was strange, but he went on down the road. As soon as he was out of sight of the creatures he sat down and started laughing. When his laughing fit was over, he continued on down the road.

He hadn't gone far when he saw somebody up ahead. It was Brer Fox. He was going toward his house with two fat chickens and Widdle-Waddle, the plumpest duck Brer Rabbit had ever seen.

Brer Rabbit hurried and caught up to him.

"Where you been?" Brer Rabbit asked. "I just come from

King Lion's and I didn't see you there. Everybody was asking about you. I told 'em you were feeling kind of feeble and were trying to put on some weight."

Brer Fox got nervous hearing that folks had been inquiring about him. "Did King Lion ask about me?" he asked anxiously.

"Sho' did. He called out your name more than once and more than twice. When he didn't get no answer, he put some language around your name that would burn a hole in my tongue if I repeated it. I hope King Lion is feeling better when you see him."

Brer Fox was real nervous now. "Did King Lion cuss?" he wanted to know.

"Well, let me put it to you this way. If you can think of something that's worse than cussing, then you getting close to what King Lion said about you."

"Have mercy, Brer Rabbit! What am I going to do?"

Brer Rabbit shook his head and said he didn't know. Brer Fox said he best be getting on down to King Lion's house.

Brer Rabbit snapped his fingers like he'd just remembered something important. He searched through his pockets and, with a sigh of relief, pulled out a piece of paper.

"Found it! After King Lion heated up the air talking about you, he give me this note and said I was to show it to you. He said you were supposed to tear off one corner and give it to him, and that'd be the proof that you'd seen it."

"Brer Rabbit? Is there any writing on that piece of paper? If there is, then it ain't gon' do me no good. I can read reading but I can't read writing."

Brer Rabbit said, "Well, that's how it is with me, except I can read writing but I can't read reading."

"Well, I see some writing on there. What does it say?"

Brer Rabbit looked at the piece of paper like he was trying to decipher what was on it. It wasn't nothing but a shopping list his wife had given him the week before, and it said, *half-gallon of milk, a pound of salami, a jar of mayonnaise, and a box of Godiva chocolate.* But Brer Rabbit scrunched up his nose, narrowed his eyes, and made like he was reading. "It say, *All and samely, whichever and whoever and wheresoever, especially the howcome and the what's-his-name, the aforesaid aforementioned and aftermentioned, let him come head first into the courthouse where the high sheriff and the law can lay him down and flatten him out, all whom this concerns, enough said.*"

Brer Fox scratched his head. "That don't sound good. What does it mean, Brer Rabbit?"

"It means that King Lion wants you to come up there where he can get his paws on you. You best get to King Lion's house quick as you can, Brer Fox. Tear off a piece of this note and show it to King Lion soon as you walk in."

Brer Fox moaned. "How am I going to get there in a hurry, Brer Rabbit? I got these two chickens and Widdle-Waddle. Maybe I better take them on home. I could get to King Lion's in no time if they weren't slowing me down. What do you think, Brer Rabbit?"

Brer Rabbit smiled. "I think that's a *good* idea."

Brer Fox headed for home and Brer Rabbit followed from a distance. He saw Brer Fox run in his house to put the chickens and Widdle-Waddle away, then hurry out again. Right behind him came his wife, hollering and yelling. "You better come back here and help me with these children of yours. I may have birthed them, but that don't mean they all mine. You act like I'm some kind of slave to you. I have to do every blessed thing there is to be done— split the wood, make the fire, do all the cooking, all the pulling and hauling, and on top of that, take care of your children. You just wait until I get to my consciousness-raising group next week."

She didn't really say that last part. That came out of my mouth when I wasn't looking.

Brer Fox didn't hear none of it 'cause he was steady moving down the road.

Brer Rabbit waited until Brer Fox was good and gone. Then he made his way up to Brer Fox's house.

He was walking slow, and the odor of politeness surrounded him like twenty-five-cent cologne. Anybody who didn't know better would've thought Brer Rabbit was a real gentleman. When Brer Rabbit acts like a gentleman, you better put your house under lock and key and call the FB and I for protection.

He walked on the porch and knocked softly on the door.

Miz Fox opened the door and Brer Rabbit, hat in hand, bowed low. "How you today, Miz Fox?"

"Don't ask, Brer Rabbit. What can I do for you?"

Brer Rabbit began to search in his pockets. "I got a note here for you, if I can lay my hands on it. Ah! Here it is!" He handed her the piece of paper.

Miz Fox took it and stared at it. "I ain't good at reading since these children broke my glasses. I don't know what I'm going to do, especially since my husband ain't got time to stay home and help me. When he does come in, it looks like the floor burns blisters in his feet and he's out the door again before I scarcely know he's been here. I tell you the truth, Brer Rabbit! If I'd known at first what I knew at last, I would've taken two long thinks and a mighty big thunk before I would've married anybody."

"Yes, ma'am," said Brer Rabbit. "Well, I met Brer Fox in the road just now. He asked me how I was doing, and I told him the truth. I said I had fallen on hard times, though it feel like hard times done fell on me. I'm a proud man and don't like to beg, I told him, but I don't have nothing to eat in my house. Everybody know that Brer Fox got a soft spot in his heart for the downtrodden, the oppressed, the impoverished, the tired, the poor, the weary, and them what's got bad feet. And he wiped his eye and say he couldn't stand it for me to be going around hungry."

"I wish he'd wipe his eye about some of my troubles," Miz Fox interjected.

"Yes, ma'am. Brer Fox say that just this very morning he had brought home two fat chickens and Widdle-Waddle Puddle Duck and he say I could have them. And he sat down and wrote it all out on that note I just gave you."

Miz Fox gave Brer Rabbit a hard look. Then she looked at the note again. She turned it upside down and round and round but she can't make out the letters without her glasses. "If this note ain't read until I read it, I feel sorry for the note. What does it say, Brer Rabbit?"

"Yes, ma'am." Brer Rabbit took the note and cleared his throat. *"To all whom it might contrive or concern, both now and presently: Be so pleased as to let Brer Rabbit have the chickens and Widdle-Waddle Puddle Duck. I'm well at this writing and hoping you are enjoying the same shower of blessings. The end."*

Miz Fox shrugged. "Well, it ain't no love letter." She went in the back and brought the two chickens and Widdle-Waddle and gave them to Brer Rabbit.

"Blessings on you," Brer Rabbit said. He went home and didn't waste no time getting there. He told his wife to cook the chickens and Widdle-Waddle Puddle Duck like they was having company for dinner, and then he hurried back to see after King Lion's foot.

When he got to King Lion's house, Brer Fox was waiting outside for his turn to go in. Brer Fox had the really-truly goodness dripping from his mouth and oozing from his hide. He looked like what folks used to call " 'umble-come-tumble." He was scared that King Lion was going to do away with him, so when he saw Brer Rabbit, he was relieved.

"Brer Rabbit! Brer Rabbit!"

"I'm mighty glad to see you, Brer Fox. After we talked, I got scared that you would go in and see King Lion without me, and that would've been mighty bad for you."

"I was going to go in like you told me to, but the other creatures told me to get in line and wait my turn. I'm sho' glad to see you."

"Well, Brer Fox, you stay right here and don't try to go in there where the King is until I give you the word. I don't know what he might do to you."

Since Brer Rabbit was the doctor, he could go in to see the King anytime, so he elbowed his way through the creatures and walked into King Lion's throne room.

King Lion's paw was wrapped up like Brer Rabbit had left it, and King Lion was just dropping off to sleep. He started snoring like he'd swallowed a horse—mane and hoof. Brer Rabbit went back out.

"What's the news?" Brer Fox wanted to know.

Brer Rabbit put his arm around Brer Fox's shoulder. "You better get out of here. King Lion is terribly upset at how you been acting. I begged for you, Brer Fox. I begged and begged. Finally King Lion said he'd let you off this time, but the next time, have mercy on you! You best go on home, Brer Fox, before your wife gives away them fat chickens and Widdle-Waddle."

Brer Fox laughed. "I'd like to see somebody get them chickens and Widdle-Waddle away from my wife. You a smart man, Brer Rabbit, and if you can get them chickens and that duck away from my wife, you're welcome to them."

Brer Rabbit bowed low. "I sho' do thank you, Brer Fox. I sho' do thank you." And he went lippity-clippiting down the road, laughing so loud that all the trees wanted to know what the joke was.

Brer Fox Tries to Get Revenge

You probably won't believe this, but there be some folks that wouldn't enjoy that tale I just told. Somebody come telling me once that it was a story about stealing and that Brer Rabbit wasn't nothing but a liar and a thief and a scoundrel. Them words hurt me in the heart so bad I had to eat a gallon of Häagen-Dazs coffee ice cream before I started feeling better.

It ain't possible to be friends with these stories without shaking off a lot of your ideas. No doubt about it. You have to shuck them ideas like you shucking corn.

Folks got their laws and the creatures got theirs, and that's just how it is. But folks have the notion that everybody got to think like they do. Like the time I painted my house yellow. Folks come around saying, how come you paint your house yellow when everybody else's house is painted white? Well, I didn't want to live in a white house. I see the color white and it makes me think of snow and ice, and what I want to be sitting up in my house shivering in the middle of summer? So I painted my house yellow, and in the winter I be sitting inside, and that yellow color on the outside make me feel all warm and cozy.

But most folks get upset if you don't think the way they do. If they had different eyes, and if their eyes were on a different level, they wouldn't see the way they do, and consequently they wouldn't think the same way either. Take Brer Turtle, for example. He looks on the world from both sides of his head. That's how come can't nobody get the best of him. He see trouble coming from the east and the west at the same time. But you and me have to turn our heads to see trouble coming from the east and while we looking east, trouble from the west done come and grabbed us and is carrying us on down the road. So that's how come creature laws ain't folks' laws.

To all them what think Brer Rabbit was a thief, well, there's clearly some things they ain't thought about. In the first place, why would anyone think that them chickens and that duck belonged to Brer Fox? From what I know about Brer Fox, that ain't very likely. On top of that, we know he didn't get them at home, 'cause that's where he was headed. He didn't get them in the woods, 'cause chickens and puddle ducks don't grow on trees, and if they did, Brer Fox can't climb no higher than he can jump. Now, you can put it down and carry four, that wherever Brer Fox laid his hands on them, he didn't buy them, and neither were they given to him. You don't have to guess about that; you know it by your nose and your two big toes.

And another thing. Them chickens and duck probably didn't belong to the one Brer Fox tuck them from. It would take a long time to hunt up and search out the nicknames and pedigrees of all who had them chickens and duck before they came into Brer Rabbit's hands.

Now, the reason I go into such a long explanation is not because I done decided to run for president but because this is what you call a two-horse tale. But just like you can't hitch two horses to a wagon at the same time, you got to tell one tale at a time. So, let me get the other horse hitched up.

Brer Rabbit and Brer Fox were outside King Lion's, and Brer Fox told Brer Rabbit that if anybody could get them chickens and Widdle-Waddle Paddle Duck from his wife, they could have 'em.

Brer Rabbit laughed so hard that the rocks in the ground wanted to know what the joke was. (Folks don't realize it, but there ain't nothing in nature enjoy a good joke more than a rock. You don't know what laughing is until you've heard a rock laugh.)

Brer Fox went on home. Brer Rabbit decided to follow to see what was going to happen when Brer Fox found out that his chickens and Widdle-Waddle Puddle Duck were gone.

Brer Fox walked in the door, and he could tell by the way his wife was standing at the stove that she was mad at him. "What's the matter, sugar-honey?" he asked.

"I'll sugar you! I'll honey you! How come you brought food home for us and the children to eat and then have me give it away? It don't make no sense for you to carry two fat chickens and a duck home and then five minutes later give them away. And how come you want to give them to Miz Rabbit? What is she to you, anyhow? I'm sitting up here just dribbling at the mouth thinking about how good them chickens and that duck going to taste and here come Brer Rabbit, bowing and scrapping and simpering and sniggering and grinning, saying you'd sent him to get the chickens and duck. He never would've gotten them from me if he hadn't had that note what you wrote, and you know good and well that since the children broke my glasses and you been too trifling to buy me new ones, I can't read *B* from *bull's foot.*"

Brer Fox didn't know what she was talking about. "I didn't write you no note," he said. "Sugar-honey, dumpling-pie, ain't we been married long enough for you to know that I can't write writing?"

"I been married to you long enough to know I made a mistake. If I'd married Brer Mink like he wanted me to, at least I would've had a coat when he died. All I want to know is how come you giving our food away to Brer Rabbit and his family? Your own children done got so skinny they can't make a shadow in the moonshine. And if you got to give away our food, why give it to the Rabbit family? You know as well as I do that I don't like to associate with folks who got big eyes. Folks with round eyes ain't got too much intelligence. Plus, they smell bad."

Brer Fox didn't know what she was talking about, but the idea had gotten through to him that the chickens and Widdle-Waddle Paddle Duck were gone.

"Woman, put the brakes on your lips and park your mouth on the side of the road. Do you mean to stand there, flat footed and right before my face and eyes, and tell me that you took them fat chickens that I brought home, and that juicy Widdle-Waddle Paddle Duck, which I also brought home, and give them to Brer Rabbit for no reason?"

"You sent me a note and that's what the note say."

"Let me get this straight. You ain't got no more sense than to believe something that's written on a piece of paper? How come you didn't ask Reginald the Fourth to read that piece of paper? He in college and he can read reading and writing in fourteen languages."

Miz Fox got mad at Brer Rabbit now. She swore that when she saw him she was going to put a hurting on him so bad that the Devil would ask her to have mercy.

Brer Rabbit was hiding alongside the house and he started laughing. He laughed so hard and so loud that Brer Fox heard him.

"I'm going to get some rabbit meat to make up for the chicken meat you gave away. You go out on the porch and be sweeping in front of the door. You pretend like you talking to me inside the house. I'll slip out the back and sneak up on Brer Rabbit."

Miz Fox went on the porch and started sweeping and talking. "You better get on up from there and go out and get us something to eat instead of trying to think up on how you gon' get revenge on Brer Rabbit. Revenge can wait. Hungriness can't."

Miz Fox was sweeping and talking, and she didn't see Brer Rabbit until he was right there on the porch with her.

"How do, Miz Fox," he said politely. "I hope you well this evening."

Miz Fox jumped but figured she'd get Brer Rabbit in a conversation so Brer Fox could catch him. "I ain't doing too well, Brer Rabbit. My husband done come down with lumbago of the brain and ain't feeling too well."

"I'm sorry to hear that. I been going around through the community this evening and seems like almost everybody is laid up there. Folks say that a plate of lasagna and wintergreen LifeSavers will clear it right up." Brer Rabbit looked at Miz Fox strangely.

"What you looking at me for like you crazy?"

"I beg your pardon, Miz Fox. I was just wondering how come you ain't got on your new dress."

"New dress? What you talking about?"

"The one made out of calico what King Lion gave to Brer Fox to give to you!"

Miz Fox laid the broom down. "You mean the King sent me a dress? I ain't never laid one eye or the other on it."

Brer Rabbit acted like he was embarrassed. "You'll have to excuse me, ma'am. I believe I done put my mouth where it didn't have no business being. I never like to come between a husband and wife, not me! But Brer Fox is right there in the house. Ask him yourself."

Miz Fox was so mad about not getting the dress and wondering who Brer Fox had given it to that she didn't care what she said. "He ain't in the house. He's sneaking around the house to grab you for taking the chickens and Widdle-Waddle Paddle Duck."

Brer Rabbit laughed. "That Brer Fox is quite a man. That he is. Now, that's the way you see it, Miz Fox. The way I see it is that Brer Fox saw me coming and is hiding out 'cause he was afraid I was going to ask you about that calico dress King Lion sent you. It was a pretty dress too, and if I'd knowed then what I know now, I would've gotten that dress from Brer Fox to give to my wife. That's just what I would've done!"

Brer Rabbit bowed and made his farewells and went and hid in some bushes.

He wasn't a minute too soon, because here come Brer Fox from around the side of the house. "Where is that molly-dodger? He was right here. I know he was. Where'd he go?"

Before Brer Fox could say another word, Miz Fox was going all upside his head with the broom. Brer Fox thought he'd been hit by lightning. He fell down on the ground and started rolling over and over, but Miz Fox's aim was deadly and whichever way he rolled, Miz Fox was right there with the broom.

Eventually the broom wore out and when the dust cleared, Brer Fox got an idea of what had hit him. "Honey! What's the matter with you? What you hitting me for? I ain't Brer Rabbit. Whatever it is, I swear to you I ain't gon' do it no more!"

"So, it's true, is it?" Miz Fox yelled and she started in on him again. Since there wasn't much broom left, she hit him with the handle.

Finally the broom handle wasn't nothing but splinters. Miz Fox had run out of breath and Brer Fox had run out of bones to break. They both just flopped down in the dust.

Then Miz Fox started crying, and that was worse for Brer Fox than the beating. That's the truth. I done seen men who could kill a herd of tigers with their bare hands be totally helpless before a crying woman.

"How come you didn't give me that calico dress King Lion give to you to give to me?" she asked him finally, sniffing and bawling.

"What calico dress? I didn't get to see King Lion today."

"But you said you wasn't going to do it no more."

"I said that to try to get you from stop beating on me."

They looked at each other and realized that Brer Rabbit

had tricked them again. They decided that if it was the last thing they did, they were going to do away with that rabbit.

For the next two weeks everyplace Brer Rabbit went, Brer Fox or Miz Fox was right with him. Brer Rabbit thought this was fun, but after a while it started to get boring. Not only that, Brer Rabbit was afraid that his luck might run out just when he needed it the most and he'd be caught.

Along about that same time King Lion sent word that he wanted to see Brer Rabbit. The place on King Lion's foot where the thorn had been had swollen up into a great big blister and it hurt so bad that the King couldn't sleep.

Brer Rabbit went straight to the place where King Lion done his kinging, and it didn't take him long to get there. When Brer Rabbit takes a notion to go somewhere right quick, he just picks up the miles with his feet and drops them off again like a dog shedding fleas.

Brer Rabbit took one look at King Lion's foot and shook his head. "King, this foot of yours is sho' 'nuf in a bad way."

"What can I do about it?" King Lion wanted to know.

"Ain't but one cure for a foot that done swole up this bad."

"What is it?"

Brer Rabbit said, "Well, it's a cure I don't like to prescribe, and if you wasn't the King, I wouldn't prescribe it. But we can't have a King with a sore foot. Ain't no two ways about that. There's only one thing that will make your foot well. You have to wrap your foot in fox hide. And not only that. The hide must be so fresh that it's warm."

Brer Rabbit started crying. "Po' Brer Fox! I'm sho' gon' miss him. Me and him done had some good times on the topside of the world. That's the truth!" He sniffed and wiped his eyes. "King, I'd appreciate it if you'd let me slip on out the back door before you do what you got to do to Brer Fox. I'll just go on off in the woods yonder and wonder at the flight of time and the changes the years bring."

He bowed to the King. "Next time I see you your foot will be well. But what will Brer Fox be?"

King Lion said, "He'll be nothing but a hide. You want me to send you his hide?"

Brer Rabbit said, "No, please don't. I couldn't bear to look at it. Just send it to Miz Fox. It might be some sort of comfort to her in her grief."

King Lion's foot got well; Brer Fox got dead, and Brer Rabbit? Shucks. Brer Rabbit got away.

Brer Wolf and the Pigs

Everybody knows the story of the three little pigs. Well, that story ain't right. It might be right for whoever tells it and don't know no better, but I know better. Anybody who believe that story is getting shortchanged, 'cause there're only three pigs in that story. In the *real* story, the one I'm about to tell you, there are five pigs.

If memory serves me right, there was Big Pig, then come Little Pig, and after that was Speckle Pig, and then Blunt, and last and lonesomest was Runt.

These pigs had a rough time. Their daddy died while they was still little, and they'd just gotten to the age where they could halfway take care of themselves when their mama came down terrible sick, and she knew she wasn't gon' get better.

She called all her children in and told them she wasn't gon' be in the world much longer. "You going to have to look out for yourselves. You'll get along fine if you always keep a lookout for Brer Wolf. As long as you live, beware of Brer Wolf!"

Big Pig, she said she wasn't scared of Brer Wolf. Little Pig say, she ain't either. Speckle Pig put her penny in the pot and say she wasn't scared. Blunt say he almost as big as Brer Wolf, so he wasn't scared. Runt, she don't say nothing but just grunt.

Not long after that, Miz Pig died, and the children were on their own.

Big Pig, she went and built her a house out of brush. Little Pig, she built a stick house. Speckle Pig, she built a mud house. Blunt built himself a plank house. Runt went to work and built herself a stone house.

Well, one morning here come Brer Wolf, licking his chops and shaking his tail.

First house he came to was Big Pig's. Brer Wolf knocked politely on the door—*knock, knock, knock.* Nobody answered.

Brer Wolf never was one to waste time on being polite, and this time his knock had some sense in it—*blam! blam! blam!*

That got Big Pig's attention. "Who's that?"

"A friend," said Brer Wolf. And then he sang:

> *If you'll open the door and let me in*
> *I'll warm my hands and go home again.*

Big Pig wasn't too big on music, so she said again, "Who's that?"

"How's your mother?" Brer Wolf wanted to know.

"My mother's dead," answered Big Pig, "and before she died she told me to keep on the lookout for Brer Wolf. You sound mighty like Brer Wolf to me."

Brer Wolf sighed. "I don't know why your mama would say something like that. I heard that Miss Pig was sick and I decided I'd bring her some corn. If your mama was here right now and feeling like herself, she'd take this corn I done brought and be mighty thankful. She'd ask me in so I would warm my hands by the fire."

The thought of the corn made Big Pig's mouth water so, she opened the door and let Brer Wolf in. That was the last anybody ever saw of Big Pig. Brer Wolf didn't give her time to squeal or to grunt before he gobbled her up and swallowed her down.

The next day Brer Wolf played the same trick on Little

Pig. He banged on her door and sang his song. Little Pig let him in. He returned the favor and let Little Pig into his stomach.

A few days later Brer Wolf paid a call on Speckle Pig. He banged on her door and sang his song. But Speckle Pig was suspicious and wouldn't open the door.

Brer Wolf started some sweet talk then. "How come you treating me this way? It's as cold as the hairs in a polar bear's nose out here. At least let me stick one of my paws inside so it can get warm."

Speckle Pig opened the door a crack and Brer Wolf stuck his paw inside. "That sho' feels good. But having this paw warm makes the other paw feel even colder. Please, could I stick it in too?"

Speckle Pig opened the door a little bit more. Well, no need to drag this out. Brer Wolf kept pleading until he had his whole body in the house, and that was the last anybody ever heard of Speckle Pig.

The next day Brer Wolf made a meal out of Blunt. Wasn't nobody left now but Runt. And that's where Brer Wolf should've left well enough alone. He would've been a smart man if he hadn't been too smart.

Runt was the littlest of the pigs, but she had so much sense that it was a bother to her sometimes.

Brer Wolf banged on Runt's door and sang his song:

If you'll open the door and let me in,
I'll warm my hands and go home again.

Runt had more sense than to believe something like that. Brer Wolf talked sweet, but Runt didn't listen sweet. Finally Brer Wolf decided to break the house in, but he

took a long look at that stone and knew that wouldn't work.

Brer Wolf decided to pretend that he'd gone home, and he went off and laid in the shade for a while.

Then he came back and knocked at the door—*blam! blam! blam!*

"Who's that?" asked Runt.

"It's Speckle Pig," said Brer Wolf. "I brought you some peas."

Runt laughed. "My sister, Speckle Pig, never talked through that many teeth."

Brer Wolf went away again and laid in the shade for a while more.

Blam! blam! blam!

"Who's that?" Runt wanted to know.

"Big Pig," said Brer Wolf, "I brought you some corn."

Runt looked through a crack in the door. "My sister never had hair on her foot."

That did it! Brer Wolf was mad now.

"I'm coming down the chimney!" he hollered.

"Come on," Runt told him.

When Runt heard Brer Wolf on the roof, she grabbed an armful of straw. When Brer Wolf started down the chimney, she put the straw on the fire. The smoke from that straw was thick. It got in his throat and in his eyes, and he was coughing so hard and his eyes were watering so much that he lost his balance and fell right smack into the fire. And that was the end of Brer Wolf.

At least that was the end of *that* Brer Wolf.

————————————

Mr. Benjamin Ram and His Wonderful Fiddle

Mr. Benjamin Ram was the nicest of all the animals. That's probably because he was a musicianer. He was an old-time fiddle player. What I mean is that he patted his foot while he played. If a fiddle player pats his foot while he's playing, he's playing that old-timey music, the kind that can turn white milk into yellow butter.

Mr. Benjamin Ram lived way back out in the woods, but he didn't get to spend much time at home, 'cause whenever the creatures wanted to have a party, and that was near about every weekend, they wanted Mr. Benjamin Ram and his fiddle.

He'd sit there in a chair, put the fiddle under his chin, close his eyes, and get to bowing and patting his foot, and next thing the animals knew, they'd be dancing as good as Baryshnikov and Sandman Sims rolled into one. When the party was over, the creatures would fill up a big bag of peas for Mr. Benjamin Ram to carry home with him.

One time Miz Meadows and Miz Motts and the girls decided to have a party. I don't know what they was celebrating. If my recollections serve me right, it was the birthday of toenail polish. Whatever it was, they got word to Mr. Benjamin Ram that they expected him to be there with his fiddle.

The day of the party came, but King Sun didn't come up that morning. The clouds were spread out all across the elements and the wind started to blow cold. That didn't matter to Mr. Benjamin Ram. He took down his walking cane and put his fiddle in a bag and set out for Miz Meadows's place.

He thought he knew the way, but the wind started blowing colder and colder and the clouds got thicker and darker, and before Mr. Benjamin Ram knew it, he was lost.

If he'd stayed on the big road, he would've gotten there without any problem, but he had tried to take a shortcut. Sometimes what seems like the short way turns out to be the wrong way and the long way. That's how it turned out with Mr. Benjamin Ram.

The minute he realized he was lost, he tried to find himself. He went this way and that way and the other way, and they was all the wrong way. Some folks would've sat right down where they were and studied on the situation, but Mr. Benjamin Ram's other name was Billy Hardhead, and thinking was not an activity he ever took much time out for. Other folks would've started bawling and calling until they woke up everybody in the county. Mr. Benjamin Ram kept on trying to find the way out and kept getting farther and farther in.

The sky turned dark like it was nighttime, and Mr. Benjamin Ram began to feel lonesome. After a while Ol' Man Night dropped down and Mr. Benjamin Ram knew he was going to have to sleep in the woods.

Just about that time he came up over a hill and down at the bottom, in the valley, he saw a light. He took foot in hand and hurried toward that light like it was the very place he'd been looking for.

Before long he came to the house where the light was and knocked on the door.

"Who's that?" came a voice from inside.

"I'm Mr. Benjamin Ram and I done lost my way. Could you take me in for the night?"

"Come in," said the voice from the other side of the door.

Mr. Benjamin Ram walked in, shut the door behind him, and bowed politely. Then he looked around and he began shaking and quivering like he'd come down with the Florida flu. Sitting there in front of the fireplace was none other than Brer Wolf, and his teeth were showing all white and shiny and sharp like he'd just polished them with car wax.

Mr. Benjamin Ram wanted to put himself in reverse and get away from there, but Brer Wolf jumped up and barred and fastened the door.

Mr. Benjamin Ram was in a mess of trouble, but he decided to act like nothing was wrong. "It's good to see you, Brer Wolf. How you and your family been?"

"Very well," answered Brer Wolf.

"Glad to hear it. I appreciate you letting me come in to warm myself by your fire. I'd appreciate it even more if you'd point me in the direction of Miz Meadows's house. Seem like I made a wrong turn somewhere and went left when I should've gone right, or went right when I should've gone left."

"Be happy to," says Brer Wolf. "But why don't you put your walking cane and fiddle down and make yourself at home. We ain't got much, but what we got is yours. We'll take good care of you." Brer Wolf laughed a wolfy laugh and his teeth were gleaming like knives.

Mr. Benjamin Ram started shivering and shaking again like he was coming down with the New Orleans pneumonia.

Brer Wolf slipped into the back room and while Mr. Benjamin Ram was sitting in front of the fire thinking he had caught the Chicago chilblains, he heard Brer Wolf whispering to his wife:

"Ol' woman! Ol' woman! Throw away the smoked meat. We got fresh meat for supper."

Mr. Benjamin Ram heard Miz Wolf sharpening a knife on a rock—*shirrah! shirrah! shirrah!*—and every *shirrah* was bringing him that much closer to the cooking pot.

Mr. Benjamin Ram knew that the end was near, so he decided he might as well play his fiddle one last time.

He took it out of the bag and tuned it up—*plink, plank, plunk, plink, plink, plank, plunk!*

When Miss Wolf heard the sound, she didn't know what it was. "What's that?" she asked Brer Wolf.

They cocked their ears to listen, and just about that time Mr. Benjamin Ram put the fiddle under his chin, got his bow, and started playing one of them old-time tunes. I believe the one he played was "I'm as Good Looking as a Rat in a Tuxedo." Then again, it might've been "Don't Cry for Me, Argentina." I don't rightly remember.

Whatever it was, he was sho' 'nuf playing it. He had his eyes closed and his foot was going, and to tell the truth he didn't know where he was anymore. When Mr. Benjamin Ram got to playing, he forgot everything except the music. That's how come he was so good.

Brer Wolf hadn't heard music like that in all his days. It seemed like the notes of the music were bouncing up and down on his hide and beating on his eyeballs and pulling at his ears, and the faster Mr. Benjamin Ram played, the more the notes of music bounced and beat on Brer Wolf. He couldn't take it no more, and he lit out through the back door and headed for the swamp, Miz Wolf right with him.

After a while Mr. Benjamin Ram stopped playing. He looked around and didn't see Brer Wolf. He listened and he didn't hear Miz Wolf. He looked in the back room. Nobody there. He looked on the back porch. Nobody there. He looked in the closet. Nobody there.

Mr. Benjamin Ram locked all the doors, fixed himself some supper, then lay down in front of the fire and went to sleep.

Next morning when he got up, it was bright and sunny and he didn't have no trouble finding his way to Miz Meadows's house.

When he got there he apologized for not making it to the party the night before. Miz Meadows say they couldn't have no party without him. But that wasn't the truth. Brer Rabbit had gone home and gotten his saxophone and them creatures had just stopped partying about a half hour before Mr. Benjamin Ram got there. But didn't nobody tell him, 'cause they didn't want to hurt his feelings.

Mr. Benjamin Ram Triumphs Again

Mr. Benjamin Ram was old, but that don't mean he wasn't vigorous. He was a sight to see, with his wrinkly horns, shaggy hair on his neck, and red eyes. And when he shook his head and snorted and pawed his feet, he looked almost as fierce as Ol' Boy.

One day Brer Fox and Brer Wolf were coming down the road and Brer Fox said, "I'm hungry in the neighborhood of my stomach."

Brer Wolf was astonished. "How can you be hungry when Mr. Benjamin Ram be laying up in his house just rolling in fat?" Seems like Brer Wolf had forgotten that he had had Mr. Benjamin Ram in his house and hadn't gotten none of that fat.

Brer Fox shook his head. "I look at Mr. Benjamin Ram and I lose my appetite."

Brer Wolf laughed. "What kind of man are you? How can you lose your appetite when Mr. Benjamin Ram rolling in fat like he ain't never heard of skinny?"

Brer Fox gave Brer Wolf a hard look. "I hear tell that you tried to get Mr. Benjamin Ram in the pot and you ended up sleeping in the swamp."

Brer Wolf's mouth started moving like he wanted to say something, but when truth slap you in the mouth, first thing you better do is be sure you still got all your teeth.

Brer Fox chuckled. "You right, Brer Wolf. Mr. Benjamin Ram is just rolling in fat and I'm hungry. Let's get us some of that fat."

Brer Wolf's jaw fell. "Well, to be honest with you, Brer Fox, I just remembered that today is the day I'm supposed to be the judge at a sneaker-smelling contest."

"This ain't gon' take long. We close to his house as it is."

Brer Wolf went on with Brer Fox. Before long they were knocking on Mr. Benjamin Ram's door. They were expecting the door to open, but Mr. Benjamin Ram came from around the side of the house.

They looked around and there he was, staring at them with his red eye. Brer Wolf jumped up in the air and started running before his feet touched the ground. When he realized what he was doing, he stopped and came back, 'cause he didn't want Brer Fox telling all the creatures that he'd gotten scared and run away.

Brer Fox laughed and laughed. "You may be puny in the mind, Brer Wolf, but you are definitely feeling good in your legs."

Mr. Benjamin Ram went and sat on the porch. "Brer Fox! I thank you for bringing Brer Wolf to me. I just about done run out of meat. My wife was telling me this morning that the freezer is almost empty. I'll just chop and pickle Brer Wolf, and that'll hold me and my family for a few months. We ain't had no wolf meat in a long time."

Brer Wolf didn't need to hear nothing else. Neither did Brer Fox. They ran away from there so fast that the wind they created almost knocked Mr. Benjamin Ram's house down.

That was one time when Mr. Benjamin Ram made the acquaintance of his brain. I wonder if he'd been talking with Brer Rabbit.

How the Bear Nursed the Alligators

Once there was a Bear who lived in the swamp in a hollow tree. She had two little bears and she loved her children more than honey.

Every morning she went out bright and early to find food for them. One day she was gone for a long time and the two children got very hungry. The little boy Bear said to his sister, "I'm tired of waiting for Mama. I'm going down to the creek and catch some fish."

The little girl Bear looked scared. "Mama said something might catch us if we go out. You better mind what Mama says."

The little boy Bear laughed. "Hush up! And don't tell mama either."

He climbed out of the tree and went down to the creek.

He was standing on the bank of the creek when a big log came floating toward him. "That's the very thing I need. I'll stand on that log and catch some fish from there."

The little boy Bear jumped on the log. As soon as he did, the log turned around and started toward the middle of the creek.

"What kind of log is this?" the little boy Bear wondered. He looked at the log more closely and what he saw made

him tremble all over. It wasn't a log. It was a great big Alligator!

The Alligator flicked her tail and hit the little boy Bear in the back. Then she turned around and opened her mouth wide so that he could see all of her teeth.

"I've been hunting breakfast for my children, and I believe I found it," said the Alligator.

The Alligator swam to her hole in the bank and slithered inside, the little boy Bear on her back.

"Children! Come see what I brought you for breakfast!" shouted the Alligator.

She had seven children. They were lying in the bed, and when they heard their mama mention breakfast, they raised up and opened their mouths.

The little boy Bear took one look at those baby alligators and all their tiny sharp teeth, and he started crying. "Please, Miz Alligator. Give me a chance to show you what a good nurse I am. I know you must worry about your children when you're out hunting food for them. I'll mind the children for you and take some of the worriment out of your gray matter."

The Alligator thought for a moment and decided that wasn't a bad idea. "I'll try you for one day," Miz Alligator said. "If you any good, I'll try you again tomorrow. If you not, we'll eat you today."

"I'm good! I'm good!" said the little boy Bear.

Miz Alligator left.

The little boy Bear sat down. After a while he started to get hungry. His stomach growled. Even a baby bear's growling stomach sounded like a thunderstorm was coming.

Time passed. His stomach growled louder. More time passed. The little boy Bear was so hungry he could hardly hold up his head.

"Ain't no way I'm gon' starve myself, especially not when I'm sitting in the same room with alligator meat."

The little boy Bear grabbed one of the baby Alligators and ate him. He didn't leave the head; he didn't leave the tail. And he ate the shadow for dessert.

When he finished chewing and belching, he patted his stomach. "I feel good now. I don't know what I'm gon' tell Miz Alligator when she comes back, but I feel too

good to worry about that. I'll worry about it when it's
time to worry, and since Miz 'Gator ain't here yet, it ain't
time to worry."

The little boy Bear yawned, crawled on the bed, and
went to sleep.

Close to nightfall the voice of Miz Alligator woke him
up. "Hey, little boy Bear! How can you be minding my
children when you sound asleep?"

Little boy Bear said, "My eye went for some sleep, but
I'm wide awake!"

Miz Alligator flicked her tail. "Where my children that
I left here with you?"

"They here, Miz Alligator." He started pulling the baby
Alligators out from under the covers.

Here's one, here's another,
Here're two on top of the other,
Here're three piled up together.

Miz Gator grinned. "You took care of my children very
well. Bring me one so I can wash him and feed him his
supper."

The little boy Bear carried one to Miz Alligator. He carried another and another and another until he counted six.
Then he got scared. Miz Alligator was expecting seven
children.

"Bring me the last one," shouted Miz Alligator.

The little boy Bear grabbed one of the babies, smeared
some mud over him, and carried him to Miz Alligator.
Them was the ugliest children anybody had ever seen, and
ugly is ugly. You can't tell one ugly from another ugly.
And neither could Miz Alligator. She washed the same

one off the second time without knowing it, and the little boy Bear carried it back to the bed.

The next day Miz Alligator left early in the morning. After a while the little boy Bear got hungry. He grabbed another one of the baby alligators and ate it. He thought it tasted like pizza with matzoh balls.

That evening Miz Alligator came home and asked to see her children. There were only five left, so two of them got washed and fed twice.

This went on for five more days, and when the last baby Alligator was eaten, the little boy Bear decided he better go home and see his mama and his sister.

And that's what he did. But he didn't go away again for a long, long time.

Brer Turtle and Brer Mink

Brer Turtle and Brer Mink both lived in the water. Brer Mink knew that Brer Turtle was a smart man, but Brer Mink knew too that Brer Turtle nor anybody else could swim like him. Brer Mink would dive and swim through the water so slick and smooth that the water didn't splash or shudder.

One day Brer Mink was getting out of the creek with a string of fish when along came Brer Turtle.

"What's happening, Brer Mink?"

"Same old same old."

"Them are sho' some good-looking fish you got there. Where'd you get 'em?"

"Where you think? Fish don't grow in trees and neither do they grow out of the ground."

"You got them fish out of the creek?" Brer Turtle asked, amazed.

"Are you going deaf? That's just what I said."

"You don't understand what I'm talking about, Brer Mink. It don't look good for a man who can swim like you to be going in a creek like this. This creek ain't worthy of a swimmer like you. If other folks find out you been swimming in this little dinky creek, they might start thinking you slowing down and can't swim like you used to."

Brer Mink said, "Looks or no looks, there's some good fish in that creek, and I'm going to get me as many of them as I can."

"Well, I'm glad to see you a man what's got a mind of his own. You know, Brer Mink, I always wished I was as good in the water as you are. I done tried to catch fish, but I just can't never seem to catch up to 'em. Maybe if you taught me a few things about swimming, I could learn to catch fish. Don't nobody know as much about water as you do."

Brer Mink swelled up with pride. "What you want to know?"

"Well, let's have a contest and see who can stay underwater the longest. Whoever stays under the longest can have these fish."

Brer Mink chuckled. "I ain't in danger of losing that bet. Let's go, Brer Turtle."

They went down to the creek and waded in.

Brer Turtle jumped back a little bit. "Have mercy! This water is cold! How can you swim in something this cold, Brer Mink? You a better man than I am!"

They got out to where the water was deep. Brer Turtle said, "When I count three, we'll dive under and the contest will start. One, two, three!"

Brer Turtle didn't have his mind on staying underwater any longer than it took him to swim back to the creek bank where the fish were.

He ate every last one of Brer Mink's fish. Then he slid back in the water and swam back out to the middle.

Time he got out there, he came up to the surface kicking and thrashing like he was dangling from the end of somebody's fishing pole. Brer Mink heard all the commotion and came to the top.

Before he can say a word and start bragging, Brer Turtle hollered out, "I should've known you would trick me! I should've known!"

"What're you talking about, Brer Turtle?"

"Don't come asking me what am I talking about! Look over there on the creek bank where you been eating the fish. I should've known you'd trick me!"

Brer Mink looked on the bank, and sho' 'nuf. All his fish were gone. He blinked his eyes once. Twice. Thrice. That's the way they used to say three when I was doing the kinging over in the Land of Aluminum Foil. But that's a story I best keep to myself.

Brer Turtle kept up a steady stream of talk. "While I was down there in the water about to die from lack of breath, you swam to the bank and ate up all the fish which by rights ought to be mine 'cause I was gon' beat you!"

"I didn't eat them fish," Brer Mink said.

"You expect me to believe that? You keep on acting the way you acting, and after a while you'll be worse than Brer Rabbit. You can't expect me to believe you didn't trick me out of them fish when I know good and well that you did."

It made Brer Mink feel proud to be compared to Brer Rabbit, 'cause Brer Rabbit was a mighty man. Brer Mink laughed and acted like he knew more than he was telling.

Brer Turtle kept the talk coming. "I ain't gon' be mad with you, Brer Mink, 'cause that was a mighty good trick you pulled. But you ought to be ashamed of yourself for playing a trick like that on an old man like me."

By this time they had drifted to the bank, and Brer Turtle crawled out and went on down the road. As soon as he was out of sight of Brer Mink, he laughed and laughed until there wasn't any more fun in laughing.

Brer Billy Goat Tricks Brer Wolf

Brer Wolf was going along the road one day and Ol' Man Hungriness was on him. Brer Wolf made up his mind that the first thing he saw, he was going to eat it, regardless.

No sooner was the thought thunk than Brer Wolf rounded a bend and there was Brer Billy Goat standing on top of a rock. This was not one of your little rocks. This rock was as big and broad as a house, and Brer Billy Goat was standing on the top like he owned it and was thinking about turning it into a condominium.

Brer Wolf didn't care about none of that. He charged up the rock to find out what goat meat tasted like.

Brer Billy Goat didn't pay him no mind. He put his head down and went to acting like he was chewing on something. Brer Wolf stopped. He stared at Brer Billy Goat, trying to figure out what he was eating. Brer Billy kept on chewing.

Brer Wolf looked and looked.

Brer Billy Goat chewed and chewed.

Brer Wolf looked close. He didn't see no grass. He didn't see no corn shucks. He didn't see no straw and he didn't see no leaves.

Brer Billy Goat chewed and chewed.

Brer Wolf couldn't figure out to save his life what Brer Billy Goat was eating. Didn't nothing grow on a rock like that. Finally Brer Wolf couldn't stand it anymore.

"How do, Brer Billy Goat? I hope everything is going well with you these days."

Brer Billy Goat nodded and kept on chewing.

"What you eating, Brer Billy Goat? Looks like it tastes mighty good."

Brer Billy Goat looked up. "What does it look like I'm eating? I'm eating this rock."

Brer Wolf said, "Well, I'm powerful hungry myself, but I don't reckon I can eat rock."

"Come on. I'll break you off a chunk with my horns. There's enough here for you, if you hurry."

Brer Wolf shook his head and started backing away. He figured that if Brer Billy Goat could eat rock, he was a tougher man than Brer Wolf was. "Much obliged, Brer Billy Goat. But I got to be moving along."

"Don't go, Brer Wolf. This rock is fresh. Ain't no better rock in these parts."

Brer Wolf didn't even bother to answer but just kept on going. Any creature that could eat rock could eat wolf too.

Of course, Brer Billy Goat wasn't eating that rock. He was just chewing his cud and talking big.

You know something? There're a lot of people like that.

Brer Fox Takes Miz Cricket to Dinner

One of the smallest things on the grassy side of the earth was Miz Cricket. Even though she wasn't big, she could make as big a fuss as anybody. Some of the creatures say she made more fuss than she done good. I don't know about that. I ain't agreeing with it and I ain't disagreeing. The way I look on it, everybody is put on this earth for something, good or bad, and the most we can do is follow our noses if we plan on getting anywhere, and if you don't fall down and get talked about, you can thank all the stars on the underside of the sky.

Miz Cricket lived in the bushes and the high grass, and all she did every day was play on her fife and fiddle. When she got tired of playing on one, she'd play on the other, and that's what she did.

One day King Sun was shining thankful like. Miz Cricket climbed up in the tall grass and fiddled away like the circus was coming to town. Of course, back in them days there wasn't no such thing as a circus, and if there had been, it probably would've been folks who would've been balancing balls on their noses and jumping through fiery hoops. But that's what Miz Cricket's happy fiddling put me in mind of.

Miz Cricket heard somebody coming along the road. She looked real close and it wasn't nobody but Brer Fox.

"Why, hello there, Brer Fox! Where you going?"

Brer Fox stopped and looked around. "Who's that?"

"Ain't nobody in the round world but me. I know I ain't much, but I'm here just the same. Where you going?"

Brer Fox said, "I'm going where I'm going. That's where I'm going, and it wouldn't surprise me if where I was going was to town to get my dinner. I was a rover in my young days and I'm a rover now."

"I know what you mean, Brer Fox. We all go the way we're pushed by mind or hand, and it don't take much of a shove to send us the way we're going. I used to be a rover myself, but I've settled down and don't do nothing but have my own fun in my own way and time. But listening to you has got me to thinking about having my dinner in town."

"How you going to get there?"

"What you mean? I got legs and feet, and I caught the jumping habit from Cousin Brown Grasshopper. He's the kind what crawls a little, walks a little, flies a little, and hops a little. What time will you get to town?"

Brer Fox thought for a minute and did some counting on his fingers. "It'll take me a good two hours. My appetite will get there first but I won't be far behind."

Miz Cricket was astonished. She held up all her hands and feet and did some counting. "Two hours!" she exclaimed. "By the time you get there, Brer Fox, I'll be belching and picking my teeth and ready to take my after-dinner nap."

Brer Fox laughed. "If you beat me to town by so much as ten seconds, I'll buy your dinner and you can order from the menu that don't have no prices on it. But if I beat you, you'll have to pay for my dinner and I'm gon' tell you now: I'm powerful hungry."

"Brer Fox! It's a deal!"

Brer Fox grinned and started off down the road.

Just as Brer Fox made his start, Miz Cricket made hers. She took a flying jump and landed in Brer Fox's bushy tail, where she made herself comfortable and went to sleep.

Brer Fox had been going down the road about an hour when he met up with Brer Rabbit. They howdied and inquired about each other's family, and then Brer Fox told Brer Rabbit about the race he was having with Miz Cricket.

Brer Rabbit saw Miz Cricket nestled in Brer Fox's tail, and she gave him a big wink. He smole a smile and rolled his eyeballs. Brer Fox wanted to know what was wrong with him.

"Well, I was just thinking about how you'd feel if you knew that Miz Cricket was winning the race," said Brer Rabbit. "She passed me on the road about fifteen minutes ago. What have you been doing all this time? You must've fallen asleep and didn't know it."

"I been coming full tilt the whole time."

"If that's so, Miz Cricket got a whole lot of talent for covering ground. She probably in town now, waiting for you."

Brer Fox took off running, but as fast as he went, that was how fast Miz Cricket went.

When Brer Rabbit saw Brer Fox kicking up dust and moving down the road, he laughed so hard that he fell over in a ditch. "I'm mighty glad I met my old friend, 'cause now I know that all the fools ain't dead—and long may they live, 'cause it gives me something to do. Don't nothing keep me fat and sassy as good as a fool."

About forty-five minutes later Brer Fox got to the gate of the town. Back in them days all the towns had walls around them, and the only way in and out was through a gate. That's an idea that ought to be revived. I know a whole bunch of folks ought to be kept outside the gate.

When Brer Fox got to the gate, Miz Cricket took a flying jump and landed on top of the wall. Brer Fox knocked on the gate.

Miz Cricket yelled down from the top of the wall, "Hey, Brer Fox! Where you been? You must've stopped and had

a snack somewhere. I done ate my dinner already, but that was so long ago, I believe I could eat another one."

Brer Fox looked up and couldn't believe his eyes. "How in the wide world did you get here so quick?"

Miz Cricket said, "You know how I travel—with a hop, skip, and a jump. Well, I hopped and skipped and jumped a little quicker this time. I run into Brer Rabbit and he wanted to stop and talk, but I know that the only way to get where you going is to go on and get there. I reckon you must've run into Brer Rabbit too and let him get you tied up in his tongue."

Brer Porcupine was the gatekeeper, and he opened it. Brer Fox took Miz Cricket to dinner at the best restaurant in town. I think it was the Chez Stomachache. Then again it might've been the House of Grease and Good Times.

Brer Fox didn't know how somebody so little could eat so much. She had a great big porterhouse steak, baked potato, broccoli with French dressing, and washed it all down with a seventy-five-dollar bottle of wine. For dessert she had French vanilla ice cream with fresh strawberries. She finished it all off with a pot of black coffee. Luckily Brer Fox never left home without his American Express card, 'cause he sho' needed it that night.

Miz Cricket Makes the Creatures Run

Miz Cricket had almost as much sense as Brer Rabbit. Back in them times the big creatures had the strength, but the little ones had the sense.

One summer day the creatures were laying out in the meadow getting suntans. Don't ask me how come the creatures wanted tans. I ain't figured out how come white folks work so hard to get tans. Deep down I think they want to look as good as us black folks do, 'cause they sho' work overtime at it. I reckon the creatures wanted to look black too.

There they were out there in the meadow slapping suntan lotion on each other and turning this way and that way to make sure their tans were even all over, and that's what caused all the trouble.

What's true for folks was true for the creatures. When folks ain't got much to do and ain't got much more to talk about, somebody will start in bragging, and trouble ain't far behind. Brer Fox was the one what started this time.

"I was just lying here thinking that I'm the swiftest one of anybody here."

Brer Elephant winked one of his tiny eyes, flung his trunk in the air, and whispered—of course, when Brer Elephant whispered, folks a mile away could hear it—"I got the most strength!"

King Lion was there and he shook his mane and showed his teeth. "Don't forget! I'm the King of all you creatures."

Brer Tiger stretched himself and yawned. "I'm the prettiest and the most vigorous."

The bragging went on this way until all the creatures had declared that he was the most something or other. The only one that hadn't bragged was Miz Cricket, and didn't nobody expect her to do no bragging, 'cause as far as they were concerned, she didn't have nothing to brag about.

So everybody was astonished when Miz Cricket said, "I can make all of you run your heads off, all of you from Brer Elephant on down."

The creatures thought that was the funniest thing they'd heard since somebody played them a record called *Luciano Pavarotti Sings the Blues.*

Brer Fox said, "I hear you talking, Miss Cricket, but what I want to know is, how you gon' do it?"

"Don't worry about it. You'll hear from me. That you will."

The creatures thought that was the second funniest thing they'd ever heard and they took to laughing some more.

They were laughing so hard, they didn't notice that Brer Rabbit wasn't laughing at all. He knew Miz Cricket was powerful in the mind, and he wanted to know what she was up to. It just so happened that Miz Cricket wanted to exchange a few syllables with Brer Rabbit, 'cause she needed some help.

Brer Rabbit and Miz Cricket sneaked off where they could talk.

"You got a big job on your hands," said Brer Rabbit.

"I know, and I can't do it if I don't get your help."

Brer Rabbit twisted his mustache and looked thoughtful. "Well, I don't know, Miz Cricket. All the creatures been after me so fierce lately that I done had to lay low. But what's on your mind?"

Miz Cricket told Brer Rabbit what she was planning and Brer Rabbit laughed. "If that's all you want me to do, Miz Cricket, I'm your man!"

The next day Miz Cricket and Brer Rabbit went back to the meadow where they knew they'd find all the creatures. The first one they saw was Brer Elephant.

"I got some bad news," Brer Rabbit told him.

"What's the trouble?"

"A big wind came up last night and blew a tree down on Miz Cricket and broke one of her legs. She can't get to the hospital to get it attended to. I was wondering if you'd be so kind as to carry her there."

Brer Elephant said he'd be glad to. He knelt down and Brer Rabbit put Miz Cricket on his back. But Miz Cricket didn't stay on Brer Elephant's back. She crawled up to his neck and down into his ear.

As soon as she was in his ear, she started fluttering her wings. Brer Elephant thought a big wind was blowing through the trees. Miz Cricket fluttered her wings faster. It sounded like a storm was coming, and Brer Elephant took off running through the woods. He plunged through the bushes and knocked over trees, but the storm kept getting louder and louder. It was good thing Miz Cricket was inside his ear or she would've been knocked off and trampled on.

Miz Cricket took out her fife and started playing on it. She played kind of low to begin with and then got louder and louder. The louder she played, the more scared Brer Elephant got, and the more scared he got, the more he ran. He ran round and round in circles, his trunk flapping in the air, and pretty soon he ran back to the meadow.

"Where you going?" King Lion asked him, jumping up.

Brer Elephant stopped, almost out of breath. "I got a singing and whistling in my ears and I don't know where it's coming from. Can't you hear it?"

The creatures listened and they heard it.

King Lion said, "Seems to me, Brer Elephant, that that whistling sound means that you about to boil over, and if that's what you going to do, I believe I want to be way away from here."

While King Lion was saying all that, Miz Cricket took a flying jump out of Brer Elephant's ear and landed right smack dab in King Lion's ear.

Brer Elephant said, "Wait a minute! I don't hear it no more." He listened. "Sho' 'nuf. The whistling done stopped." He smiled. "I'm cured. I don't know which one of you is a doctor, but I thank you for curing me."

By this time Miz Cricket had gotten comfortable in King Lion's ear and took out her fife and started playing.

King Lion cocked his head to one side and listened. "You might not hear it no more, Brer Elephant, but I can still hear it. I think I done caught what you was just cured of."

Miz Cricket played louder and King Lion started getting fidgety, like there was someplace he had to go but he don't know where it is. He waved his tail and shook his mane. Miz Cricket played louder and fluttered her wings.

"I hear the wind blowing," said King Lion. "I got to go home and see after my family." He took off and he ran and he ran trying to get away from all the noise in his ear. He ran to where he didn't know and come back to where he did know which is where he'd started from but he didn't know that.

"What y'all chasing me for?" he asked the other creatures. "I left y'all back yonder where I came from."

"We ain't moved out of our tracks," Brer Elephant said.

"You ran away and left us here and now you come back," added Brer Tiger. "What's the matter with you?"

"I got a whistling in my head and can't get away from it. I don't know what I'm going to do."

"Ain't nothing you can do except do like I did and stand it as best you can," Brer Elephant offered.

Brer Tiger said, "I hear it and it sounds like you gon' boil over any minute. I know I don't want to be here when you do."

While Brer Tiger was saying that, Miz Cricket took a flying leap out of King Lion's ear and landed right smack dab in Brer Tiger's. Soon as she got comfortable, she began playing on her fife and flapping her wings. Brer Tiger started getting fidgety and moving around.

"Has the disease got you now?" Brer Elephant wanted to know.

Brer Tiger didn't wait around to answer, 'cause he was galloping across the meadow like a racehorse.

Brer Rabbit walked up to the creatures, chuckling. "Miz Cricket said she was going to make y'all run, and that's just what she done. If you just wait here, Miz Cricket will bring Brer Tiger back in a few minutes."

Sure enough it wasn't long before Brer Tiger came back with his tongue dragging on the ground. Miz Cricket jumped out of Brer Tiger's ear and bowed real low to all the gentlemen.

"Howdy do, everybody."

But the creatures didn't want any "howdy-doing" with Miz Cricket after that.

It serves 'em right for laying out there slapping suntan oil on themselves and trying to get tans. If the Lord had wanted them to be as pretty as black folks, they would've been born black. But they wasn't and they should've been content with what the Lord blessed 'em with.

The Story of the Doodang

I know the first thing you want to know is, what is a Doodang? Well, I can't tell you, 'cause I ain't never seen one. However I have seen them what say they heard tell of them who had seen him.

The way I heard it was that the Doodang lived in the mud flats down on the river. Didn't nobody know exactly what kind of creature he was. He had a long tail like an alligator, a great big body, four short legs, two short ears, and a head that was uglier than a rhinoceros's. His mouth went from the end of his nose to his shoulder blades, and his teeth were big enough and long enough and sharp enough to bite off the left hind leg of a bull elephant.

The Doodang could live in the water and he could live on dry land, but his favorite place was the mud flats. He could sit on the mud flats, reach out in the water, and catch a fish, or he could reach up in the bushes and catch a bird.

To you and me it might seem that the Doodang had the best of both worlds, dry and wet, but that ain't the way it seemed to the Doodang.

He got dissatisfied and started wanting things he didn't have. What he had didn't satisfy him and he started worrying. His worrying turned to growling and groaning all through the day and all through the night.

His groaning and growling kept all the creatures, fur and feather, wing and claw, wide awake for miles around.

After a week without any good sleep Brer Rabbit had had quite enough. He went down to the river to see the Doodang.

"What is the matter with you?" Brer Rabbit said right

off. He didn't waste no time with howdy-dos and all like that, and to tell the truth Brer Rabbit didn't phrase the question as politely as I did.

You would think that a creature as big as the Doodang would've had a deep bass voice. Truth is his voice was high pitched, and when he talked it sounded like he was whining. "I want to swim in the water like the fish do."

Brer Rabbit shivered. "You make my blood run cold when you talk about swimming in the water. The Lord put the water on earth so we'd have something to make Kool-Aid out of, but if you want to swim, swim on dry land! Swim on dry land!"

The Doodang talked so loud that the fish heard him. Like everybody else they hadn't been able to get any sleep, and they were so tired they had started biting at fishing worms. They held a meeting out there in the river.

"Did you hear that fool Doodang say he wants to swim like we do?" said Brer Catfish.

"I wouldn't mind teaching him how to swim," said Brer Mackerel, "but he ain't got no scales and fins."

"That's it!" said Miz Goldfish.

"What's it?" all the other fish wanted to know.

"Why don't we lend him one scale and one fin apiece?"

The fish agreed that that was the thing to do, and no sooner said than done.

They swam over and told the Doodang what they were going to do. He was so happy that he gave a loud howl and rolled over in the water.

The fish surrounded him and each one took a scale and a fin and put it on the Doodang. When they got through, the Doodang took a deep breath and plunged into the water.

He skeeted about in the water, waving his tail from side to side. He swam up the river and down the river and went back and forth across the river. He swam on the topside of the water and underneath the water. He had a good time being a fish—for about an hour or so. Then he got tired and bored and started walking out of the water.

"Hey!" the fish yelled out. "Where you going?"

"It's not fun being a fish," said the Doodang.

"Then give us back our fins and scales!"

The fish were so mad they were ready to fight, so the Doodang gave them back their fins and scales and crawled onto the mud flats to take a nap.

He hadn't been asleep long when a big noise woke him. He looked up and the blue sky was black with birds, big ones and little ones. They were coming to roost in the trees on the island in the middle of the river.

The birds had scarcely gotten settled before the Doodang started howling and growling and carrying on like he had eaten too many hot dogs.

The King-Bird flew over to the mud flat. "What is wrong with you?" he screamed at the Doodang.

The Doodang rolled over on his back and started howling louder.

"WHAT IS WRONG WITH YOU?"

The Doodang just lay there and howled and howled. Finally he raised his head and said, "I want to fly."

"You doofus Doodang! You can't fly. You too big to fly!" the King-Bird yelled.

"If I had some feathers, I bet I could fly. I bet I could fly as good as you—if I had some feathers."

The King-Bird flew back to the island and held a meeting with all the birds.

"Listen up, everybody!" said the King-Bird. "We got to get us some sleep. Ain't no two ways about it. The Doodang said if he had some feathers he could fly, and if he's flying, he ain't hollering, and if he ain't hollering, we can get some sleep. I say each of us lend him a feather."

The King-Bird hadn't finished his speech before the birds started taking off feathers. They took 'em to the Doodang and put them on him.

The Doodang looked at his new feathers and he was as

proud as a little boy who's been playing in the mud. "Where should I fly to?" he wanted to know.

Brer Buzzard said, "There's another island about a mile down the river that ain't got nothing but dead trees on it. Why don't you see if you can fly down there?"

The Doodang got a running start, jumped up in the air, and started moving his wings. Wouldn't nobody ever say that the Doodang looked pretty flying, but he stayed in the air, and that was the main thing.

In a little while he landed with a splash in the water next to the island. He was spluttering around in the water when Brer Buzzard said, "I don't want my feather getting all wet. Won't be good for flying then." He swooped down and grabbed his feather off the Doodang.

Soon as he did that, the other birds swooped down and took their feathers back. And then they flew away.

There the Doodang was on the island with the dead trees and no way to get back to the mud flats.

All the creatures went to sleep that night and they slept that night, all the next day, the next night, and half of the following day.

On the day after that Brer Rabbit happened to run into Brer Buzzard. "Say, Brer Buzzard, what happened to the Doodang?"

Brer Buzzard pointed down the river to the island where the dead trees were. "You see my family sitting in them dead trees?"

Brer Rabbit nodded.

"That's where the Doodang is. If you'll get me a bag, Brer Rabbit, I'll bring you his bones."

Brer Rabbit laughed and laughed and laughed.

Brer Deer and King Sun's Daughter

One of the problems with telling tales like these is that it ain't always easy to get the story fixed in the time it's supposed to be in. That's because there're so many different kinds of time.

There's daytime and nighttime, bedtime and mealtime. There's sometime, any ol' time, and no time. There's high time, fly time, good times, bad times, and the wrong time, not to mention a long time and time to go. All the different kinds of time are enough to give a body a headache and turn him white. I've been trying to count up all the different times, and my calculator can't count that high. There's new time and old time, cold time and due time, and then there's once upon a time.

Some folks say that this story happened "once upon a time," but I ain't sure about that. The once-upon-a-time stories got people in them, but this story took place before then. So I can't start it off with "Once upon a time." Let me think a minute.

All right. I got it.

Way back before there was a time, Brer Deer fell in love with King Sun's daughter. Back in the time what I'm talking about, King Sun wasn't like he is now. He was as different then as them times are from these times. For one thing he was a lot closer to the earth then. For another he didn't go off and hide at night like he does now. King Sun was a lot more neighborly in them days than he is now, when he don't talk to nobody.

Back in them times he lived so close that he used to send one of his servants down to the spring for drinking water. Three times a day he'd climb down with a bucket in his hand and climb back up with the bucket on his head.

All the creatures knew King Sun had a pretty daughter, but none of 'em had ever seen her. That didn't matter to Brer Deer. He made up his mind that he was going to marry her. The only problem was that he had to find a way to ask her.

He was sitting beside the road trying to figure out a plan when along came Brer Rabbit.

"Well, Brer Deer. How is your copperosity segashuating?"

"My copperosity is segashuating just fine, Brer Rabbit, but I got trouble in my mind and I can't get it out."

"I'm sorry to hear that." Brer Rabbit sat down looking like he knew all there was to be known. "When I was a little rabbit, I heard the old folks say that a light heart make for a long life. They knew what they was talking about, 'cause I been here longer than anybody."

Brer Deer sighed. He blinked his eyes real fast to keep the tears in 'em from falling out. "I know you telling me the truth, Brer Rabbit, but I can't help myself. I am what I am and I can't be no ammer. I feel more like crying than eating, and I seem to get angry for no reason. Just a little while ago Mr. Benjamin Ram told me howdy, and for no reason I ran at him and butted him with my horns. Now, I know that wasn't the right thing to do, but I couldn't help myself."

Brer Rabbit got up and put a little distance between himself and Brer Deer. "Now that you mention it, them horns of yours have always made me a little nervous."

"I ain't gon' do *you* no harm, Brer Rabbit. We been knowing each other a long time, and I'm glad you come by. If I don't tell my troubles to somebody, I'm going to bust wide open."

Brer Rabbit sat down close to Brer Deer again. "What's your trouble?"

"I'm in love with King Sun's daughter. I don't know how it happened, but it did. I ain't never talked to her. I ain't never laid eyes on her, but I'm in love with her just the same. You can laugh at me if you want to, but truth is truth."

Brer Rabbit didn't laugh. He felt sorry for Brer Deer. Falling in love was hard on the appetite and on your sleep. I don't want to have nothing to do with something that makes me leave food on my plate and lie in bed at night tossing and turning. Brer Rabbit knew that the best cure for falling in love was getting married, so he decided to help Brer Deer out of his misery.

Brer Deer perked up. "If you help me through this, I'll be your friend forever."

Brer Rabbit shook his head. "Having a friend forever would make me kind of nervous. To be truthful I been feeling kind of bored the past few weeks, so this will give me something to occupy my mind." Brer Rabbit got up and brushed the dirt off his pants. "I hope to have some good news for you the next time we meet in the big road."

Brer Rabbit went on down the road and Brer Deer found him a cool spot in the woods and got the first sleep he'd had in weeks.

Brer Rabbit went to the spring where King Sun's servant came to get water. He had to carry a lot of water too. The more water King Sun drank, the more he wanted, so the servant was carrying water almost all day every day.

Brer Rabbit got to the spring and it was just as clear as glass. He leaned over, looked in, and saw himself. "Whoever you are, you as pretty as sin." He laughed.

Down at the bottom of the spring was Ol' Man Spring Lizard. He was taking his morning nap and woke up when he heard somebody talking. He looked up to see Brer Rabbit looking at himself in the water.

"Maybe you ain't as good looking as you think you are," the Spring Lizard hollered up.

"I ain't never had my reflection talk back at me before," Brer Rabbit said.

Mr. Spring Lizard swam from under the green moss and came to the top. He asked Brer Rabbit what he was up to.

Brer Rabbit told him about Brer Deer being in love with King Sun's daughter.

"I seen her once. A few months back she came down here to the spring. She's got an Afro that's light and fluffy like clouds and eyes that shine like love."

"Do tell!" said Brer Rabbit. "Well, I got to figure out how to get word to her that Brer Deer wants to marry her."

"That's easy."

"Talk to me, Mr. Spring Lizard."

"When the servant comes from King Sun's house, he has to let down a ladder. When he does, you can just slip up it."

Brer Rabbit wasn't too sure he wanted to met with King Sun face to face. "I'm a homebody, you know, and don't like going off on long trips."

"Well, if Brer Deer will write a note, I'll get in the bucket and take it up."

"That's a good idea. Brer Deer can't write, but I can. I be back in a little while."

Brer Rabbit went home, wrote the note, and brought it back. "Don't let this note get wet."

Mr. Spring Lizard acted disgusted. "How can the note get wet when I'll have it in my pocket? You land creatures got the wrong idea about water. What's wet to you ain't wet to us, excepting on rainy days."

Before long King Sun's servant let down the ladder and came to the spring with his bucket. He dropped the bucket in and filled it with water. The Spring Lizard swam in at the last minute and hid down at the bottom. The servant took the bucket, climbed back up the ladder, and pulled it up after him. Then he went along the path to King Sun's house.

He brought the bucket of water to King Sun, who grabbed his dipper and drank and drank until it looked like his fire might go out. But he had his fill before that happened and he went on in the back to take a nap.

Soon as he was gone, Mr. Spring Lizard leaped out of the bucket, put the note on the table, and jumped back in.

In a little while King Sun's daughter came bouncing in the room to get herself a drink of water and saw the note. She picked it up.

"Daddy! Daddy! Here's a letter for you."

King Sun came in the room, pulled his fingers through his beard, put on his glasses, and read the note, "Well, well, well. I ain't never heard of such impudence."

"What does it say, Daddy?"

"Dear King Sun: I would be most honored and proud if you would permit me to be the one to marry your daughter. I will take care of her better than anybody. If you grant my request, it will make me very happy. (Signed) Brer Deer."

King Sun's daughter got all red in the face and she got mad and she got glad and she didn't know what to think. That was the sign that she had fallen in love.

King Sun got out his pen and some writing paper and wrote a letter back to Brer Deer. *If the one who wrote the letter will send me a bag of gold, he can marry my daughter. (Signed) King Sun.* He gave the letter to his daughter and she put it on the table where she'd found the other one.

When they left the room, Mr. Spring Lizard jumped out of the bucket, got the letter, and jumped back in without making a splash.

A little while later the servant came in, took the bucket, let down the ladder, and went to the spring. Mr. Spring Lizard jumped into the water and waited for Brer Rabbit.

Brer Rabbit had been hiding in the bushes, waiting, and as soon as the servant left, he went to the spring, got the letter from Mr. Spring Lizard, and went directly to Brer Deer and read it to him.

In no time at all Brer Deer had gathered up a bag of gold. Don't come asking me where he got the gold. That information must not have been important, 'cause it wasn't in the story when the story was handed to me, and I'm too tired to put it in today.

Brer Deer left the bag of gold at the spring and waited. Wasn't long before he saw the ladder being let down, but it wasn't the servant who walked down. It was King Sun's daughter herself. She was coming to see what kind of man Brer Deer was.

Brer Deer looked at her and was glad that he had listened to his heart, even though what his heart had been saying hadn't made no sense to his brain. King Sun's daughter had an Afro that curved around her head like a shining halo. Her skin was a deep brown like earth that had just been turned over by a plow. Her eyes glistened like they were the place where joy had been born.

Brer Deer got up his courage and stepped out from hiding, so King Sun's daughter could see him. She looked at him and he looked at her, and it was over for both of 'em. And from what I understand, they were happy with one another, except on Sundays, when Brer Deer didn't pay her no attention 'cause he was watching football on TV.

———————

Teenchy-Tiny Duck's Magical Satchel

Once there lived a man and a woman, and they were very poor. They didn't have any money. They didn't have a farm. They didn't even have a garden patch.

All they had in the whole world was a little puddle duck who walked around all day singing the hungry song: "Quack! Quack! Give me a piece of bread!" It wouldn't have taken much to feed her because she was so tiny, which was why folks called her Teenchy-Tiny Duck.

One day she was paddling in the river when she found a money purse filled with gold. As soon as she saw what it was, she started quacking: "Somebody lost their pretty money! Pretty money! Pretty money! Who lost their pretty money?"

Just about the same time a rich man came walking along. He had a walking stick in his hand, and every few steps he stopped and made some marks in the dirt, trying to add up all the money he had. He heard Teenchy-Tiny Duck making a lot of racket, and his eye lit on the money purse.

"That's mine! That's mine! I lost it and came back to look for it." He picked up the money purse and dropped it in his satchel.

Teenchy-Tiny got mad! "That rascal just came and took all the gold I found and didn't even give me none for finding it!"

She waddled home and told the folks what had happened. The poor man was so mad that he started pulling his hair out. "Get out of my house!" he yelled at Teenchy-Tiny Duck. "Get out and don't come back until you get the gold what that rich man took!"

Teenchy-Tiny didn't know what to do. She went back to the river and sat on the bank and started crying.

Well, it just so happened that Brer Rabbit was laying over in the weeds trying to figure out how come he was so smart, and he heard Teenchy-Tiny crying. "What's the matter, little puddle-duck?" he asked her.

She told him about finding the gold and the rich man taking it from her. Brer Rabbit cried with one eye and winked the other. "Well, go after him and get the gold back."

"How am I going to do that?" Teenchy-Tiny wanted to know.

"There's always a way, if not two."

Teenchy-Tiny started off down the road after the man, waddling and quacking as fast as she could. "I want my pretty money! I want my pretty money!"

After a while she came upon Brer Fox.

"Where you going?" he wanted to know.

She told him.

"What you gon' do when you find that rich man?"

"I'm gon' get my money and take it back home."

"You want me to go with you?" asked Brer Fox.

"Wouldn't nothing suit me better."

"Well, I have to hide."

Teenchy-Tiny had brought a satchel with her to carry the gold in when she got it back. "Get in my satchel."

"It ain't big enough," said Brer Fox.

"This here is a stretching satchel."

Brer Fox jumped in.

Not long after that Teenchy-Tiny met Brer Wolf.

"Where you going?" he wanted to know.

She told him.

"Maybe I can help you, but I'm tired and I can't go too far."

"Get in my satchel."

"It ain't big enough," Brer Wolf said.

"This here is a stretching satchel. Jump in."

Brer Wolf jumped in and Teenchy-Tiny Duck went on down the road.

The next somebody she ran into was Uncle Ladder, who was taking his noonday rest by the side of a tree. He wanted to know where Teenchy-Tiny was going.

She told him.

Uncle Ladder felt sorry for her. "You think I could help you out?"

"No doubt about it."

"Well, I be glad to, but I can't walk fast as you."

"Don't need to. Just get in my satchel and I'll carry you."

Uncle Ladder got in the satchel and off Teenchy-Tiny went down the road, quacking and squawking about getting her pretty money back.

The road curved and Teenchy-Tiny Duck found herself next to the best friend she'd ever had, Grandpappy River. He stopped running. "What's the matter? When I saw you this morning, you were happy. Now you look like you in bad trouble. How can I help you? I'd go along with you if I had legs."

"Just get in the satchel, Grandpappy."

Grandpappy River got in the satchel and didn't drown nobody. Teenchy-Tiny went on down the road. "I want my money! I want my money!"

After a while she came to a big beehive. Ol' Man Drone was sunning himself and he started laughing at the little duck toting a satchel that was seventy-eleven times bigger than she was. But when him and all the Bees saw how sorrowful Teenchy-Tiny was looking, they asked her what was wrong.

She told them all about her troubles and it seemed like the more she talked, the bigger her troubles got.

The Bees said they'd be proud to go with her.

"Get in the satchel, but don't be stinging nobody."

The Bees got in the satchel and kept their stingers to themselves.

Teenchy-Tiny went on down the road, and late over in the evening she came to the rich man's house. She went up to the gate. "Hey, stupid rich man! You bring me my money!"

The rich man laughed and told one of his servants, "Go get that duck. I believe I'll have her for supper tomorrow."

The servant grabbed Teenchy-Tiny and threw her and the satchel in the henhouse.

Soon as she was inside, the chickens started pecking and beating on Teenchy-Tiny something awful.

Teenchy-Tiny wasn't in no mood for nothing but her money, so she opened up the satchel. "Brer Fox!"

Brer Fox jumped out, saw all those chickens, and knew he was in paradise. Wasn't long before there was nothing but silence in that henhouse.

Next morning when the servant came to the henhouse, there wasn't a chicken there. However there were a whole lot of chicken feathers.

The servant couldn't believe his eyes, and while he was standing in the door wondering what to do, Teenchy-Tiny picked up her satchel and marched out, shouting, "I want my money! I want my money!"

When the servant told the rich man and his wife what had happened, the wife said, "That ain't no duck. That's a witch. You better give her that money!"

The rich man just laughed.

All day long Teenchy-Tiny stood outside the house, shouting, "I want my money! I want my money!"

Night came, as night is prone to do, and the rich man told the servant, "Put that duck in the stable with the mules and the horses. They'll take care of her."

The servant put Teenchy-Tiny and her satchel in the stable.

Teenchy-Tiny was scared that the horses and mules might step on her during the night. She opened up the satchel. "Brer Wolf!"

Brer Wolf leaped out, saw all the horses and mules, and thought he was in paradise. The next morning when the farmhands came down to the stable to hitch up the horses and the mules, every last one of 'em was stretched out cold.

When they told the rich man what had happened, his wife started crying. "Give that duck her gold! If you don't, it's gon' be the end of us!"

The rich man was mad now. He told his servant, "Throw that duck in the well!"

The servant threw Teenchy-Tiny in the well. Teenchy-Tiny squawked and yelled until Uncle Ladder heard her. He got out of the satchel and stretched himself, 'cause a satchel ain't a comfortable place for a ladder. He managed to make his way over to the well and let himself down so that Teenchy-Tiny Duck could climb out.

That's what she did, and wasn't but one thing on her mind. "I want my pretty money! Give my my pretty money!"

The rich man was sho' 'nuf mad now. He told his cook, "Get the oven heated up!"

All while the oven was getting red hot, Teenchy-Tiny

was yelling, "I want my money! Give me my pretty money!"

The rich man told his servant, "Throw that duck in the oven!"

The servant grabbed Teenchy-Tiny and threw her in the oven.

"Grandpappy River!" hollered Teenchy-Tiny.

Grandpappy River came pouring out of the satchel and headed straight for the oven and drowned the fire. Teenchy-Tiny came marching out of the oven, hollering, "Where's my pretty money? I want my money!"

The rich man's wife begged and begged, but the rich man wasn't listening. "I'll take care of that duck myself."

Late that night the rich man sneaked out in the yard. Teenchy-Tiny was hollering so loud for her money that she wouldn't had heard the man if he'd driven up in a fire engine with the siren on. The first thing she knew, the rich man was beating her with his walking stick. He was about to beat her into soup or pâté, depending on your preference, when Teenchy-Tiny yelled, "Bees!"

The Bees came swarming out of the satchel. The way they stung that rich man was enough to make you smile or cry, depending on which way your mind leans. The rich man couldn't run fast enough to get that money. He gave it to Teenchy-Tiny Duck and told her to please leave him alone.

Everybody thanked Teenchy-Tiny for the fun adventure and got in the magical satchel so she could take them back where she'd found them. Brer Wolf and Brer Fox didn't like the way the Bees were buzzing and said they'd get home on their own. Teenchy-Tiny carried the Bees back to the hive, the Ladder to the tree, and Grandpappy River to his bed.

Then, Teenchy-Tiny went home and gave the gold to her master and mistress, and after that Teenchy-Tiny had plenty to eat and she got right fat and plump.

But folks called her Teenchy-Tiny just the same.

Julius Lester is the critically acclaimed author of books for both children and adults. His first two collections of Uncle Remus stories, *The Tales of Uncle Remus: The Adventures of Brer Rabbit* and *More Tales of Uncle Remus: Further Adventures of Brer Rabbit, His Friends, Enemies, and Others,* have won numerous awards. Both were ALA Notable Books, Coretta Scott King Honor Books, and *Booklist* Editors' Choices. Other books for Dial include *To Be a Slave,* a Newbery Medal Honor Book; *Long Journey Home: Stories from Black History,* a National Book Award finalist; *This Strange New Feeling;* and *The Knee-High Man and Other Tales,* an ALA Notable Book, *School Library Journal* Best Book of the Year, and Lewis Carroll Shelf Award Winner. His adult books include *Do Lord Remember Me,* a *New York Times* Notable Book, and *Lovesong: Becoming a Jew,* a National Jewish Book Award finalist.

Mr. Lester was born in St. Louis and grew up in Kansas City, Kansas, and Nashville, Tennessee, where he received his Bachelor of Arts from Fisk University. He is married and the father of four children. He lives in Amherst and teaches at the University of Massachusetts.

ABOUT THE ILLUSTRATOR

Jerry Pinkney, a 1989 Caldecott Honor Book artist, is the only illustrator ever to have won the Coretta Scott King Award three times. He illustrated *The Patchwork Quilt* (Dial) by Valerie Flournoy, which in addition to the Coretta Scott King Award also won the Christopher Award and was an IRA-CBC Children's Choice, an ALA Notable Book, and a Reading Rainbow Selection. Mr. Pinkney's recent work for Dial includes illustrations for *The Talking Eggs* by Robert D. San Souci and *Rabbit Makes a Monkey of Lion* by Verna Aardema, which won First Place in the 1989 New York Book Show. His artwork has been shown at the Bologna Book Fair, the AIGA Book Show, the Society of Illustrators Annual Show, and in museums around the country.

Mr. Pinkney is Associate Professor of Art at the University of Delaware. He and his wife Gloria are the parents of four children. They live in Croton-on-Hudson, New York.

The Last Tales of Uncle Remus

The Tales of Uncle Remus
The Adventures of Brer Rabbit

More Tales of Uncle Remus
Further Adventures of Brer Rabbit,
His Friends, Enemies, and Others

Further Tales of Uncle Remus
The Misadventures of Brer Rabbit,
Brer Fox, Brer Wolf, the Doodang,
and Other Creatures

The Last Tales of Uncle Remus

•

Long Journey Home
Stories from Black History

This Strange New Feeling

The Knee-High Man *And Other Tales*

To Be a Slave

The Last Tales of Uncle Remus

as told by JULIUS LESTER

illustrated by Jerry Pinkney

DIAL BOOKS

New York

Published by Dial Books
375 Hudson Street
New York, New York 10014

Text copyright © 1994 by Julius Lester
Illustrations copyright © 1994 by Jerry Pinkney
All rights reserved
Design by Jane Byers Bierhorst
First Edition

Library of Congress Cataloging in Publication Data

Lester, Julius.
The last tales of Uncle Remus : as told by Julius Lester
illustrated by Jerry Pinkney.—1st ed.
p.   cm.
Summary : Retells the final adventures and misadventures
of Brer Rabbit and his friends and enemies.
ISBN 0-8037-1303-7.—ISBN 0-8037-1304-5 (lib. bdg.)
1. Afro-Americans—Folklore. 2. Tales—United States.
[1. Folklore, Afro-American. 2. Animals—Folklore.]
I. Pinkney, Jerry, ill. II. Title.
PZ8.1.L434Las 1994
398.2'08996073—dc20   93-7531   CIP   AC

The publisher wishes to express its sincere thanks to the estate
of Joel Chandler Harris for its gracious support during the
publication of this new version of *The Tales of Uncle Remus.*

*Each black-and-white drawing is made of pencil and graphite; and
each full-color picture consists of a pencil, graphite, and watercolor
painting that is color-separated and reproduced in full color.*

Since the first volume of my retelling of *The Tales of Uncle Remus* appeared in 1987, a question I have been asked often is, "Why did you keep the name of Uncle Remus?"

Behind the question I hear a concern that by retaining the name, I may have also retained the unpleasant historical memories evoked by a name of plantation slavery. My response has been that the title, *The Tales of Uncle Remus,* identifies a particular collection of Afro-American folktales, the largest single body we have.

However, as I completed work on this, the fourth and last volume, I began wondering why *The Tales of Uncle Remus* have endured in people's affections to an extent far greater than anything else in American folklore. Since 1987 I have met many people who grew up being read *The Tales of Uncle Remus*. I have seen their bodies relax into childhood as they share memories of the experience of being read to by a mother or father.

The expressions of awe and wonder on their faces indicate that the memories evoked include more than the stories themselves, especially because often they do not recall particular stories, though they do remember Brer Rabbit. The memories are of a total experience, encompassing the tale, the setting in which the tale was heard, and the storyteller, the one in the flesh— parent, relative, teacher—and the one on the page, Uncle Remus. The experience evoked by the memories is of a relationship, a relationship for which the adult still yearns.

It is this relationship that is absent from many of the stories that appear in print today. As the function of storytelling has been taken over more and more by books, the voice of storytelling has become a disembodied one. The story has become words on pages supported and vivified by illustrations.

But storytelling is a human event, an act of creating relationship. In a traditional setting, storytelling creates and re–creates community, making a bond between the living and the living, the young and the old, the living and the dead, the human and the animal, the human and the vegetable and the mineral. The storyteller resides at the vortex of mystery, resolving it by means that do not rob us of mystery.

The genius of Joel Chandler Harris was creating Uncle Remus. It is difficult to separate the tales from the figure of Uncle

Remus. Quite rightly, Harris made story and storyteller one. If he had simply published the tales without the distinctive voice of the narrator, the stories would not have endured. It is Uncle Remus's belief in their veracity that enables us to suspend our rationality and be blessed by the magical act of the story.

Uncle Remus is more, however. He is the archetypal good father. He jokes, he teases, he pretends to be annoyed, he feigns anger and hurt when offended. But we know the truth of the man is his dignity, his self-respect, and above all, his love.

It is a love that is difficult to describe, especially in a time when love is sentimentalized in an unceasing effluvium of popular music, television dramas, and films. Thus, we forget or never learn that love is tough, that love has the brilliant hardness of diamonds, the cutting clarity of the most rational thought.

Uncle Remus loves tradition. For him tradition is not an act of preserving the past, but an understanding of values, values that a newer age has increasingly little sense of. Uncle Remus knows what is right and what is wrong and suffers no confusion or doubt about which is which. This is part of the comfort and safety generations of children have found in him and his story-telling. He represents certainty; and childhood, with its constant change and growth, is anything but secure and safe.

Uncle Remus also loves language. The language of storytelling is supposed to be a specialized one of startling images, absurd words, and amusing paradox. It is the language that gives these tales their special aliveness because the language startles us from the complacency of the ordinary into the vibrancy of the extraordinary. The language is so convincing, however, that we are not left in the world of fantasy but are returned to the ordinary where we find ourselves wanting to address a rabbit on the lawn as "Brer" and feeling disappointed that it won't answer.

Of course, I am aware that Harris's Uncle Remus also represents a slave plantation type—the servile "darky," loyal to white people, disparaging of other blacks, the privileged faithful servant who identifies with his oppressor and condition of oppression. As I pointed out in the introduction to the first volume of this series, I do not quarrel with history. Such blacks existed during slavery. Those who would criticize Uncle Remus for his accommodationist politics overlook the fact that it is the same Uncle Remus who preserved the culture through the tales. Without the Uncle Remuses, how much of black folk culture would have survived?

I note that Harris's Uncle Remus was in many respects an Uncle Tom. This should not blind us to his contribution or cause us to withdraw respect from him. Each of us is as complex and contradictory, and that is the beauty of being human.

So as I conclude this retelling, I understand that I retained the name of Uncle Remus and created my own version of him because the storyteller is as important as the story, if not more so. I wonder if generations have not read these tales as much for the tale-teller as for the tales themselves. And is this not logical? Do not our souls hunger for genuine experiences of others? Are not our spirits revived through contact with others whose spirits touch our spirits in a way that makes us feel better for having sat with them for a while? Is not the essence of our lives the desire to live in relationships that will return to us an image of ourselves that we can love?

This is the function of the storyteller and his or her story— to wed us with ourselves by wedding us to the mysteries that will always be, and at the same time animate us with laughter and love.

While a book may have a single author, the final product is a collaborative effort. I want to thank Jerry Pinkney for his wonderful illustrations in these four volumes. His work has enhanced the wonder of the tales, enriched their spirit, and complemented the language to create a whole bigger than the words could have alone.

Phyllis Fogelman, the editor-in-chief and publisher of Dial Books for Young Readers, and I have worked together for almost twenty-five years now. Since the publication of *To Be a Slave*, she has been the midwife who has scrutinized the manuscripts to be certain that I was saying what I wanted to say as well as she knew I could. And then, she has taken words on manuscript pages and transformed them into books that are inviting to read and beautiful to behold. It is she who, in collaboration with Atha Tehon, the art director, and Jane Byers Bierhorst, the designer, decides on typeface, page size, design, layout, kind of paper, and more details than I know. Phyllis and Atha have repeatedly said that the Uncle Remus books have been the most difficult to produce. Whatever the difficulties, Phyllis never sought the easy solution, or even the least expensive. She wanted and obtained only the best solution. Her creative diligence has been indispensable in bringing these tales to a new generation.

Julius Lester
February 25, 1993

Contents

The Last Tales of Uncle Remus

Why the Cricket Has Elbows on His Legs

The first thing you have to understand is that the world today is different than it was back when these stories took place. For one thing, folks were bigger then. My great-grandaddy said his great-grandaddy's great-grandaddy's great-grandaddy was so big that it took three of him to make one of him, if you understand what I'm saying and didn't get lost among the hims. People have swunk up since them days. My great-grandaddy's great-great-grandaddy said it's because folks have stopped eating raw meat and gone to messing with tofu and bean sprouts. That will certainly swunk you up.

In any event, it stands to reason that if the people were bigger, the creatures and the creeping and crawling things were also bigger. And they were! They had bigger houses and if they had bigger houses, then, they had bigger chimneys on the houses. And since that's so, we can proceed to learn about Grandaddy Cricket who, back in the old times, was about goat-size.

During the summer Grandaddy Cricket lived in the woods. He had his fife and his fiddle and he didn't need anything else. One day he would fiddle for the fish to dance. The next he would take out his fife and teach the birds some new tunes.

Over in the autumn, however, when the weather started to get cool, Grandaddy Cricket had to keep his hands in his pockets from early in the morning until close to noontime. By the time he got them warmed up and had played a tune, the sun started going down, on account of the days being shorter. His hands would start getting cold, and he would have to put them back in his pockets before he had finished two tunes.

Well, one year autumn turned to winter and it was the coldest winter there'd ever been in them parts. It was too cold for Grandaddy Cricket to play the fiddle and fife, the dozens, the lottery, or solitaire. He was so cold and hungry all he could do was creep along and try to keep on the sunny side of the world.

That's what he was doing one day when he saw smoke curling into the air. Grandaddy Cricket knew that where there's smoke there is fire. He crept a little faster, and after a while he saw that the smoke was coming from a chimney built at one end of a house.

This house wasn't like the houses you see today. This was an old-timey house. It sat on blocks, which raised it up off the ground, and was made out of logs. The spaces between the logs were stopped up with clay. The chimney, however, was made out of sticks and stones and mud.

Grandaddy Cricket crawled underneath the house, thinking it would be warm there. Not only wasn't it warm, but that was where the wind came to rest when it was out of breath. Ain't nothing colder than the wind setting around huffing and puffing, trying to catch its breath.

Grandaddy Cricket made his way over to the chimney to get some of its warmth. But it was built tight and all the warmth was inside where it was supposed to be.

It didn't take Grandaddy Cricket long to figure out that

if the warmth was inside the chimney, that was where he needed to be too. He gnawed and he sawed, he scratched and he clawed, he pushed and he gouged, he shoved and he scrouged, and after a while he made a hole through the mud-and-rock chimney. Before long Grandaddy Cricket was warm. When Grandaddy Cricket is feeling warm and cozy, he's happy, and when he's happy guess what he has to do?

That's right! Make music!

There wasn't enough room in the crack to play the fiddle, but there was plenty for fife playing, which is what he proceeded to do.

During the day he stopped playing whenever he heard a noise from inside the house. At night, however, when it was dark and the house was quiet, he would play up a storm. The children what lived in the house would lie in their beds and listen and laugh at the happy music. Their father didn't see nothing to be happy about. How could he sleep with all that racket?

Grandaddy Cricket played like he was getting paid for it. Pretty soon he was playing day and night. He played the children off to school in the morning. He played them home at lunchtime. He played to their momma while she baked bread and made soups that didn't have no tofu in them. He played to her when she sat in her rocking chair by the fire and dozed off, dreaming about the times when she was a little girl—the olden times that would make her grandchildren feel funny when they would hear about them.

After a while, the father got tired of all the fifing.

"I'm going to get that cricket out of there."

"You leave that cricket alone," his wife told him. "Crickets are good luck."

"Well, I'd rather have less luck and less fifing," the man yelled into the chimney. "Hush up all that racket!"

Grandaddy Cricket was doing his thing and didn't pay the man no never mind.

"If you don't stop that fifing, I'm going to pour boiling water on you."

Grandaddy Cricket heard *that*. He stopped fifing long enough to sing back:

Hot water will turn me brown,
And then I'll kick your chimney down.

The man said, "We'll see about that."

He put a kettle of water on the fire. When the water was boiling, he took the kettle and poured the scalding water through the cracks in the chimney.

Well, you don't have to be a genius to figure out what happens when you pour water on hard mud. Water plus hard mud will get you soft mud every time. Before the man knew it, the chimney started to sag. As it did, Grandaddy Cricket put his fife in his pocket and started kicking. He kicked and he kicked and the chimney fell down and buried the man.

When the man's wife and children finally dug him out, he was one eyed and splayfooted. His nose was where his ear used to be 'cause his ear was on his lip. His wife and children didn't know him. They had to ask him his name and where he came from and how old he was. After he satisfactorily answered all the questions, the woman said to him, "Didn't I tell you that crickets were good luck?"

"You call this good luck?" the man answered.

Grandaddy Cricket wasn't the same either. He had kicked so hard and kicked so high that he unjointed both of his legs. When he crawled out of the chimney, his elbows were down around his knees, which is where they have stayed.

Grandaddy Cricket didn't mind. He had found himself a home that was cool in the summer and warm in the winter. That's why to this day, crickets live in chimneys.

Why the Earth Is Mostly Water

If you look at a map of the world, you'll see something peculiar. We are surrounded by water and outnumbered by fish!

What kind of sense does that make? If it had been me what made the world, I would've turned the thing around and made more dry than wet. I'm not friendly with water, though I will speak to that in my bathtub every now and then.

Being outnumbered by fish and surrounded by water has always made me nervous, so I did some investigating. I learned that this is not how the Lord first made the world. I always knew the Lord had as much sense as me. He made the world the way I would have—a lot of dry and a little wet. But that's not how things are today.

So what happened? The first thing that happened is that folks got their stories confused. Everybody knows about Noah and the ark and the time it rained forty days and forty nights and the whole world was covered with water. What folks don't know is that that flood was the *second* flood. That's right! There was another flood that happened a long time before Noah was born. Now that I think about it, the flood I'm going to tell you about happened before "Once upon a time." And stories that happened that long ago happened when the animals ruled the world, topside and bottom too.

Back in those days animals had as much sense as people. Maybe more, 'cause people don't have as much sense as they think they do. But back before "Once upon a time," the animals could read and write and do arithmetic, slam dunk a basketball and anything else you can think of.

Once a year the animals had a big convention where they would talk over any problems or grievances they might have with one another. One year the big point of dispute was between the fish and the alligators. Fish said the alligators was moving into the neighborhood and sending it to ruination. Seems like the alligators would sit out on their lawns at night and grunt. Another year the big complaint was about the coyotes and dogs howling at the moon all night and keeping everybody awake.

Well, this particular year the time was at hand for the convention, and the animals come from near and far. The Lion was there, because he was the king. Couldn't be no meeting without him. The Hippopotamus was there, of course. The Elephant came, as did the Giraffe, Griffin, and Pterodactyl. All the animals were there, from the biggest all the way down to the Crawfish.

When everybody was assembled, the Lion shook his mane and roared loud enough to make Jell-O shake. That was the sign for the convention to begin.

The animals started making speeches and screaming and yelling and hollering and cussing and flinging language around like a big wind tossing trees in a storm. Didn't nobody take it too seriously. Animals liked to hear themselves talk same as people.

While all the speech-making was going on, the Elephant

accidently stepped on one of the Crawfish. I don't have to tell you that when an Elephant steps on you, you have been stepped on. When the Elephant lifted up his foot, there was not even a memory of that Crawfish left. To make matters worse, the Elephant didn't even know he had done it.

All the other Crawfish got mad. They had a caucus, which is a little meeting which nobody could come to except Crawfish. They drew up a resolution to protest what the Elephant had done. It was a good resolution too, filled with wherefores and therefores and whereats and be-it-re-solveds, and all the other kind of things that make a resolution a resolution and not just a bunch of running off at the mouth.

They got up to read their resolution to the convention, but the Leopards were reading one to the Tigers about the superiority of spots over stripes, and the Hyenas were laughing, and the Beavers were eating all the chairs, and the Snakes were crying because they wanted to hug folks and nobody wanted a hug from them. The Crawfish kept on reading while the Unicorn and the Bull compared horns, and the Cat walked around looking at everybody like they was crazy, and you know what happened? The Elephant squished another Crawfish!

The Crawfish were sho' 'nuf hot now, the few that were left. They drew up another resolution filled with where-fores and therefores and whereats and be-it-resolveds, and tried to read it out to the convention. But that was just the time Brer Rabbit come by selling the latest issue of *Animal* magazine. I don't remember who was on the cover. It could've been Jackie Opossum. Naw, I believe it was Michael Jackass. Then again it could've been Madonna

Llama. Well, whoever it was, everybody got so excited that it busted up the convention for that day.

The Crawfish were seriously upset now! You can do a lot of things wrong in this life, but don't ever cross swords with a mad crawfish. It might be one of the littlest things in the world, but 'cause something is little don't mean it ain't powerful. That's what the animals were about to find out.

The Crawfish nodded to their cousins, the Mud Turtles. The Mud Turtles nodded to their cousins, the Spring Lizards. All of them together started boring holes in the earth. Down and down and down into the earth they went, all the way to the center.

Back in that time that's where the water was. But after the Crawfish and the Mud Turtles and the Spring Lizards got through boring all them holes, that is not where the water stayed. No, indeed! Them little creatures unloosed all the fountains in the earth!

The water started spouting up out of the earth, and it spewed and it spewed and it spewed. Noah thought he saw something when it rained forty days and forty nights. Shucks, Noah didn't know what water was. The water he saw was coming from on high. The water the Crawfish, Mud Turtles, and Spring Lizards let loose was from within, and it spouted out of the center of the world for three months, seventeen days, and forty-'leven minutes.

Finally the rain stopped, and as far as the eye could see, water covered everything. It covered the tallest trees; it covered the tallest trees on the tallest mountains, and even some low-flying clouds. For a few days, the Almighty thought He might have to raise heaven's skirts up.

Well, quite naturally, all the animals drowned, all of them, that is except the Mud Turtles, Spring Lizards, Crawfish, and all the other kinds of fish. The Earth animals died because they thought they was too big to listen to something as little as the Crawfish.

So, the Lord had to make the world all over again. This time He decided to put most of the water on *top* of the earth instead of inside.

Which is why most of the world is water today. If the Crawfish ever get mad again and bore down to the center of the world, they are going to be in for a surprise. Nothing down there now but fire.

The Origin of the Ocean

Some folks say the story I just told you is not the real one of why the world is mostly water. There's another story that also explains the matter. Sometimes things are so perplexing that one story don't satisfy everybody. That's fine with me, 'cause it means another story.

It used to be that all the animals lived on the same side of the world. That's because the world only had one side, and that was all over. Wasn't no oceans separating folks. Back in those times you would've found tigers in Toledo, lions in Louisville, apes in Arkadelphia, and baboons in Boston. It probably would've stayed that way too if Brer Lion hadn't messed with Brer Rabbit.

One day Brer Lion decided to go hunting and he asked Brer Rabbit to go with him. Brer Rabbit was ready for every kind of fun on the topside of the ground.

Off they went. Whenever they found some game, Brer Lion would leap at it but would miss. Brer Rabbit would chase it down and catch it. The instant he did Brer Lion roared, "It's mine! It's mine! I killed it!"

Brer Lion was so big that Brer Rabbit wasn't about to dispute him. But Brer Rabbit didn't forget. All that day Brer Lion would leap at the game and miss. Brer Rabbit would catch it and Brer Lion would roar, "It's mine! It's mine! I killed it!"

That evening they were so far from home they had to camp out next to a creek. They built a fire, cooked their supper, and afterward sat around the fire. Brer Rabbit started bragging long and loud about what a great hunter Brer Lion was. Brer Lion leaned back on his elbows and swelled up with pride.

Brer Rabbit bragged so hard, he soon wore himself out. He yawned. "I believe it's time to get some shut-eye, Brer Lion. You may be a powerful hunter, but when it comes to sleeping, I don't know as there is a creature in creation that can do more serious sleeping than me. So, I'm going to apologize in advance for disturbing your rest."

Brer Lion was insulted. "Don't be too sure, Brer Rabbit. When it comes to sleeping, I ain't no amateur."

Brer Rabbit was doubtful. "What do you sound like just as you're falling asleep?"

Brer Lion made a sound like a saw sawing trees.

"And what do you sound like after you're sleeping good?"

The noise that came out of Brer Lion sounded like a mountain falling down. Brer Rabbit was amazed. "That's some sho' 'nuf sleeping you be doing, Brer Lion."

"I'm the king, ain't I?"

"That you are. That you are."

Brer Lion smiled, stretched out on his side, and soon he was snoring like he snored when he wasn't too far asleep.

Brer Rabbit listened.

After a while it started to sound like a mountain was falling down. Brer Rabbit knew Brer Lion was sho' 'nuf asleep.

Brer Rabbit went to the fire. He took cold ashes and sprinkled them on himself. Then he took some hot coals out of the fire and threw them on Brer Lion.

Brer Lion jumped up. "Who did that? Who did that?"

Brer Rabbit was lying on the ground, kicking and screaming and yelling, "Ow! Ow! OW!"

Brer Lion saw Brer Rabbit covered with ashes and kicking and squalling like he was burning alive. It was obvious somebody had tried to set both of them on fire. Brer Lion peered into the darkness but didn't see anybody.

He lay down and was soon asleep, mountain after mountain crumbling.

Brer Rabbit went to the fire. He sprinkled cold ashes on himself, then threw hot coals on Brer Lion again.

Brer Lion jumped up, screaming. Brer Rabbit lay on the ground, kicking and squawking, "Ow! Ow! OW!"

When Brer Rabbit caught his breath, he got up and looked at Brer Lion. "You ought to be ashamed, trying to burn me up like that."

Brer Lion held up his hands. "Wasn't me, Brer Rabbit. I swear it wasn't."

Brer Rabbit looked like he didn't believe him. Then, he sniffed the air. "I smell rags burning."

Brer Lion sniffed. "Me too." He smelled some more. The more he smelled, the closer the odor. The more he smelled, the warmer he got. "That ain't rags. That's my hair!" He rolled on the ground and put the fire out and fell back to sleep. Soon, the mountains started falling again.

Brer Rabbit got up and sprinkled himself with cold ashes and threw hot coals on Brer Lion.

As Brer Lion jumped up, Brer Rabbit was hollering, "I saw him, Brer Lion. I saw him. He came from across the creek. He sho' did!"

Brer Lion roared a roaracious roar and jumped across the creek. As soon as he did, Brer Rabbit cut the string that held the two banks of the creek together.

When he cut the string, the banks of the creek began to fall away from each other. They got farther and farther and farther away, and the creek got wider and wider and wider. After a while it was so wide that Brer Rabbit couldn't see Brer Lion and Brer Lion couldn't see Brer Rabbit. It got so wide that Brer Rabbit couldn't even see land. And neither could Brer Lion. All the animals that was on one side with Brer Lion had to stay there, and all them what was on the same side as Brer Rabbit had to stay there. And that's where they been from that day to this, with the big water rolling between.

Now, I know what you're thinking. How could the banks of the creek be tied together with a string? Well, it's a strange thing about stories. You have to take them as you get them. But I promise you this: The next time the Tale Teller comes through here, I'll ask him. If you aren't too far away, I'll send word for you to come quick and you can hear what the Tale Teller has to say about that. So, don't be getting upset with me 'cause I don't know how the creeks could be tied together with a string. Who put the string there, I don't know about that either. But I do know who cut the string. I sure do!

Brer Rabbit and Miss Nancy

There have been three periods in the life of the world. There was the time before people. That's when the animals were in charge of everything.

Then there was the time when people and animals lived with each other like there wasn't no difference between them. People could understand animal talk, and the animals could understand people talk, and it was hard to tell who was animal and who was person.

Finally, there's today, when the people are in charge of everything. To my mind the world was a lot better off when the people and the animals lived with each other like everybody was part of the same family.

For instance, back then there were easy times and hard ones just like today. One year the economics turned bad. First there was a recession, and then the recession got depressed and by the time the recession took its depression to a therapist, well, hardly anybody could find a job. Brer Rabbit felt very lucky the day Mr. Man offered him one.

"I can't pay you, but you can eat for free."

"That's payment enough!" Brer Rabbit responded.

Brer Rabbit worked hard, hoeing potatoes, chopping cotton, weeding the vegetables. Mr. Man said that Brer Rabbit was one of the best workers he'd ever had. He told his daughter that if she wanted to marry somebody who wasn't afraid of hard work, Brer Rabbit was the man.

Well, one hot day Brer Rabbit had been working out in the sun for a long time and he was hungry and thirsty.

"It's hot today!"

Mr. Man agreed. "Well, there's the bucket and you know where the creek is. Go get yourself a drink."

Brer Rabbit filled the bucket and drank it empty. However, all that water and no food made his stomach mad. It started growling and complaining: "Give me some food! I want some food!"

Brer Rabbit's stomach was growling and fussing so loud that Mr. Man heard it. "Go on up to the house and tell my daughter to give you some bread."

Brer Rabbit went up to the house and knocked on the door. When Mr. Man's daughter saw who it was, she said, "Why, Brer Rabbit! What're you doing here? My daddy said that you are the best worker he has, but if you call standing out here on the porch working, I think there's something wrong with my daddy's eyesight."

"I'm here, Miss Nancy, because your daddy sent me."

"And why would he send you up here?"

"He sent me to get two dollars and some bread and butter."

Miss Nancy gave Brer Rabbit a suspicious look. "I don't believe you. I'm going to ask Daddy about this."

Before Brer Rabbit could say a word, Miss Nancy was running down the path to the field. "Daddy! Is you say what Brer Rabbit say you say?"

Mr. Man yelled back, "That's what I said!"

Miss Nancy went back to the house and gave Brer Rabbit two dollars and some bread and butter.

A few hours later Brer Rabbit went up to the house and asked Miss Nancy for two more dollars and some bread and butter. She went to the field and asked her daddy, "Is you say what Brer Rabbit say you say?" Her daddy said that he had. She gave Brer Rabbit two more dollars and some bread and butter.

This went on for some days. Mr. Man was almost out of money and didn't know it. However, Brer Rabbit knew that one day soon Mr. Man would look in his money box and see more box than money.

Well, it just so happened that Miss Nancy had a new boyfriend. I don't remember what his name was. Seems I heard my great-granddaddy tell my great-uncle's nephew's cousin's wife that his name was Doofus McGoofus. Whatever his name was, Brer Rabbit didn't like him. And if Brer Rabbit don't like you, you are in trouble. Sometimes you in trouble if he does like you.

One day Mr. Man and Brer Rabbit were working in the field together. Mr. Man heard Brer Rabbit talking under his breath, but he couldn't make out the words.

"Brer Rabbit? What're you talking about?"

"Who? Me?"

"Ain't nobody else here."

Brer Rabbit looked around like he wasn't quite sure. "I was just concentrating on learning a song I heard a blue jay singing this morning." Brer Rabbit went back to hoeing and mumbling.

This didn't satisfy Mr. Man. "What did the blue jay sing?"

Brer Rabbit stopped, scratched his head, and squinted. "I believe it went something like this:

The boy kissed the girl and called her honey;
He kissed her again and she gave him all the money.

"What money?" Mr. Man wanted to know.

"How should I know?" Brer Rabbit answered. "I'm not in the song. Anyway, it's just a song."

But Mr. Man couldn't get the song out of his mind:

The boy kissed the girl and called her honey;
He kissed her again and she gave him all the money.

The song went round and round in Mr. Man's head. The more times it went round, the more worried he got.

That evening when he went home, Doofus McGoofus was sitting on the porch with Miss Nancy. Mr. Man said a polite "Howdy do" and went in the house. He didn't go to the kitchen to wash his hands like he usually did. He went straight to his office, opened the cabinet, and took out his money box. He looked inside and it was almost empty!

"Where's my money?" he yelled, running onto the porch. Miss Nancy said she didn't know.

"Yes you do!" Mr. Man declared. "You gave almost all

my money to Doofus. Pack your things and you and Doofus get out of here right now!"

Miss Nancy pleaded and cried. Mr. Man would not change his mind. So Miss Nancy packed up her things and went on off with Doofus.

As for Brer Rabbit and Mr. Man—well, Brer Rabbit was just being Brer Rabbit. Faulting him for that would be like faulting winter for being cold. Can't say as much for Mr. Man, though. But, that's how men can be—adding two and two and coming up with seventy-seven.

The Old King and the New King

Nothing in this world will get you in trouble quicker than your mouth. A lot of times your mouth goes in motion while your brain is still asleep. Other times your brain is telling you to say, "No," and your mouth says, "Yes." But even if your mouth and brain are good friends, don't go to thinking that you're as smart as God. There's always somebody else whose mouth and brains are like twins.

That's what happened, this king learned.

I don't know whether the king had a name. He probably did when he was a baby, but once he became king, well, that's what everybody called him. After a while even he forgot his name. So, if *he* thought his name was king, we don't have any reason to think it was Junebug Jabbo Jones.

The other thing that's not in the story is where he did his kinging. It could've been in Zimbabwe, Zanzibar, or Zululand. Then again, he might have been king in Cambodia, Canada, or Cameroon. But who knows? He also could've been king in Des Moines, Dubuque, or Dallas. But the story don't say where he was king at, so anyplace you put him is all right with me and him.

The king had been kinging for a long time. Seemed like he started kinging before water was wet. He had been kinging so long that his hair had fallen out, all his teeth were loose, and his toenails had whiskers. Worst of all, his brain and his mouth had not spoken to one another in many years.

It was time for a new king. There were things that needed deciding, such as whether the grass in the kingdom should be painted yellow and orange like some folks wanted. Another decision to be made was whether folks should breathe through both nostrils at the same time or breathe through the right one on Monday, Wednesday, and Friday, the left one on Tuesday, Thursday, and Saturday, and breathe how they wanted on Sunday.

A delegation went to the king.

"King? We don't want to hurt your feelings, but it is time for somebody else to do the kinging."

The king listened. The more he listened, the tighter he sat in his chair. That night, the king didn't go to bed, but slept in his throne chair. The next day he ate all his meals in his throne chair. It was obvious he was not going to get off the throne until he died.

The people decided they couldn't wait for that. They had a large meeting, and everybody agreed on who would make the best king. They went to the person and asked him to be the new king. He said he would.

The delegation went to the palace and told the old king that he had to make room for the new king.

"Who is he?" the old king wanted to know.

Nobody said anything. The old king might kill him if he knew.

"Is he an old man?" the king wanted to know.

If the king thought the new king was old, he would have all the old people killed. If he thought the new king was young, he would have all the young people killed.

"Older than some and younger than others," somebody responded.

The king got angry. He roared and he yelled and he screamed and he threatened. But no one would tell him who the new king was going to be.

The king got very quiet. Finally, he said, "You think I don't have any sense. Well, tell this new king that before he can be king he has to send me a beef. But it can't be a bull and it can't be a cow. When he can do that, then I'll know he has sense enough to be king."

How could there be meat that was not from a bull or a cow? The man chosen to be king was a young man. Maybe he didn't have enough sense to be king if answering questions like this was what kinging was about.

The delegation went to see the young man they wanted to be king.

"The old king said you can be king if you send him some beef that is not from a bull or a cow."

The young man smiled and winked one eye. "Tell the old king that I've got a steer in my pen, but he has to come and get it. And he can't come in the day and he can't come at night."

They ran back to the palace and told the old king what the young man had said.

The king scratched his head. He scratched his stomach. He scratched in his armpits. But wherever he scratched, he couldn't come up with an answer. So, he took off his crown and his robe and walked out the door and down the road.

It just goes to show that your mouth and your brain might make folks believe water is running backward. But there's always somebody who can make 'em believe water can dance.

And don't *ever* forget: There is always somebody younger right outside the door.

Brer Bear Comes to the Community

Brer Bear didn't always live with the other animals. He was born and raised way off in the woods with his family. His daddy taught him all he needed to know—how to rob a bee tree and dig for sweet potatoes, get roasting ears off a cornstalk, and whatever else he needed to know.

Brer Bear decided he wanted to see what was on the other side of the woods. When the day came for him to go, his father gave him seven pieces of honey in the comb. "I don't have much to give you, but this will be more than enough. Whoever eats a piece of that honey will have to wrestle you every morning for seven years and give you everything he has."

Brer Bear put the seven pieces of honeycomb in his bag, slung the bag on his back, and went his way. He walked all that day. When night came, he made camp and went to sleep.

The next morning he had scarcely gotten his eyes open

when he heard a rustling in the bushes. It was Brer Tiger looking for his breakfast.

Brer Bear howdied Brer Tiger. Brer Tiger howdied back.

Brer Bear opened his bag, took out a piece of the honeycomb, and started eating.

Brer Tiger watched. Brer Bear knew Brer Tiger was hungry. "I would invite you to join me in eating some of this honeycomb, but whoever eats it will have to wrestle me every morning for seven years and give me all their possessions."

"I'm a very good wrestler," Brer Tiger responded. "And I'm also very hungry."

Brer Bear shrugged. "Don't say I didn't warn you."

Brer Tiger grinned and proceeded to eat his fill of honey. "This honey is so good I'll wrestle you eleven years."

After a while Brer Tiger had his fill of honey. He thanked Brer Bear and headed for home. He didn't get very far, though, before he felt a zooming in his head and a crawling on his hide. It got so bad that all he wanted to do was to go back to Brer Bear.

When he got there Brer Bear was curled up taking a nap.

"Wake up!" Brer Tiger shouted. "I feel like wrestling!"

Brer Bear put his grin on and it looked like it fit him. "You can have all the underholds, Brer Tiger, and you got to promise not to use the inturn, the hamtwist, and the kneelock."

Brer Tiger didn't know what Brer Bear was talking about. But he found out when Brer Bear grabbed him, swung him around and around, snorted in his face, squeezed him tight, hit him in the head, and then lay on top of him.

Brer Tiger's pants were split, and his head felt as big as the moon. He limped home and went to bed.

Early the next morning Brer Tiger heard a knock at his door. He looked out, and there was Brer Bear standing on the doorstep. "I come to wrestle you. We got six years and three hundred and sixty-four days to go."

Brer Tiger went outside, and Brer Bear twirled him around in the air, slammed him down on his back, jumped on his midsection a time or two, twisted his legs around, bit his ear, and fell on top of him.

When Brer Tiger got up, didn't a soul recognize him except his wife and Brer Rabbit.

Brer Rabbit shook his head and said, "Brer Tiger, what you need is a change of scenery."

Brer Tiger agreed that was so. He moved out of his house and didn't take a thing with him. Brer Bear moved in, took over all Brer Tiger's possessions and has been living with the animals ever since.

The Snake

Once there was a woman by the name of Coomba. Some say she was from Africa.

One day she went for a walk through the woods. She happened on a Snake nest with an egg in it. A very big Snake sat atop the egg, and it was a very big egg.

Coomba thought about the omelet she could make from an egg that size. But the Snake was looking at her like it knew what she was thinking and that her thinking included the green peppers, onions, and cheese she would put in the omelet.

Coomba looked at the Snake.

Snake looked at Coomba.

Coomba decided to let the egg stay where it was.

But it's a strange thing when something gets in your mind. You can't forget it, no matter how hard you try. Whatever Coomba did, the thought of that egg followed her like it was her shadow. Wherever she went, the egg was there too, beckoning, beckoning.

The next morning Coomba hurried through the woods and across the field and hid behind a tree until she saw the Snake slide away to go hunt its breakfast.

Coomba grabbed the egg and hurried home. Before King

Sun had finished gathering the dew to make his morning coffee, Coomba had cooked the egg and eaten it.

When the Snake came back to its nest and saw that the egg was gone, it put its nose on the ground and followed the scent to Coomba's house.

"Where's my egg?" the Snake asked plaintively.

"I haven't seen your egg," Coomba responded.

Snake saw the snakeskin which had been over the egg hanging from a nail on the wall. "What is that?"

Coomba didn't say anything.

"Why did you take my egg?"

Coomba pretended like she hadn't heard the Snake.

"You hear my voice crying out," the Snake said. "You took my egg. You destroyed my children. Take care of your own, woman. Take care of your own."

Snake left.

Time passed. Coomba gave birth to a little girl whom she called Noncy. Coomba didn't know she could love anything as much as she loved that little girl. Coomba loved her hard and everywhere Coomba went, she carried Noncy next to her.

As soon as Noncy was born, however, Snake hid itself in the grass outside Coomba's house. Snake watched all day. Snake watched all night, its tongue flickering in and out, in and out.

Snake waited.

Noncy grew. Noncy grew until she was too big to carry. "I can't carry you with me anymore when I go out to work in the fields. And you are too young to come and not get in the way. I must leave you at home."

Coomba showed Noncy how to lock the door. "When I come home, I will sing this song:

Walla walla witto, me Noncy,
Walla walla witto, me Noncy,
Walla walla witto, me Noncy!

When I do, you sing:

Andolee! Andoli! Andolo!

And then you open the door."

Snake lay in the grass, listening.

Throughout the day, every day, Coomba came home from the field to be sure Noncy was all right. Each time she sang:

Walla walla witto, me Noncy,
Walla walla witto, me Noncy,
Walla walla witto, me Noncy!

And from inside came:

Andolee! Andoli! Andolo!

The door would open and Coomba would go inside.

After listening for several days, Snake slid up to Coomba's door one morning after she left.

Wullo wullo widdo, me Noncy,
Wullo wullo widdo, me Noncy,
Wullo wullo widdo, me Noncy!

Snake tried to make its voice like Coomba's, but Snake's voice sounded like graveyard dirt rattling in a tin can. Noncy didn't say a word.

"Open the door," Snake yelled.

"My momma don't holler like that," Noncy replied.

Snake tried to sing the song again, but Noncy was quiet. Snake tried and tried. No luck. Finally, Snake flickered its tongue and slid away.

Soon, Coomba came.

Walla walla witto, me Noncy,
Walla walla witto, me Noncy,
Walla walla witto, me Noncy!

Noncy said, "That's my momma." And she sang:

Andolee! Andoli! Andolo!

Snake listened closely and practiced hard.

The next morning when Coomba went to the fields, Snake slid up to the door and sang:

Walla walla witto, me Noncy,
Walla walla witto, me Noncy,
Walla walla witto, me Noncy!

Noncy thought it was her mother and she sang:

Andolee! Andoli! Andolo!

She opened the door and Snake swished inside like a cold wind. Snake hugged the little girl and twisted its tail around her, twisted and twisted until Snake was coiled around Noncy from toe to head.

Noncy hollered and screamed and squalled.

Snake squeezed and squeezed until Noncy was as thin as a tear. Then, it swallowed her whole.

When Coomba came home, she sang out. No song came back. She sang louder. The silence came back louder.

Coomba touched the door. It opened when it should have been locked. She looked inside. The house was empty. Coomba stood in the doorway, wondering where her daughter could be.

Then she looked down. There, in the dust, were the swirling grooves left by Snake.

"Oh, no!"

Coomba went to the swamp and cut a piece of cane. Then, she followed the snake track.

Snake was so full carrying Noncy inside that it could not go fast. Snake was so full carrying Noncy inside that it became sleepy. Soon it was not moving at all.

When Coomba caught up to Snake, it was lying in the path, asleep. Coomba hit Snake over the head with the piece of cane until its head was as flat as a broken promise.

Then she cut Snake open. There, inside, was Noncy, sound asleep.

Coomba took her home and washed her clean. Noncy opened her eyes, saw her mother, and sang:

Andolee! Andoli! Andolo!

And Coomba and Noncy lived happily for many, many years.

A Ghost Story

Some folks don't believe in ghosts, which is fine with me. You believe what you believe.

However, if you had seen all that I have seen since I peeped out of the womb, you would be as nice to the dead as you are to the living. Maybe nicer.

Once there was a man and a woman. If they had names, I don't recollect what they were. Could've been Rick and Ilse, or Rock and Doris, Fred and Wilma, or Homer and Marge. Names didn't count for as much back in them times, so it don't make no never mind. If you need them to have names, you stick them on. I don't, so I'll just call 'em a man and a woman.

They grew up together in the same community and liked one another since they were little things. Everybody knew that when they got grown, they would marry one another. Strange thing was that they didn't.

I don't know why. They probably didn't either. Maybe he never asked her. Maybe there wasn't a reason. There ain't a reason for everything, you know. Some things are because they are and other things ain't because they ain't.

Just as no one knows how come the two of them didn't get married, nobody knows how come the woman's health began to fail. One day she took to her sickbed. Wasn't long before her sickbed became her deathbed.

In a community as small as that one, there wasn't no undertaker to do things for folks. Folks did everything for themselves.

When the woman breathed her last breath, folks laid her out real pretty and lighted some candles and put them at her head. They put two big round silver dollars on her eyes to keep them shut. Don't nothing mess with your appetite like having a dead person staring at you.

Folks told the man that since he knew the woman better than anyone, he should go dig her grave and bury her.

The man took the body out to the cemetery and dug her grave. Just as he was about to put her in the ground he saw those silver dollars on her eyelids, shining like hope.

He picked one up. It felt good in his fingers. He picked up the other one. It felt good too.

The woman's eyes opened. She was staring at him. Quickly, he threw her body in the grave and covered it with dirt. The two silver dollars were jingling and jangling in his pocket.

He hurried home and put the two coins in a tin box. He shook the box. The money jingled like it was music. But the man didn't feel so good. Regardless of where he looked, regardless of whether his eyes were open or closed, the woman seemed to be staring at him. The man decided to go to bed early.

He hadn't been asleep long, before the wind began to

rise. At first it was a small wind and made a small sound—
Woooooo—as if it were just being born.

But the wind got stronger and stronger and louder and
louder.

WOOOOO! It blew on top of the house.

WOOOOOO! It blew under the house.

WOOOOOO! WOOOOO! It blew on all four sides of
the house.

WOOOOOOOOOOOOOOOOOOOOOOOOOOOO-
OOOOOOOOOOOOOOOO!

"Ain't nothing but the wind," he told himself, and tried
to go back to sleep.

The wind hollered and cried. It blew on top of the house.
It blew under the house. It blew on all four sides of the
house. And it found the cracks in the walls and whistled,
EEEEEEEEEEEEEEEEEEEEEEEEEEEEEEEEEEEE-
EEEEE!

The man started trembling and shaking. Then, he heard
something at his money box.

Clinkity, clinkalinkle!

"Hey! Who's stealing my money?"

OOOOOOOOOOO! EEEEEEEEEEEE!

Clinkity, clinkalinkle!

The man got out of bed and looked around. He didn't
see anything. He double-locked the door and went back
to bed.

His head had just touched the pillow when—*Clinkity,
clinkalinkle!*

"Must be a rat in my money box," the man said.

He got out of bed again and looked at his money box
on the mantelpiece. It was closed tightly.

He opened it. The two silver dollars shone like dreams.

He closed the box, and as he put it down there came a voice:

"Where's my money?"

Clinkity, clinkalinkle, clink!

"Where's my money?"

The man put a chair against the front door. Then he jumped in bed and pulled the covers over his head.

Clinkity, clinkalinkle, clink!

"Where's my money?"

The man shook and the man shivered; the money clinked and clanked; the voice came nearer and nearer.

"Where's my money?"

"WHERE'S MY MONEY?"

"WHERE'S MY MONEY?"

The front door flew open. The chair the man had stacked against it went tumbling across the floor.

The man peeped over the covers. It was the woman!

Clinkity, clinkalinkle, clink!

"Where's my money?"

"Oh Lordy, Lordy, Lord," said the man.

The woman groped through the room touching the table and the chairs and the wall. She got close to the bed and felt the mattress. Then she jumped on the man and hollered, "YOU HAVE MY MONEY!"

The next morning folks found the man just as dead as dead can get. They laid him out like they had the woman and thought it would be nice to put him in the same grave with her. Now they could be together as folks had thought they should've been.

The man didn't have to give up the silver dollars, though. Except this time, they were on *his* eyes.

———————

Brer Bear Exposes Brer Rabbit

One Saturday when all the creatures had finished their work for the week, they were sitting around talking politics. When they had solved all the problems in the world, which is easy to do when you ain't got none of the responsibility, they got to talking about which one of them could eat the most.

Brag breeds brag. Brer Wolf said, "I don't know how much I can eat because there has never been a day when I've been able to eat as much as I wanted to."

Brer Bear said, "I could eat a horse if I had enough salt."

Brer Fox said, "I'll match any man here, chew for chew and swallow for swallow."

Brer Rabbit was laying back with his eyes closed. They heard him chuckle. "If you will buy the food, I guarantee you that I'll eat more than all of you put together. If I don't, I'll give you my hat."

I don't know what was so special about Brer Rabbit's hat that anybody else would want it, but the animals agreed to the deal.

The next Saturday they got together for a big barbecue. They had hogs and they had sheep and they had cows and they barbecued all the meat and were ready for the eating contest to begin. They looked around for Brer Rabbit and didn't see him.

"Where's Brer Rabbit?" they wondered.

Just about then they saw Brer Rabbit coming across the hill. He had on a long cloak and was walking with a cane, walking slow like he had gotten old between moondown and sunrise.

"I'm sick. Mighty sick. If I was a little more sick, I would not have gotten this far in the world."

"What's the matter, Brer Rabbit?"

"I got a headache. I got a backache. I went down in the swamp after some calamus root and got my feet wet. That gave me a bad cold and the cold flew to my head, spread to my back, dropped down in my legs, and I almost died."

By the time Brer Rabbit finished telling everybody how his coporosity come to be segashuating that way, the creatures were very suspicious. And why wouldn't they be? He had tricked each of them and more than once.

"If you're so sick, how can you beat us eating?" they wanted to know.

Brer Rabbit sighed. "It's a fact that I'm feeling bad and my pulse is slow and I ain't got no appetite and I can hardly stand up on three legs, but I didn't want nobody to think I was trying to get out of nothing and that's why I came. If I can't beat you eating, that's how it is. But if I can, then I will."

The creatures were satisfied.

They took all the meat and piled it on a long table, making the biggest pile in front of Brer Rabbit. Brer Rabbit bent over backward to see the top, and it was in the clouds.

"Don't forget," Brer Rabbit said, "you got to eat the meat and the bones."

The creatures looked at one another. "The bones?"

"Bones!" Brer Rabbit repeated.

They started into eating. Brer Rabbit was going at it so fast that he made a blur. Before anybody had had a good belch, Brer Rabbit was done and talking about how hungry he was. They gave him more meat and he started in on that.

Brer Bear was sitting off to the side. He had one eye on Brer Rabbit and saw him drop meat in his cloak. Brer Bear didn't say a word. He waited.

After a while, all the meat was gone, and the creatures agreed that Brer Rabbit had outeaten everybody. Brer Bear walked over to Brer Rabbit like he was going to shake his hand. Instead he reached out and grabbed Brer Rabbit's cloak and pulled it off. Hidden inside the cloak was a great big bag. In the bag was all the meat Brer Rabbit was supposed to have eaten.

Brer Rabbit didn't wait around. He dropped his cane and dashed into the bushes.

The creatures might could outeat Brer Rabbit, but there was no way they were going to outrun him.

Brer Rabbit Teaches Brer Bear to Comb His Hair

Brer Bear shouldn't have done what he did. Brer Rabbit was just having fun. He wasn't going to hurt nobody by playing that trick. But when Brer Bear exposed him like that, Brer Rabbit decided to teach Brer Bear a lesson.

Brer Rabbit took to primping himself every day. He put grease in his hair and slicked it down real slick. He put on cologne. He was gleaming like sunlight on dew and smelling like honeysuckle in May, and every morning he went and promenaded past Brer Bear's house.

Miz Bear would be outdoors hanging up clothes on the

line or working in her garden. When she saw Brer Rabbit, he would tip his hat and bow, as polite as he could be.

Miz Bear saw how nice Brer Rabbit looked and she started taking closer looks at Brer Bear. His hair was matted and tangled, and he smelled like a, well, like a *bear*!

"How come you don't look nice like Brer Rabbit?" she asked.

"I don't want to look like that scoundrel."

"Scoundrel or not, ain't nothing wrong with having your hair combed. You look like a rat's bed."

Brer Bear's feelings were hurt. He didn't want his wife thinking Brer Rabbit was more handsome than he was. One day he saw Brer Rabbit going along the road and asked him, "How do you keep your hair so slick?"

Brer Rabbit said, "I don't comb my hair, Brer Bear."

"You don't? Then, how do you do it?"

"My wife does it for me. She combs my head every morning."

"She does? How does she get it to lay down and gleam like that?"

"She takes the axe and chops the hair off. That's so she can get at it good and have it separate out. Then she puts it back on and there it is, all combed."

Brer Bear thought that over for a minute. "Don't it hurt?"

"Hurt? I ain't no coward!"

Bear Bear thought some more. "Don't it make your head bleed?"

"What's a little blood if it means keeping up appearances?"

Brer Bear nodded.

He went home and told Miz Bear how Brer Rabbit combed his hair. Miz Bear got the axe. Brer Bear put his head down on a log. Miz Bear raised the axe up high. Brer Bear closed his eyes and hollered, "Cut if off easy!"

WHOP!

And that took care of Brer Bear. If it had been me, I would let Brer Rabbit have that meat. I sho' would have.

Why Brer Possum Has No Hair on His Tail

There aren't too many tales about Brer Possum. That's because he never did that much. Why would he? Brer Possum is one of the laziest animals in creation. One time, though, his laziness got him in trouble.

On this particular day Brer Possum woke up hungry. If you and I wake up hungry, we go to the refrigerator, get a slice of cold pizza, and tell our stomachs that it is time to go to work. Brer Possum woke up hungry and did not know what to do. He hung there in the tree, upside down, his tail curled around a limb, listening to his stomach. His stomach was saying, "Fool! Go find some cold pizza!"

Brer Possum was too lazy to go anywhere. He thought if he hung there long enough, food would come to him. He changed his mind, however, when he overheard his stomach tell Ol' Man Death, "Come get this fool!" Brer Possum decided it was time to do something.

He dropped out of the tree at the very minute Brer Rabbit was walking by, and almost landed on him.

"You trying to hit me?" Brer Rabbit hollered angrily.

"No, no, Brer Rabbit. Why would I do that? You and me always been the best of friends."

"That's true," Brer Rabbit agreed. "So tell me. How you be?"

"I'm hungry," said Brer Possum.

"A body has to be smart to keep a full stomach these days," Brer Rabbit agreed. "But I believe I know where you can get as much to eat as you want."

"Where's that?" Brer Possum asked eagerly.

"Brer Bear's apple orchard. Brer Bear don't care nothing about apples. He's a honey man. He watches the bees when they come to the apple blossoms. When the bees leave he follows them to their hive and gets the honey."

Brer Possum lit out for Brer Bear's apple orchard. Sure enough, the trees were full of the reddest, juiciest apples you can imagine. Brer Possum climbed to the top of the biggest tree and proceeded to do away with some apples.

While Brer Possum was getting fat on the apples, what do you think Brer Rabbit was doing? He was banging on Brer Bear's door.

"Brer Bear! Brer Bear! There's somebody in your apple trees."

Brer Bear came barreling out of the house. He couldn't afford to have somebody eating his apples. That's what he filled up on before he went into hibernation every winter. He lit out for the apple orchard.

Brer Possum thought he heard somebody coming. "Just one more apple."

He ate another one. He heard something again, and it was closer this time.

"Just one more."

The noise was closer now. Brer Possum looked out over the landscape and there was Brer Bear running toward the orchard like a runaway horse.

"Just one more," said Brer Possum.

That was one more too many.

Brer Possum was still chewing when Brer Bear started shaking the tree with all his strength, and down came Brer Possum like a leaf in a November wind.

But Brer Possum's feet were moving before he touched the ground, and when he did, those little legs shot him five feet down the road.

Brer Bear took off after him. Brer Bear may be big but he ain't slow. Uh-uh. It wasn't long before Brer Bear caught up to Brer Possum and grabbed him.

That didn't mean a thing to Brer Possum. Caught or not, Brer Possum didn't stop moving his legs. They were churning and turning and kicking up grass so bad that Brer Bear's grip was slipping. He bent over and grabbed Brer Possum's tail in his teeth.

That didn't slow Brer Possum down either. His little legs were still flinging dirt and grass back into Brer Bear's eyes. Brer Possum kicked and scratched and scratched and kicked until you would have thought a little tornado had landed. He kicked and scratched until he kicked and scratched his tail right out of Brer Bear's teeth. And all the hair on his tail came off in Brer Bear's mouth.

Brer Bear started coughing and gagging and he might've strangulated to death if Brer Rabbit hadn't come along and beat him on the back until Brer Possum's hair came out of his throat.

The hair may have come out of Brer Bear's throat, but it didn't go back on Brer Possum's tail. That's why, from that day to this, the Possum has no hair on his tail.

Why Brer Possum Loves Peace

Brer Possum might've had a naked tail, but it didn't seem to embarrass him. Neither did it make much difference to his best friend, Brer Coon.

Brer Possum and Brer Coon were about the best buddies that could be. They got together every day to chat about this, that, and the other, and every evening, just before the stars came out, they took a little stroll through the neighborhood.

One evening they were out strolling when they met Brer Dog, who was out taking *his* stroll. He didn't like them and they didn't like him.

Brer Possum and Brer Coon always gave Brer Dog as

much room as he wanted. This evening, however, they looked this way and that way and there wasn't much room to give Brer Dog.

"What we gon' do if he comes for us?" Brer Coon asked.

Brer Possum laughed. "Nothing to worry about. If he comes, I'll stand by you. What you want to do?"

"Only one thing to do. If he runs up on me, I'll make him wish he'd stayed home and scratched his fleas."

The words had hardly covered the distance from his mouth to Brer Possum's ears before Brer Dog ran straight for them.

Brer Dog swung at Brer Possum's stomach. Brer Possum giggled and fell over like he was dead. Brer Dog then went after Brer Coon. That was where he made his mistake.

Brer Coon grabbed Brer Dog and turned him ever-which-a-way-but-loose. He kung fued his eyeballs; he judoed his tail, jujitsued his ears, sat on his wet nose, and karated his bow-wow. Have mercy! Brer Dog felt worse than he did the time he ate a pepperoni, green pepper, anchovy, onion, and sauerkraut pizza for breakfast. He ran away from there so fast, his shadow had to hitchhike home.

Brer Coon was feeling pretty good until he looked down and saw Brer Possum lying on the ground like he was dead. After a minute or so, Brer Possum raised up, gave a weak grin, and ran off.

A couple of days later Brer Possum came over to Brer Coon's house for supper.

"How you doing, Brer Coon?"

Brer Coon don't say a word.

"Something the matter?" Brer Possum wondered.

"I don't run with cowards."

"Who you calling a coward?" Brer Possum wanted to know, rolling up his sleeves like he was ready to fight.

"You! I don't want nothing to do with them who lie down on the ground and play dead when there's a fight to be fought."

Brer Possum started laughing. "Have mercy, Brer Coon! You think I did that 'cause I was scared. Why, I wasn't a bit more scared than you are right now. I knew you could whup Brer Dog and I was just laying there watching you do away with him."

Brer Coon wasn't about to buy a lie that sounded that much like a lie.

But Brer Possum insisted. "I tell you I wasn't scared of Brer Dog. When he come running at us, I was getting ready to give him a taste of my right uppercut, when the first thing I know, his nose was in among my ribs. Well, I'm about the most ticklish thing in the world. When his nose touched my ribs, I just fell out like I was dead. That's a fact. Tickling is the one thing in this world I can't stand. Now you put me in a fight where there ain't no tickling and you'll see some fighting!"

And you know something? To this very day, if you want peace from a possum, just touch him in the ribs. He'll fall over like he's dead every time.

The Baby Who Loved Pumpkins

There was a poor woman who had a lot of children. She went down to the creek one day to wash all the clothes.

When she got there she saw an old man sitting on the bank.

"Howdy," he spoke.

She howdied back.

"If it ain't too much trouble, would you mind washing my coat for me?" the old man asked.

The woman said it wouldn't be a bit of trouble. She washed his coat, wrung it real good, and gave it back to him.

The man thanked her. He reached in his pants pocket and pulled out a string of black beads. He gave them to her and said, "When you get home, go behind your house and you will see a pumpkin tree filled with pumpkins. Bury the beads at the root of the tree and then ask for as many pumpkins as you want."

The old man went his way. When the woman finished her washing, she went home and did as the old man had told her. She asked for a pumpkin and a plump pumpkin floated out of the tree and landed at her feet. The woman did not believe her good fortune. She didn't want to be greedy, but for the first time she and her children would have enough to eat.

I know that you think a pumpkin ain't good for nothing except to make a jack-o'-lantern out of at Halloween. Well, you wrong about that. You can make pumpkin fritters and pumpkin bread. You can bake it like squash; you can boil it like turnips. You can toast the seeds and eat them like peanuts. Anybody who knows their way around a kitchen can do a lot with pumpkins, and this woman definitely knew her way around the kitchen! Soon, the woman and her children were healthy and feeling all right about the world.

One morning the woman opened her front door and there, on the doorsill, was a little baby. She looked up and down the road, wondering who had left the baby. She didn't see anyone.

She took the baby and put him with her other children. This was a witch-baby, however, and when the woman served pumpkins to her children, the witch-baby ate all them pumpkins. The woman took the baby and put it back outside.

As soon as she did, the baby turned into a grown man. The man walked down to the creek where he saw an old man sitting on the bank.

"Would you please comb my hair?" the old man asked.

"Comb it yourself!"

"Would you like some pumpkin?" the old man wanted to know.

"Now you talking my kind of talk."

The old man told him where the pumpkin tree was. "But it is very very very important that you only ask for one pumpkin."

The man nodded and went off to the pumpkin tree. When he saw how many pumpkins were in that tree, he hollered, "I want all the pumpkins!"

The pumpkins fell out of the tree and smashed him, knocked him flat, broke his giblets, pounded him into peanut butter and jelly, and killed him dead, which is what he was supposed to be.

———————————

Impty-Umpty and the Blacksmith

Back when folks knew a lot more and a lot less than what they know now, a blacksmith had a shop at the big crossroads. I can hear you getting ready to ask me where was the big crossroads? That's a good question, but it has a curious answer.

It seems that when people were going somewhere and coming back from that where, they passed the blacksmith's shop and it didn't matter which way they went and came. That was confusing to the folks who were doing the going and the coming, since they didn't always go and come back the same way. It didn't matter. Somewhere during their going and coming they would hear a whanging and a clanging and would look up and there was the blacksmith's shop, red inside from the fire.

In the wintertime the blacksmith's shop wasn't a bad place to be because the fire going all day kept it quite warm. It was so warm, in fact, that the shop held a lot of the warmth through the night, a fact that Brer Rabbit discovered one cold night.

After the blacksmith went to his quarters in the back of the shop, Brer Rabbit made himself at home by the fire. But one morning he overslept, and the blacksmith caught him.

If the blacksmith didn't want Brer Rabbit enjoying any of his heat, he should've said so. Instead, he threw a hammer at Brer Rabbit. If that hammer had hit him, there wouldn't have been enough left of Brer Rabbit to fill the navel of a gnat. But Brer Rabbit dodged the hammer and got away from there.

He went home to the briar patch and thought about

what he was going to do. He hadn't done no harm to the blacksmith's fire. The blacksmith didn't have to throw the hammer at him.

Along about that time Brer Rabbit saw ol' man Billy Rickerson-Dickerson coming down the road. They passed the time of day and caught up on all the news, and when Mr. Billy Rickerson-Dickerson was about to go, Brer Rabbit said, "Could you do me a favor?"

"Don't see why not."

"When you pass the blacksmith shop, stick your head in the door and say, 'Friend, you'll have company soon,' and go on your way. The next person you meet, tell them to do the same."

Word got around fast. Before long, everybody who passed the blacksmith's shop put their head in the door and said, "Friend, you'll have company soon."

The blacksmith wondered what was happening. What did everybody know that he didn't? The blacksmith got so worried that he couldn't sleep and he stayed up, working with his hammer and anvil. Who was the company and how come nobody would tell him who it was?

One night people were sitting in the shop getting warm and watching the blacksmith work. The flames from the forge made their shadows large against the wall. Every time the blacksmith's hammer hit a piece of iron, the sparks flew up in a red shower. It was natural that people started talking about the Bad Place, and quite naturally, that led them to talking about Impty-Umpty, the one who's in charge down there.

The blacksmith worked and listened to the talk. They said Impty-Umpty walked through the world every day and could turn himself into anything except a hog, a monkey, and a cat. If that was the way it was, one of them might be Impty-Umpty. They looked around like they didn't want to know one another anymore.

The blacksmith finished what he had been working on. It was a big iron box with the sides all welded together, and a top that made a tight lid.

Everybody was admiring the box when the door opened and a tall black man stepped inside and bowed.

"Howdy, folks!"

Everybody looked. They had never seen anybody who looked like him. He was black but he didn't look like a black person. His eyes shone like pieces of glass in the moonlight. He was tall and slim and looked like he was clubfooted and doublejointed.

"I hope that you all will excuse me for coming in so suddenly. I used to be a blacksmith and wanted to see the shop and warm myself by the fire."

He walked over to the forge and held his hands over the live charcoals. The fire sprung up like somebody had poured gasoline on it. The flames burned white, then blue, then green, and got bigger and bigger until they wrapped around the Black Man's hands like snakes.

Nobody said a word.

After a few minutes, the Black Man took his hands out of the fire and looked at the blacksmith. "I hear you expecting company soon."

"Who told you?" the blacksmith wanted to know.

"I saw ol' man Rickerson-Dickerson this morning. He told me. When he did, I told him to sit down in the rocking chair and make himself at home. I left right then to see who this company was that's coming to see you."

The people looked at each other. Ol' man Rickerson-

Dickerson died two days ago and had been buried yesterday.

"Where did you see ol' man Rickerson-Dickerson?" somebody asked the Black Man.

"I saw him coming down the road. He looked like he was cold and I invited him in to warm by my fire."

"Did he warm himself?"

The Black Man laughed until smoke came out of his mouth. "He sho' did!" He laughed again. "He sho' did!" The smoke that came out of his mouth had a sharp odor like the smell when you strike a big wooden match.

When the people heard that laugh, when they saw and smelled the smoke that came out of the Black Man's mouth, they started easing toward the door to get away from there. They had a feeling that the blacksmith's company had come!

Soon nobody was left in the shop but the blacksmith and the Black Man. Oh, and outside Brer Rabbit was peeping in through a crack.

The Black Man said, "I've had my eye on you for a while. I used to be a blacksmith, like I said, and you are going at the thing in the wrong way. You don't need a fire and bellows and all that."

"How am I going to get the iron hot enough if I don't have a fire? How can I make what I need to make if I don't have a hammer and tongs?"

"Watch!" The Black Man picked up a piece of iron, held it close to his mouth and blew on it—once, twice. The iron got hot. It got red-hot. It got so hot, it turned white! He put it on the anvil and hit it—once, twice—and there was the prettiest shovel you have ever seen.

"Who are you?" the blacksmith asked, afraid.

"Folks got a lot of different names for me. I'm not proud.

I respond to all of them—Satan, Old Boy, the Devil."

"Impty-Umpty!"

"That one too."

"Folks say that there're three things you can't do."

"And what might those be?" Impty-Umpty asked.

"Folks say you can't change yourself into a hog, or a monkey, or a cat."

Impty-Umpty grinned, jumped in the air, twisted around like he was a gymnast or an ice skater and when he hit the ground, he was a hog. He grunted and scurried around the shop, snuffling the floor and licking up any crumbs he found. Then he lay on the floor and wallowed around and became a monkey. He ran up the wall and sat on the rafters. Then he dropped to the floor and when he landed, he was a little black cat.

The blacksmith grabbed the cat, shoved it in the iron box he had just finished making, slammed the lid tight and locked it! Then he laughed and laughed.

Brer Rabbit had seen everything. He beat the ground hard with his hind foot. It sounded like a loud drumbeat.

"Who's that?' the blacksmith called out.

"I'm the man you put in the box," Brer Rabbit responded.

The blacksmith laughed. "You can't fool me. Impty-Umpty is in here where I put him at, and he'll be impty-umptied before he's emptied."

"Shake the box, man! Shake the box!" Brer Rabbit answered.

The blacksmith shook the box. He didn't hear anything. He shook it again. Still no sound from inside the box.

The blacksmith scratched his head. He put the box on the floor, unlocked the lid and opened it a crack. He didn't

see anything inside. He raised the lid a little higher and when he did, a big bat flew out of the box, hit him in the face, and flew out the door.

Time passed. The day came, like it comes to everybody, when the blacksmith died. The blacksmith knew there wasn't much chance of him getting into heaven, so he went on down to the Bad Place to see Impty-Umpty. He knocked on the door.

"Who's that?" Impty-Umpty wanted to know.

"Ain't nobody but me."

"If you that blacksmith who locked the cat in the box, you can't come in here." Impty-Umpty hollered to one of his children, "Bring the blacksmith a piece of fire and give it to him. He can go start a hell of his own."

I don't know if the blacksmith did that or not, and I hope I don't find out.

The Angry Woman

Strange things went on in the world back in the old times. Like the time the pot chased the angry woman. This was not one of the kinds of pots folks put on the stove today. Those pots are made out of steel or aluminilium, and they shine and you can see your face in them. Whoever heard of such nonsense? If I want to see my face, I'll go look in the mirror.

The kind of pot I'm talking about are the old-timey pots that were black 'cause they hung in the fireplace. These pots had legs, three little stubby legs, and you could set the pot right in the fireplace if you wanted. After being in the fireplace a while, that pot would get right black. You could tell how good the food was going to be by how black the pot was. The blacker the pot, the better the eating. Food out of a shiny pot might be all right for your stomach but it ain't gon' do nothing for your soul.

Long time ago before shiny pots and stoves with electricity in them, there was a woman who lived in a little house back in the woods near a creek. Now this house might've been in Yallerbammer or Georgy. We know it wasn't in Massachewsits or some foreign place like that.

Some folks say the woman was a black woman. Others say she was white. Everybody says she was nine parts evil and it don't make no never mind about the part what was left over. That's about as close to the truth as we can get in this kind of weather.

From what I heard—and I been keeping both ears wide open—she was a very angry person. She had a bad temper. Neighbors said her tongue was long and loud and mighty well hung.

The woman was married, and her husband tried to get along with her. But she always found something to quarrel about. When he chopped the wood, it was either too long or too short. When he brought home meat, it either had too much fat or not enough. When he wanted breakfast, she cooked supper, and when it was time for supper, she put scrambled eggs on the table. When it came to low-down meanness, this woman was rank and ripe.

The woman didn't know her husband was a conjure man. A conjure man is the kind of man who says hello to a tree, and the tree knows it better say, "Howdy-do" back. He could turn dandelion fluff back into yellow flowers and compose songs for the birds. So the man was not afraid of his wife.

For a while he tried patience and goodness on her. It didn't work. The man knew he had to do something else.

One day when the woman wasn't home, he spit in the fireplace. Then he made an X mark in the ashes, turned around two times, and shook a gourd-vine flower over the pot in the fireplace. That was that.

Don't come asking me what all that meant. I don't know, and I'm not too sure I want to. There's some things you're better off not knowing and how to conjure folks is definitely one.

Whatever it was the man did, there was peace in the house for a few days. The woman acted halfway nice, at least nice for her. One morning, however, she scared the sugar off the frosted flakes and told the yellow in the eggs to get out of the house. It did. The man knew it was time to try something a little stronger.

When she left the house, he made another X in the ashes and put some thunderwood buds and calamus root in the pot. Then he sat down and waited.

When the woman came back, she was snorting and fuming and carrying on like she had been eating fried nails with red-hot peppers.

She started making supper. She made some dumplings and threw them in the pot. Then she threw in some peas and chili peppers. On top of that she flung a sheep's head. She was making sheep's-head stew. Naw, they don't have that at McDonald's, and it wouldn't sell if they did. But my great-grandaddy's half brother's aunt's third cousin told me that it was some sho' 'nuf good eating.

The man stared at the X he had made in the ashes. After

a while, he smelled the calamus root he had put in the pot. Things were about to start happening.

The sheep's head started bumping against one side of the pot and then the other. Suddenly, the head bumped all the dumplings out. A minute later the peas bounced out and across the floor.

"What's wrong with you?" the woman yelled at the pot. "You been fooling around with me for a long time and I'm sick of it. I'll show you a thing or two!"

The woman hurried toward the door.

"Where you going?" the man asked.

"I'm going where I'm going. That's where I'm going!"

She went to the woodpile to get the axe. She was going to turn that pot into scrap metal. The axe was lying on top of the woodpile and saw her coming.

I reckon I should push the pause button on this story 'cause you want to know how the axe could see her coming. How am I supposed to know something like that? Do I look like an axe? Do I talk like an axe? Since I am not an axe, how am I supposed to know how the axe saw her coming? I don't even know if an axe has one eye, two eyes, or seventy-four eyes. All I know is that the axe saw her coming, and that's what I told you. If you want to worry yourself about *how* it did its seeing, well, you just go right ahead, but I'm going to go on with the story.

Now as I was saying before your loud thinking distracted me, the axe was lying on top of the woodpile and saw the woman coming. The axe didn't want anything to do with her. It dropped down behind the woodpile.

The woman went to get it. The axe climbed back on top and fell down the other side. The woman and the axe kept going back and forth for some time.

Although we don't know how many eyes an axe has, we do know this: It has only one leg. So it was only a matter of time before the woman caught it.

The woman hurried back in the house with the axe, ready to murder that pot.

"You better let that pot alone," the man said. "You'll be sorry if you don't."

"You gon' be sorry if you don't keep your mouth off my business."

"If you don't listen to me, it'll be your last chance to listen to anything."

The woman raised the axe. The pot got up from the fire and headed out the door.

How dare that pot run away from *her*! Out the door she went.

The pot had three legs to the woman's two, but the race was on.

Into the woods and over the hill they went, but it wasn't to grandmama's house. The pot took her up hill and down hill, across the creek this way and back across that way. The pot went so fast and so far that after a while the woman was huffing and puffing and feeling weak.

The pot stopped, came back, and started dancing in a circle around her. Around and around it danced, faster and faster, until, dizzy, the woman fell to the ground.

The pot threw a hot coal of fire at her. I don't know where it got the coal from. I don't know if the fire fell on the woman. I do know she was never seen again. Some say she burned up. Others say she ran away and is now living in Massachewsits, but why would she want to do that?

As for the pot, well, the pot danced and laughed until

it had to hold its sides to keep from busting open. It danced all the way back to the house. Then, it washed its face and scraped the mud off its feet and sat back down in the fireplace.

All the while, the man hadn't moved from his chair. In a few minutes he heard some boiling and bubbling in the pot. He got up and looked in. The sheep's head and the peas and some rice were cooking just as sweetly as you please.

That evening the man had a quiet and peaceful supper.

Brer Rabbit Throws a Party

One time all the animals were sitting around, all of 'em, that is, except Brer Rabbit. And 'cause Brer Rabbit wasn't there, he became the topic of conversation.

The animals started remembering all the things he had done to them. Brer Wolf and Brer Fox had the most memories. These were not the kind of memories the animals wanted to remember or memorize, and by the time they finished remembering, they were upset and out-of-sorts. They agreed that the time had come to take care of Brer Rabbit once and for all.

But how were they going to accomplish this?

They thought with their right brains. Then they thought with their left brains. Finally, they thought they had the perfect plan. They would have a big party. Brer Rabbit wouldn't miss a party if he was dead. When he got there, they would do away with him.

Maybe the plan would've worked. Then, maybe it wouldn't have. We'll never know because Brer Rabbit had been stretched out in the shade of a nearby tree listening all the while. So, after the animals had their plan set, Brer Rabbit sneaked away and doubled around, and the animals looked up to see him coming down the big road—bookity-bookity—galloping like a horse that won the Kentucky Derby.

"Well hello, friends! Howdy! I haven't seen any of you since the last time! Where have you been these odd-come-shorts? If my eyes ain't gon' bad and my breath still smells sweet, that looks like Brer Bear over there with his short tail and sharp teeth. And ain't that Brer Coon down there? My goodness! Looks like everybody is here. Well, that saves me a whole lot of running all over the community to spread the news."

"What news, Brer Rabbit?" the animals asked anxiously.

"Miz Meadows and the girls are going to have a big party tonight and told me to invite everybody. They say they want Brer Bear to do the Roastin' Ear Shuffle. And Brer Coon? They want you to dance the Rack-Back-Davy. I'm gon' play the fiddle, something I haven't done since my oldest child had the mumps and measles on the same day. I took my fiddle down from the shelf this morning. I tuned it up and tightened the bow, and my whole family forgot about breakfast because they were having such a good time dancing to them old-time fiddle tunes I was playing. Miz Meadows say for everybody to put on their Sunday best and she'll see you tonight."

And with that Brer Rabbit went on down the road.

The animals rushed to their homes and spent all afternoon bathing and getting ready for the party.

That night they went over to Miz Meadows's house and knocked on the door.

Miz Meadows come to the door. "My goodness! What are you all doing here? And all dressed up?"

"We come for the party!" they announced.

"Party? I'll party on your heads. You better get out of here before I call the police. How dare you come banging on my door in the middle of the night?"

She slammed the door.

The animals looked at each other very sheepishly and slowly went home.

Brer Rabbit had given them another memory.

Why Brer Fox's Legs Are Black

Now I know you don't know too much about foxes and the like. You probably don't even know that some foxes are red and some are gray, but they all got black legs. How you figure something like that? Well, this is how it came about.

One time Brer Rabbit and Brer Fox was out hunting. Don't ask me what they were hunting for. They could've been hunting lions or tigers. Then again, they might've been hunting for a bargain. Whatever it was, they weren't finding it.

After a while their stomachs started talking, and what their stomachs were saying cannot be put into a book designed for family enjoyment. However, Brer Rabbit had brought along a piece of corn bread to nibble on. Brer Fox hadn't brought anything. Brer Rabbit thought about sharing his corn bread with Brer Fox, but if he did that, then there wouldn't be enough for him. So he walked behind Brer Fox and nibbled on the corn bread whenever his stomach said something that I can't put into a book.

As the day went on, they managed to kill a squirrel or two, but they hadn't brought any matches to make a fire. By now Brer Fox was so hungry that his stomach was talking about him in fourteen different languages. If that wasn't trouble enough, his head was hurting. Plus it was getting late, and the sun was hanging low in the sky and shining red through the trees.

"That's where you can get some fire," Brer Rabbit said.

"Where?"

"Yonder where the sun is. Won't be long before it goes into its hole. As it does, you can get a big chunk of fire

off it. You leave the squirrels here with me and go get the fire. I'd go myself 'cepting you are bigger and more swift and can go faster."

Brer Fox took off to where the sun lived. He trotted; he loped; he galloped; and after a while, he was there. By that time, however, the sun had gone in its hole to get some shut-eye, and Brer Fox couldn't reach down far enough to get a chunk of fire.

"Hey, Mister Sun!" yelled Brer Fox. "Wake up!"

Sun was snoring so loud, he didn't hear a thing.

Brer Fox was determined to get himself a chunk of fire, so he lay down on top of the hole and went to sleep.

The Sun woke up before Brer Fox did. Because the Sun

is the Sun, there is only one thing it can do when it wakes up—and that's to rise.

Sun started climbing out of its hole. Brer Fox was asleep on top of the hole.

In a situation like that, there's got to be a winner and a loser. We don't have to think too long about who was which.

Sun was rising. Brer Fox was asleep. The higher the sun rose, the hotter it got at the top of the hole.

Brer Fox started sweating and moaning in his sleep and woke up just in time to see this ball of fire coming at him. If he hadn't jumped out of the way, he would've gotten burned up. But he didn't jump quite quick enough, because Sun scorched Brer Fox's legs as it went by. And from that day to this, they have been black.

Just goes to show: You got to be careful where you sleep.

How the Witch Was Caught

Sleep is a funny thing. Some nights I go to bed and I'm asleep before my eyes are shut. Other nights I shut my eyes and sleep is on the other side of town. Some nights I sleep a little bit and wake up feeling as if I had slept all night. Other nights I sleep a lot and wake up more tired than if I had stayed up.

When you sleep a lot and wake up tired, it can mean only one thing: A witch was riding you during the night. That's what the ol' folks used to say. Don't ask me why a witch would want to ride somebody. Better than riding the bus, I guess.

I have never seen a witch. At least, not to my knowledge. I have known a few people who I thought might be close relatives, but I myself have never personally sat down face-to-face with a witch and talked about the news of the day. Which don't mean that witches don't exist.

Right here in this town there used to be a man lived down there by the river. He worked hard, saved his money, and bought a house to rent to people so he could make even more money.

But something was the matter with the house he bought. A person would move in in the morning. When they went to bed that night, they felt like they shouldn't go to sleep, because if they did, something told them they wouldn't hear the Sun knock on the door the next morning. They moved out that very same night.

One rainy evening a preacher came along who needed somewhere to stay. He asked around and people told him about the man's empty house.

The preacher went to him.

The man said, "I can't let you stay there. The house is haunted."

"I'd rather stay inside with the ghosts than outside in the rain," the preacher said.

The man took the preacher to the house, made a big fire in the fireplace, and went his way.

The preacher drew a chair up before the fire and waited for the ghosts or the witches, or whatever it was. Nothing came.

After a while the preacher fixed his supper. When he was done eating and was about to wash the dishes, he heard a scratching on the wall.

He looked around. A big black cat was sharpening its

claws on the door. The preacher knew this wasn't a cat you set a bowl of milk out for.

This cat had long white teeth that glistened like stars in the sky on a winter night. It had great big yellow eyes that shone like two moons. And it grinned like it knew something you wished you knew but wouldn't until it was too late.

The cat sidled up to the preacher. Preacher shooed the cat away like it was nothing.

The cat went off.

Preacher wasn't fooled. He washed and dried the dishes. Then he took one of the kitchen knives, sat down by the fire, and waited.

Wasn't long before the black cat came back with twenty black cats just like it, marching behind. They paraded into the room and headed toward the preacher.

The big black cat howled and leaped at the preacher's eyes. The preacher ducked. The cat howled and leaped again. The preacher took a swipe at the cat with the knife and cut off one of its toes.

The cat yowled and ran up the chimney. The other cats followed.

The preacher looked around carefully until he found the cat's toe. He picked it up, wrapped it in a piece of paper, and put it in his pocket. Then he went to bed and slept soundly until Mr. Sun banged on the window the next morning.

Preacher got up, said his prayers, had his breakfast, and prepared to go. He reached in his pocket and felt the piece of paper with the cat's toe in it. The paper felt funny, though. He unwrapped it. Lo and behold, what had been a toe last night was now a finger with a ring on it. The preacher wrapped it up again and put it back in his pocket.

He went to the man's house and thanked him for letting him sleep in the house. "I sure would be obliged to have the opportunity to extend my thanks to your wife and give her my blessing," the preacher finished.

"My wife ain't feeling well this morning, but I'll take you in to her."

The wife lay in bed with the covers pulled up to her chin. Her eyes looked like she hadn't had a wink of sleep.

The preacher held out his hand to the woman. The woman put out her left hand. Preacher took his hand back, like he didn't want to shake her left hand.

"My right hand is crippled," the woman told the preacher.

"Ain't nothing the matter with your right hand that I've ever noticed," her husband put in. "Let me see this hand."

The woman slowly took her right hand from beneath the covers. And guess what? That's right! One of her fingers was missing.

"How did this happen?" the man wanted to know.

"I cut it off," the woman said.

"How did you cut it off?"

"I knocked it off."

"Where did you knock it off?" the man insisted.

"I broke it off."

"When did you break it off?" he said, getting angrier.

The woman got real quiet.

The preacher reached in his pocket, took out the finger, and tried it on the woman's hand. It fit!

"This is the witch what's been haunting your house," the preacher told the man.

The woman yowled like a cat. And right before their eyes, she changed into a big black cat.

The preacher and the man caught the cat and made sure that cat wouldn't haunt anybody's house ever again. After that, the man was able to rent his house, and the folks who lived there were very happy. And so was the man.

————————————

The Man Who Almost Married a Witch

I don't know whether there are witches going around today. Seems to me that all the electricity and neon lights and waves from the TVs and radios would make it mighty hard for a witch to know night from day. If I was you, I wouldn't be worried about witches. I'd just enjoy the stories and leave it at that.

Long, long time ago, when the moon was a whole lot bigger than it is now, there was a Witch-Wolf that lived way back in the swamp where the alligators and snakes laid around in the moonshine, flossing each other's teeth.

This Witch-Wolf was about as evil a creature as ever walked the earth without leaving a footprint. When she wasn't making trouble, she was thinking about it, and her thoughts could cause a body misery.

The Witch-Wolf usually took the form of a big black wolf with long claws and green eyes. But when she was hungry she would close her eyes, smack her mouth, and turn into the prettiest woman you ever laid eyes on.

I reckon I got to interrupt the story right here to tell some of you boys who ain't got sense enough to keep your toenails cut short not to go around thinking that every pretty girl might be a witch. That ain't what the story say. The story is about *this* woman and her alone.

The Witch-Wolf's favorite activity was eating men. But before she ate them she would change into a pretty woman, make the man fall in love with her, and marry him. The "I do's" wouldn't be cold before she would shut her eyes, smack her mouth together, and change back into a wolf. Then she'd eat the man up, and that would be that.

One day word got back to her in the swamp that a new

man had moved to town. He had land, but she didn't want the land. He had horses, but she didn't want the horses. He had cows, but she didn't want the cows. She wanted the man.

She closed her eyes, smacked her lips, and there she was, as pretty as a sunrise on a spring morning. Off she went.

The man was sitting on his porch in the cool of the day when a woman walked by, looking as good as a lawn that stays green and never has to be mowed.

"Evening," she said, real sweetlike.

"Good evening to you," he responded, sweating and trembling and grinning all at the same time.

"Mighty nice out this evening, ain't it?"

"It is that."

But before the man could say anything else, the woman walked on down the road, leaving him so eager to see her the next evening that he scarcely slept that night.

Every evening he sat on the porch and waited for her, and every evening she came by. Before long they were sitting on the porch drinking iced tea and talking about the kinds of things men and women talk about.

The woman pretended that she was in love with him. He wasn't pretending about anything. He was sho' 'nuf in love, but something was holding him back. He wanted to ask her to marry him, but the words wouldn't come out of his mouth.

The man was in love but he wasn't dumb. Something about the woman didn't feel right. For one, where did she come from? She wouldn't tell him. Where did she live? She wouldn't tell him. Who were her people? How did she make a living? She wouldn't tell him.

He decided to do some asking around. But who should

he ask? He studied on the situation for a while and finally decided to go see Judge Rabbit. He'd been living in them parts longer than anybody else.

The man went to Judge Rabbit's house and knocked on the door.

"Who's that?" Judge Rabbit called out.

"It's me," answered the man.

"Mighty short name for a grown man," Judge Rabbit said. "Give me the full entitlements."

The man gave out his full name, and Judge Rabbit let him in. They sat down by the fire, and the man started telling Judge Rabbit about the beautiful woman he had met.

"What's her name?" Judge Rabbit asked.

"Mizzle-Mazzle."

Judge Rabbit got very quiet. He made a mark in the ashes in the fireplace. "How old is she?"

The man told him.

Judge Rabbit made another mark. "Has she got eyes like a cat?"

The man thought for a moment. "I guess she does."

Judge Rabbit made another mark in the ashes. "Are her ears kind of pointed at the top?"

The man did some more thinking. "They might be."

Judge Rabbit made yet another mark in the ashes. "Is her hair yellow?"

The man didn't need to worry his mind over that one. "Yes, it is."

Judge Rabbit made another mark. "She got sharp teeth?"

The man nodded.

Judge Rabbit made still another mark and frowned. "I thought Mizzle-Mazzle had moved out of the country. But here she is galloping around, just as natural as a dead pig in the sunshine."

"What're you talking about, Judge?"

"If you want trouble with trouble that doubles and triples trouble, marry Mizzle-Mazzle."

The man looked scared. "What should I do?"

"You got any cows?"

"Plenty."

"Well, here's what you do. Ask Mizzle-Mazzle if she is a good housekeeper. She'll say yes. Ask her if she can cook. She'll say yes to that. Ask her if she can clean pots and pans. She'll say yes. Ask her if she can do the laundry. She'll say yes. Then, ask her if she can milk the red cow. And watch what she says."

The man thanked Judge Rabbit and went home. When he got there, the woman was waiting for him.

"How you doing today?" he asked her.

"Fine. How you?"

"I ain't feeling too good," the man said.

"How come?"

"I'm not rightly sure. It might be because I'm lonely."

"Why are you lonely?"

"I guess it's because I ain't married."

The woman started batting her eyes real fast and running her tongue over her lipstick to make it shine. "What you looking for in a wife?"

"Well, I need somebody who can take care of the house when I'm gone and somebody to keep me company when I'm home. Are you a good housekeeper?"

"Why, yes. I am."

"Can you cook?"

"Why, yes."

"Can you clean pots and pans?"

"Indeed."

"Can you do the laundry?"

"Yes."

"Can you milk the red cow?"

The woman jumped and screamed so loud, the man almost fell over. "You don't think I'd let some cow kick me, do you?"

"The cow is as gentle as a baby."

The woman was still upset, but after a moment she said, "Well, I suppose I could try to milk the cow, if that's what you wanted me to do. But first, let me show you how well I can take care of a house."

Bright and early the next morning the woman came and

cleaned the house from attic to cellar and back again.

The day after that she fixed him the best meal he had ever had. The day after that she cleaned the pots and pans. They shone so much like mirrors that Mr. Sun stayed a little longer at the man's house to look at himself in them.

The day after that she did the laundry and got the whites whiter than white, and the colored clothes stood up and started singing a commercial.

The day following that one, she came to milk the red cow. The man watched from a distance.

She walked into the cow pen with a pail. The cow smelled the witch in her blood. Cow snorted, pawed the ground, and lowered its head like it was going to charge. Before the woman knew it, that's just what the cow did.

The woman leaped the fence, and as she did so, smacked her lips together. She changed into a wolf and disappeared. She hasn't been seen from that time to this.

Why Dogs Are Tame

Back in the days when people and animals lived on the earth like kinfolk, Brer Dog ran with the other animals. He galloped with Brer Fox and loped with Brer Wolf, and cantered with Brer Coon. He went through all the gaits and had as good a time as the other animals and as bad a time too.

It was after one of them bad times that Brer Dog started thinking. Somewhere between Monday morning and Saturday night Brer Dog was sitting in the shade, scratching and thinking about the winter that had just ended. The wind had carried knives and cut through everything standing in its path. Hungriness built a skyscraper in Brer Dog's stomach and moved in with all his kin. Brer Dog was so thin he would've counted his ribs if he had known his numbers. He didn't want to go through another winter like that.

That's what Brer Dog was thinking when Brer Wolf came meandering along.

"Howdy, Brer Dog!"

"Howdy back, Brer Wolf!"

"Brer Dog, you look like you and food are angry at each other. Not that I'm on the friendliest of terms with food myself."

"I hear you," Brer Dog responded.

They commiserated with one another for a while and then Brer Wolf asked, "So what are you up to today?"

"It don't make no difference what I'm up to if I don't find dinner."

"You can't have dinner if you don't have a fire."

"Where am I going to get fire?"

Brer Wolf thought for a minute. "Well, the quickest way I know is to borrow some from Mr. Man and Miz Woman."

"That's a risky proposition."

"I know it."

Mr. Man had a walking cane that he could point at you and blow your lights out.

Brer Dog was desperate, though. "I'll go for the fire," he told Brer Wolf, and off he went.

Before long he was sitting by the gate outside Mr. Man's house. If the gate had been closed, Brer Dog would've gone back from where he came. But some of the children had been playing and left the gate open. Brer Dog didn't want to go through the gate 'cause he didn't want to get his lights blown out. On the other hand, his lights were getting dim because he was so hungry. He walked through the gate as scared as scared can be.

He heard hogs grunting and pigs squealing and hens cackling and roosters crowing, but he didn't turn his head toward grunt or squeal, cackle or crow. He started toward the front door, but it looked too big and white. He went to the back door, and from inside he heard children laughing and playing. For the first time in his life, Brer Dog felt lonely.

He sat down by the back door, afraid to knock. He waited. After a while somebody opened the door and then shut it real quick. Brer Dog didn't see who it was because his eyes were on the ground.

A few minutes later Mr. Man came to the door. In his hand was the stick that would put your lights out. "What you want?" he asked Brer Dog.

Brer Dog was too scared to say anything, so he just wagged his tail.

"As far as I know, you ain't got no business here, so be on your way," Mr. Man said.

Brer Dog crouched down close to the ground and wagged his tail some more. Mr. Man looked at him real hard, trying to decide whether or not to shoot him.

Miz Woman wondered who her husband was talking to. She came to the door and saw Brer Dog crouching on the ground, wagging his tail, his tongue hanging out of the side of his mouth, his eyes so big and wet that he looked like he was going to cry at any minute.

"Poor fella," Miz Woman said. "You not going to hurt anybody, are you?"

"No, ma'am," Brer Dog responded. "I just come to ask if I could borrow a chunk of fire."

"My goodness! What you need a chunk of fire for?" she wanted to know.

"He wants to burn us out of house and home," Mr. Man put in.

"I wouldn't do that," Brer Dog said. "I need the fire so that if I get something to eat, I can cook it. And if I don't get nothing to eat, at least I'll be able to keep warm on these chilly nights."

"You poor thing. Why don't you come in here to the kitchen and get as warm as you want."

"I don't want that animal in my house," Mr. Man protested.

"He's so cuuuuute," Miz Woman said.

Brer Dog didn't say anything. He just tried to look cute as he trotted in the house.

There was a big fireplace in the kitchen, and he sat down on the hearth. The children were sitting around the table eating their supper. After a while, Brer Dog was feeling right splimmy-splammy.

But he was still very hungry. He looked up with his big eyes and saw the children eating corn bread and collard greens and ham hocks. His eyes followed the children's hands from plate to mouth, mouth to plate, plate to mouth, mouth to plate.

Miz Woman saw Brer Dog watching the children. She went to the cabinet and got a plate and put some ham, corn bread, and juice from the greens on it and set it down in front of Brer Dog.

Brer Dog gobbled it up with one gulp. It wasn't enough to satisfy his hunger, but he was afraid that if they saw how hungry he really was, they wouldn't let him stay.

So he stretched out in front of the fire, yawned loudly, and put his head across his paws and pretended he had fallen asleep.

Wasn't long before he smelled a familiar smell. He smelled the familiar smell of Brer Wolf. He raised his head and looked toward the door.

Mr. Man noticed the dog looking toward the door. "Is there something sneaking around out there?"

Brer Dog got up, trotted to the door, and growled a low growl.

"There's a varmint out there, ain't it?" Mr. Man said, getting his rifle from over the fireplace. He opened the door, and what should he see but Brer Wolf running out the gate. Mr. Man raised the rifle and—*kerblam!* Brer Wolf howled. The shot missed Brer Wolf, but the scare was a bull's-eye.

After that Mr. Man had a new appreciation for Brer Dog. Brer Dog showed he could be useful in many ways. He headed the cows off when they made a break to go into the woods. He took care of the sheep. Late up in the night, he warned Mr. Man if any varmints were lurking around. When Mr. Man went hunting, Brer Dog was there to keep him company. And he played with Mr. Man's and Miz Woman's children as if he was one of them. And for all that, Brer Dog didn't want anything more than food to eat and a place in front of the fire.

Before long Brer Dog was fat and sleek. One day he was out by himself in the woods when he met up with Brer Wolf.

"Howdy, Brer Wolf."

Brer Wolf don't say nothing for a while. Finally, "So why didn't you come back with the fire that day?"

Brer Dog pointed to the collar around his neck. "See this? I belong to Mr. Man and Miz Woman now."

"You look like you haven't missed a meal in a long time. How come I can't come there and have them own me?"

"Come on!"

The next morning Brer Wolf knocked on Mr. Man's door. Mr. Man looked out to see who it was. When he saw Brer Wolf, Mr. Man got his rifle and went to the door.

Brer Wolf tried to be as polite as he could. He smiled. I don't know if you've ever seen a wolf smile. It is not a pleasant sight. Mr. Man saw a mouth full of teeth as sharp as grief. Mr. Man raised his rifle and—*kerblam!*—took a shot at Brer Wolf.

Some folks say he missed. Others say he gave him natural air-conditioning. I don't know how that part turned

out. What I do know is that Brer Dog has been living in people's houses ever since.

How Tinktum Tidy Recruited an Army for the King

This is a story about a short, ugly man. That's the first indication that this is not a fairy tale. In fairy tales the man is always a tall and handsome prince. But there are a lot more short and ugly people in the world than tall, handsome ones. Why, then, are all the fairy tales about somebody who there ain't many of?

Well, the man in this story may have been short and ugly, but he was as smart as he was ugly, which means that he was *very* smart. He was also prosperous and owned hundreds of acres of land.

His name was Linktum Lidy Lody. That was his given name. His family name was Tinktum Tidy. Other folks called him Linktum Tidlum Tidy. One or two called him Tinktum Tidlum. But me, I call him Tinktum Tidy and Linktum Lidy Lody Tinktum Tidy, so that's who he'll be.

When it came to brains, Tinktum Tidy had enough for two people. Everybody knew it, and whenever they had a problem, they'd bring it to him and he would solve it for them.

Word eventually reached the king that Tinktum Tidy was the smartest man in the kingdom. The Lord had not been kind to the king in the brain department. Didn't make any difference. You don't have to be smart to be king or president. (I could name presidents who didn't have *any* brains.) You just have to know who the smart people are and get them to work for you. So, that's what the king did. He sent word that he wanted to meet Tinktum Tidy.

Tinktum Tidy set out for where the king lived. When he got there, he told the royal guards that the king had sent for him. They took him into a big room where there were many other people.

Everybody looked at Tinktum Tidy 'cause he was so short and ugly. Tinktum Tidy looked back at them like they were crazy.

The king came in and sat down on his throne. He looked at everybody, and his eyes stopped at Tinktum Tidy. "You the shortest and the ugliest thing I've ever seen. What do you want?"

"I'm Linktum Lidy Lody Tinktum Tidy."

"So what?"

"You sent for me."

"I did?" The king was confused. "Why did I send for you?"

"How should I know?"

One of the king's counselors whispered for a long time in the king's ear.

"Now I remember," said the king. "I understand you got more brains than anybody in the kingdom." The king reached in his pocket and took out eleven grains of corn. "If you're so smart, take these eleven grains of corn and bring me back eleven strong men to put in my army."

Tinktum Tidy took the corn, tied it in his handkerchief, bowed, and went his way.

All that day he traveled. When night came, he stopped at an inn, which is what they called hotels and motels back in that time.

"What's your name and where you from and where might you be going?" the innkeeper wanted to know.

"I'm Linktum Lidy Lody Tinktum Tidy. I'm from Chuckerluckertown, and I'm on a long journey."

The innkeeper showed Tinktum to his room. Tinktum Tidy heard a loud squawking noise. "What's that?"

"That ain't nothing but Molly the Goose."

Tinktum Tidy took out the handkerchief and untied it. "Here are eleven grains of corn the king gave me. I'm afraid Molly the Goose will come in here and eat them."

The man said, "Don't you worry none about that. I'll make sure all the doors are shut tight."

Way up in the night when everybody was sleep, Tinktum Tidy took the corn and dropped it through a crack in the floor.

The next morning, when everybody was waking up, they heard Tinktum Tidy yelling and screaming, "I told you so! I told you so! Molly the Goose has eaten the king's corn! Molly the Goose has eaten the king's corn!"

When the innkeeper heard that, he got scared. He grabbed Molly the Goose and gave her to Tinktum Tidy. "Here! You can have the goose! Now, get away from here before the king comes looking for his corn."

Tinktum Tidy took the goose and went on down the big road. He traveled all day, and close to nightfall he came to another inn.

When it came time to retire for the night, Tinktum Tidy tied Molly the Goose to the bed and called the innkeeper.

"My name is Linktum Lidy Lody Tinktum Tidy. This here is Molly the Goose. She ate the eleven grains of corn the king gave me." Just then a noise came from outside. "What's that?" Tinktum Tidy wanted to know.

"That's nothing but Boo-Boo Black Sheep."

"I'm afraid Boo-Boo Black Sheep will come in here during the night and eat Molly the Goose, who ate the king's eleven grains of corn."

The innkeeper said, "Don't worry. I'll make sure all the doors are locked tight."

In the middle of the night when it was hard to tell the sleeping from the dead, Tinktum Tidy broke Molly the Goose's neck. Then he sneaked outside and threw her body in the barnyard next to Boo-Boo Black Sheep.

The next morning, when everybody was starting to wake up, they heard Tinktum Tidy hollering and yelling, "I told you so! I told you so! Boo-Boo Black Sheep killed Molly the Goose, who ate the eleven grains of corn the king gave me. The king is going to be very angry at somebody."

The innkeeper got scared 'cause the king's corn was inside the goose, and the goose was now dead, and the king might blame the innkeeper. He gave Boo-Boo Black Sheep to Tinktum Tidy. "Here! Take the sheep and get away from here. You brought me bad luck!"

Tinktum Tidy took Boo-Boo Black Sheep and went on down the big road. He traveled all day until he came to another town and in that town was an inn.

When bedtime came he tied Boo-Boo Black Sheep to his bed and called for the innkeeper. "I see you have a cow. What's your cow's name?"

The innkeeper said, "That's Brindle Cow."

"Well, this is Boo-Boo Black Sheep, who killed Molly the Goose, who ate the eleven grains of corn the king gave me. I'm afraid Brindle Cow will kill Boo-Boo Black Sheep."

"I'll make sure all the doors are locked tight."

Sometime between moondown and sunup, Tinktum Tidy

killed Boo-Boo Black Sheep and put him in the pen with Brindle Cow.

The next morning, about the time folks started yawning themselves awake, they heard Tinktum Tidy hollering and yelling, "I told you so! I told you so! Brindle Cow done killed Boo-Boo Black Sheep, who killed Molly the Goose, who ate the eleven grains of corn the king gave me."

The man heard the king's name and got scared. "Here! Take the cow! Get on away from here before you bring me more bad luck."

Tinktum Tidy took Brindle Cow and went off down the big road. He walked all that day until he came to the next town and got a room for the night at the inn.

He said to the innkeeper, "I noticed you got a horse tied up outside. Well, this here is Brindle Cow, that killed Boo-Boo Black Sheep, that ate Molly the Goose, who ate the eleven grains of corn the king gave me. I'm afraid your horse is going to kill Brindle Cow."

"Whoever heard of a horse killing a cow?"

The innkeeper should not have said that. Way up in the night, Tinktum Tidy killed Brindle Cow and put the carcass in the pen with the horse.

Next morning Tinktum Tidy woke everybody up hollering and yelling, "I told you so! I told you so! The horse killed Brindle Cow, that killed Boo-Boo Black Sheep, that ate Molly the Goose, who ate the eleven grains of corn the king gave me."

The mention of the king's name scared the innkeeper. "Here! Take the horse and go on about your business!"

Tinktum Tidy got on the horse and went trotting down the big road. He rode and he rode until he came to a creek. Sitting between the road and the creek was an old man. Linktum Lidy Lody Tinktum Tidy stopped and looked at the old man. The old man looked at Linktum Lidy Lody Tinktum Tidy.

"How do?" the old man said.

"How do?" Tinktum Tidy returned.

"Some dust blowed in my eyes, son. Would you wipe my eyes for me?" the old man requested.

Tinktum Tidy got off the horse and wiped the old man's eyes.

"Thank you," the old man said.

"You're welcome," Tinktum Tidy responded. Then he got back on the horse and prepared to go his way.

"Come scratch my head," the old man said.

Tinktum Tidy got off the horse and scratched the old man's head.

"Thank you, son. Thank you."

"You're mighty welcome." Tinktum Tidy got on his horse and prepared to ride away.

"Come help me get up," the old man said.

Tinktum Tidy got off the horse and helped the old man up. A strange thing happened. As the old man began to get up, youth and strength came back into his body. By the time he was standing erect, he looked like a young man.

"Son, I been sitting here for almost ten years. You're the first person who ever did what I asked. Some laughed at me. Some cursed me, and all went by. But it's a funny thing. Everyone that passed me was set on by the eleven robbers who live just down the road. The robbers took all their money and clothes and kicked them back out in the world. Now, seeing as how you did what I asked you, I'll be more than pleased to do what you ask."

Tinktum Tidy told the man that he had to get eleven strong men for the king's army.

The man said, "Well, them eleven robbers are strong enough to be in the army. Here's what you do. Keep on down the big road until you come to a big white house. Ride around the house seven times to the right and seven times to the left and say whatever words come into your head."

Tinktum Tidy went down the big road and came to the big white house. He rode around it seven times to the right and seven times to the left. "This is the horse that killed the Brindle Cow, that killed Boo-Boo Black Sheep, that ate Molly Goose, that ate the eleven grains of corn the king gave me. I want eleven strong men for the king's army."

The front door of the white house opened and the eleven robbers came marching out. They got on their horses and Tinktum Tidy led them right to the king.

After that Linktum Lidy Lody Tinktum Tidy didn't look so short to people, and Linktum Lidy Lody Tinktum Tidy didn't look so ugly either.

Why Guinea Fowls Are Speckled

This story is about the guinea fowls. A guinea fowl is a bird of the pheasant family. It come from Africa, which is why it's called a guinea, 'cause it's from Guinea. It's about the size of a pheasant, which is about the size of a turkey. Its feathers are kind of blue-black, with white spots all over.

But that ain't how it always was. The guinea used to be

spotless. This story is about how come they aren't that way now.

One day Sister Cow was grazing in the field with her calf. After a while along came a drove of Guineas.

"Howdy, Sister Cow!"

"Howdy!"

The Guineas pecked around in the ground while exchanging the news of the neighborhood with Sister Cow. Suddenly, they heard a curious noise from the other side of the field. The Guineas looked around but didn't see anything. Sister Cow looked around. She didn't see anything either.

The Guineas went back to pecking and Sister Cow went back to chewing her cud. Before long the noise came again, only this time it was closer. The Guineas and Sister Cow looked up. Standing between them and sundown was a great big Lion!

The Lion loved cow meat more than anything in creation. He shook his hairy head, roared a hairy roar, pawed the ground a couple of times, and made a rush for Sister Cow.

The Guineas ran this way and that, and they ran around and around. However, Sister Cow stood her ground. When the Lion charged, Sister Cow dropped her head, pointed her horns toward him, and pawed the earth.

The Lion stopped and began circling slowly around the Cow. Every way the Lion went, Sister Cow turned, keeping her horns always pointed at the Lion.

The Guineas were watching all this. They saw that Sister Cow wasn't afraid, and this gave them heart. Next thing you know one of the Guineas ran out between Sister Cow and the Lion, turned her back to the Lion, and began scratching and kicking up dirt and grass in the Lion's face.

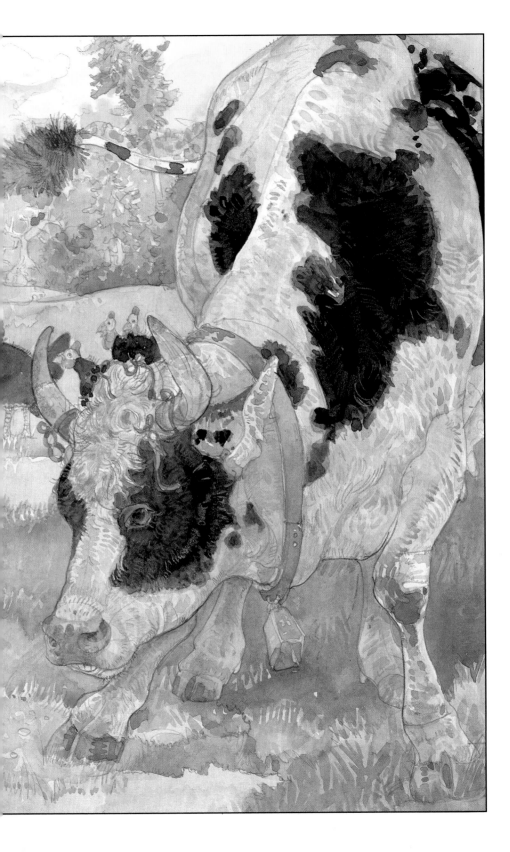

When that Guinea had had enough fun, she ran back to the group and another Guinea ran out and had her some fun kicking up dirt and grass on the Lion.

Before you know it, the Lion had so much dust and dirt and grass in his eyes that he couldn't see his hand in front of his face. He was growling and roaring and snapping at the air, and he got so mad that he made a blind plunge at Sister Cow.

Sister Cow dipped her head and caught the Lion on her horns. That was the end of the Lion.

Sister Cow called the Guineas to her. "I want to thank you for all your help."

"Don't concern yourself with us, Sister Cow. You had your fun and we had ours."

"That's true, but I would like to show you my gratitude. What can I do for you?"

The Guineas conferred among themselves for a while, then one said, "What we need doing for us, you can't do it. But I wish you could."

"And what might you need?"

"We need to be fixed so that we can't be seen from far away. We look blue in the sun, and we look blue in the shade, which makes it hard for us to hide."

Sister Cow chewed her cud and thought. "Somebody get me a pail," she said finally.

"What you want with a pail?" one of the Guineas asked.

"Get it. You'll see."

When the Guinea came back with the pail, Sister Cow stood over it and let down milk until the pail was full. Then she told the Guineas to get in a row. They lined up. Sister Cow dipped her tail in the milk, and sprinkled each Guinea, and as she did so, she said, "I loves this one." Then she would sing:

Oh, Blue, go away! You shall not stay!
Oh, Guinea, be Gray, be Gray!

She sprinkled all the Guinea hens. When she finished they sat in the sun until they dried. That's why until this day, guinea hens are speckled.

Why the Guineas Stay Awake

Every night when it came time for the Guineas to go to bed, they were asleep the minute their heads hit the pillows. Don't come asking me what kind of pillows they had. I suspect they were feather pillows, however.

One night Brer Fox decided to be sociable and visit with the Guineas after they had gone to sleep.

Along toward the shank of the evening, and if you look carefully on the clock you'll find the shank between midnight and 3:00 A.M., Brer Fox arrived at where the Guineas were sleep. Some folks when they go somewhere to be sociable would turn around and go back home if they found everybody asleep. Brer Fox was not that kind of man.

Brer Fox looked at the Guineas. They looked so fine and so fat, Brer Fox felt like they were kinfolk. "I believe I'll just shake hands with one and then I'll go."

That's what Brer Fox did, but something happened. When he grabbed a Guinea hen, his grip must have been too tight, because when he tipped his hat and left, the Guinea hen went with him.

You should've heard the racket the Guineas made when

they discovered that Brer Fox had made off with one of them. They squalled and squalled until they woke up the whole neighborhood. The dogs were barking, the owls were hooting, the horses were whinnying, the cows were mooing, the chickens were clucking and crowing, and all the people were yelling, "SHUT UP!"

The next night the Guineas were so scared that they refused to shut their eyes. And from that night to this, Guineas don't sleep at night. I don't know when they do sleep. I reckon they nod off during the day, but I don't know anybody who has ever seen them. I do know this, though: Guinea hens stay awake all night. I hope the one Brer Fox took was good eating, 'cause that was the last one he ever ate.

Brer Fox and the White Grapes

One day Brer Rabbit was going through the woods. Don't come asking me where he was going because I don't know. Brer Rabbit probably didn't know where he was going. If *he* didn't know where he was going, I cannot be expected to know what he didn't know. And, no, I don't know where he was coming from either.

I do know that while he was going through the woods he happened to run into Brer Fox.

"How you, Brer Fox?"

Brer Fox shook his head. "I ain't."

"What's the problem?"

"I'm hungry, Brer Rabbit."

"I'm glad I'm me and not you."

"Why so?"

" 'Cause my stomach is full of white grapes," Brer Rabbit told him.

"White grapes!" Brer Fox started to dribble at the mouth. "Brer Rabbit, where did you find white grapes, and how come I didn't find them?"

"Well, I don't know why you didn't find them, Brer Fox. Seems that some folks see straight. Some folks see crooked. Some folks see in curves, and some folks see around corners. And then some folks have their eyes open and don't see a thing. Me, I saw the white grapes and I ate every last one of them."

"Don't tell me that, Brer Rabbit," moaned Brer Fox.

"Well, I ate all the white grapes growing off the vine covering this one particular tree. There're probably white grapes growing off the vines on other trees in the same vicinity."

"Well, don't just stand there, Brer Rabbit. Let's go. Show me where this vicinity is."

Brer Rabbit shook his head. "I don't know, Brer Fox. You want to get me way out there deep in the woods by myself where nobody could hear me holler if I had to. Once you get me out there, you'll try and do away with me."

Brer Fox was hurt. "Brer Rabbit, I ain't got no such a thing in mind. What kind of person do you think I am? I will tell you what kind of a person I am, Brer Rabbit. I am a hungry person. That is who I am."

Brer Rabbit looked like he still wasn't sure. "Brer Fox, you have played so many tricks on people, I'd be a fool to go way off in the woods with you."

The conversation went back and forth until Brer Fox promised Brer Rabbit that he wouldn't play any tricks on him or try to do away with him. If Brer Fox had the sense he was born with he would've gotten Brer Rabbit to promise the same thing.

Off they went until they came to a big tree covered with grape vines. The grapes were not ripe, however, which Brer Rabbit knew and Brer Fox would've known if he would've seen what his eyes were looking at. But all he could see was his hunger. When a man looks at the world through hungry eyes, everything looks good to eat.

Brer Fox looked up at the tree. "How am I going to get the grapes?"

"Do like I did."

"How did you did?"

"I climbed for them."

"Climb? How am I going to do that?" Brer Fox wanted to know.

"Grab with your hands, climb with your legs, and I'll push your bottom."

So, Brer Fox grabbed and climbed and Brer Rabbit pushed. Soon, Brer Fox was high enough to grab the lowest limb. From there he made it on his own until he was high enough to eat the grapes. He shoved some in his mouth.

"Ow!" he hollered. "These grapes are bitter!" He spit them out.

"Well, they *looked* ripe," said Brer Rabbit. "I guess you better come on down, Brer Fox, and we'll go hunt for another tree."

Brer Fox started down the tree. He was doing fine until he got to the lowest limb. It was a long way from there to the ground. What was he going to do? He didn't have

any claws to cling by and not enough leg to do any serious clamping.

"Come on down, Brer Fox! Come on down!" Brer Rabbit yelled.

"How am I supposed to do that?"

"I'll tell you what, Brer Fox. Jump, and I'll catch you." Brer Rabbit stood out from the tree with his arms out. "I'm ready, Brer Fox!"

Brer Fox looked up. He looked down. He looked all around.

"Come on, Brer Fox! My arms are getting tired!"

Brer Fox took a deep breath, closed his eyes and jumped.

The instant he jumped, Brer Rabbit hopped out the way, crying, "Ow! Ow! Ow! I got a thorn stuck in my foot! Ow! It hurts!"

It didn't hurt half as bad as Brer Fox hurt when he hit the ground! KERBLAMABLAM BLAM BLAM! It took Brer Fox a while to pick himself up and feel all around to make sure he still had all his parts and they were in working order.

As for Brer Rabbit, he laughed so much, that laughter got fat.

Why the Hawk Likes to Eat Chickens

One of the most awesome sights in nature is a hawk diving from the belly button of the sky and catching something to eat. It's not a sight you see often. You got to be at the right place at the right time and looking in the right direction, 'cause it happens faster than a flea can blink.

Just as Brer Fox was having a problem keeping his belly full, there was a day when Brer Hawk was having the same problem. He flew this way. He flew that way. He even flew the other way. There was nothing to eat in any direction.

Finally he noticed the Sun up in the elements, and he flew up to see him. "Howdy."

The Sun howdied back, and the two got to talking about first one thing and another the way folks do when they are striking up an acquaintance.

Finally, Brer Hawk told the Sun the troubles he was having finding something to eat.

"Well," offered the Sun, "if you can catch me in bed, I'll show you where to find all you can eat."

Brer Hawk was up bright and early the next morning, but the Sun was already strutting across the sky. Every morning Brer Hawk got up earlier and earlier but he was never early enough. He sat up all night and still the Sun managed to get out of bed before Brer Hawk could catch him.

Not only was Brer Hawk losing sleep, he was also getting skinnier and skinnier. One morning after he had failed to catch the Sun in bed again, he was sitting in the top of a great big pine tree, wondering what to do. Just then he heard something on the ground calling him.

"Yo! Brer Hawk!"

He looked down and saw Brer Rooster. "What you want?" Brer Hawk hollered. "Stop bothering me. Go scratch up your little worms and cackle over them, but leave me alone."

"What's the matter, Brer Hawk? You in a mighty bad mood. And how come you look so pale? How come you look so lonesome?"

Brer Hawk didn't know if Brer Rooster had a degree in psychotherapy but he sure knew how to ask the right questions and that was good enough. He dropped out of the tree and settled on the fence rail where he could talk to Brer Rooster.

Brer Hawk told him that he had been trying to catch the Sun in bed.

Brer Rooster laughed so hard he almost lost his cock-a-doodle-do. When he managed to stop, he said, "Brer Hawk, why didn't you come to me? I catch the Sun in bed every morning. I'm his alarm clock!"

"You are!"

"I are!"

"Well, I'll be!"

"You'll be what?"

"Never mind," Brer Hawk said.

"If you say so. Tell you what. Sleep here tonight. In the morning when I'm ready to wake the Sun up, you can fly off and catch him in bed."

And that's what happened. The next morning along about three-ninety-seven, Brer Rooster woke up Brer Hawk. "Go get him!"

Brer Hawk stretched his great wings and he was off. Ain't nothing in creation can fly like a hawk. He flew straight up until he passed the morning star. Then he took a left and a right, did a loop-de-loop, and went through the black of night, and there on the other side was where the Sun lived. (The Sun had decided that living in a hole was dangerous after Brer Fox had fallen asleep on top of it.) Brer Hawk walked through the door, past the living room, and right into the bedroom.

There, lying in bed, the covers pulled up to his chin, snoring, was none other than the Sun.

"Time for daybreak!" hollered Brer Hawk. "What you doing laying in bed, you lazy scoundrel. Folks are waiting to eat breakfast and you gon' make 'em late."

"Who that?" the Sun said.

"Me!"

"What you want to wake me up for? Now I'm going to have a headache all day."

"Tough. I'm hungry and you said that if I caught you in bed, you would show me where to find food."

The Sun was mad at having been woken up early. "Who told you where to find me?"

"Brer Rooster."

The Sun raised up from the bed and gave Brer Hawk a big wink with his right eye. "Brer Rooster knows where you can find a meal."

Brer Hawk flew back down to earth and told Brer Rooster what the Sun had said.

"Why would he say something like that? I'm having trouble finding enough food to take care of my own family."

Brer Hawk was desperate now. "Brer Rooster, I'm hungrier than your family. I have got to find something to eat."

"You're welcome to dig here in the dirt with me. The worms are big and juicy this time of year."

Brer Hawk shook his head. He needed a lot more than worms. He flew to the top of the pine tree and sat there wondering what he was going to do.

He hadn't been there long before Miss Hen with all of the children came to help Brer Rooster hunt for worms. That was when Brer Hawk understood why the Sun had winked and sent him back to Brer Rooster.

Brer Hawk dropped out of that tree like bad news. Before anyone knew what was happening, he had grabbed one of the little chickens in his sharp talons and flown away with it.

From that day to this, the Hawk has never been hungry. And from that day to this, Brer Rooster has never told anyone else where the Sun sleeps. It just so happens that I know too, but I think it best if I keep my mouth shut.

The Little Boy and His Dogs

Once upon a time there was a woman who lived in a house beside a road. She had a little boy who, seems to me, was about your size. He might've been a little broader across the shoulders and a little longer in the leg, but if you looked up one side and down the other, he was just about your size. And like you, he was also very smart.

This little boy had a sister. But one day someone came along and kidnapped her. Quite naturally this made the mother and the little boy very sad.

Every day the little boy climbed to the top of the tallest tree and looked in every direction for some sign of his sister. She had vanished without a trace.

One day when he was at the top of the tree, he saw two finely dressed women walking down the road. He hurried and told his mother.

"How are they dressed, Son?"

"Mighty fine, Momma. Mighty fine with puffed out dresses and long green veils."

"How do they look, Son?"

"Like they brand-new, Momma."

"Well, they don't sound like none of our kinfolk, do they, Son?"

"No, they don't, Momma."

The finely dressed ladies came down the road and stopped at the house where the woman and the little boy lived.

"Could we trouble you for some water?" they asked.

The little boy got the dipper and filled it with water. The ladies put the dipper under their veils and drank and drank and drank like they hadn't had water since Adam was a baby.

The little boy said, "Momma? They lapping up the water like animals."

"I reckon that's the way rich folks drink," she responded.

Then the ladies asked for some bread. The little boy got some from the kitchen. The women ate the bread like they hadn't put anything in their stomachs since Eve was in diapers.

"Momma? The women got big long teeth that curve and sparkle in the light."

"I reckon that's how rich people's teeth are, Son."

Then the ladies asked for water to wash their hands. The boy brought the wash basin and filled it with water.

He watched them wash their hands. "Momma? The ladies got hairy hands and arms."

"I reckon that's how rich folks' hands and arms are, Son."

Then the ladies asked the woman if the little boy could show them where the road forked.

The little boy didn't want to go. "Momma, don't nobody need to be shown where the road forks."

"I reckon rich folks ain't got much sense, Son."

The little boy started to sniff and cry because he did not want to go with the two women. His mother told him that he should be ashamed of himself. "Go show the ladies what they want, Son. And who knows? You might find your sister."

The little boy had two dogs. They were bad dogs too. One was named Minnyminny Morack. The other was named Follamalinska. They were so bad that they had to be tied up day and night with great strong ropes.

The little boy got a pan of water and put it in the middle of the floor. Then he got a limb from a willow tree.

"Momma? If the water in the dish turns to blood, let Minnyminny Morack and Follamalinska loose. If the limb from the willow tree starts shaking, set the dogs on my track."

The little boy took some eggs and put them in his pocket in case he got hungry. Then he set off to show the two ladies where the big road forked.

He hadn't gone far before he noticed the two ladies panting like wild animals. He guessed that was how rich folks breathed when the weather was hot and they were tired.

When the ladies thought the little boy wasn't paying them any attention (but he was), one of them dropped down on all fours, just like a wolf. A minute later the other lady dropped down on all fours and started running.

The little boy thought to himself, Well, if that's how rich folks rest themselves when they tired, I better be thinking about resting myself.

He saw a big pine tree and climbed up it quickly.

The animals turned back into ladies and one of them hollered, "What're you doing, little boy?"

"I'm resting myself."

"Why don't you rest on the ground?"

"I can rest better up where it's cool."

The ladies walked around and around the tree. "Little boy, little boy! You better come down and show us how to get to the fork in the big road."

"It's easy, ladies. Keep going straight until the road forks. You can't miss it. And anyway, I'm afraid to come down. What if I fall and hurt one of you?"

"You better come down or we'll tell your mother how bad you are."

The little boy answered, "While you're telling her that, tell her how scared I am."

The ladies were angry now. They growled and snorted. They pulled off their bonnets and their veils and their dresses, and lo and behold, guess what the little boy saw? Two great big panthers! They had great big yellow eyes and long sharp teeth and great long tails. They looked up at the little boy and growled. The little boy shivered. The panthers tried to climb the tree but they had clipped their claws so they could wear gloves, which meant they couldn't climb anymore.

Then one of the panthers sat down in the road and made some marks in the sand.

BOING! The tails of both panthers turned into axes. One panther was on one side of the tree; the other panther was on the other side, and they started axing away. Before long, the tree was ready to fall.

The little boy remembered the eggs in his pocket. He took one, broke it, and said, "Place, fill up!"

The places where the panthers had cut the tree filled right up. The tree looked like nothing had ever happened to it.

That didn't bother the panthers. They started whaling away at the tree again. When the tree was almost ready to fall, the boy broke another egg and said, "Place, fill up!" The tree became like new again.

The little boy had only one egg left, and the panthers were once again axing the tree.

Just about this time the little boy's mother noticed the pan of water turning to blood. She went to the yard and untied Minnyminny Morack and Follamalinska. As soon as she returned to the house she saw the willow limb trembling and shaking. She hollered to the dogs, "Go!" The dogs took off!

The little boy heard the dogs coming. "Come on, my dogs! Come on!"

The panthers stopped axing and listened. "You hear anything?" one asked the other.

"I don't hear nothing," said the little boy. "Go on with your chopping."

The panthers went back to axing, but they couldn't shake the feeling that dogs were coming. Before they could change from panthers to ladies, Minnyminny Morack and Follamalinska caught them.

The little boy hollered to the dogs, "Shake 'em and bite 'em. Drag 'em round and round until you drag 'em ten miles."

So the dogs drug the panthers ten miles. By the time they drug them back, those panthers were cold and stiff.

The little boy climbed down from the tree and decided to see if he couldn't find his sister. Off into the woods he and the dogs went.

They hadn't gone far before he saw a house sitting off by itself. The dogs smelled around the house. The hair on their bodies stood straight up. The boy saw a little girl carrying wood and water. She was very pretty, but she was clothed in rags and crying. Minnyminny Morack and Follamalinska were wagging their tails. The little boy had found his sister.

He went up to her and asked her her name.

"I don't know," she said. She had been scared for so long that she had forgotten.

"Why are your crying?" he wanted to know.

"Because I have to work so hard."

"Whose house is this?"

"It belongs to a huge black Bear. He's the one who makes me work so hard. The water is for the big pot. The wood is to make the water boil, and the boiling water in the pot is how the Bear cooks the people he feeds to his children."

The little boy didn't tell her he was her brother. Instead he said, "Well, I believe I'll stay and have supper with the Bear."

"Oh, no! You mustn't! You mustn't!"

But the little boy walked in the house. He saw that the Bear had two big children. One was sitting on the bed. The other was sitting by the fireplace. The little boy sat down and waited.

The Bear was a long time in coming home, though. So, the little girl cooked supper for herself and the boy. After they ate, the little boy told her that he would love to comb her hair. Her hair hadn't been combed in so long, however, that it was all tangled up. She started crying at the thought of a comb going through it.

"Don't worry," he told her. "I'll be very gentle." He warmed water on the stove, worked it into her hair and combed it until it was soft and curly.

Finally, the Bear came home. He was surprised to see

the little boy sitting there. He was very polite, though, shook the little boy's hand, and admired how pretty the little girl's hair was.

"How did you make her hair look so nice?" the Bear wanted to know.

"It's easy," said the little boy.

"Well, if that's the case, would you mind curling my hair?"

"Why, not at all. Fill the big pot with water."

The Bear filled the big pot with water.

"Build up the fire under the pot and heat the water."

The Bear built up the fire.

"When the water is scalding hot, stick your head in. And your hair will curl right up."

When the water was scalding hot, the Bear stuck his head in. The scalding water curled his hair until it came right off. That was the end of the Bear.

The Bear's children were upset when they saw what happened to their daddy. They started biting the little boy and the little girl. Minnyminny Morack and Follamalinska got hold of them bear children and when the dogs were finished, there wasn't enough left to figure out who they used to be.

Then, the little boy told the little girl he was her brother and they went home to their mother.

The Man and the Wild Cattle

Once there was a man who lived next to a great woods. I don't believe there're any woods in the world big as that woods was. If you got on a horse and rode in a straight line for seven days and seven nights, that's how wide the woods were. If you got on the same horse and made him go as fast as he could go for eleven days and eleven nights, you would go as far as the woods was long.

In these woods were herds of horned cattle. Might've been some deer and moose and other creatures in there, but most of the creatures were horned cattle.

The man would hunt the cattle for their hides. He had

a bow and arrow and two big dogs. What cattle he couldn't get with his bow and arrow, the dogs would get. These dogs were almost as big as the cattle, and they were as ferocious as lion's breath. One dog was named Minny-minny Morack and the other was called Follamalinska.

That's right. The man in this story is the little boy in the last story, after he grew up.

The man and the dogs hunted the horned cattle day and night. Things finally got so bad for the cattle that they had a meeting. They conferred and debated and caucused. Finally they concluded that the only way they had a chance was to get the man by himself. But that would be hard to do because the man never went anywhere without the dogs.

One of the calves said she would change herself into a pretty young woman and make the man marry her. Then, she would tie the dogs so they couldn't go out, and then the man would be alone.

The next time the man went hunting in the woods, he was surprised to see a beautiful young woman. She was as pretty as red shoes with blue shoelaces. The man looked at her. She looked at him, and that took care of that.

Don't come asking me how a calf could turn itself into a woman. Back in them days animals could do all kinds of things they can't do now. At least, we don't think they can. But what do we know? I know some folks that act like animals and, for all I know, they might be.

Anyway, with the look the man gave her and the look she gave him, it wasn't long before they were looking at the preacher and saying, "I do."

They hadn't been married too long before the man announced that he would get up the next morning, take the dogs, and go hunting.

When he went to sleep, his wife took the dogs off in the woods and tied them to a big tree. The next morning the man couldn't find his dogs. He wasn't concerned because sometimes they went off by themselves. And if he needed them, all he had to do was call their names and no matter how far away they were, they would come running.

Off the man went into the woods.

The horned cattle saw him coming. When the man saw them, they ran. The man followed. Each time he came close, they ran and he followed. Deeper and deeper into the woods they went and deeper and deeper into the woods the man followed.

Finally the cattle came to a clearing. When the man arrived, it looked as if all the wild cattle in the world were there.

The man put an arrow in his bow and let it fly. At the same time he hollered for his dogs: "Minnyminny Morack! Follamalinska! Come, dogs! Come!"

He listened. He didn't hear the dogs coming. The man kept shooting at the cattle, but they moved out of the way of his arrows. Soon, the man was down to his last three arrows.

"Now we got you," the horned cattle said. "Let's see how you like it when we take *your* hide."

The man stuck one of his arrows in the ground. The arrow grew to be a huge tree, and the man was resting on the highest limb.

The horned cattle were angry now. They butted their heads against the tree. The tree didn't budge. They pawed and snorted. That might have made them feel better but it didn't do a thing to the tree. Some of the cattle got some axes and started cutting down the tree.

I understand you might not understand how cattle could cut a tree down with an axe. That's simple. If the cattle could talk and think, using an axe wasn't nothing. Now, if I'd said the cattle set the clock on my VCR, that would be unusual!

The man was sitting in the top of the tree, hollering, "Minnyminny Morack! Follamalinska! Come, dogs! Come!"

At the base of the tree, the horned cattle were chopping on the tree. "Blam! Blip-blip-blam! Blip-blip-blam!"

The tree started to shake. The man called the dogs, but they didn't come. The axes called the tree, and it came— right down to the ground—KERBLASHITY BLAM!

But the man stuck another arrow in the ground, and the tree grew up twice as tall and twice as big around as the first time.

"Minnyminny Morack! Follamalinska! Come, dogs! Come!"

The axes called the tree. "Down! Down! Dip-dip-down! Down-dip! Dip-down! Dippy-dip! Dippy-down!"

The dogs didn't come, but the tree did—KERBLASH-ITY BLAM!

The man stuck his last arrow in the ground and the tree grew up twice as tall and twice as big around as before.

The horned cattle started working their axes again. "Down! Down! Dip-dip-down! Down-dip! Dip-down! Dippy-dip! Dippy-down!"

"Minnyminny Morack! Follamalinska! Come, dogs! Come!"

The dogs could hear the man calling for them. They pulled at the ropes as hard as they could, but the ropes were big and strong. Finally, the dogs began chewing and gnawing on the ropes. Just as the last tree started to sway, the dogs got free.

The man heard them coming. "Minnyminny Morack! Follamalinska! Come, dogs! Come!"

The axes talked. "Tree-down! Tree-down! Trip-trip-tree-down!"

Just as the tree came down—KERBLASHITY BLAM!—the dogs rushed up. They did away with the horned cattle in a hurry.

When the dogs were finished, the man looked at the dead horned cattle and happened to notice a very pretty young cow.

When he went home, his wife wasn't there. He looked all over for her, but he never saw her again.

———————————

"Cutta Cord-La"

One winter times got sho' 'nuf hard among the animals. The times was so hard that they didn't even get soft when spring sprung. And spring didn't sprang too high that year, 'cause they wasn't any rain. If there wasn't any rain, nothing grew. If nothing grew, there wasn't much for the animals to eat.

I don't know if you ever been hungry. I remember one time one of my children come running in the house and said, "I'm starved." I told him not to be using that word around me! No, sir! He don't know what starving is and never will.

Starving is when you don't have no food, and there is no food to be had. Starving is when you're too weak to cry, and if you could cry, there wouldn't be enough water inside you to make tears. But maybe the worst thing about starving is that it twists your mind. Just plain being hungry does funny things to my mind. You know what I mean? When I'm real hungry and you ask me a question, I might try to bite your head off. But when my belly is full, you ask me the same question, I'll be as nice as warm syrup on hot pancakes. Well, if being hungry makes you grouchy, starving can make you crazy. That's what happened to Brer Wolf.

One day he and Brer Rabbit were talking about how hungry they were and how they were afraid they might die.

"What we gon' do?" Brer Wolf asked.

Brer Rabbit sighed and shook his head. "Naw, we can't do that."

"Do what?"

Brer Rabbit shook his head again. "Forget I brought it up. It's just too gruesome to think about."

"How do I know it's gruesome if I can't think about it?"

Brer Rabbit sighed deeply. Then he started crying.

"What's the matter?" Brer Wolf wanted to know.

Brer Rabbit sniffed. "I don't know what else we can do except kill your grandmother."

Brer Wolf started crying.

The two of them cried for a while. Finally, Brer Wolf said, "I'm so hungry."

"Me too!" howled Brer Rabbit.

Brer Wolf got up, went home, and killed his grandmother. He took her body into town and sold it to a hunter. With the money he bought a lot of groceries and him and Brer Rabbit were able to eat for a while.

But the day came when the food ran out.

Brer Wolf said, "I ain't had nothing to eat in three days, Brer Rabbit. It's time for you to kill your grandmother."

Brer Rabbit looked at him like he was crazy. "It's time for me to do what? I can't kill my grandmother."

Brer Wolf was angry, very, very angry. "I'll make you kill your grandmother."

Brer Rabbit knew that Brer Wolf was serious. So, the first chance he got, Brer Rabbit sneaked away, took his grandmother, led her off in the woods, and hid her at the top of a coconut tree.

Don't come telling me that there're no coconut trees in the United States. There ain't none *now*! Back in them days, however, bananas grew in New York where the Empire State Building is now. That's what King Kong was looking for when he was up there with that skinny white woman.

Brer Rabbit gave his grandmother a basket with a cord tied to it and every morning he came to the tree and sang:

"Granny! Granny! O Granny! Jutta cord-la!"

When his grandmother heard his sweet voice, she would let the basket down with the cord, and Brer Rabbit would put in it whatever he had managed to find to eat. She would pull the cord and haul the basket up.

This was the routine, and every morning Brer Wolf watched from hiding. Finally, one day after Brer Rabbit left, Brer Wolf went to the base of the tree and sang out:

"Granny! Granny! O Granny! Shoot-a cord-la!"

Grandma Rabbit listened. "My grandson don't sound like that."

The next morning she told Brer Rabbit that somebody had come and sung, "Shoot-a cord-la." Brer Rabbit laughed because he knew who it had been.

When he left, Brer Wolf came out of hiding again.

"Granny! Granny! O Granny! Jutta cord-la!"

Grandma Rabbit listened. "You sound like you have a bad cold, Grandson. Your voice sound mighty rough." Grandma Rabbit peeped out of the tree and saw who it was. "Go 'way from here, Brer Wolf! You can't fool me! Go away!"

Brer Wolf was ten times mad now. He went off in the woods to think. Then he went to the blacksmith and asked him how he could get a fine voice like Brer Rabbit.

"Let me put this red hot poker down your throat. That'll make your voice smooth."

Brer Wolf gave his consent.

The blacksmith stuck the poker down Brer Wolf's throat. It hurt something fierce. When his throat was all healed, his voice was as smooth as chocolate pudding.

He went to the coconut tree.

"Granny! Granny! O Granny! Jutta cord-la!"

Grandmother Rabbit heard the voice and it sounded just like Brer Rabbit. She lowered the basket. Brer Wolf climbed in. Grandmother Rabbit started to pull.

"My! My! My grandson loves me so much that he bring me lots of food this time."

She pulled and just as the basket got close to the top, she stopped to rest.

Brer Wolf looked down. When he saw how far it was to the ground, his head started to swim. He looked up, and Grandmother Rabbit was staring at him with a strange smile on her face. He looked down again and there, at the base of the tree, was Brer Rabbit!

"Granny! Granny! O Granny! CUTTA CORD-LA!"

Brer Rabbit sang out.

Grandmother cut the cord. Brer Wolf dropped to the ground and broke his neck.

Brer Wolf was never hungry again.

Why Brer Bull Growls and Grumbles

I wonder what it was like back when animals could change themselves into people and back again. Goodness gracious! You wouldn't know whether you were talking to a person or buzzard. On the other hand, it must've been a lot of fun too. I probably would've turned myself into a cat so I could sleep all the time.

Brer Bull was lonely. All day he stood in the field and ate grass. How would you like to spend your life eating grass by yourself? Brer Bull was not only tired of being alone, he was also tired of eating grass. He decided to change himself into a man and find a wife.

There was a woman who lived with her son in a little

house on the other side of the road from the field where Brer Bull lived. Brer Bull changed himself into a man and showed up on the woman's doorstep, asking for a cool drink of water. Wasn't long after that but the man was at her house every night for supper.

The little boy's name was Simmy-Sam, and he was smart. He noticed that when the man came for supper, Brer Bull was not in the field. When Brer Bull was grazing in the field, the man was nowhere to be seen.

One day when Brer Bull was eating grass in the pasture, Simmy-Sam hid behind a tree and waited and watched. Close to suppertime, Brer Bull sat down like a dog. He shook his head and said, "Ballybaloobill!" His horns shrunk, his tail shriveled, and quicker than you can blink your eye, Brer Bull had become a man.

Simmy-Sam ran home so he could be there before the man came. All during supper, Simmy-Sam was quiet. He was afraid his mother was going to marry Brer Bull. His own daddy had died, but he didn't want a bull to be his new one.

A day or two later his momma told him she was going to marry the man.

"You can't do that, Momma," blurted Simmy-Sam. "You can't do that! He ain't no man. That's Brer Bull! I seen him change his shape. That's Brer Bull!"

His momma was in love, and when you in love, you wouldn't know sense if it walked up and hit you over the head with a brick.

His momma told him to stop making up stories or she would snatch him baldheaded. She left the hair on his head, but she didn't leave much skin on his bottom because she took a belt and gave Simmy-Sam a good whipping for telling tales.

Simmy-Sam didn't say anything. But every night when the man left the house, Simmy-Sam followed him. When the man got to the pasture, he said, "Billybalooball!" And the horns grew out of his head, and the hooves came out on his hands and feet. His clothes dropped off, and he was a bull again.

One evening when the man was sitting at the table eating supper, Simmy-Sam said, "Billybalooball!" The man put his hands up to his head, but there wasn't a thing he could do. The horns started to grow as his face changed into that of a bull; the hooves came out of his hands and feet; his clothes dropped off and before the man could get out

the door, he had changed into Brer Bull. His tail curled up on top of his back, and he ran to the pasture.

Simmy-Sam's mother apologized for thinking he was telling tales, but her apology didn't help his bottom much. Ain't no apology in the world ever made swelling go down or a bruise go away. Maybe it's better to be sorry *before* you hurt somebody.

Simmy-Sam was smart enough to know that Brer Bull was not done. Sure enough. Every time Simmy-Sam went to the yard to play, Brer Bull watched him.

Creatures are very patient. Brer Bull waited. He waited until the day Simmy-Sam's mother sent him into the woods to get kindling wood. She gave Simmy-Sam some pancakes to eat in case he got hungry.

Off Simmy-Sam went. Soon as he was deep in the woods, Brer Bull leaped over the fence and took off after him.

Simmy-Sam heard Brer Bull coming and climbed a tall tree. Brer Bull hit the tree with his horns—kerblip! He got a running start and hit the tree again—kerblam! Tree didn't move.

Guess what Brer Bull did then? Changed himself into a man. Guess what the man had in his hands? An axe!

"I got you now!" the man said, and he started in with the axe. "Come on down and save me the trouble of bringing you down."

"I'm scared."

"Scared or no scared, you better come down."

The man was chopping on the tree as fast as he could—blip! blap! blip! blap!

Simmy-Sam reached in the bag where the pancakes were. He dropped one on the man. The man's arm fell off. The man didn't stop to put the arm back on. He chopped with the arm he had left.

Simmy-Sam dropped another pancake on the man. His other arm fell off. The man couldn't cut anymore, but Simmy-Sam was still scared. So he dropped the last pancake, and the man's head fell off. Simmy-Sam climbed down and went home.

The man put all his body parts back on, changed himself back into a bull, and from that day to this, that is what he has remained. However, from that day to this, Brer Bull has growled and grumbled like somebody hurt his feelings.

And have you ever noticed that bulls don't like little children to come close to them? Well, now we know why.

Brer Rabbit, King Polecat, and the Gingercakes

Brer Polecat was king of all the creatures that run about after dark. You might have thought that Brer Lion was the king, and he was. But he was the king of all the creatures that run about in the morning, afternoon, evening, *and* night. Except that Brer Lion didn't like to be awakened at night to do any kinging, and that's when Brer Polecat took over.

Brer Rabbit noticed how much Brer Polecat enjoyed kinging. It seemed to him that Brer Polecat might enjoy it a little *too* much.

One afternoon when King Polecat and all the animals were together, Brer Rabbit cleared his throat. "Hear! Hear! I have an announcement to make!"

Everybody gathered around to listen. "I think every creature, winged and paw, feathered and skin, can agree that when it comes to kinging, can't nobody do it better than Brer Polecat."

The creatures certainly agreed with that.

"Seeing as how that is the case, I propose a new law. Every time any of us meet Brer Polecat in the road we have to shut our eyes and hold our nose."

The creatures thought that was a good idea except some of them weren't too eager to shut their eyes.

"If I close my eyes, Brer Hawk might eat me," said Brer Mouse.

"If I close my eyes, I might walk into a a tree," Brer Bear put in.

"If I close my eyes, I might go to sleep," said Brer Dog.

Brer Rabbit ignored their objections. "Seems to me there ain't no risk too big to honor such a king as Brer Polecat."

So, it was agreed. Anytime any of the creatures saw Brer Polecat in the road, they would close their eyes and hold their noses until he had passed.

Brer Polecat lived in a big house with Brer Coon and Brer Mink. Brer Coon was known far and wide for the gingercakes he made. There wasn't a party or function of any kind held without a stack of Brer Coon's gingercakes being served.

If Brer Rabbit thought about Brer Coon, his stomach started growling for gingercakes. That's what happened the very next morning after the new law was passed. Brer Rabbit thought about Brer Coon and his stomach started growling. Brer Rabbit headed for Brer Coon's.

When he got there, he bought a stack of gingercakes. He was getting ready to eat them when he remembered that he didn't have any garlic to eat them with. Brer Coon said he didn't like garlic on his, so he didn't have any.

"Please watch my gingercakes," Brer Rabbit asked Brer Coon. "I'm going to hurry home and get some garlic."

Brer Coon said he would and off Brer Rabbit went.

Brer Rabbit was hardly out of sight before King Polecat showed up. Brer Coon shut his eyes and held his nose. Brer Polecat ate the gingercakes Brer Rabbit had just bought, and off he went.

A little later, Brer Rabbit came lippitin' back with the garlic. "Brer Coon? You said you would watch my gingercakes."

Brer Coon didn't know what to say. "I didn't see anybody take them."

Brer Rabbit wasn't too happy, but his stomach wanted some gingercakes real bad. He ran his hand in his pocket and bought another stack.

"I got my garlic with me, so I'll watch these gingercakes my own self."

Brer Rabbit sat down, pulled out his knife and fork, and put some garlic on the cakes. Just as he was about to do away with that stack, here come King Polecat.

Brer Rabbit jumped up, held his nose and shut his eyes. Well, not really. A rabbit's eyes are so big that he can't shut them all the way. So as soon as King Polecat reached for the gingercakes, Brer Rabbit hollored, "Drop them cakes!"

King Polecat jumped back. "You didn't play fair, Brer Rabbit! Your eyes were supposed to be shut! No fair! No fair!"

Brer Rabbit apologized and explained that he couldn't shut his eyes. "Give me back my gingercakes or I'll tell all the creatures what a low-down thief you are and then you won't be king anymore."

King Polecat was angry, but what could he do? If he was going to be king, he had to stay on Brer Rabbit's good side. Of course, when all the creatures saw how nice Brer Polecat treated Brer Rabbit, always asking his advice, they understood who was *really* king.

The Fool

Once there was a man who acted strange. Some mornings he put on one shoe and forgot the other and walked around all day with one shoe on and the other foot bare and he never noticed. Folks said he was cripple under his hat. But he worked hard, and when he finished his harvesting he had a crib full of corn. Every morning when he went out to admire his corn, the pile seemed to be a little lower than it had been the day before.

The fool watched his corn day and night and didn't see even an ear disappear, but the pile kept getting lower and lower.

The fool lived on the river. On the other side of the river was a deep woods. Somebody told the fool that squirrels were crossing the river, taking his corn, and hiding it in the woods.

The fool laughed. "If the squirrels can carry off my corn, they're welcome to it."

The fool got up early the next morning to see what he could see. Wasn't long before the squirrels came. They climbed in the crib, took an ear of corn, and started for the river.

When they got there, they took pieces of bark, put the corn on the bark, and perched on top of the corn. They raised their tails like sails and went across the river.

The fool could not believe his eyes. The next morning he watched. The same thing happened. Each squirrel took an ear of corn, laid it on a piece of bark, climbed on top, raised his tail and sailed on across.

The fool thought that squirrels were the most clever creatures he had ever seen. He laughed and laughed and told his neighbors what the squirrels were doing.

They asked him why he didn't stop them from stealing his corn.

He winked and grinned.

"You the biggest fool around here," they told him.

He winked and laughed.

With the squirrels coming every morning and taking his corn, it wasn't long before the fool didn't have much corn left. So, one morning he took his gun and his axe and went across the river to get his corn back.

He hadn't been looking for the squirrels long, before a rabbit jumped out of the woods. The fool raised his gun and fired. The rabbit ran into a covey of partridges. The sound of the gun scared a turkey, who flew up in a big tree. The man fired the other barrel, and the turkey fell dead across a tree limb.

The fool looked around and saw one dead rabbit, eleven dead partridges, and up in the tree a dead turkey. One partridge wasn't dead, though, and it ran off into the bushes. The fool followed, and what should he come upon but a nest of turkey eggs.

He took the turkey eggs and then climbed the tree to get the dead turkey. When he climbed up there, however, the turkey had dropped into a hole in the tree. The fool pulled the turkey out and guess what was in the hole? His corn!

The fool climbed down, took his axe, and started to chop down the tree. He hadn't been chopping long, before he noticed something sticky oozing out of the tree. He tasted it. You know what it was? Wasn't nothing but honey!

The fool plugged up the hole to keep the honey from oozing out. He picked up the dead rabbit, dead turkey, eleven dead partridges, and the turkey eggs, and started for home. As he was walking through the woods, another rabbit jumped out in front of him. The fool's gun wasn't loaded, so he threw it at the rabbit but missed.

The man went to pick up his gun, and the ground beneath his feet gave away. The next thing he knew he was in a dark hole. He felt around and touched something hard and cold. You know what it was? That's right! A barrel of money!

The hole wasn't that deep so the man lifted the barrel of money out and rolled it down to the river and loaded it on his canoe. When he got home he counted the money and discovered he was a rich man! There was forty-'leven thousand dollars in that barrel.

The next day the fool hitched up his horse and wagon and drove the long way around and went over the bridge to cross the river. He had some empty barrels in the wagon, and he filled them with the honey. The day after that he came back with more barrels and filled them with all the corn that was in the tree. There was a lot of corn in that tree because the squirrels had been stealing from more folks than him.

Just think. If the man hadn't been a fool, he never would've gotten rich.

How Brer Lion Lost His Hair

The lion might be the king of all the animals, but, if you ask me, I've always thought the lion was kind of funny looking. He has a lot of hair around his head and a little on his tail. But in between head and tail, why, he's buck naked.

That wasn't how the Lord made him. Uh-uh. Brer Lion used to be hairy all over. He had so much hair it drug on the ground like a cape. That's how come the Lion was king. Anybody with that much pretty hair couldn't be expected to do no work. Well, here's how the lion lost his hair.

One day over in the autumn, right after the first frost, Mr. Man knew it was hog-killing time. He laid wood in a pile and put rocks between the wood. Then he lay the barrel across the wood and the rocks at an angle, and set the wood on fire. He killed the hogs and took the rocks he had set between the wood. They were red-hot now, and he threw them in the barrel of water. Before long the water started boiling. Mr. Man soused the hogs in the water. When he took them out, the hair on the hogs was ready to drop off. Mr. Man scraped the hides until no hair was left.

After Mr. Man had soused and scraped all the hogs and took them to the barn where he would cure the meat, and everything was as still as a setting hen, Brer Rabbit came out from behind a bush. He went over to the fire to warm his hands.

He hadn't been there long before Brer Wolf and Brer Fox came along.

"Hello, friends," Brer Rabbit greeted them. "Howdy and welcome! I was just getting ready to take a warm bath like Mr. Man just gave his hogs. Would you care to join me?"

Brer Wolf and Brer Fox treated water like they treated work—they wouldn't go near it.

"Well, would you help me put these hot rocks in the barrel?"

They didn't see any harm in doing that. Soon, the water in the barrel was bubbling again. About that time, here come Brer Lion.

He growled. "What y'all doing?"

"I was just getting ready to take a bath," Brer Rabbit answered.

"That's what I need," Brer Lion roared. "How do I do it?"

"Just back right in," Brer Rabbit told him.

Brer Lion backed in. The water was hot, very, very hot. Brer Lion roared the loudest roar a lion would ever roar. AAAAAAAAARRRRRRRRRRRRRRRGGGGGGG-GGGGHHHHHHHHHHHHHHHH!!!!!!!!!!!! He scrambled trying to get out of that barrel, but he slipped in deeper, until he was in up to his shoulder blades.

When he finally got out, all the hair dropped off his body, except that around his neck and head and a little bit at the end of his tail. The only reason he had any hair there was because the end of his tail had been sticking out of a hole in the barrel.

He was a funny sight, but because he was the king, the animals didn't laugh at him. At least, not while he was in hearing range.

The Man and the Boots

There was a man who had a pair of new boots with red tops. He was sitting beside the road when he heard a wagon coming. He hid in a ditch and watched the wagon go by. It was filled with all kinds of things—new dishes, a VCR, a microwave, and a popcorn popper. The man with the boots wanted all them things for himself.

He ran through the woods until he was ahead of the

wagon. He took one of his boots and threw it in the road. Then he hid in the bushes to see what the man in the wagon would do.

In a few minutes the man in the wagon came along, saw the boot, and told his mule, "Whoa!" He looked at the boot and thought for a minute.

"If there were two of you, I'd take you. But one boot can't do me no good, not if I ain't got one wooden leg. Giddap!" And he drove on.

The man who owned the boots ran through the woods until he was ahead of the man in the wagon again. He threw the other boot in the road.

When the man in the wagon came along and saw this boot, he said, "Whoa! It looks like I'm in business. This boot makes the first one good for a man with two legs of flesh and bone." He jumped off the wagon and went back down the road to find the other boot.

As soon as he did, the man who owned the boots came out from hiding and took the VCR and the popcorn popper and the other things and hid in the woods with them.

Before long the man who owned the wagon came back. He had two boots now, but that was all he had. His wagon was empty! He didn't say anything. He didn't even act shocked or surprised.

He climbed in the wagon and started laughing. He looked in the boots and laughed harder.

The man who had put the boots in the road couldn't understand what was so funny about the boots.

He sneaked through the woods and came walking down the road toward the man in the wagon. The man in the wagon was laughing so hard, tears were coming down his face.

"I ain't never seen a man have so much fun by himself," the thief said to the man in the wagon.

"Well, if you had these boots, you would be happy too!"

The man in the road furrowed his brow. "What's wrong with the boots?"

"Not a thing! Not a thing!" the man in the wagon said, and started laughing again.

"You ain't losing your mind, are you?"

The man in the wagon said, "Well, if you were driving along a road and found what I found in them boots, you would be laughing just as hard."

The man in the road said, "I had a pair of boots just like them, and they didn't make me laugh."

"I guess the boots you had didn't have thousand-dollar bills inside them."

"Let me see them boots! Let me see them boots! I bet they're mine. You hand them over right now. I lost them boots yesterday."

"Are you sure these are your boots?" the man in the wagon asked.

"Absolutely, positively, and certainly. I got proof!"

The man in the wagon said, "Well, come up here and show me your proof."

The man in the road climbed up in the wagon but before he could do or say anything, the man in the wagon flung him down, tied him up, and carried him to town, where he handed him over to the high sheriff. There the man confessed to taking the VCR and the popcorn popper and the other stuff, and he had to make his home in jail for a long time after that.

Of course, the man in the wagon hadn't found anything in them boots. What the man who owned the boots didn't understand was that it's all right when the creatures take what don't belong to them, and play loose with the truth. They are creatures. But when folks try it, they will come to a bad end every time.

Why the Goat Has a Short Tail

Brer Billy Goat and Brer Dog were promenading around and being sociable one day when, suddenly, a big rainstorm came up.

"I left my umbrella at home," Brer Billy Goat said.

"Rain don't bother me," Brer Dog said.

"Well, I don't like the rain," Brer Billy Goat said and trotted as fast as he could until he came to a house. Brer Dog went along with him.

Brer Billy Goat knocked on the door and said, "Baaaaaa!"

Brer Dog wagged his tail and said, "Arf! Arf! Arf!"

The peephole in the door opened, and guess whose house it was? Brer Wolf! He looked at Brer Billy Goat and Brer Dog out there in the rain. "Well, well, well. Why don't you all come in out of the wet?"

Brer Dog shook his head and began kicking up dirt and gravel with his back two legs. You know why? He smelled blood from inside Brer Wolf's house. Brer Billy Goat saw how Brer Dog was acting and he decided that he shouldn't go in either.

"Come in and sit by the fire and dry yourselves off," Brer Wolf implored.

Brer Billy Goat and Brer Dog shook their heads.

Brer Wolf thought that if he could get Brer Billy Goat and Brer Dog to dancing, then he could get them in the house and have them for dinner. He took down his fiddle and started in to playing. Brer Billy Goat wouldn't dance.

Finally, Brer Wolf asked, "Tell me something. How do you all get meat?"

"I depend on my teeth," Brer Billy Goat said.

"Me too," answered Brer Dog.

"Well, I depend on my four feet," Brer Wolf said, and he opened the door and started after Brer Billy Goat and Brer Dog.

Off they went through the rain. They ran until they came to a big creek.

"What we going to do?" Brer Billy Goat asked Brer Dog.

"I'm going to swim," Brer Dog responded.

Brer Billy Goat started to cry. "I can't swim a lick."

Brer Dog said, "Don't worry." He reached in his pocket and pulled out a rabbit's foot. He touched Brer Billy Goat with it. Brer Billy Goat turned into a white rock. Brer Dog leaped into the creek and swam across.

Brer Wolf came up about that time, but he was scared of the water. Brer Dog was on the other bank now and he hollered over, "You look like you scared, Brer Wolf. You made Brer Billy Goat drown, but you scared of me. I dare you to throw that white rock at me!"

Brer Wolf was mad. He reached down, picked up the rock and threw it as hard as he could at Brer Dog. The instant the rock hit the ground it turned into Brer Billy Goat.

Brer Billy Goat shook himself a time or two and then hollered, "What you trying to do? Break my neck?"

Then, Brer Billy Goat looked at himself, and that's when

he noticed that his long tail had broken off when he hit the ground. But he was so happy that the rest of him was all right that he didn't mind one bit. Not one bit.

Brer Buzzard and Brer Crow

One day Brer Buzzard and Brer Crow found themselves perched in the same tree together. They spoke politely, but that was about it.

Brer Crow had heard that Brer Buzzard had been going through the community bragging about how he could outfly Brer Crow. Before long Brer Buzzard said that very thing to Brer Crow's face.

"Can't do much flying with them squinchy wings of yours, can you?"

A crow ain't no sparrow-sized bird, if you know what I mean. Their wings make a nice-sized shadow. But compared to Brer Buzzard's, they were not large at all.

They got to arguing back and forth and forth and back about whose wings could stir up the most wind and who could fly the farthest and who could fly the fastest and who could fly the highest, and someone would've called the police if there had been any to call.

Finally, Brer Crow admitted, "You can probably outfly me, Brer Buzzard, but I know this. You can't outsing me."

"How you know? I ain't never tried."

"I'll bet you a new suit and a hat that I can sit here and sing longer than you can."

"Let's get to it," Brer Buzzard declared.

"Not so fast. I just thought of something. This ain't a fair bet because you are bigger than I am. You got a bigger wind chamber and can hold more air, and therefore, you can probably sing longer than me. Well, no matter. I'm going to beat you singing if I die trying."

They shook hands and Brer Crow shut his eyes and started singing:

> *Susu! susu! gangook!*
> *Mother, mother, lalho!*

Brer Buzzard shut his eyes and he started in to singing:

> *Susu! susu! gangook!*
> *Mother, mother, lalho!*

Don't come asking me what the song was about. That's the way it was given to me. If you can get on the inside of it, more power to you. If you can't, don't fling none of

the blame on me. Young as you are, you know just as much about that song as I do and probably more, because you ain't been trying to figure it out as long as I have.

They sang and they sang. Brer Buzzard would stop for a minute every now and then to catch his breath and then he would go right back to it:

Susu! susu! gangook!
Mother, mother, lalho!

Brer Crow would stop to catch his breath and then he would go back to it:

Susu! susu! gangook!
Mother, mother, lalho!

It went on like this until they both began to get hungry. But Brer Buzzard was the biggest, and it looked like he was going to win the contest. Brer Crow was very hungry, and his voice was getting weak, but he hadn't given up.

Somewhere between hungriness and starvation Brer Crow saw Miss Crow flying over. He sang out as loud as he could, "*Susu*! go tell my children—*susu*!—to bring my dinner—*gangook*!—and tell them—*mother, mother*—to bring it quick—*lalho*!"

Wasn't long before the Crow family brought Brer Crow more food than he could eat. Brer Crow got his strength back and he sang so loud his kin began to wish they had let him starve.

As for Brer Buzzard, well, he didn't have no kin to bring him any food, but he wasn't about to lose the contest. He sang and he sang. He got hungrier and hungrier. He got weaker and weaker. Finally he dropped out of the tree.

You know? There're folks who would rather die than lose.

The Blacksmith and the Devil

I was sitting here thinking about the days when the creatures and the people could talk to one another, the days when creatures could turn into people and back again. Don't none of that go on anymore, and you know why? There ain't no more darkness.

Think about it! In the cities where most people live, night don't never come. Things go from daytime to neon time. And it never gets quiet. You can't hear a cricket sing if it's noisy. And you can't see a Jacky-My-Lantern in neon time.

I saw a Jacky-My-Lantern once when I was growing up down South. I was coming along the big road on my way home. Where I had been and what I was doing is my business! Suddenly I saw this strange light hovering off at the edge of the woods. It looked like lightning bugs, but the light burned more intensely. It looked like it wanted me to follow it. I knew better than that. You follow a Jacky-My-Lantern, you won't come to the dinner table anymore. This is the story my daddy told me about where the Jacky-My-Lantern come from.

One time there was a blacksmith. This blacksmith was an evil man. He was so evil that red roses turned green when he walked by. He was so evil that rain turned to steam when it tried to fall on him. He was so evil that his shadow walked a block behind, so as not to be seen with him.

Word about the blacksmith got down to the Devil. Sounded like the kind of man whose acquaintance he wouldn't mind making. The Devil said the magic formula that only he knew, and his horns and tail and hooves disappeared and he dressed up in a suit and tie and appeared at the blacksmith's door.

"I don't care who you are or what you want!" the blacksmith said to his visitor. "Get out of my face!"

The Devil liked that. "I heard you were almost as evil as me."

"I'm so evil the grass asks my permission before it grows. And if I tell it no, it won't come up."

The Devil laughed. "You are definitely my kind of man."

The blacksmith was curious. "And who might you be?"

"I'm the Devil, and I've come to take you back to hell with me. I can use your talents."

The blacksmith preferred to use his talents on earth. He begged and pleaded and cried. "Please, Mr. Devil. Please don't take me! Let me stay right on earth where I can do your work for you. I'm more beneficial to you here."

The Devil thought it over. That was true. "I'll make you a proposition. You can live for one more year if you do as much evil as any man has ever done."

"You just watch me!"

The Devil was pleased. "To help you in your work, I'm going to give you something." The Devil put a spell on the blacksmith's chair and his sledgehammer. "Anybody who sits in your chair will be stuck there until you tell the chair to let him go. Any man who picks up your sledgehammer will have to pound with the hammer until you tell the hammer to quit." Then he gave the blacksmith enough money to last him a year even if he spent a hundred dollars a day. Then the Devil disappeared.

The blacksmith had a year that was not soon forgotten. If folks enjoyed doing good as much as the blacksmith enjoyed doing evil, the world would be free of problems.

The blacksmith was having so much fun doing evil that he forgot about the contract he had made with the Devil. He forgot until he looked out the window one morning. There was the Devil coming up the road. The blacksmith looked at the calendar and the year was up that day.

The Devil came in the house without knocking on the door. To tell the truth, the Devil came in without even *opening* the door. The blacksmith was pounding on a horseshoe and didn't pay the Devil no mind.

"It's time to go," the Devil announced.

"Give me a couple of minutes to finish up these jobs here."

"Ain't got time."

"What's the hurry? Ten minutes ain't gon' make that much difference, is it?"

"Compared to eternity, I guess not."

"There you go. Sit down in that chair and take it easy. I won't be long."

The Devil sat down in the chair, the same chair he had put the spell on. There he was, stuck. Blacksmith laughed and laughed. Devil tried to get up, but the chair held him tight.

Finally, the blacksmith made the Devil a proposition. "Tell you what. I'll let you out of the chair if you'll give me another year."

What could the Devil do? So the deal was struck. The Devil went back to hell, and the blacksmith had another year to do evil.

The year went by so fast that the morning the black-smith looked out the window and saw the Devil coming up the road he was sure somebody had stolen some pages off his calendar. But when he checked, they were all there. Time goes by so fast when you're having a good time, don't it?

"Let's go!" the Devil said. "And no, I am not going to sit down and wait until you finish what you're doing. The year's up, and you're coming with me this minute."

The blacksmith was beating on a piece of iron with his sledgehammer. "Well, all right," he said, resigned to his fate. He handed the Devil the sledge.

Without thinking the Devil took it, and remembered too late that he had cursed the hammer.

The hammer started hammering. It flung the Devil this way and that, that way and this, up and down, side to side, round and round. The blacksmith laughed and laughed.

"Give me one more year, and I'll tell the hammer to stop!"

"You got it!" the Devil hollered.

That year passed by quickly. The morning the Devil came for the blacksmith, there wasn't a thing the blacksmith could do. The Devil grabbed him and stuffed him in a sack and off down the road he went.

He hadn't gone far before he passed a lot of people at a barbecue. The Devil knew there had to be at least one evil person at a barbecue, so he stopped to see if he could find him. He put the sack underneath a table and began to mingle with the people.

As soon as the sack hit the ground, the blacksmith began to work his way out. Soon he was free. He saw a large bulldog. He stuffed it in the sack and sneaked away.

The Devil came back for his sack. He had found a lot of evil folks at the barbecue, but they needed ripening. He'd come back in a year or two.

He slung the sack over his shoulder and headed for hell. When he got there, his children came running up to him. "Who'd you bring back today, Daddy?"

"The most evil man on earth."

"Ooooo! Let's see him!"

The Devil untied the sack and the bulldog charged out, grabbed the Devil's children, and had almost done away with them before the Devil got a hold on him and dragged him outside the gates.

The years went by. The blacksmith was on the topside of the world doing evil. Finally, he choked to death on his bad breath.

The blacksmith didn't mind being dead because now he had eternal life. He just wasn't sure where he was supposed to live it. He went up to Heaven and rang the doorbell on the Pearly Gate. Saint Peter looked through the peephole, saw who it was, and said, "Get away from here! Get away!"

The blacksmith headed to hell. He rang the doorbell on the gate down there. The Devil looked through his peephole, saw who it was, and said, "I know you! I know you! If I let you in here, next thing I know I'll be working for you. Get away from here! Get away!"

Since that time the blacksmith has been wandering between Heaven and earth, looking for a home. Folks out in the country say on dark nights you can see him hovering at the edge of woods and swamps looking for somebody to go home with. But he hasn't found anybody yet.

Why Chickens Scratch in the Dirt

There were two large farms next to each other. One time the chickens and fowls on one place decided to throw a big party and invite the chickens and fowls from the other farm.

They sent invitations, and the other chickens and fowls sent back their RSVPs saying that not only were they coming, but they were bringing their appetites.

The day of the party came. The chickens and fowls who were the *invitees* were all excited. Mr. Rooster blew his horn and assembled them together and off they marched, Mr. Rooster in the lead, his head held high. Behind him was Miss Hen and behind her was Miss Pullet, and next was Mr. Peafowl and Mr. Turkey Gobbler and Miss Guinea Hen and Miss Puddle Duck, and then all their aunts and cousins and children and whomsoever else was in the fowl family. They marched out of their barnyard, across the field, down alongside the creek, up the hill, past the corral and the outhouse, and before long, they were there.

The fowls what done the inviting were happy to see

everybody, and they proceeded to have themselves a party. They danced and sang for a long time. Their favorite song was the one that went like this:

> *Come under, come under,*
> *My honey, my love, my own true love,*
> *My heart been a-weeping*
> *Way down in Galilee.*

They partied and sang and danced until they were hot and thirsty. Mr. Peafowl blew on the dinner horn, and everybody went and washed their faces and hands and went in for dinner.

All they saw was a big table. On it there was nothing but a pile of corn bread. Mr. Rooster looked at the corn bread and put his head in the air. He was insulted that there wasn't anything more, and he strutted out.

All the fowl who had come with him were upset. Miss Hen and Miss Pullet cackled and squalled; Mr. Gobbler, well, he gobbled. Miss Puddle Duck shook her tail and said, "*Quickty-quack-quack.*"

Mr. Rooster wouldn't change his mind, though.

The other fowl didn't know what to do. Should they walk out with Mr. Rooster? Before they could seriously consider the matter, however, their gullets had a thing or two to say, and what their gullets said was, "Let's eat!" And that's what they did.

They started pecking at the corn bread and before too many pecks they made a discovery. Underneath the corn bread was a whole pile of hot meat and greens and baked sweet potatoes and okra.

Mr. Rooster was outside and heard all these noises coming from inside. He peeked through a crack. When he saw

how much food was under that corn bread, he felt mighty foolish. Some of the other fowls went out to him and begged him to come in and get some of the food. But he was too proud.

He learned his lesson, though. From that day to this, chickens peck and scratch before, during, and after they eat, just to be sure that what they see is all there is.

Brer Rabbit and Aunt Nancy

Once a year all the creatures—winged and claw, big and little, long-tail, bobtail, and no-tail—had to go see Aunt Nancy. Aunt Nancy was the great-grandmother of the Witch-Rabbit, Mammy-Bammy-Big-Money. She ruled all the animals, even King Lion. When she wanted them to know that she was watching their every move, all she had to do was suck in her breath and the creatures would get a chill.

One year it came time for the creatures to go pay their respects.

"I ain't going!" Brer Rabbit announced.

"You got to go," the other animals argued with him.

"Says who? I don't feel like going way up in the country and into that thick swamp just to see Aunt Nancy."

"You better go," they told him.

"I done already been and seen. But, when you get where you going, ask Aunt Nancy to shake hands with you. Then you'll see what I saw."

The creatures went off. After a while they came to Aunt Nancy's house. If you had seen her house, you would've said it looked like a big chunk of fog.

Brer Bear hollered, "Hallooooo!"

Aunt Nancy came out wearing a big black cloak and sat down on a pine stump. Her eyeballs sparkled red like they were on fire.

"Let me call the roll to be sure everybody is here," she said in a voice like chalk on a blackboard.

"Brer Wolf!"

"Here!"

"Brer Possum!"

"Here!"

Finally she got to the last one. "Brer Rabbit!"

Silence.

"Brer Rabbit!"

More silence.

"BRER RABBIT!!!!!"

Silence and more silence.

"Did Brer Rabbit send an excuse as to why he ain't here?" Aunt Nancy asked the creatures.

Brer Wolf said, "No, he didn't."

Brer Bear added, "He said to tell you howdy and he told us to tell you to shake hands with us and remember him in your dreams."

Aunt Nancy rolled her eyes and chomped her lips together. "Is that what he told you? Well, you tell him that if he'll come, I'll shake hands with him. Tell him that if he don't come, then I'll come and shake hands with him where he lives."

Brer Bear persisted. "Why won't you shake hands with us? You're hurting my feelings."

Aunt Nancy rolled her eyes again. She got up. But her cloak got caught on the tree stump and slipped off. The creatures looked. She was half woman and half spider, with seven arms and no hands. That's why her house looked like fog. It was a web.

The creatures got away from there as fast as their legs could take them.

When they got back and told Brer Rabbit what they had seen, he chuckled but didn't say a word.

That was the last time the animals went to see Aunt Nancy.

The Adventures of Simon and Susanna

Once upon a time there was a man who had a very beautiful daughter named Susanna. Susanna was so beautiful that all the young men wanted to marry her.

Her father sent out the word that the man who could clear six acres of land, cut all the wood into logs, and pile up all the underbrush in one day could marry his daughter.

Nobody could do something like that, and even if he could, the question was if he would. And if he could've and would've, Susanna wasn't worth that much work.

There was one young man, however, who thought she was. His name was Simon. Simon loved Susanna. Susanna loved Simon. That made it convenient for both of them.

Simon went to Susanna's father. "I accept your challenge. If any man can clear that land, cut the trees into logs, and pile up the brush in one day, I am the man."

The father grinned. "We'll see about that tomorrow."

What Simon did not know was that the man was a witch. But what the man did not know was that his daughter had learned all of his tricks and had a few of her own.

The next morning when Simon came by the house, Susanna got an axe for him. She sprinkled black sand on it and said, "Axe, cut. Cut, axe." Then she rubbed her hair across the axe, gave it to Simon, and said, "Go down to the creek and get seven white pebbles, put them in this little cloth bag I'm giving you, and whenever you want the axe to cut, shake the pebbles in the bag."

Simon got the seven white pebbles and put them in the cloth bag Susanna had given him. Then he went off in the woods and shook the bag. The axe started cutting. As the trees fell they broke up into logs and rolled themselves into piles, while the brush uprooted itself and fell into piles.

About two hours before sundown, the man came down to see how Simon was doing. He almost fainted when he saw the six acres cleared, the logs and brush piled up, and

Simon sitting down, his back resting against a stack of logs.

The man didn't know what to say. He didn't want to give up Susanna, but he didn't know how to get out of it. He walked around and around, thinking and thinking.

"You're a mighty good worker," he said finally.

"Yessir! When I start a job, I don't stop until I get it done."

"Well, since you got so much energy, there's two more acres across the creek. Get them cleared up before supper and you can come to the house and get Susanna."

"I'll get right to it."

Simon took the axe and the bag of pebbles across the

creek. He shook the bag, and the axe set to work. The two acres were cleared and all the wood and brush piled up, and there was still an hour to go before supper.

Simon went to the house and knocked on the front door. "I'm finished."

The man went down to see for himself. Sure enough, the two acres were clear. He came back to the house and called Susanna. "Looks like you gon' have to marry Simon tomorrow."

But the man still didn't want to let his daughter go. That night he told her that after she and Simon got married they had to go upstairs to the front room and she had to make Simon get in the bed first.

The man went upstairs and sawed the floor under the bed in the front room until the floor was weak. When Simon got in the bed, the floor would give away. The bed and Simon would go through, and Simon would be killed.

The next evening Simon and Susanna were married, and they went upstairs and into the front room. As soon as they were inside Susanna grabbed Simon's hand and put one finger to her lips to tell him to talk softly.

"We got to run away from here before daddy kills both of us," she whispered. "Pick up your hat and button up your coat. Now, take this stick of wood from behind the door and hold it above your head."

Susanna got a hen egg, a meal-bag, and a skillet. "Drop the wood on the bed."

Simon did so. The bed went crashing through the floor. Susanna grabbed Simon's hand and they ran down the back stairs and out the back door.

Her father heard the bed come crashing through the ceiling. He ran into the room, expecting to see Simon lying there, dead. But there was no Simon. He ran upstairs. There was no Simon *or* Susanna.

He was mad now. He ran outside and saw Simon and Susanna running down the road, holding each other's hands. He grabbed his knife and took out after them.

Before long he was close enough to smell their fear. And that's when Susanna said to Simon, "Drop your coat!"

Simon flung his coat to the ground. A thick woods sprang up. Her father cut his way through it with his knife and had soon caught up to Simon and Susanna again.

Susanna dropped the egg on the ground. A big fog rose up, and her father was lost for a while. He conjured up a wind to blow the fog away and was soon after Simon and Susanna again.

As he got close, Susanna dropped the meal-sack and a large pond of water covered the ground where it fell. The man drank as much of the pond as he could. Then he blew his hot breath on it and dried it up and took out after Simon and Susanna again.

They were running as fast and as hard as they could. But no matter how fast or how hard they ran, her father ran faster and harder. As he got close again, Susanna dropped the skillet. A big bank of darkness fell, and the man didn't know which way to go. He conjured up light to suck the darkness up and took after Simon and Susanna again.

"Drop a pebble," Susanna told Simon.

He did so, and a hill rose up, but her father climbed the hill and kept gaining on them.

"Drop another pebble."

Simon dropped another one, and a mountain grew up. Her father climbed it and kept gaining on them.

"Drop the biggest pebble!"

A big rock wall rose up. It was so high, her father got a crick in his neck trying to see the top of it. He ran along the wall but he couldn't see to the end of it. He ran along the wall in the other direction but couldn't see to the end that way either. He couldn't go over and he couldn't go around. There wasn't a thing for him to do but to go home.

Simon and Susanna went their way and from what I heard, they lived happily ever after.

And I hope you do too.

Julius Lester is the author of books for both young people and adults. His first three retellings of Uncle Remus stories, *The Tales of Uncle Remus, More Tales of Uncle Remus,* and *Further Tales of Uncle Remus,* have received many awards and honors, including three ALA Notables; two Coretta Scott King Honors; as well as two *Booklist* Editors' Choices; *American Bookseller* Picks of the Lists, *School Library Journal* Best Books, two Parents' Choice Awards; and three NCSS Notable Children's Books in the Field of Social Sciences. Mr. Lester's other books for Dial include the ground-breaking *To Be a Slave,* a Newbery Honor Book and ALA Notable; *Long Journey Home: Stories from Black History,* a National Book Award finalist; *This Strange New Feeling,* an NCSS Notable Book in the Field of Social Studies; and *The Knee-High Man and Other Tales,* an ALA Notable Book, *School Library Journal* Best Book of the Year, and Lewis Carroll Shelf Award winner. His adult books include *Do Lord Remember Me,* a *New York Times* Notable Book, and *Lovesong: Becoming a Jew,* a National Jewish Book Award finalist.

Mr. Lester was born in St. Louis and grew up in Kansas City, Kansas, and Nashville, Tennessee, where he received his Bachelor of Arts from Fisk University. He is the father of four children. He lives in western Massachusetts and teaches at the University of Massachusetts at Amherst.

Jerry Pinkney, a two-time Caldecott Honor Book artist, is the only illustrator ever to have won the Coretta Scott King Award for Illustration three times. *Back Home,* written by Gloria Jean Pinkney, his wife, was a 1992 ALA Notable Book and *Booklist* Editors' Choice. *The Talking Eggs,* by Robert D. San Souci, was a Caldecott Honor Book and won the Coretta Scott King Award. Valerie Flournoy's *The Patchwork Quilt* received numerous awards, including the Coretta Scott King Award, the Christopher Award, and it was also an IRA–CBC Children's Choice, an ALA Notable Book, and a *Reading Rainbow* Feature Selection. Mr. Pinkney's other books for Dial include *I Want to Be* by Thylias Moss, *The Sunday Outing* by Gloria Jean Pinkney, and *David's Songs: His Psalms and Their Story* selected and edited by Colin Eisler.

Mr. Pinkney has taught art at the University of Delaware. He is the recent recipient of the Hamilton King Award of the Society of Illustrators in New York, the David McCord Award from Framingham State College, and the Drexel Citation for Children's Literature from Drexel University. His art has been exhibited at the Art Institute of Chicago, the Indianapolis Museum of Art, Cornell University, the University of Delaware, the Philadelphia Afro-American Historical and Cultural Museum, and the Schomburg Center for Black Culture in New York. He and his wife have four children and six grandchildren. They live in Croton-on-Hudson, New York.

INDEX